A Teaspoon of
Desire

Alex Danvers

Riptide Publishing
PO Box 1537
Burnsville, NC 28714
www.riptidepublishing.com

A Teaspoon of Desire

Cover art: L.C. Chase, lcchase.com
Editor: Carole-ann Galloway
Layout: L.C. Chase, lcchase.com

ISBN: 978-1-62649-927-0

First edition
May, 2022

Also available in ebook:
ISBN: 978-1-62649-926-3

A Teaspoon of
Desire

Alex Danvers

RIPTIDE
PUBLISHING

For M.

Table of Contents

Chapter One

San Francisco whirred past the taxi's windows, skyscrapers and bright sun and somehow even more people than Seattle. San Fran was the only big PNW city Henry Isaacson hadn't visited. Until today. Bubbles danced under his skin and his belly fluttered with butterflies. He couldn't keep the smile from his lips, not that he tried all that hard.

The cabbie—a twisted tree-trunk troll of a man—didn't pull over to the curb, stopping instead in the street in front of the Hotel Majestic, a cracked-stucco building that didn't even begin to live up to its name. "Here, right?"

Henry glanced up, double-checking the sign to maake certain *this* was actually the Hotel Majestic. And it sure appeared to be, in spite of the overwhelming weight of irony. "As far as I know." He reached into his back pocket for his wallet. "What do I owe you?"

The cabbie pointed a gnarled finger at the red-numbered counter mounted on the dashboard: $24.57.

Frisco is spendy. And I called it Frisco. Off to a great start. Henry thumbed out a ten and a twenty and handed them through the tight opening in the plexiglass shield. "Keep the change. Just let me get my suitcases out of the back?"

"Sure. Hurry, though."

Henry jumped out and ran to the back. The trunk popped open, and he hauled out three new suitcases and a duffel bag that was embarrassingly ratty and worn. *I haven't been to the gym in two years. You'd think it would be in better condition.*

A couple of people whizzed around the parked cab, middle fingers extended.

He slammed the trunk closed and waved through the back window. Off drove the beaten-up yellow chariot. Henry lugged his stuff onto the sidewalk, doing his best to make apologetic faces at everyone who had to go around him. Not easy. He could hardly feel *bad* about what he was doing. In spite of his churning stomach acid, joy buoyed in his chest more and more with each step closer to the revolving hotel door.

Once he reached the entrance, Henry set everything down and gazed across the tableau around him. The buildings shot up high, but a single two-story across the street was low enough to leave him a perfect view of the Golden Gate Bridge, which stood bright red against the sea, and truly massive.

"Can I help you with your bags?" An older white gentleman stepped up, pushing a faux-brass bell cart in front of him. "You look like you're laden down pretty well."

"Thank you. Stopped to take in the city. Probably shouldn't block up all the foot traffic." Henry loaded his suitcases and duffel bag onto the carpeted base of the cart, then slid his wallet free again. He handed the . . . in his fifties could he be called a bellboy? He handed the man a couple of bucks. "Have a good day."

"You as well, sir. You as well."

There was no line at the desk—a stroke of luck. *Maybe it's a good omen*. If the rest of Henry's trip went so smoothly, he wouldn't be caught complaining. He pushed the cart up to the front desk. "Hi, I'm checking in. Name's Isaacson."

The woman behind the desk—ruddy-skinned with sleek black hair—tapped her keyboard a few times. "First name?"

"Henry. I'm here for *Get Baked*."

"We get that a lot since they legalized weed. Just don't do anything stupid. Public intoxication's still illegal."

"No . . . *Get Baked*. The competition? We're supposed to tell you when we check in."

She finally looked at him, nodding rapidly and smiling. "Right. My bad. The coffee machine is broken, so I'm running on empty." She glanced at the screen again, made a few more entries. "There you are. They hide these room blocks behind special codes. Stupid system, but you're definitely here. I will need a credit card."

"Yeah. One second." He dug his card out of its pocket and laid it on the faux-granite laminate. He hadn't necessarily planned on paying for the visit—a network like Eatery TV should have had plenty of money to comp a few hotel rooms—but it would be a drop in the bucket once he took home that prize money.

She ran the card. "So, big bad baker man. You going to win? Should I get your autograph now, while it's still free?"

"I didn't come all the way down here to walk home with empty pockets." Henry chuckled, leaning against the bell cart. "And as for my autograph, you can always give me a receipt to sign." He certainly *wanted* to win. A competition for the best bakers and pastry chefs in America, and put on by Dexter Wilson of all people? Money aside, the sheer clout that victory could award was dizzying. Not that he was about to turn down the prize money, either.

The clerk handed back his card. "Okay, we've got that on file in case there's any damage, but it looks like the costs of the room are covered for your stay. So, nothing else to worry about." She grabbed a key card and put it into the little encoding machine, then passed it across. "You're on the fourth floor, wing two. Away from most of the noise and bustle. They booked the whole wing, so you'll probably get a peek at who you're up against."

Henry grinned, both at her and at the notion that he could spy on some of his competition. "Have a nice day."

"You too. And good luck."

She said the last of it to his back as he pushed his cart to the elevator doors. Henry pressed Up and the doors slid open. No wait there, either. *Auspicious*. He tapped Four. The whole carriage shuddered and a faint smell of smoke filled the space. Henry only spent a few seconds imagining himself hurtling to his death.

Eventually, the doors slid apart to reveal a tacky hallway: Overactive party-vomit wallpaper and muted, paisley floors bedecked with the odd divot or cigarette burn to break things up.

Henry followed the faded signs to Wing Two, then he checked the key sleeve for his room number: 4208. Down toward the *end* of the wing. It did seem fairly quiet, though. God knew he'd probably need his sleep if he was going to keep up with the competition.

Henry was good at what he did. He'd built a successful pâtisserie in Seattle with his own damn hands and a pastry bag. That was apparently why the network had approached him in the first place. Young, gay baking entrepreneur with a well-reviewed business and a handful of awards under his belt. What wasn't to like? But he was facing the worst sort of opponents he could imagine: the unknown. Maybe all of them had gone to Le Cordon Bleu or worked at Le Cinq or did something else French that he couldn't translate.

Then again, the whole point was to overcome the impossible foe. He wanted to test his mettle against the best of the best. That was what Eatery TV had promised him when he'd gotten the invite. That was what they'd promised in that promo trailer making the rounds online too. So they could throw all that at him and more: Henry was there to fight. And he liked his odds.

Henry nodded at his own thoughts, thankful no one else was around to see him. He rounded a corner toward the single-digit rooms and, at last, wasn't alone. Someone else was crouching down in front of one of the doors. Henry's eyes bobbed straight down to a pert ass wrapped in navy denim. *Have company* and *a view. Nice.* He stared longer than polite society would have allowed, but there was no harm in window-shopping.

His gaze raked up to a gray and fuchsia long-sleeved shirt, riding high at the hem to reveal a Hanes waistband and a small—but definitely present—barbed-wire tramp stamp. Higher still, those striped sleeves hugged tight to the stranger's biceps, and cleanly coiffed chocolate hair swirled atop his head. A cigarette sat behind Mr. Surprise Sexy's right ear.

And finally, Henry looked to the bags piled by his door. He could learn plenty about someone by seeing what they carried with them. One in particular was halfway unzipped with chef's whites peeking out. *At least I'll have some eye candy while I'm here.* He wasn't so hopeful to think he'd get laid, but he wasn't so *hopeless* to squash that dream yet.

Henry cleared his throat, earning a jump of surprise from the stranger. "You need a hand?"

"No, no, I'm fine." Surprise Sexy waved off the offer, still not turning. "Need to stop trying to do forty-seven things at once."

Sexy voice too. Familiar? Maybe. Sounded like one of those Hollywood hunks. It was rough with barbs, the kind of voice that hooked the listener in and refused to let go.

Henry stepped closer. "Let me hold the door open for you."

"Well, thanks." The stranger righted, pulling the hem of his shirt down. But when it looked like he was about to finally turn around, he jerked back and ducked to zip up the bag with the chef's whites. "You here for the show? Or you just unlucky enough to be put out in the middle of bumfuck Egypt?"

"Show. My flight got in today."

"Mine too." He hauled his bag up onto one shoulder, then slipped his key card into the slot.

Henry stepped over and held the weighted hotel door open . . . right as Surprise Sexy shifted himself around again to grab a piece of luggage. So still no face. Henry sighed. "Well, we'll probably be seeing a lot of each other."

Sexy shrugged. "Unless one of us gets sent packing week one."

Henry snickered, smashing himself as far back against the door as he could manage. "I would have to change my name and disappear for a while if that happened."

The stranger's laugh held onto Henry tight and left a trail of warmth in its wake. "Solid plan." He loaded in his last two bags, then stepped back into the hallway. "So, I should probably introduce myself."

At last, he faced Henry head-on. Smiling . . . and then not smiling anymore as his eyes locked on, hardening. "Isaacson. I guess we've already met."

Henry couldn't keep his jaw from dropping. *Casablanca* played through his head. *Of all the cooking competitions in all the hotels in all the world, you had to walk into mine.* "Tristan." As quickly as it had dropped, Henry's jaw clenched tight. "Congrats on making the cut."

"Yeah. Thanks." Tristan closed his eyes and sighed. "How's the shop?"

"Fantastic, as usual. How's the catering?"

"Going well. Word of mouth."

Yeah, no shit. "I should get into my room. Shower off the plane funk."

"Well . . . bye."

Tristan slipped inside with no other word than that. Henry stared at his door as though he might be able to bust it down by force of will. Tristan goddamn Delgado. The pastry chef who had put Carlita's Catering Services at the top of the list for wedding season . . . and knocked Henry to the wayside before he could establish a foothold in the Seattle catering world.

Henry headed for his room, a couple of doors down. What were the odds? Had the showrunners picked the pair of them on purpose, figuring two Seattleites inside the industry would know each other? Had they somehow known that there might be drama with the two of them? *Right. I'm sure these TV execs are following internal Seattle catering happenings.* It wasn't even like he and Tristan had a *real* feud. Not up to Bette Davis and Joan Crawford levels, at least. They simply had . . . animosity.

A healthy dollop of animosity, which the Seattle high-life circulars, newsletters, and magazines did their part to keep alive, intentionally or not. For the past three years, Henry and Tristan had traded back and forth for various awards and recognition from all those stupid publications.

They were mainly stupid because Tristan was up by two awards on Henry.

The first time Henry had run into him had been at an awards event. It had been just after he'd started to get his feet under him at the shop, when he'd already been setting the groundwork to bust into catering. A small awards ceremony, because it wasn't like the Washington LGBT Culinary Society had been about to rent out Benaroya Hall. But pleasant enough, and he'd been happy to get the nod.

It had been nice hobnobbing with his peers. He and his boyfriend at the time, Lance, had been checking out the local sexy chefs, and they'd both—of course—been drawn over to Tristan. Not only because he was lovely, which he undoubtedly was, but because he was lovely and had been standing by himself, tucked away in a corner.

"Hi. I'm Henry. You all alone?"

"Yeah." Tristan stared at a nearby centerpiece as he spoke, not at Henry. Didn't even try to make his lack of eye contact covert. But Henry

was persistent, and they'd eventually gotten talking, mostly about food, of course.

They must have been standing there talking for an hour when Henry reached out to take his arm, lead him back to Lance, since they were getting on so well.

And that's when Tristan freaked, shoving Henry's hand away, and darting out of the room.

After that, he'd avoided Henry the rest of the night. For what? Fucking nothing. Daring to try to be nice, that's all Henry had done. It hadn't been as if Tristan had suddenly had to run home or something He'd reappeared ten minutes later. But he'd patently avoided Henry at every turn.

Triple the slight when *Tristan* had won the Culinary Society Award for Best New Pastry Chef.

Henry forced himself to leave everything behind when he walked through door 4208. Leave the competition and ego and strife out there for when they would be useful instead of bringing them into his one place of respite.

The room was okay enough. Nothing worth posting about—not that he could post a damn thing until the competitors were announced, anyway. Media silence or he'd be tossed out. He'd had to tell everyone but Carrie he was taking an extended vacation down in California. Only she and Athena knew what was really going on, out of pure necessity. Athena because she had to run the shop, and Carrie because she was his roommate and best friend in the entire world. He hadn't even told his parents why he was going down.

His phone buzzed, apparently prompted by the universe. He slipped it from his pocket to see a message from Carrie. *You make it in one piece?*

Henry tapped back a quick response. *Of course. Don't you think I'd be haunting your ass if I'd died in a fiery crash?*

He could be playful with her, act like himself. *Something* that felt normal. She was trustworthy, too. She wouldn't spill. Henry sighed and unloaded his bags on the foot of the bed, then pulled the blinds aside. A somehow better view of the Golden Gate Bridge and the silver, sparkling water crashing against the pylons. He could have done with tighter quarters, though. The room felt massive, like it would swallow him. Massive . . . and lonely. Henry didn't live alone. He'd tried it once and had barely made it through his lease. Alone, he could only distract himself so long, then he had to face his thoughts.

And chances were high that those thoughts would be drifting toward Tristan a lot, whether he left that all outside or not.

It figured things would turn out this way, didn't it? He'd assumed the worst part of the competition would be the unknowns: his opponents' pasts, their training, their raw talent.

But now he was faced with Tristan, who was definitely not an unknown. Who was a damn good pastry chef. And that drove home the reality of the whole contest: he was going to need to work his ass off to prove himself.

The hopeful bubbles in Henry's stomach slowly popped.

"Henry's here. Henry fucking Isaacson." Just when Tristan had left Seattle behind for the moment, here he was, presented with a constant reminder of the city and all the stresses it brought with it. He unpacked his bags, sliding his clothes into the drawers beneath the flat screen. He'd tossed the Bible into the closet to make room for more important things. He'd try to remember to put it back before checkout so the cleaning staff didn't have to locate it.

"Henry *fucking* Isaacson!" As though saying it louder could make the universe understand his indignation better. Henry owned a perfect little pâtisserie, right in the U District. *He* ran it, *he* controlled it. And damn it all if it wasn't successful . . . and if the baking he put out of that shop wasn't completely fucking delicious. Delicious baking that *Henry* got to decide on himself, day in, day out.

On the other hand, Tristan worked for a curt, semi-militaristic woman, making wedding cakes and petit fours and everything else with sugar in it for the bride's special day. He knew he was good enough to run a shop, but with his bills stacking up faster than his paychecks lately, there was no way he could even take a swing at owning his own business. And with his sister now living with him indefinitely, those bills would be stacking even faster and higher.

Which is why I can't let Henry get into my head. He needed the money—both the winnings and the money Eatery would pay for his appearance on each episode . . . and the bonus Carlita had offered him for going on the show. Since the publicity from this show was likely to be strong, she'd promised him five hundred bucks for every episode he appeared on. With his student debt, it was hard to say no to any of that.

Most importantly, he didn't want to leave any excuse for Lucia to go back to Robert, and if she thought she was a burden on his finances . . .

Tristan packed away the last of his clothing, then sat gingerly on the edge of the bed. He slid his phone out of his pocket and dialed home.

One ring. Two rings.

"Hello?"

"Hey, I made it in." Tristan pulled the cigarette from behind his ear and twiddled it between his fingers. "You doing okay?"

"You've only been gone for four hours," Lucia's voice creaked out. "I think I can make it four hours without my big brother."

"I know you can. It's your big brother's job to worry anyway."

"I'm okay. Karen's coming to stay with me for a while."

Thank God we held on to her after high school. Most of their friends had peeled off, as tended to happen, but not Karen. Which was a blessing for both of them. She had a reasonable head on her shoulders. She'd been right there alongside Tristan, telling Lucia to leave that bastard husband of hers for the last couple of years. Plus she was a cop's daughter. "And you know what to do if he tries to contact you."

"Come on, Tristan."

He pressed the issue. "Don't pick up. You promised me you wouldn't talk to him while I was gone. That was the deal."

"I *remember*. I don't need you to keep bringing it up." A bit of her old fire still peeked through. Robert hadn't *totally* beaten that out of her. "Stop thinking about me. You keep your head in this thing, not back home. You promised me you'd try if I stayed."

"I haven't even seen the kitchen yet. I only got to the hotel ten, fifteen minutes ago."

"Still: you promised."

"And I'll keep my promise." When she'd shown up in tears at his door again, he'd nearly canceled on the competition. Family was family. Period. He'd have found a way to make ends meet, even if it had meant more debt and credit cards and who knew how many more years working for Carlita with his creativity on a choke chain. But Lucia had made him swear, said she'd walk right out the door if he put off this trip for her. And there'd been too much of a chance she could have ended up back at her old house if she'd walked out. At Robert's house.

At the mere thought, he clenched and unclenched his fingers around the phone. "I'll keep my ringer on the whole time."

Lucia sighed. "They won't let you do that. You could be cheating somehow."

"I'll work it out. You call me if you need *anything*. I can be home in a few hours if you need me." He'd still get however much pay he'd already earned. From the show and Carlita. "You call me, Lucia. I mean it. I'll take the signing bonus, flip them off, and head back."

"I'm pretty sure you're lying. But thanks." Her voice softened slightly. "And you'll call me every night?"

"Of course. I'll find out when we finish up every day and we'll plan from there."

"Thank you." Another little crack in her voice. "I mean, I don't know where I'd go—"

"I'm your brother. It's what family does." Anything to get her away from Robert. Even a temporary fix was preferable to the alternative. "Now go on and enjoy your day. I need to get in the shower before they call us down to tour the kitchen. You have no idea how disgusting I look."

"I'm sure you look fine." She sighed. "Good luck, Tristan. I know you're going to do great."

"We'll see. Maybe I'm up against Julia Child reincarnated."

"You could smoke Julia Child. Unless they ask you to roast a chicken. Then I don't know."

He chuckled. "I love you."

"I love you too. Night." She hung up.

Tristan set his phone down and flopped back on the bed. A king-size, where he could actually stretch out. A *room* where he could spread out. No one else to bother him—thank God they weren't sharing, because with his luck he'd have ended up with Henry fucking Isaacson—just a place to relax and sleep.

That was the intention, anyway. But after two seconds, Tristan snatched up his phone to watch the promo trailer yet again. He knew almost nothing about the show he was walking into. Not really. The producers had reached out to him through Carlita a few months prior—apparently his awards and write-ups had caught their attention—and he'd had an interview with them over video call. Some basic info had been traded back and forth, about his past employers and his training. Then seven weeks ago, a representative from Eatery TV had flown out to Seattle to talk with him in person and try his food. After that, he'd been signing contracts and getting the rundown on what they were willing to tell him. Which hadn't been a lot. Filming dates, location, compensation. Nothing that would *"give away the game,"* as the rep had said, but a baseline. If not a very useful one.

However, he had access to their teaser trailer. Fifty-three seconds of heavily edited footage that he kept watching and watching, hoping he'd be able to glean *something* from it that hadn't shown up the last half-dozen times.

One last attempt. He queued up his obsession once again. An acid-green background, followed by a glint of silver. A butcher knife whistling past before slamming through a big, white-frosted cake and revealing the pale brown interior. The knife stuck into the green wall behind it with a satisfying thud as the words began to flash by.

America's Top Bakers
Competing for a Quarter Million
Nine Won't Make the CUT
One Will Rise to the Top

The knife was pulled out, smeared with white frosting and little brown crumbs. Probably spice cake or carrot cake. *Which still tells me nothing.*

A sharp musical sting gave way to the next bevy of words floating past.

An All-American Baking Showdown
Judged by Dexter Wilson

That was the most concrete fact the trailer provided, but it was info he'd also gotten from the Eatery TV rep. It wasn't that useful. Dexter Wilson was famous for writing *Everything You Need to Know About Baking*. Which meant his competition show could be pulling from *anything*.

Get Ready

Get Set

Get Baked!

The show's logo pushed onto the screen for the last few seconds, followed by *Coming Soon to Eatery TV*. And that was it. Still providing no clues, but it brought up all his worries about competing yet again. In front of Dexter Wilson, no less. Plus two other judges yet to be revealed.

Honestly, the only thing this trailer made clear to him was that they were trying to sell themselves as bigger, bolder, and more American than any other big baking show on air. *Sounds like a perfect fit for my personality. And while I'm lying to myself, maybe I'm queen of the lizard people.*

Tristan shook himself and shut the phone off, placing it facedown against the pillow for good measure. This was his only sanctuary during his time here. He needed to stop polluting it. *Relax and sleep, don't fret and overthink.*

Relax and sleep and shower. He needed to wash up and change clothes before he had to head to the studio for the first time. His outfit was cute enough, but hardly professional. Plus his shirt rode up in the back, and the last thing he wanted was to show skin and maybe have to answer uncomfortable questions if the hem went a little too high. Not here.

Tristan rose and strolled into the bathroom, which was right by the door. He shook his head up at the universe. "Henry fucking Isaacson."

Chapter Two

The TV station's white kidnapper van trundled along the San Francisco streets. Tristan kept his gaze fixed out the window at the endless industrial expanse of neutral-toned buildings and jerky traffic, patently ignoring Henry *fucking* Isaacson sandwiched right against him. All hot and muscular and smelling tantalizingly of coconut.

The contestants had been packed into two of these Free Candy vans, five apiece. Tristan and Henry, along with three women in this one. Three guys and two women in the other van. Tristan took a deep breath—trying not to speculate too much about his competition—and fucking *coconut* filled his lungs. It *had* to be a smell he loved, didn't it?

Tristan wasn't blind or stupid. Henry was a sexy son of a bitch. He had been as long as they'd been running in the same circles. Expressive, nutmeg eyes, perfect teeth, the right amount of scruff on his chin, and fit. Very fit. If he wasn't so infuriatingly successful—and if his ego wasn't quite so large—Tristan would have been happy to hit him up for a roll in the hay. After enough vodka sodas to get him into a hookup mood, anyway.

Vodka sodas in his own house where he didn't have to deal with crowds, preferably.

He might have had the chance at that first meeting if he hadn't blown that introduction, and Henry hadn't shown his true colors after that. They'd had such a nice conversation, then Henry tried to lead him somewhere—by the arm. And he'd wrapped his fingers around one of Tristan's scars, launching him into a panic attack. He'd realized it was irrational after a breather in the bathroom. But when he tried to come back out and apologize, there had been no opening, just icy indifference . . . which had only intensified when Tristan had beaten him.

The van stopped and so did Tristan's train of thought. The driver, a rotund, gray-haired man, turned his head and smiled back at everyone. "Okay, let's load out. You've all got a busy day ahead of you."

Tristan opened the door without hesitation. Anything to get away from the overbearing coconut and all the useless thoughts that came along with it.

They were in a crowded parking garage, now, under bright white fluorescent lights. It smelled slightly of exhaust and tar, but not too bad.

The three women piled out along with Henry. They'd all exchanged names on the drive over, but otherwise, it had been pretty silent inside. Hezzie was dusky-skinned, middle-aged, with broad hips. Willa brought to mind a scarecrow, with frizzy silver hair framing a wrinkled, pink face. The last one, Nina, had red hair and was so pale she could have burned in the moonlight.

"You've all made it, that's wonderful!" A tiny white woman in a business suit scurried into sight, wringing her hands and wearing a slightly manic grin. Blonde hair hung in a tight ponytail between her shoulder blades. "Come on, no need to stand out here in this smelly old garage all day." She waved them toward the door as the second van pulled in, and that was their entire introduction.

Tristan still hadn't talked to anyone other than Henry, but there was no time right now. The squirrelly blonde had already darted through the door. Tristan made sure to hang back and fall out of coconut range from Henry. Of course, that was perfectly inside of stare-at-his-ass range, which really didn't help matters any. The khakis hugged Henry's curves *very* well. Those taut, squeezable curves. *Maybe I should bang him and get it out of my system. Then I can move on.*

They tracked through a lot of dark, cluttered hallways. Tristan could barely see their guide darting around ahead of the group. People rolled huge stacks of boxes and chairs at dangerous clips, celebrity chefs he recognized from overpriced cookbooks strolled around, and a general miasma of noise and unpleasantness floated through the space.

"It's right over here, guys." The blonde's squeaky, overly adorable voice carried all the way back, as though she were standing directly in front of Tristan. "Now remember, smiles make for happy judges, and happy judges let you stick around longer!"

Tristan forced his lips to curve up. After all, what could it hurt to try to act personable if it made him money? Sure, his *baking* should be what made him stay, but when in Rome.

They exited the dark backstage and walked into the cleanest kitchen on Earth. There was no ceiling. Instead, scaffolding hung with huge, bright lights. Other than that, the whole space was beyond perfect. Ten individual stations, each with an oven, a range, a proper KitchenAid mixer—probably product placement—and an array of other appliances. The space was decorated in lurid, candy-bright colors, including the big acid-green Get Baked logo at the back of the set, looming high above everything else. The walls, a dark teal, made a workable backdrop, but largely faded amidst the vivid cacophony.

His eyes skated around the kitchen and over to the empty front. Empty of any cooking stations, anyway. Four people stood there. Two men and a woman grouped together and a second woman off to the side, with a massive camera, snapping away.

Squirrel Assistant cleared her throat, the least threatening sound Tristan had heard in his life. But four heads turned. She stepped up to the three getting their pictures taken. "Your contestants are here."

"Perfect." The most recognizable of them stepped away from the herd. Dexter Wilson: six feet of dark Jamaican baking prowess. He patted the assistant on the shoulder. "Thank you, Kristin."

"Not a problem, Mr. Wilson. This is what they pay me for, after all." She winked at him. "I'll leave them with you."

He nodded and she scurried off. Then he smiled wide at all ten of them. "Well, I'm Dexter Wilson, and we're going to be spending a lot of time in this kitchen." He stepped aside and waved the other two up. "These are your other judges. I'll let them introduce themselves."

As though they needed introduction. The culinary world was only so large, and even smaller when you drilled down to pastry and baking. The Indian woman smiled gently. "You know Dexter, I'm sure. I'm Rita Prasad. I own Rita's on Sunset." A high-end pastry shop in Los Angeles. Well-reviewed, well-regarded, and expensive enough to sit on Sunset Boulevard. "And I promise I don't usually wear heels in the kitchen." She rolled her eyes. "I only wore them today because the publicists practically shoved them onto my feet this morning."

Their final judge nodded curtly. Eli Castle. The pretty boy of the NYC pastry scene. He was white, in his early twenties, clean-shaven. A little too clean-cut for Tristan's tastes—he preferred someone a little rougher and scruffier and more like Henry, unfortunately—but pair his looks with his talent and Tristan could definitely see the appeal. "I'm Eli Castle. I'm currently the pastry chef at La Bernardin in New York."

Dexter scanned them again, his smile never once faltering. "I want you to know you're here because you're not merely good. You're incredible. Each and every one of you. Good news for me, and for the show. But maybe bad news for you, because there can't be any slacking off. Not with competition this steep."

Tristan shifted uncomfortably beneath the weight of that reminder. Dexter was laughing, along with a few of the other contestants, but it didn't seem funny at all. Seeing Eli and Rita, that gave him a *little* more idea what caliber of contestants they might be expecting—neither of them had the celebrity pull more amateur shows tended to lean on for judges, which drove home the stakes. Still, he kept his forced smile on. Whether he thought it was fair or not, he'd grin like an idiot if it might actually get him a couple of more days. He was here for the long haul, here to get this money. For his loans. For his piling bills. For his credit card debt.

For Lucia's extra expenses and Lucia's moving costs and Lucia's divorce lawyer, God-willing.

Dexter took them all in with one final turn of the head, then sighed. "Right. While we have the photographer here, we need to get the publicity shots done. Then we can get into the fun stuff." He pointed behind him. "There are full chef whites back there. Just slip those on long enough to take the picture, then you can get back out of them and be comfortable the rest of the day."

I would have brought mine if they'd told me. Wearing borrowed whites, and over his jeans no less? *Why not add one more layer of discomfort?*

Henry smiled for the flashing camera. Four shots. Five shots. Then the lens dipped down, and he wiped his forehead on the underside of his sleeve. They'd been standing in different configurations for fifteen minutes. He was hot—no amount of Borax was going to get the sweat stains out of this jacket, and Tristan wore the whites *way* too well for Henry's comfort. No one should look *sexy* in chef's whites. Sophisticated, put together, high class, often uncomfortable . . . but not sexy.

Tristan looked sexy. Maybe they were a size too small and *that* was why the coat seemed to hug his biceps and his shoulders. And maybe the way he filled out the uniform accounted for some of his popularity at weddings. He might be off-limits to the bride, but there would still be plenty of bridesmaids—and maybe even some groomsmen—who would appreciate the extra eye candy on top of the sweets.

"I think that's enough." The photographer lowered her camera. "I'm going to get this back up to the big wigs, so you're done for today." She slipped a pair of Coke-bottle glasses onto her nose. "Best of luck, everyone."

She scampered over to her lights, and Henry immediately loosened the collar of his jacket to let in a little air. Dexter stood up and walked over to the group. "Okay, you never have to wear those again if you don't want to. Unless the execs want another picture for something."

Immediately, all ten chefs stripped off their jackets. Shoes flew from feet and pants shimmied down . . . There was that waistband again. *Why do I keep watching Tristan? Not helpful, dude. Not helpful.* But his gaze lingered, staring at the flash of ridged spine and the gray and white Hanes logo beneath barbed wire.

When they'd all shucked their whites and carried them to the waiting bin in the back, Dexter handed a sheet of paper to each of them. "Now, this has everything you're going to be expected to make during your stay here. Each round will be filmed in a single day, with three individual sections so that we can fully put you through your paces. We've got the times listed next to each item so you know what to prepare for. You'll get three days in between each filming session for you to test and develop your recipes. You'll all have access to the kitchens here for practice, but the crews will want a couple hours to clean up and test the equipment before we actually begin shooting, so make sure you're not cooking right up to the wire." He rubbed his chin, gaze pointing upward. "I'm likely forgetting something vital. But I suppose if it's important enough, word will get around. For now, you're all free to go."

The group dispersed throughout the studio . . . leaving only Henry and Tristan before too long. They locked eyes—Tristan's were a stark hazel, flecked with hints of gray and gold and *Stop it*—then went to stations on opposite sides of the room.

But that didn't mean Henry got left *alone*. A little old white lady with a curly perm tottered over to him, smiling wide and warm. "You're a young thing, aren't you?"

"Not as young as our judges, apparently."

She chortled like a bird. Her voice bore out the tiniest hint of an accent. Southern? Probably Southern. "I'm Bertha. Hideous name, I admit, but it's the one I've got to work with." She moved to the other side of his otherwise private station and set down her list. "Pie's coming up. Not my forte, but I can manage. No self-respecting grandmother could fail at pie."

Henry looked at the list himself. Round one: apple pie, lemon meringue, and a three-course meal, all in various pies. That last one would be tricky, but the other two he could make blindfolded. Nothing else seemed scary either. Not for a while. Cakes for round two, then cookies, bread . . . and Germany? *What the hell is bienenstich? Have to research a bit.* Individual pastries, choux pastry products, chocolate, and then the grand finale.

"You're not going to introduce yourself?" asked Bertha.

"I'm sorry. I got caught up reading. I'm Henry." He smiled at her. "What's your background, anyway?"

"Oh, I'm just a cake lady down in Georgia." She chuckled softly. "Not anything fancy like the rest of you, but seventy-some years floating around should have taught me one or two things. I guess we'll see." She brushed a stray curl back into place. "What about you?"

"I have a pâtisserie in Seattle." He couldn't fully commit to the conversation with Bertha. Not *only* because he didn't put much stock in her career, although that was certainly part of it. But, mostly, because his mind was whirring through ingredients and possibilities and flavors that could dance across his tongue. Nothing mundane would do, of course. *Apple pie, but not mundane. As American as apple pie. Non-American apple pie. Swedish with rolled oats and breadcrumbs. French tarte tatin. Too obvious. Everybody and their dog makes tarte tatin nowadays.*

Something. *Something* would click into place.

Lance used to love when I made a tarte tatin.

The sudden arrival of his ex into his thoughts was the terrible icing on this already substandard cake of a day. Shouldn't have been too much of a shock. Henry wanted to prove himself to the world, but a part of him also wanted to prove that he *was* worth the effort, even though Lance hadn't thought so. Luckily, Henry had a year's worth of practice shoving Lance back into whatever dark corner of his mind those memories occupied, so he could keep that little burning seed of spite to fuel himself.

A new voice helped pull him back into reality. "Well, looks like there's someone else my age here." Willa, with her explosions of frizzy silver hair, slinked over, smiling wide at Bertha. "And what's this, hitting on the young'uns? Is that even allowed?"

"Oh, I don't think she's hitting on me." Henry chuckled. "I'm sure Bertha knows better. I mean, when was the last time you saw a straight man working in a bakery?"

"Yesterday, but that's because I hired him." The new woman winked. "See all sorts of strange sights in New York City, though. Even straight pastry chefs."

Henry laughed. "So, you must be in one of those fancy restaurants, living in the Big Apple?"

"Oh God, no one calls it the Big Apple. And no, it's just me and my bakery, plodding along in Brooklyn." She laughed at her own . . . misfortune? Joke? Nervous chatter? Henry didn't know, but he put on his best fake laugh all the same.

"So we got New York, Seattle, and I rode over here with a young man who got sniped out of Ireland to come work in the states too." Bertha shook her head. "I'm going to go out on a limb and say you won't see me around long."

Henry certainly hoped so. He was here not solely for the money, but to prove himself against real chefs and bakers. The tradition of cake ladies had its place in the Southern states, and no doubt she made delicious cakes. But cards on the table, all things being even, she was a hobbyist, not a pastry chef.

Willa waved Bertha's concern away. "Little old Southern ladies aren't exactly slouches in the kitchen. May not be high-class, but we'll see how the challenges play out."

Ouch. Henry got grazed by that shade as it shot past him. Like, damn. He at least had the civility to not say it out loud. Willa apparently . . . didn't.

Bertha had definitely felt it too, her smile deflating a second before she caught herself again. "I'm just happy to have been asked on here."

"You should be." Willa's smile was saccharine and sharp. "That's an honor in itself, right?"

There was that New York attitude. Tell it like it is. As Henry turned to lean against the counter—and get himself squarely out of Willa's sights before she came for him—he saw Tristan standing alone, poring over the list with furrowed brows. Of course he was that hot guy, too good to even pretend to mingle. Henry rolled his eyes. Maybe it wasn't nice, but there'd certainly be *some* appeal in trouncing Tristan. Partially because he *was* so good. But, also, it would once and for all put them into a hierarchy. If Henry won head to head? There'd be no question who was the better baker.

Now all that remained was winning.

Chapter Three

Tristan stood under the hot, pelting flow of water, letting it drain in rivulets off his hair and down his body. The hotel soap and shampoo smelled like coconut. *That explains Henry.* Everyone would probably smell like coconut while they were here, which was a way better option than just Henry.

He leaned his forehead against the stone-tiled wall. The issue at hand wasn't who smelled like what. The coconut scent was an inconvenient coincidence. He was attracted to Henry fucking Isaacson because the pastry-shop-owning bastard was sexy as hell, with chocolate eyes and skin the color of slivered almonds and clove-colored hair. He was a piece of cake Tristan wanted to eat. And he could bake. Damn it, he could bake. That skillset didn't make Henry *less* sexy, to be sure. The thought of him flexing his arms while kneading dough or whipping the crap out of some cream . . . maybe in nothing but an apron . . .

Tristan turned the water off, grabbed a towel, and dried himself enough that he wouldn't slip and die walking out. He stopped in front of the full-length mirror next to the door. Without his glasses, even his own reflection was slightly blurry. A better view. No scars showed up when he was blurry. All the cigarette burns and deep-cut belt marks vanished.

Oh, it's late and I'm alone. Of course my brain's dredging up the past. He pulled a white, fluffy bathrobe out of the closet. *Let's try to relax.* He slipped it over his shoulders, then dropped onto the bed. He grabbed his glasses first, then his phone. On with the glasses and he dialed the house again.

It picked up after one ring. "Hello?"

"Hey, it's me."

"I know, you have caller ID." Lucia sighed. "Long day?"

"Not too bad. I wanted to hop in the shower before I called, though."

"Are you talking to me naked?"

"I'm in a bathrobe." He rolled his eyes. "Did Karen show up?"

"Yep. It's like a big slumber party, now." Her voice dripped sarcasm. "How did everything go? Come on, you're on a TV show, you're in California. Who cares about what's happening in the boring old Seattle apartment?"

"Well, I do. It's my house, and my little sister's living there while I'm gone." He chuckled. "But okay. I met Dexter Wilson today. Kind of."

"The *Everything You Need to Know About Baking* guy?"

"Yeah. And he's as gorgeous as in his pictures." Not Tristan's type—like Eli, Dexter was too put together and clean around the edges—but he was objectively attractive. *I guess I like them scruffy. And infuriatingly arrogant. And maybe I like it when they own stupid pastry shops too.* "They gave us the rundown of what we're going to have to cook, so that's helpful."

"Anything tricky?"

"The bread round might be a bit of a challenge." He was a *pastry* chef. He worked in sugar and chocolate and spices, not yeast and rye. "I'll make it work, though. They give us a few days to practice, so I think I can figure it out."

"You'll do great. You know how to make bread, Tristan. I've been eating your homemade bread all weekend."

"That's with a bread machine." His best garage-sale find, bar none. "I don't see them letting us use one here."

"Hey. Don't psych yourself out. You didn't make it in because you're bad at baking, right?"

"Right."

"*Right*, Tristan? If you're going to lie, make me believe it."

"Make *me* believe it and we'll talk."

"Oh, come on. You do this all the time. Something good happens and you sit there and worry the fun out of it. You got picked to go be an awesome pastry man on national TV. Enjoy yourself for a little bit. Take in the sights. Get blisteringly high. Sleep around, maybe. Something. Or else I'll find my way down there and yell at you in front of the fancy chef people."

Tristan stifled a laugh. There wasn't a ton of sightseeing time in his schedule, and he didn't partake of weed often enough to ever get "blisteringly high." And as for sleeping around . . . he didn't need to spread the clusterfuck that was the Delgado family's track record with men across state lines. Besides, he was currently swearing off men again, specifically to avoid winding up with a bastard like his father or Robert. "I'll do my best. But no promises."

"I'll let it go this time."

"So can I talk to Karen real quick?"

"About me?"

Of course about you. "I want someone to check in with Carlita. I haven't been able to get hold of her and she wanted updates."

"It can't be me?"

"I don't want to put any extra pressure on you. This is your vacation." Until Robert inevitably figured out where Lucia was staying. No more vacation once he started trying to worm his way back in. Tristan didn't want to say it, but he couldn't help wondering if he'd convince her to return again. Karen or no Karen, would Lucia still be there when Tristan got home? Robert had always managed to get a new foothold in her life, and Tristan could only hope this time would be different. "Can you just put her on?"

A moment of silence. "Yeah. Sec."

Tristan waited until a thick, heady voice rasped over the line. "You rang?"

"Yeah. Thanks for being there."

"No problem. Andre has the kids under control, so I'm here as long as you two need me."

"Good. I officially owe you more than I could possibly pay back."

"I know. Don't worry, I won't let you forget it either."

Tristan offered a weak laugh. "I don't want to take up a whole bunch of your time, but . . . look, if anything happens, I want you to call me. I don't care if Lucia wants you to, you call me. And *please* keep this between us, because I don't need her stressing out over this while she's supposed to be relaxing and recuperating."

"Of course. It's not a problem."

"And if Robert shows up at my house, you call the cops. He's not welcome in my apartment. He's trespassing or harassing or— I don't know, maybe he's not doing anything, but the cops will scare him off." Karen had plenty of contacts with the local cops, so even if there was no actual crime, she'd be able to get someone to show up with a badge. Being friends with a sergeant's kid had its perks.

"I'll take care of it. No worries." Her voice grew quieter, a bare whisper nearly swallowed up by telephone static. "She's in really bad shape, Tristan."

The words stung, even though he already knew it. Someone else confirming it somehow made the truth wriggle deeper under his skin. "Yeah. We made an ER visit when she showed up." What else could he say that he and Karen hadn't talked about a dozen times already? They both wanted Lucia away from Robert. They'd both be there for however long it took her to find her own way out. They both hoped this was the time that path would make itself clear. And this competition could give Tristan the chance to make it easier on her. "If I can win this thing, I'll have enough money to help her out, you know?" He didn't know how much of a hurdle her finances were, but he knew Robert had a firm grasp on the purse strings, and he hadn't let her get a job. He "liked the house kept nice," which had meant she'd better damn well stay home and clean. Or else.

A couple seconds of silence before Karen came back, her voice still soft. "Then you better rest up and make sure you win this thing."

Yeah. No pressure. Tristan's shoulders slumped as he blew out a long, slow breath. "Thank you. Like I said, I owe you. And if it comes up, I asked you to get Carlita a message for me, since I couldn't get hold of her."

"Got it. I'll take a trip down there when she opens up." Her voice was back to normal, thankfully. Serious time over. "Go kick some butt."

"Bless you, sweet virgin."

"I'll take the blessing, but I'm no virgin. At least not according to my kids. You want Lucia again?"

"Yeah. And thanks."

Lucia's voice came over once more. "You finish your plotting?"

"Plotting for her to talk to Carlita, I told you." Tristan flopped over on the bed, staring at the ceiling. "I'm gonna get off the phone, but I wanted to say I love you before I go."

"You don't need to tell me all the time."

"Yeah, I do, Lucia." He pulled the bathrobe a little tighter around his middle, holding in the warmth as long as he could. "I love you."

"I love you too. Now rest, please. And stop worrying about me."

"Not going to happen. But I'll talk to you tomorrow. Let's make it five o'clock?"

"I'll be here."

"And I'll be here. Possibly in a bathrobe." He hung up the phone to a disgusted laugh from his sister, then set it aside and stretched his arms out wide. *Stop worrying about you?* They both had scars on their bodies from their father. But Lucia had plenty of new marks from Robert too. Including fresh bruises. Thankfully no breaks this time. "I don't think I ever *could* stop worrying about you."

His family had poor luck with men. Sure, there was a whole stock of good ones out there somewhere. Karen had managed to find one. But his father was an abusive son of a bitch. Lucia had gotten caught up with the same kind of bastard, and even though he knew better than to blame her for what had happened, it was painful to hear her make the same excuses as their mother had.

Tristan shook his head, trying to dislodge this old, too-familiar stream of thoughts. He was already doing all he could, including being here to try to make up the difference in the bills. All he could do now was wait. Wait, and vow to never get caught in the same trap. Eighteen years with his father had been more than enough.

Tristan rose and stripped out of his bathrobe. He was ready to leave it there on the floor . . . but this was his home. If he let it get messy, it would just lead to clutter in his head that he couldn't afford. So he grabbed it and hung it up, then slipped into his lounge pants.

He pulled out his laptop and started in on his brainstorming. "What are we going to make for that three-course pie dinner?" *That* was a much better topic than the constant failures of the Delgado family's romances. "I wonder if chicken pot pie would be too trite?"

Henry stood in the back row, waiting as the basket of numbers went around. He took a little folded piece of paper when it came around to him but, as instructed, didn't open it yet.

When everyone had received one, Dexter clapped his hands. "All right, check your number to see which station you're at. We'll keep you there as long as we can manage, but when people start to leave, we might have to move you around. Production crew likes you more evenly spread out."

Henry unfolded his paper: station six. He walked along the aisle bisecting the room and slid into the middle right station.

So of course Tristan took the one in front of him. He wasn't in that entirely too-tempting gray and fuchsia top, but his jeans still hugged tight and his arm muscles still bulged in all the best possible places under a black long-sleeved T-shirt, and none of that was conducive to Henry winning this competition. Even when Henry won, Tristan just appearing on the show would bring more fame and notoriety and business to the sexy son of a bitch and his damn catering business.

It's pretty ridiculous to hold a grudge against him because he's getting the catering gigs. And I'm not. Or because of the awards. But acknowledging that didn't make the grudge suddenly disappear. If anything, it locked his distaste harder into place.

Right as Henry had started to get some real clientele built up for his own wedding services—cakes, petit fours, all that stuff people wanted to feel fancy on their big day—along had come this hotshot new pastry chef for Carlita's, and there had gone Henry's chances of chipping out a spot for his own shop. It had been the first major stumble since he got the shop off the ground, and falling after such a long run of successes had hurt. Bad. Then to have Tristan constantly lauded up at the same level as him? Yeah, it was annoying on the best of days.

It didn't help that Tristan was so damn desirable. A pastry chef with a body like that? Henry knew firsthand that hauling wedding cakes was a good arm workout, and it showed on Tristan in a perfect way. Running back and forth between stations kept your legs working. Dealing with annoying customers stressed you out, which probably burned calories too. *It better. That's my whole excuse for eating as much ice cream as I do.*

Tristan likely had a lot of other muscles worth experiencing up close and personal. And, looking around as the other guys passed him on the way to their stations, Henry could confidently say Tristan was the sexiest one of them all. *And* he was for sure into dudes. And sleeping down the hall from Henry's hotel room.

Stop it. Last thing I need is another fuckboy. They were cheaper than disposable piping bags back home. All the "marrying types" seemed to be either paired off already or frustratingly not into dick. Henry wasn't likely to get the kind of relationship his parents had. Not never, but certainly not with Tristan.

Besides, I'm too selfish for a real relationship, right? That's what fucking Lance said.

"Okay, everyone squared away?" Dexter walked from the front table all the way to the back of the studio, by the doors to the massive pantry room. "Now, I know it's only been a day or so, but if anyone has a list of ingredients they want, you can hand it in now and I'll make sure it gets to one of the production assistants." He sighed and glanced upward. "What else? Don't try to sabotage anyone, obviously. Not even during these practice runs. You'll be getting key cards to get you in here whenever you need. They're giving you free rein, so don't abuse it and wreck things for the chefs next season."

Next season, huh? If they were already planning a second season, then this might be a bigger career boon than Henry had planned on. *All the more important I stick around.*

Dexter clapped loudly. "For now, I think you'll all want to get cooking. I hope you won't mind me watching for a while. I want to get a look at what you're really like, without the cameras going."

He started to walk away, but Tristan stepped out and stopped him. "List?" He held out an envelope. "I might ask for more later if that's all right?"

"Fine by me." Dexter patted Tristan on the shoulder, then headed back up front, folding and pocketing the envelope.

Of course he had a list of ingredients ready. Henry rolled his eyes as he stepped away from his station and into the pantry, a truly massive room at the rear of the set, lit by stark hanging fixtures. There were shelves and shelves of all sorts of ingredients, and three massive refrigerators, one set aside for meat. It was hard to believe there was a whole lot someone would *need* to bring in from the outside. Maybe specific extracts or oils or baking emulsions, particularly uncommon fruits or—God forbid—weird organs or sweetbreads.

Henry grabbed a container of bread flour, a block of butter and a block of lard, and a miniature jar of salt. He needed to work out the meat pie first, the "entrée" pie for the last hurdle of the round. That one was going to give him some problems. Hell, so would his soup course. They had five hours on filming day to do all of this. On paper, it sounded like plenty of time to make three pies. In reality, it would likely flash past him in a breath.

Which meant practice. Lots and lots of practice.

The first option that came to mind was beef Wellington. Maybe a bit too boring, but the flavors worked, and it was something Henry knew how to make. Nothing better to riff on than that. It used to be his go-to first-date meal . . . when he'd bothered to date.

Henry had made it a lot of times over the years. Lance had been the last one to eat it who'd actually stayed past a brief tangling of the sheets. *I guess I need a higher class of men to appreciate it. Or Cupid's a vegetarian.*

He grabbed some chestnut mushrooms, shallots, a bottle of Madeira, some cream, and beef tenderloin to get chopped up. Tarragon too. Cursed, loveless recipe or not, they were solid flavors no one could complain about.

And hell, maybe someone would taste it and finally decide to settle down with him.

Tristan came back to his station not long after, carrying his own basket of ingredients. He eyed Henry's station. "Beef wellington's not exactly a pie, is it?"

Henry shrugged, failing to keep the ice out of his voice. Not that he tried *too* hard. "Maybe you shouldn't assume you know what I'm doing."

Tristan rolled his eyes and turned back around.

With them working this close to each other, it was going to be a long show.

Tristan walked back and forth outside of the studio. They'd practiced for three days, and he'd seen amazing food. Incredible apple pies, some thin and golden and shining, some half a foot high with flaky, bronzed crusts.

He took a short drag on his cigarette, letting heat and heady smoke fill his lungs. It failed to release the tension balling between his shoulder blades, but it gave him something to do until they let him onto the set.

A cab pulled up next to him. Tristan glanced at it and scowled, because fate was a nuisance on her best days. Out of the cab stepped Henry. He handed some cash to the cabbie, grabbed a receipt, then straightened up and locked eyes with Tristan. "Guess I'm not the only one here early."

"Everyone else probably has jetlag. We're still in the same time zone." Tristan sucked down harder on his cigarette.

"They'd be waking up earlier than us if they hadn't adjusted."

"Well then, I don't know. I'm just waiting until they let us in." He twiddled his key card between two fingers. "Tried this and it doesn't work."

"That's ridiculous." Henry pulled out his wallet and slipped his own key card free.

"I told you I tried already."

He slid the card into the slot and the lights flashed green. "Maybe yours got demagnetized. Don't keep it next to your cell phone."

"Thanks for the tip." Tristan sucked the last bit of his cigarette down, leaving behind a huge trail of blue-gray ash. Such a *great* start to the day.

They walked in together, through the backstage area, and out onto the kitchen set. Willa and Hezzie stood around chattering with Finn, a tall, pale man with a thick Irish accent. They all waved to Henry but hardly glanced at Tristan. Which made sense. He hadn't plunged into socializing at all. He didn't need to start now, either. It wasn't important how the other competitors felt about him, just that they hadn't all arrived yet this morning. *At least the stupid key didn't make me miss the whole thing.*

Tristan slid into his station and swept his hair back into place. *Should have brought another cigarette. Or a pack.* He shouldn't be this nervous about making pie. Pies he'd practiced *endlessly* for the past three days, for Christ's sake.

But he was about to make them on camera. With a time limit. In front of Dexter Wilson and Eli Castle and Amrita Prasad. Not to mention he'd have Henry fucking Isaacson standing behind him the entire time, judging him. Even through the miasma of cigarette smoke, there was coconut on the air. *Everyone smells like coconut. It's not only him. It's not. It's not.*

More people trickled in over the next quarter hour: competitors, judges, and some squirrely-looking tech guys. They attached mics and battery packs to everyone, never once speaking. Tristan stood indignant and still as one of them attached the gear to him. No *asking*, not even a mention that they were about to functionally grope his ass to get the pack on his belt. He swallowed an admonishment when they lifted his shirt up a little too high for comfort.

The judges received the same rough-and-ready treatment for their mics, so fair was fair. But Tristan only watched them for a few seconds. Then the cameras were pushed in and the rest of the crew stormed in with them. Jesus, Tristan had severely underestimated the number of people necessary for a show like this.

"Things are moving! Are we all excited?" A man in a suit swept in, a wide smile beneath a dark, bushy mustache. "I'm Mark McCall. Don't worry, don't worry, I won't be around that often. I'm the producer for the show. Well, alongside Mr. Wilson. I wanted to wish everyone the best of luck and say how *excited* I am to see this project go forward." He scanned over the lot of them. "I will admit, I might be back now and then for some unofficial taste-testing." He boomed out a laugh. "I know we're running a bit of a tight schedule, so I'll get out of your hair. Good luck, godspeed, et cetera."

Tristan rolled his eyes once McCall had turned his back. *I get the impression we were an item on his checklist for the morning.*

Just as McCall's footsteps faded into the hum of the set, a new woman stepped into view. She was dressed nothing like any of the chefs on the set, and nothing like any of the production assistants, either. Even Rita, true to her word, had dressed in sensible flats and an easy, breathable top. But this stranger had on a bright blue blazer, a pleated skirt, and strappy heels. Not stilettos or anything *that* unconscionable, but she stood out. "I'm here, now. You can all relax."

Tristan couldn't help a minor hit of panic. *Are we supposed to know who she is?*

Dexter stood. "I'm sorry this is so last minute, ladies and gentlemen, but her flight from Philly kept getting delayed. This is the show's host, Sylvia Kwan." He smiled at her. "I insisted on using her. She was on every infomercial back at home, and she convinced me to part with far too much of my money, so I thought she deserved a chance to work during waking hours."

"Honestly, I don't know what to do with myself. What is that exceptionally bright circle in the sky?" She winked at Dexter, then turned back to the contestants. "We're starting very soon, so say your prayers and get out your rolling pins."

Soon. Did *soon* mean five minutes? Ten? Two? *I should have brought more cigarettes.* Not that they would be getting a smoke break. Even if they did, Tristan wouldn't be able to afford to take it. He had to use every second available if he wanted a shot at making it through.

Some crewmember jogged past, and Tristan overhead them on their headset. "I know, ten minutes left. I'm on the move."

Ten minutes to filming. Great. No problem. *Screw a cigarette. I need a fifth of vodka.*

Henry drummed his fingers on the countertop, waiting for *something* to finally happen. He couldn't still his gaze, and his belly flipped and flopped. How could the competition look so calm while Henry exploded inside?

Apple pie first. Preheat. Crust. Spices. Filling.

"Quiet on set!" A dumpy little man waddled into sight, a headset plastered to his face. "We're filming intro footage in one minute!"

One minute? One minute. Okay. Only one more minute of waiting to go, then. On the plus side, Henry wasn't focusing on Tristan anymore. Roiling stomach acid demanded the entirety of his attention. *Don't puke before appearing on national television. Don't puke while appearing on national television. Zero puking.*

This wasn't practice. This was his chance to prove his skill against the crème de la crème. He was going to make his mark come hell or high water. He'd been thrust aside one too many times over the years. By Lance when he'd dared to pursue his dream. By his peers after he'd come out. By the remarkably attractive pastry chef stepping into the catering scene.

That trend ended today.

Up front, the judges settled into their seats around the oversized café table. Sylvia smoothed her skirt, then pasted a clearly practiced smile on her face.

The little man with the headset cleared his throat. "Roll in five, four, three, two . . ."

Cameras swept around the room.

Don't. Puke. Henry did his best to appear presentable. He couldn't keep track of that many cameras, so he'd have to stay en pointe the whole time.

"And cut!" The little man—apparently the director—piped up. "We'll get your voice-over recorded later, Syl." He turned toward the competitors. "From here, we're live. Watch your language, get all your cussing out now. Make it easier on the editors."

Nobody said a damn thing, except Sylvia, but he couldn't hear her quiet response. The competitors were stone silent. Tension hung palpable in the air, lacing every breath Henry took. *All I have to do is not forget how to make a stupid apple tart. That's it.*

He closed his eyes, waiting for some calm to drop on him. Of course it didn't. It wouldn't until they started baking. Henry opened his eyes again and *somehow* they ended up pointing at the curve of Tristan's lower back. *Goddamn it. Can't catch a fucking break, can I?*

"Okay, big roll starting! Quiet on set!"

Henry waited through the countdown, then Sylvia's voice burst out. "Welcome, all you baking and pâtisserie *wunderkind*. I'm excited to see all your bright shining faces. And I'm even more excited to see what you pull out of the oven. I have my dietician on speed dial, so I'm all prepared."

Henry offered a weak chuckle. He didn't want to open his mouth too far in case vomit spewed forth.

Sylvia clasped her hands, her smile bright white and wide. "Now, today we want to really see your creativity, but also those superb baking skills we all know you have. The judges are expecting to be wowed. You're some of the best bakers and pastry chefs in the country. We gathered you together to find the quintessential American baker, so we're starting with the quintessential American bake: apple pie—and you don't even have to start by creating the universe."

That must have been a reference, but not one Henry understood.

"Basically everything is open to your own discretion. It can be double-crusted or open-faced. Any flavors you want to bring, any design. It can be in a tin or hand-raised. The only requirements are that it a) has a crust and b) is filled with apples. Beyond that, you're free to fly as close to the sun as you dare." Sylvia pointed to a massive digital clock above the judges' table. Two hours filled in the blank space.

I can do this.

"Get ready."

I can do this. It's a pie.

"Get set."

It's a fucking pie, Henry. Do it.

"Get baked!"

Chapter Four

Tristan didn't run, but he certainly walked *briskly* to the pantry. "Preheat the oven when you get back," he whispered to himself. The last thing he needed was to make a rookie mistake. Especially during the first episode. He snatched one of the wire baskets from in front of the door and headed in, dodging the other bodies bustling alongside him. A block of butter, a container of flour, a little thing of salt. It would get him his basic pastry dough. Then apples. Golden Delicious. He'd get enough tartness from the cherries to counterbalance them. Some honey. Allspice berries. A cinnamon stick. A finger of ginger. And a couple of eggs. Then he took another "brisk walk" back to his station.

In his head, Tristan knew that two hours was more than enough time to make a stupid little apple and cherry pie. His heart and stomach disagreed, insisting he had all of thirty seconds left.

He popped the oven up to 375°F, then pulled out a mixing bowl and started dumping. Flour, butter, salt, crumble.

With his hands in the mix, Tristan's doubts began to melt. He baked every day. This was the same as being in a tent out back of a wedding. Easier, really. He had air conditioning and a proper stove and range and all the ingredients he could possibly need and an audience of millions and he had to make the entire dish in one go and this was *nothing* like working at a wedding, oh my *God*.

Tristan closed his eyes. How many cigarettes was too many? Surely one of these cameramen or judges or another chef had one he could bum. "Focus on the pie."

His dough had turned to crumb. He popped into the miniature freezer for ice and dumped it into a second bowl, then filled it with water. A glance around told him he at least wasn't behind the pack. But not significantly ahead, either.

The dough came together quickly, only taking five tablespoons of the ice water. He smacked it into some plastic wrap, then dashed it into the fridge. His oven chimed gently to say it was preheated. He pulled a high-brimmed skillet out of cupboard and popped it on the range. *So far, so good.*

"Tristan!" Dexter marched up to him and then leaned on the edge of his counter, smiling. A cameraman followed him. "How's everything going?"

"It's fine." Tristan pulled his apples over. "I'm making good enough time." He glanced at the clock—it had only taken ten minutes or so to get to the pantry and get his crust started. "I'm about to get going on my filling."

"And what exactly are you making?" Dexter examined the ingredients, his dark eyes sparkling. "I see apples and cherries?"

"I'm from Washington. What's more Washingtonian than that?" Tristan started peeling his apples, shedding off golden slips of skin, and hoping the conversation wouldn't distract him enough to slice up his hands. "Rainier cherries are a nice pale color so they won't stain everything. And also very Washingtonian."

"I would have expected apples and coffee out of Washington." Dexter winked.

"Well, you know." People always seemed to associate coffee with Washington. Tristan may not be prone to state pride, but it was always a niggle when people overlooked things like cherries and potatoes for coffee.

"Well, it sounds like you have some good flavors going. It's not going to be too sweet with those apples?"

"It should be fine." When was Dexter going to leave Tristan in peace to work? And why was it so fucking difficult to work and talk and be on camera? TV chefs did it all the time. "The cherries will help balance it out, but I do like my desserts sweet."

Dexter nodded. "I'll let you get on with it. It's fairly simple, so make sure you're hitting your flavor balance."

Lucia's words from before played through his mind, and in his distraction, they shot out of his mouth before he could censor himself.

"I didn't make it in because I'm bad at baking, right?" *Fuck, just had to smart off.* Dexter was a judge. But Tristan's mouth had gone too dry for him to correct himself, so he simply had to stand in his shame, peeling apples.

"No, you're not here because you're bad at baking." Dexter laughed, low and loud, then knocked on the counter and moved on, taking the blasted cameraman with him, thankfully. When there wasn't a stupid *interview* happening, Tristan could focus. He got his apples peeled and cherries pitted, then tossed some butter into the skillet. Allspice went into the grinder, then into the foaming fat. Same with the cinnamon. Soon their strong, heady perfume wafted up. Once again, a wave of calm pushed through him as he settled into familiar territory. Tristan dropped in his apples, and they immediately began to sizzle. He tossed them in the butter and added honey, waiting for a little softness in the flesh before adding in his flour-coated cherries.

This was nothing. Not the kind of thing he made every day, but wedding pies had a bit of a cult following, and living in Seattle *of course* there were people who wanted them, if for no other reason than to be contrary and shock their mothers-in-law.

He'd do it today, in this fake kitchen with all the cameras, and the air perfumed like a spice market on a hot summer day. He'd do it well enough to make up for his smart mouth. He'd do it in spite of Henry behind him, smelling of coconut and—Tristan looked over his shoulder—slicing apples into thin strips without even watching his hands, the blade of the chef's knife gliding cleanly against the edge of his knuckles. *Maybe I'll even do it* to *spite him.*

Tristan did his best to focus in the time remaining. He added his cherries and cranked the heat down on his pan so the flour wouldn't scorch or thicken too quickly. The cherries created a new plume of steam, fragrant and sweet and only slightly acidic on the nose. He stirred and tasted and adjusted with salt and a dash more honey, then stirred and tasted and finally ran a spoon through the liquid collecting in the bottom of the pan. It was a perfect nappe, coating the back of the spoon and, when he ran his finger down the center, it didn't flow in to fill the empty space. A slight smile pulled at the edges of his lips. *Maybe I actually will pull this off.*

His filling went into a bowl, and that went into the fridge. It didn't need to be stone-cold, but putting hot filling into his pie case would melt all the fat and leave his crust stodgy. There were a lot of moving pieces, and with the clock above them ticking down, Tristan felt like he could see each one ten times more clearly than usual. The chilling of the fat in the dough, blooming the starch for the filling, controlling the heat of the fruit against the need for structural integrity in the crust. From a bird's eye view, pie was simple, but when a quarter million dollars was on the line, when taking care of himself and his family was on the line, each detail became a monumental hurdle to leap.

While he waited for everything to settle, he prepped the rest of his ingredients: sanding sugar and egg wash and extra flour to roll out the dough.

He also couldn't resist checking behind him to see what the competition was bringing to bear. At the very back, Ricky was . . . hopeless. He was struggling to manipulate the crust into the pan. Bits of apple scrap littered his station, and flour caked his apron. Plus that dullness in his eye . . . Tristan wasn't prone to bouts of confidence, but even he felt a little more secure in his position looking at Ricky.

But the real source of interest lay in front of Ricky. Henry was carefully arranging his apple slices into his tart shell, overlapping them like rose petals as he circled inward. It was impressive, that was for damn sure, and Tristan couldn't help noticing the serenity on his face, the calm set of his jaw, and focus in his eyes. Henry truly was lovely, and when he wasn't talking, his ego and his pastry shop were much easier to forget.

"You know, I may not be some highfalutin caterer like you, but I'd be using my time a little more efficiently than just watching me arrange my tart." Henry didn't lift his head, but his eyes flashed upward to Tristan as he spoke. "I admit I'm pretty, but you're going to rob my victory of any actual value if you don't try."

And there came that ego, as soon as Henry fucking Isaacson opened his mouth. *A highfalutin caterer? Really?* "Right. You want to trade? You can be Carlita's pastry bit—lackey and I'll run my own pâtisserie in the U District. Done deal."

Henry paused for a second, just long enough to shake his head, then went back to arranging in silence. Tristan turned and bent down to the fridge. *All the snobby caterers out there in the world, and he calls me highfalutin. I wish.* Highfalutin caterers *definitely* struggled to pay off their debts and support their families. Anyone who knew a damn thing about Tristan wouldn't call him highfalutin.

His dough was chilled enough, and his filling was on its way there, so Tristan got back to work. He split the dough and made a quick case, shearing off the edges with a paring knife. His filling was down close to room temp now. Close enough, anyway, so he piled it in and smoothed it out, then placed his top on and crimped it shut. His crimping took a lot longer than usual, or at least it seemed to. But he wanted perfection: evenly spaced finger waves along the edge. He sliced a vent in the top and then brushed on the egg wash and sprinkled chunky, coarse sanding sugar over the whole pie before getting it in the oven.

Then it was all finished, save for waiting. He tidied up and watched as more and more chefs joined the waiting game. Ricky was the last man standing, and even when he got his pie in to bake, an almost palpable miasma of disorder and anxiety crept up from his station. This was the sort of mess Tristan would have normally cleaned up, but that wasn't his kitchen. So he took the time to quickly whip some cream, lightly sweetened. A bit of fat to counterbalance the tart cherries and all the sugar.

Somehow, the waiting got worse. The kitchen was all but silent before long as the clock ticked away. Tristan resisted every urge suggested by his nervous energy. No needlessly opening the oven. No extra whipping of his cream. Certainly no adding extra elements to a fully complete pie.

And no thinking about the coconut that, in spite of all the wonderful spices and fruits filling the air, crept up from Henry's station and into Tristan's nose. No thinking about that at all.

Finally the first timers started to go off and pies came out. Less than ten minutes remained, barely enough time for the pies to cool, then get touched up. The cameramen pushed forward as each chef pulled their work from the oven, vultures ready to snap up the carrion of a failed pie. Tristan's stomach churned at the thought, and when his timer joined the symphony, he had to hold back his guts from flying out of his mouth.

But when the pie was revealed, his crust was solid, sanding sugar sparkling like crystals on bronzed pastry, no visible leakage, steam gently wafting up from the vent hole. His body relaxed as soon as he had it on the cooling rack, and the camera moved on, seemingly unsatisfied by his lack of failure.

Henry also pulled out his tart. It had a beautiful pattern, but seemed dry. However, as soon as he glazed the surface, it took on a sheen under the fluorescent lights that made it infinitely more appealing. The studding of lavender buds helped as well.

"You all have five minutes left," Sylvia's voice projected from the front of the set. And sure enough, the clock up above ticked right past the five-minute mark. Tristan forced his thoughts to run smoothly. He took his whipped cream out of the fridge and dished up a healthy portion of it into a ramekin—couldn't serve it on top of a hot pie. He wiped down the sides to make sure everything was neat and silently prayed that his pie was fully cooked. There was no knowing for sure until it was cut.

"One minute remaining!"

The other pies were garnished and finished and moved off the cooling racks, onto the counter for presentation. Tristan couldn't resist a peek back at the train wreck of Ricky. He had his pie out, but the crust looked utterly unappetizing, a splotchy cream and brown color. That glance back also let Tristan see Henry's tart again in its full, shining glory.

A loud buzz filled the space as the clock flipped to zero. There was nothing they could control anymore. Now it was down to Dexter, Rita, and Eli.

Henry waited motionless at his station as the judges meandered back, dragging the camera crew with them. Of *course* they started on the opposite side, and spoke quietly enough that he couldn't hear what was said. But nobody burst into tears, so the results couldn't be *too* bad.

Now Dexter, Rita, and Eli stood around the station at the front of his row. Still too far away for him to hear, so he watched as they examined Willa's offering. It was a big damn pie, hand-raised with a crumble on top in place of a crust. Dexter tapped the outside and Rita scratched one of the golden forks through the crumble. Then finally, Eli grabbed the knife from the counter and sliced in. When he transferred it to a plate, it held together. They ate, they nodded, their mouths moved, and Henry wished he'd learned to read lips at some point.

Then they moved one station back. This time, Henry could actually hear their conversation.

"Tristan." Eli smiled at him. "Let's see what we've got. Apple and cherry is one of my favorite flavor combinations."

Rita picked up the knife and tapped the tip against the top of the pie. "You have lovely decorations, a firm crust. You work for a caterer, right?"

Tristan nodded. "In Seattle. Suffice it to say pie isn't demanded all that often, but I've still made my fair share."

"And Washington is known for its apples, of course." She chuckled softly as she cut the tiniest, most delicate sliver of pie. It also stayed intact, a brilliant red because of the cherries. "You used Golden Delicious, right?"

"I like the sweeter flavor. It balances out well with pie cherries."

Rita dropped it onto the plate, then scooped out whipped cream and placed a gentle dollop next to the pie. "It holds up nicely. The apples aren't dissolving or collapsing, which can sometimes happen with Golden Delicious, and it's got a lovely aroma."

They dug in, chewing quietly as the camera zoomed and shifted around. Henry was maybe too interested in this, since one of the cameras focused squarely on him. Then again, why wouldn't he be focused? Tristan was competition. Real competition.

Dexter spoke up first this time. "I was suspicious of your apples, which is not a sentence I ever foresaw myself saying. But you've pulled it off. Your crust is buttery and delicate, and the cherries pop against the honey and the apples. This would be a star at a Fourth of July picnic."

Tristan hesitated a few seconds before finally responding. "Really?"

Dexter smiled and chuckled. "You shouldn't sound so surprised. After all, you didn't get here because you're bad at baking, right?"

Tristan's head jerked around so he was fully facing Dexter. His mouth hung open slightly, and he ran his fingers through his hair. "I, umm . . . Yeah." That brief show of embarrassment struck Henry right in his middle. *As though he needed help being a sexy son of a bitch.* But the way his expression put his lips on display, the way his hair parted around his fingers, the shy smile that toyed across his face as they passed him by . . .

As they passed him by. Shit. That meant Henry was next. Suddenly he judged his pie all over again, pointing out every flaw to himself. An uneven lip of crust here, a misplaced bit of lavender there, an unintended pool of glaze that he should have evened out.

Dexter first. They must have been taking turns to keep the footage fresh and interesting. "Now that is something to look at, isn't it? What exactly is in here?"

"It's traditional apple-pie flavors infused with lavender."

"With lavender? It's such a delicate flavor, can it really hold up to all those spices?"

Henry winked, putting on the best show he could. "I guess we'll find out."

Dexter chuckled and Eli started slicing yet another sliver of pie. "Your crust is firm, not too thick. The apples aren't holding together quite as well as I would have liked, but they aren't completely collapsing. A shape like this is normally held together with caramel or toffee or frangipane, so the fact it's holding at all is pretty good."

Henry did his best to stay chill as they continued to pick his tart to pieces. He'd considered a stronger base, of course, but toffee or caramel both seemed too sweet and would have covered up the delicacy of the Braeburns he'd used, and certainly would have masked the floral notes of the lavender.

Rita broke Henry from his thoughts. "I am impressed. You've set your flavor bar high. It takes skill to handle lavender like this, and it's a hell of an opening card to play." She put a hand to her mouth. "Can I say that?"

"They said it on Disney, we can say it here." Dexter sighed and leaned forward. "I don't like lavender, so this was always going to be a hard sell for me. But it's a good apple tart. The lavender isn't perfumey in a bad way, though it's definitely present. I could do without it, but it doesn't ruin the tart."

Henry sighed with relief. They liked it. "I wanted it present, being from Seattle and everything."

Eli's head tilted to one side. "Lavender in Washington?"

Yes, lavender in Washington. Where do you think it comes from? "There's lavender fields all around Seattle. I grew up in Sequim, so it was all over the place."

Eli nodded. "I might have to make an excursion. Dexter may not enjoy it, but I love lavender and rose and violet. Done well, at least, and this was done well."

That was apparently all they had, because the posse moved on. Henry slumped back on his stool. It was only the first hurdle, and apple pie wasn't exactly a *high* hurdle to clear. But he'd still put out a strong showing, a gay boy from Seattle. And although he wouldn't know for sure until the end of the day, it felt as though he'd been deemed worthy.

Once the "competing in front of judges and a million cameras" dam had broken, the other rounds moved quickly for Henry. His lemon meringue was solid, though unfortunately not nearly as photogenic as Tristan's. He didn't run into any great problems with his three-course pie meal, either.

After each round, the remainders of the pies had been carried up to a large table off-camera, where contestants and crew alike could taste them between shootings. Henry gazed longingly at that collection of baked goods. At the start of filming, he hadn't wanted that much sugar, afraid it might leave him jittery. Twenty pies wasn't exactly a balanced meal, and while craft services were decent, those sandwiches weren't enough to overcome that influx of sweetness.

Now, as he stood drenched in the smells of roasting meat and vegetables, his stomach growled. *I'll eat next time. I'll definitely eat. The hotel must have a gym, right? I can make use of that duffel bag.*

In spite of his growling stomach, the time slipped by faster than Henry liked. Soon enough, all their pies were out and he had to wait for final judgment. He had to be through. His pies were all beautiful. A "potato soup" pie, full of bacon and potatoes and onions and all sorts of good, hearty fare. His beef wellington pie with the flaky layers of rough puff, because who the hell had time to make full puff *and* three pies? And his dessert pie, because of course one of his three courses would be dessert. Peach and hazelnut with a thick amaretto syrup drizzled over the top. It certainly looked impressive . . . though not as much as Tristan's.

Everyone went to the judges' table one at a time, with cameras and production assistants trekking behind, carrying the pies up to the front and then disappearing before the judging began. Henry's whole body tightened as he watched them, the way they walked without watching where they were going. Even though it wasn't his pies yet, that level of carelessness didn't instill confidence. At all.

After a remarkable critique—"impeccable decorations" and a "command over classic flavors" in a boeuf bourguignon pie—Tristan walked back to his station, smiling. Tristan rarely smiled. It suited his face: pushed his cheeks up and revealed all-too-charming dimples. *Not that I noticed. Stupid caterer. Stupid sexy caterer.*

A few seconds' waiting, then the cavalcade of staff arrived at Henry's workstation. They stood just out of shot as Sylvia smiled wide. "Henry, come on up and wow the judges."

He grabbed the entrée, like he'd been instructed, and the two assistants snatched up his dessert and soup course. Henry suppressed a cringe at how close their thumbs got to the top of the pie, wrapping too tight and threatening to puncture the crust. Together, they all moved to the front where Henry would face his final judgment of the day. So far, things hadn't gone well for the majority of the contestants. The judges had loved Tristan's, Willa's, and Finn's spreads, but the rest all sounded middling at best. At least one girl had royally fucked herself over. Fish pie didn't seem appetizing. Sure, it would have been impressive to see someone pull it off . . . but she hadn't. She'd served some overdone catfish monstrosity that wasn't likely to be salvaged by her other two pies. You didn't make Dexter Wilson spit food out into his napkin and stick around very long.

Once his pies were arranged on the table, Sylvia cut back in. "So, tell us what you have here. Whet my appetite."

Henry nodded. "The first pie is all the flavors you'd get in a traditional potato soup. Then the entrée is my take on beef Wellington, and you'll end with a peach and hazelnut cream pie, which is a riff on the traditional sort of peach and frangipane."

Dexter cut thin slivers and put them on individual saucers. The judges ate a bite of each without comment, and Henry watched for any tics or tells or foaming-mouthed collapses. But nothing.

Dexter set his fork aside. "You definitely emulated the potato soup well. I wasn't sold on the texture of a soup in a pie, though, and I'm still not. If it had been pot pies, maybe, but even with it thickened up, it's making more mess than I would have liked."

Eli nodded and Rita twiddled her fork between her fingers as she started in. "But the beef wellington was great. The crust was perfect, and your meat had a lovely flavor. I particularly enjoyed the tarragon. You used a lot of it and I was nervous, but it seems like you knew what you were doing."

Of course I did. I know how to cook. But Henry nodded and looked over to Eli, because after one day he'd gotten it figured out—they were going to talk in order.

And Eli did exactly as was expected. "Now, I think all of us know what that peach and frangipane tart is supposed to taste like. It's a summery little dish. There's a French bakery in New York. Barely a door with a hallway. They make the best galettes in the summer, and that was one of my favorites to order." He leaned forward, elbows on the table. "This is something else, and I like it. It feels . . . Christmassy. The hazelnut is something I always associate with the holidays, and I do love it with the peach. It's different, a bit deeper than almond. And doing it set into a cream filling makes it feel more decadent than frangipane." Leaning back, he nodded. "It's good. I don't have any better notes than that."

Henry waited for any extra comments. When none came, his pies were whisked back to his station and lined up on the counter, uncut sides facing front. He followed shortly behind, sliding into place. They were nearly finished, now. Before long, one of them would walk out the doors for good.

Tristan and the other chefs stood behind their stations, waiting in silence as the judges continued to deliberate and scribble notes at the café table. They were at it for a good five minutes before they finally called Sylvia over and slipped her a piece of paper. She checked it and nodded, then stepped up to the front.

And in case that wasn't enough strain on his nerves, the coconut smell still lingered, forcing Tristan's thoughts onto Henry when they should have been fully focused on his own anxiety.

Sylvia sighed, rolled her shoulders back, then smiled out at the room. "There were of course some real hits this week, and some misses."

It wasn't obvious what or who she was referring to, as they stood there in person. On TV, Tristan imagined the cameras zooming in on people's faces and dramatic sting music playing. Nothing of the sort now. Just nerves on top of nerves.

Sylvia clapped her hands together. "First, the good news. The best pies of the week. These came from a very experienced baker, someone who knows how to utilize simple, classic flavors to the best of their ability." She paused a moment, then gestured to the station at the front of Tristan's row. "Willa, you had the best pies. Congratulations, you'll be coming back next week. And that was a fantastic apple pie."

Willa nodded. Tristan did his best to shut up his own thoughts. The screaming doubt in his skull wouldn't do any good and wouldn't change a damn thing now. So he stood there and let it scream and pretended as hard as he could that it didn't bother him.

Sylvia shook her head. "It's only been a week. Unfortunately, only the upper crust can stay after making these pies." She paused and Tristan did his best not to vomit all over his shoes. When she finally broke the silence, her words cut clean through the adrenaline clouding his brain. "We'll have to say goodbye to Ricky this week."

With a snap, the screaming stopped and Tristan had to hold back a laugh of relief. They hadn't said his name. He was safe. He was staying. Ricky had struggled the entire time, barely seeming to hold himself together well enough to get *anything* out for the judges. Objectively, Ricky made sense. And more importantly, he wasn't Tristan.

Ricky stepped out from his station, smiling. It took every muscle in Tristan's face to avoid smiling along with him. Tristan wasn't going to provide the crying zoom shot, so distraught about Ricky leaving. He was too relieved to still be around, still bringing in that extra money and publicity.

I hope it's not this stressful every week. I don't think my heart can take it.

Sylvia put on a good show. She wrapped her arms around Ricky. The experience so far wasn't nearly as brash as Tristan had been expecting. In large part because of Sylvia's general joyful demeanor. She was the sort of person who would . . . well, hug a perfect stranger in front of God and everyone.

Cameras swung past the embrace and the director stepped out from backstage. Not into the shot, but he stepped up, waited for a few seconds, then his voice burst out: "All right, we need to get a final shot of the losing pie, and then we're clear."

Dexter shook his head as he walked over to Ricky's station, carrying an impressively large cleaver in one hand. A single camera followed behind him, along with a couple of production assistants. They coaxed Ricky's entrée pie, a coq au vin pie that had immediately leaked all over when it was sliced, onto the cutting board. A little quiet back and forth, then Dexter raised the cleaver high and brought it down with a satisfying, all-too-final thud. Ricky had been cut. Maybe the metaphor was a bit literal, but it got the message across.

He'd seen the play of it in the trailer, of course, but somehow Tristan hadn't thought they would actually take a cleaver to anyone's work. But when you lost . . . you lost.

"All right, then." The director waved his arm through the air. "We'll call that a wrap. Ricky, we'll get your exit interview before you leave. Everyone else can do their weekly confessional now or in the morning. Your call."

Production assistants carried all the pies up from the stations to the café table, and all of the previous rounds' pies out from backstage, as Dexter slid around to the front. "You all did exceptional work. I know this isn't what any of you are used to, so we were impressed with what you managed to pull off under the circumstances." He clapped, then gestured behind him. "If you all want to take a run through everyone else's final pies, you're more than welcome. Everything else is going home with the crew."

That, Tristan would take part in. He moved forward, right alongside Henry, who hadn't bothered to taste anyone else's pies during the rest of the day. Probably didn't think anything was up to snuff for his refined fucking palate.

They stopped at the same pie first. A giant pastry parcel filled with butternut squash and walnuts that Katherine had banged together. Tristan served a small slice onto one of the provided plates, then reached out with his fork, addressing Henry as nonchalantly as he could. "Finally decided to join the party?"

Henry said nothing, just carried on around the table, staring at the pies laid out.

Tristan put the squash and walnut pie in his mouth and chewed rather than sniping off. It was a pretty decent pie, nicely balanced flavors. They were only slightly marred by Henry's dickishness.

Tristan swallowed and scanned over the other pies. What looked good? People were milling all around, and he couldn't just stand there. His stomach tightened, thinking how close this crowd was about to be to him if he didn't move his ass. Too close, too handsy. He knew from experience that he didn't always behave with the best decorum if someone got too close to a scar, and he wouldn't risk some irrational reaction. Not here.

Henry had pulled ahead, so Tristan stuck next to him. It left enough of a gap between himself and the others that he could hopefully breathe. Plus Henry would keep him on the path of good pies. If he spit something out, Tristan would know to stay away from it.

Of course, following raised Tristan's anxiety. He had to talk, say something. "So, Sequim?"

"Until I was ten, yeah." Henry poked and prodded one of the lemon meringues before moving on, still not taking a bite of anything. "Why?"

May as well be honest. Tristan didn't owe him the nicety of a lie. "I trust your judgment because your food is good, so I'm letting you eat pie before I do, and I thought it would be more socially appropriate if I made small talk with you instead of creepily following behind." At least the animosity with Henry loosened Tristan up. He could say what he meant without filtration around Henry fucking Isaacson.

"Oh, so you trust my palate. You made a good decision."

"I'm still here and Ricky's not, so I made at least two."

Henry's lips turned up into a slight grin for a second. Then he stopped at . . . Tristan's pies. "You may be a pastry bitch, but I happen to trust your palate too." He dove straight into the pear and stilton tart Tristan had put together. "You'll make kicking your ass worthwhile, anyway."

"So I'm a talented pastry bitch."

Henry nodded. "More talented than Ricky."

Not exactly a high bar, so not exactly a compliment. But Tristan let it go and moved on to the beef wellington pie Henry had made. He did *love* a good beef wellington. Plus he could trust Henry's palate, so in he went. Tender beef met his tongue, earthy mushrooms, and tarragon forward, all paired with flaky puff pastry.

"It's good, isn't it?" Henry was smiling a little too smugly over his shoulder. "Go ahead, you can admit it. You already complimented me once."

Damn that smug bastard. Being nice would have been a hell of a lot easier if Henry wasn't right. That stupid pie tasted like a fine fucking beef wellington, and it was already cut apart, so even more tender. It had been a good choice for a pie, and it pushed Tristan into thoughts of sharing actual beef wellington . . . with a shirtless Henry in a candle-lit room.

Rather than respond and feed that ego, Tristan slipped past him. He'd eat in his hotel room, with nobody shirtless except maybe himself. *Boy doesn't that sound like an exciting night?*

Chapter Five

Henry stretched out on his bed, staring at the knockdown ceiling of his hotel room. He should be sleeping. If he wasn't afraid of the hangover, he would have gone out looking for a drink or six to send him crashing into dreamland. Instead, he played the filming session over and over in his head, examining it from twice as many angles as the cameras had captured. What went on behind the scenes gave him more mental footage to scrub through.

After they'd wrapped, Henry had found out that Ricky wasn't even the chef who was supposed to come, originally. The actual pastry chef from his restaurant cut a deal with Eatery TV to send her sous chef, because she didn't want to leave the business behind that long.

Her sous chef, who apparently had such bad nerves he didn't like his *picture* being up on the restaurant's website. He had basically been doomed from the outset, but Henry still flashed cold when he thought about how quick his stint had ended. One day's baking and *poof*. Gone.

The next round was cakes, and that pressed into Henry's mind almost as much as the suddenly real threat of being sent home. Henry could make cakes. His career had been built on the back of a stiff buttercream and bourbon vanilla chiffon. But Tristan, at least, was a caterer. His lifeblood was making big, impressive, multi-tiered cakes. He might be "Carlita's pastry bitch," but he knew what he was doing. Henry wouldn't admit it in public, of course, but Tristan could likely turn out a better product than him, particularly under pressure. A TV show was nothing compared to the burning gaze of an exacting Seattleite bride.

What if not being on top meant Henry would go home? That he'd be another failure, pushed beneath the societal steamroller?

"I don't know if you can do this."

He'd still been in high school when his mom said that. He'd been filling out his applications for culinary programs, and she'd kept suggesting alternate options. Accounting degrees and computer science.

"What's going on, Mom? If it's about the money, there's scholarships and even loans. When I get my own business, I'll pay them off no problem." He had a list of several he could use to go to culinary school, depending where he got accepted. The sort of schools that would set him up for his own restaurant if he played his cards right. And another list that would help him go to community college until he could get to culinary school.

She sat down in the chair next to him and shook her head, blonde ponytail shaking. *"It's not the money. It's . . . I don't know if you can do this"*

Henry stiffened, sure he'd misheard. But he hadn't. *"Mom, what?"*

She sniffled, waving her hand at him. *"That came out wrong. I didn't . . . I'm not trying to dissuade you, but being gay will make your path harder."* She grabbed his hands. *"So much is stacked against you from the outset. If you trip and fall . . . there won't be a lot of hands offering to pick random gay kids back up."*

"And you don't think I can do it?" The words barely came off his lips they were so heavy.

"I think you can do anything." She slid her hands up to his shoulders. *"But I don't know if the world is going to let you. And there are ways to make life easier on yourself. If you're an accountant, you'll always have work, no matter what anyone might think about your love life. But you have to rely so much more on good will to make it in cooking. Maybe established chefs and restaurateurs won't let you get a foot in the door, or landlords will refuse to rent premises to you. And if you get a place, then what? Smashed windows, slurs spray painted on your door, constant harassment—"*

"Mom, this is what you're thinking about?" His intestines twisted into an icy knot. *"Most of that can affect me if I'm an accountant too."*

"I know. I know that." She blew out a long breath and shook her hands out. *"But . . . you're my son. I can't help but worry about these*

things. And any time I think you might be at risk, that stupid voice pops up."

"The voice that tells you I'm not going to be able to make it in the real world."

She hesitated a moment, then nodded, wiping her eyes with the back of her hand. "I told you it was a stupid voice. But sometimes I can't help but listen to it. All things being equal, I don't think there's anything beyond your reach. But it's not equal. And the thought of you getting hurt terrifies me."

It was the first time Henry could recall seeing his mom so human. How often did she butt up against those fears, that voice? How often did she think he would fail? And how many times over the last eighteen years had he proven those fears right? He'd put money down on "more than once."

She didn't make any further comment, but the words played as a constant chorus in the back of Henry's mind, even as he filled out his applications for the Northwest Culinary Institute and the Culinary Institute of America. He didn't want to be a burden on her thoughts like that.

Henry had vowed before he even graduated high school that he'd erase any need for her to worry. As long as he never stumbled, he could never fall and he'd never feed her fears . . . which might have become his own fears too.

He rolled over and padded to the bathroom. It really could all fall apart if he couldn't keep up with Tristan and Willa. Or even Bertha. The most in-demand cake ladies down south might make a dozen a week or more. Good, classic cakes. She hadn't seemed intimidating at first . . . but she did now. And what kind of training did the others have?

Thinking like this isn't doing you any good. He turned the faucet on and splashed some cold water across his face. He couldn't think of anything else to do that was nonalcoholic. Maybe it would shock some sense into him.

Or more likely, it would do nothing and he'd get some good practice making cakes while exhausted tomorrow. Times like this, he'd have turned to a friend to calm him down. Probably Carrie. She was always good at keeping him on the level. It had been that way since they'd met back in culinary school. He slipped out his phone to check the last text from her, received a few hours ago. Just a series of kissy faces, but he smiled anyway.

He tapped out a late response, knowing she wouldn't be awake to get it this late. *San Fran sucks without you. We had to make pies.* And a frowny face.

Texting was something, but in the big empty hotel room, it wasn't close enough to real contact. So he took another splash of cold water, for all the nothing it did, then headed back into his bedroom to stare at the ceiling.

A tiny, stupid voice in the back of his mind reminded him that there *was* someone here he knew. There was someone he could potentially talk to. The problem with that stupid voice was that somebody was Tristan Delgado.

He was sexy, yes. He was good at baking, yes. But there was zero love wasted between the two of them. Professional respect was there, yet that wasn't enough excuse to get them chatting about Henry's problems. *Maybe we don't have to talk.* They could just make out and fuck until they were both too tired to have any concerns left. *I bet Carrie would tell me to go for it.*

She lived to meddle in relationships. She'd kept him from running back to Lance after the big argument. She'd convinced him to go home with a few guys who were shockingly good lays. It was a gift.

Henry's phone buzzed, and he checked it to see a late-night response from Carrie. *Yeah, well, Seattle sucks without you.* And a crying face.

Maybe she would be enough to keep him level, even from afar. Maybe.

"So they're keeping you around for another one?" Lucia failed to stifle a yawn. "That's awesome, Tristan."

"Thanks, but you didn't have to answer. Voice mail is a thing." It had been approaching ten by the time filming had wrapped and he was back in the hotel, showered, and feeling moderately human. "I was planning to leave a message and apologize. They have us shooting the whole round in one day, so I don't know how late I'm going to be during those. But I'll call you at five on the three practice days in-between."

"You call me whenever. When have I ever been an early riser?" She chuckled slightly. "Okay, I admit ten is pretty close to bedtime, but it's fine. You're not allowed to freak out if I don't pick up at one in the morning, though."

He wished he could say he'd never take that long, but what did he know? Any one of these filming days could drag on that late. Bread week would, maybe viennoiserie with all the leavened doughs and puff pastry that came along with it. "If it's one, I'll wait for a reasonable hour."

"Deal."

Tristan sighed. "So I told you about Henry Isaacson?"

"No." She paused a moment. "You're saying he's there too? The guy with the pastry shop in the U?"

"Yeah. The one with the ego. He's still a prick, too, but I want him." Telling his sister that was embarrassing. But not as embarrassing as telling anyone else, and maybe if he said it, the lust wouldn't be so all-encompassing inside him. "It's stupid, but he's sexy, and he's good at cooking, and if he wasn't an egotistical dick, I'd probably be even more tempted."

"Wow. Sleeping with the enemy, huh?"

"Not exactly sleeping with him. But frustratingly turned on to the idea of it, that's for sure."

"Would it be so bad?"

"What?" Tristan shook his head and rolled his eyes. "Come on, Lucia, no. That's not happening. He called me a damn highfalutin caterer today. 'Highfalutin' of all things! Plus he *knows* he's good and has no problem reminding everyone of that fact." Thinking about him raised Tristan's blood. "There wouldn't be enough room in the bed for me, Henry, and his ego."

"Then do it on the floor."

Tristan squirmed. "I'm not getting into *that* situation with anyone who comes along. Especially not someone I don't like." There was too much on the line, too many potential emotions and too much of *himself* out there. Tristan wasn't showing off his body to any Tom, Dick, or Henry who made the blood rush to his crotch.

Especially when the Henry didn't like him all that much.

"Well, look, I don't know what to tell you. You can either bang it out of your system or you can ignore it." Lucia sighed. "'Highfalutin caterer,' huh?"

"Yeah."

"He straight-up spouted that off?"

"Pretty much."

"Didn't you recently get another mention from that restaurant critic? Tommy Wilbanks?"

Tristan was a little shocked that she was following his reviews— he certainly hadn't told her about that one. "He happened to be at a corporate event we were catering. What does that have to do with anything?"

Lucia sighed again. "Sounds to me like Henry's a little jealous of you."

"Jealous?" Tristan snorted. "What would he have to be jealous of?"

"Grass is always greener, right?" She badly stifled another yawn. "Look, I need to get to sleep, but call me tomorrow and let me know if you decided to take Henry to bed."

"Right. Yeah. Good night, Lucia."

"Night."

Tristan put the phone down, shaking his head. "Henry fucking Isaacson jealous of me. Sure." He flopped back onto his bed.

If it *was* true, there'd be some leverage he could use to needle Henry. But it wasn't true. Nobody could be jealous of some creatively restricted, mass-production catering pastry chef.

Tristan sure as hell wouldn't have been jealous of himself. Throw in this bullshit with Robert, his finances, his relationship woes . . . Henry was an ass, but he wasn't stupid enough to want in on all that.

Chapter Six

Henry stood waiting for the director—he'd finally revealed his name as Jacob Maxwell—to start the day's filming. Henry had delivered a list after the first day of practice—nothing drastic, but a few ingredients that weren't on hand. And sure enough, today a bottle of Chambord sat at his station. The label had been hastily covered by a strip of paper that read *black raspberry liqueur*, but it was there.

The director waddled into sight. "All right, are we ready to go?" An affirmative murmur answered him, and he nodded. "Okay, opening shot, monologue from Sylvia, then we're going to go right into filming, so make sure everything's ready and you're set to get right into baking."

Henry nodded. He had a game plan. He had two hours. Fifteen minutes of it was for mixing, forty for baking, another fifteen for cooling the damn cake—twenty or more if he could swing it. Then the rest of the time for decorating and finishing. He'd even worked in time to slow down and talk to the judges when they inevitably swung by for their interview.

The director stepped back into the off-screen. "Five, four, three, two." Point.

Cameras danced again. Sylvia was *not* wearing heels this time. Perfectly sensible Mary Janes matched her black blazer. Black pants with a white blouse. She would have looked exceptionally grave if not for the smile stretched over her face.

"Last week on *Get Baked*, we saw pies of all shapes, sizes, and flavors. Some remarkable, and some leaving a bit to be desired." She produced a cleaver from behind her. "And one pie that left it all on the table. Literally. This week, we're testing our chefs and bakers on another staple of dessert tables across the country. Decadent, sweet, and the reason elastic waistbands were invented: cakes!"

There was a brief pause, then Jacob's voice shot out across the whole set. "Rolling nonstop, now, so be on your game!"

The cameras turned around, all but two. One to focus on Sylvia, one on the judges in case something interesting happened, presumably. Henry was definitely being picked up by at least a couple of them, but he wasn't *quite* so fidgety this time around. This kitchen still didn't feel familiar to him. However, it wasn't entirely foreign anymore. He knew the layout. He knew how to work the oven, had an idea of the actual heat from the range burners. And he'd been into the pantry so many times he could quickly collect his supplies. He had *some* command over his space.

Over his emotions? Well, judging by the magnetic way his gaze kept locking onto Tristan, he didn't have much command over them yet. Maybe Henry was too focused, but he would have sworn those pants were tighter over Tristan's ass than his usual ones.

As it had done too many times over the last few days, Henry's mind drifted into fantasies. No matter how much he jerked off, the fantasies didn't cool or fade.

And Henry had been jerking off like a fifteen-year-old the past few days.

Henry missed most of Sylvia's spiel explaining the competition, but he had the sheet with all the specifics in front of him. They had two hours to make a bundt cake. All that mattered was that it had a classic ring shape and was delicious and attractive and proved that their skills were worth a quarter million dollars. No pressure.

Sylvia slapped her hands against her sides. "Get ready. Get set. Get baked!"

Henry headed straight for the pantry, grabbing flour, baking powder, salt, sugar—everything for the basic sponge. He grabbed some plums and peaches as well, plus crystallized and fresh ginger. Cream and butter from the fridge. It was plenty to get him started.

Back at his station, he set the oven to 355°F. His chiffon recipe came from the UK, and those extra five degrees put the oven in the right range to compensate for the Celsius-to-Fahrenheit conversion. Then he started in, measuring up his ingredients, sifting his dry, separating his eggs, whipping the whites. He'd made probably ten thousand chiffon cakes using this recipe. Making this cake was nearly mechanical. He even had the same model mixer in his kitchen—at the shop and at home. A tiny flicker of familiarity and comfort flashed in his middle. He watched for the right beat on the egg whites. He added his yolks into the dry, then milk, then folded it together. Halfway through, he added some of the crystallized ginger, chopped super fine and tossed in flour so it wouldn't settle while baking or deflate the egg whites too badly. He'd amp up the flavor with his Chambord and ginger syrup. Plus that would add an extra pop of color, give his cake a chance to shine. Maybe it wasn't for everyone, but he didn't need it to be. It was for him.

With the batter fully mixed, he greased and floured his pan—they'd provided a dozen options for bundt pans. He chose the starkly cut, angular one—then poured his batter in and popped it into the oven. Forty minutes, maximum. He'd check it at thirty. He still had to work on the syrup, the filling, the other decoration pieces . . . God, that was a lot. Could he really finish it? Glancing at the clock, he was right on time. He didn't have any reason to panic.

But his stomach still clenched tighter and Henry couldn't resist the urge to glance around at the other competitors . . . especially Tristan. He was just getting his cake in too, and his station had a ton of shit spread across it: a bunch of bright-yellow Rainier cherries, some red wine, a massive block of chocolate, coconut, rock salt. It looked intriguing, and a lot more complicated.

Did I go too simple? Mine has good flavor. He'd made it twice in the last three days, and it was good. It was *really* good. Sell-it-in-his-shop good. Was that enough? He glanced to the right to see what Bertha had, and what she had was a cake in the oven and two pans on the range. She was another person to watch, and hardly the only one. Finn, that Irishman, he'd studied at Le Cordon Bleu. The proper one. In Paris.

Focus, you stupid bastard. Henry turned back to his station. He needed to blanch his fruit to get the skins off, then cook it down in time to cool all the way through. He couldn't worry about anything else. *Especially* not Bertha or Finn.

There wasn't enough room in his brain to worry about them *and* what Tristan was doing.

"So, Tristan!" Dexter marched over. "What do we have to look forward to today?"

What we have is another series of interruptions. But Tristan kept that perturbance off his face. "It's a chocolate fudge bundt with stewed Rainier cherries and rock salt for a little depth and crunch."

"Interesting. Sounds like it's going to be a pretty moist cake."

"Assuming everything goes according to plan." At least he wasn't *quite* so frantic as he'd been last time they'd done this interview. He had the cherries bubbling away gently. He needed to glaze a few he'd left whole and whip some cream with a bit of the stewed mixture, but not so much as to leave the cream slack. Plenty of time to get things done, and plenty of solid flavors on the table. How could you screw up cherry and chocolate?

Dexter looked around, leaning his hands on the counter. "It certainly smells like chocolate. And with whipped cream? A bit like a *Schwarzwälder Kirschtorte*, then."

Tristan nodded. "Without the bite from the alcohol, and with a little more intensity, I think, but the flavors are all in there."

"And is this something you would make for an event?"

"I haven't. But if someone asked, or I thought it was a good fit for a theme, I would. Non-vanilla flavors have been big in wedding cakes the last few years." He gave his cherry mixture a quick stir, releasing a puff of cinnamon-and-wine-scented steam. "Haven't met anyone this adventurous yet, but I'm sure I will sooner rather than later."

"And I guess you'll be prepared, now." Dexter clapped him on the shoulder—he was *awfully* touchy, not something Tristan cared for—then walked to the other side of the room. They were switching up the order this time. There were probably executives mapping out exactly who each judge should talk to at which time for every filming session.

At this point, his cake was down to a waiting game. He had everything in place. His mixing bowl and the balloon attachment from the mixer were in the freezer so his whipped cream would stiffen up better and faster. His coconut had already been toasted off and was cooling, and the rest of his decorations were heat-sensitive, so they were hanging out in the fridge until he needed them.

"Black forest cake?" Henry sat on the stool at his station, looking right at Tristan with bright chocolate eyes. "It flies out the door back home."

"Yeah, I'm sure you do a great business on it. Must be nice."

Henry shrugged. "They have a fair markup, so decent profit margins. I'll have to make sure to try this one of yours, see if it's up to snuff."

Tristan's belly tightened. "You don't think my work's up to snuff?"

"It's a competition." Henry smirked. "I'm sure it'll be fine."

"Fine," huh? Was Henry *trying* to press his buttons, or was it accidental? Either way, buttons were getting pressed. *And I'm going to be the bigger person, even if I strain a muscle in the process.* If Henry *was* jealous of him, acting unfazed in the face of stiff competition was as good a way as any to get under his skin. Hopefully. "I wasn't really going for black forest cake. I'm not quite *that* basic. I was thinking about these cookies when I got the idea. I don't know anyone who makes them, but they sort of appear at Christmas parties."

"Chocolate chip with the maraschino chunks?"

"Those are the ones."

"And they always have too much salt in the dough?"

Tristan nodded, proud to be able to answer up to that one. He picked up the container of rock salt. "Hence the garnish."

"Well, I hope it turns out." Henry shrugged, then ducked behind the counter with his perfect teeth and hair and muscles. Tristan still couldn't tell if there was any direct antagonism in that conversation, or who had come out on top if there had been. *Probably not me.* Henry had seemed completely *unflapped*.

Tristan thrust those musings aside, refocusing on his recipe and double-checking his components were ready.

He'd have time to overthink their conversation tonight.

Breathe, Henry. Almost finished. Henry and Tristan had both gotten glowing reviews on their bundts. Henry's stone fruit bundt had apparently been quite sophisticated, and Tristan's, on tasting, had perfectly captured all the best elements of those damn cookies. Meanwhile, Katherine had made a decent Victoria sponge, but the judges had seemed unimpressed. And Bertha had bested them all when it came time to judge the coconut cakes, but that was a Southern thing, so she had the advantage.

Now Henry stood in front of three tiers of flavored chiffon, covered in a perfect mascarpone buttercream. He'd gone with spumoni for his flavor profile: pistachio, cherries, and chocolate. They all looked identical, covered in the rich white frosting, but each one was flavorful... he hoped. He'd never made a pistachio cake, and never tried to impart so much cherry flavor into a cake before. Not before the practice rounds, anyway. Those cakes had been flavorful, but...

Stop it. The clock gave him only fifteen minutes to finish decorating. He'd worked on his buttercream flowers while the cakes baked. All he had to do now was get them in place, then fill in and make everything presentable. It was a largely traditional wedding cake in appearance, and he had to stand on a step stool in order to reach the top. He'd start there and cascade his blossoms down.

From so high up, he got a good view of what Tristan was doing as well. *Not* a traditional wedding cake would be the answer. Each tier was a different lurid, acidic color. Green—almost the exact same color as the *Get Baked* sign—orange, and electric blue. It was undeniably bold and striking and unlike anything else in the room. He'd pulled out some strange flavors for it too: Cotton candy, butterscotch, and peppermint. Henry had smelled them baking, and it was like a candy shop in an oven.

Now Tristan embossed and etched out a quilting pattern on the sides of his cakes. Would he manage to finish in time? *I sure won't get mine done if I keep watching him.* Henry pulled his attention back to his flowers. Those were easy enough. A dollop of buttercream followed by his frozen flower. He piled up a mass at the top, then trailed down in an offset wave so no part of the cake was left undecorated.

After a while, Sylvia's voice barked across the space. "Five minutes, everyone, five minutes."

Henry finally attached the last of his premade flowers. He had to go in with a leaf tip, now, fill in all the gaps so none of the buttercream peeked through where it wasn't supposed to. He glanced at Tristan and . . . Damn, he was fast. He'd finished all the embossing and outlining. Now he was placing dragées into each vertex, driving home that quilted appearance.

Henry's hands didn't shake as he squeezed out his piping. Better than he could say for his knees or his confidence, as he rushed up and down the step stool. He finished as the clock hit thirty seconds. A quick check for anything that needed cleaning up revealed nothing. So he sat and waited and relished in the camera zooming on him. It would be great footage, make him seem a lot more relaxed and competent than he actually was. Hopefully.

"And that's time, everyone!" Sylvia's voice cut across again. "Spatulas down, piping bags to the side, and gird your loins!"

Henry looked at his cake. It was fucking pretty. Any blushing bride would love it, aside from it probably upstaging her dress. He looked around and behind him, and nothing held up in the same way. There were nice cakes. Beautiful cakes. Intricate cakes. But his was the only one that stood out in that classic, virginal-white style. He couldn't say for sure if that was what the judges wanted, but if so, he had clearly delivered the best.

Then there was Tristan's cake. Crayon-colored, clean-lined, and easily as tall as Henry's, with silver dragées sparkling. It was a breathtaking cake in its own way. *And if I'm honest, give me those flavors any day.* Gentle, more-nuanced flavors weren't bad, but those candy tastes had been a bold decision, whether they worked out or not. Henry appreciated boldness.

The cameras resituated, production assistants appeared from backstage, and Sylvia stood with the judges in preparation for the final presentation. After a few minutes moving around and adjusting, Rita started it off. "Hezzie, why don't you come on up, now?"

There was very specific wording during these sections. No one could say anything that denoted time or order. That way the judging could be effectively cut together in any order to maximize drama. At least the show staff was honest about their needs instead of shooting a million times to get things right.

Hezekiah carried her three-tiered naked cake up with the help of a couple of assistants. Henry failed to avoid rolling his eyes. Who knew when they'd decide to cut *that* into the episode, but come on. A naked cake in five hours? *Hopefully she didn't strain herself.* Henry *hated* the stupid naked-cake trend. He hadn't learned to perfectly ice, cover, and decorate cakes so he could show off his goddamn crumb coat.

She got her critique: A mixed bag. Hezzie had good flavors, but the judges agreed she could have done more with her five hours. Then they went down the line. Nina, with the long red hair, and Finn had solid flavors and good decorations, but nothing that seemed to blow the judges away. Dorian, a Black guy with short hair and a slightly hawkish nose, and Willa were strong contenders all the way around. Dexter and Rita *both* went in for a second bite of Willa's maple and whiskey cake.

Then it was Bertha's turn. She was approaching seventy, if not over—Henry wasn't about to ask—so she didn't carry her own cake up. The two production assistants lifted it . . . but one lifted on *three* and one lifted on *go*, and her cake tipped at a forty-five degree angle. Henry had never seen so many people simultaneously gasp and clench their assholes. Well, he couldn't be sure that every asshole in the room clamped tight, but his sure did until they got that cake back on the counter again. It made it up to the café table intact, got middle-of-the-road critiques from the judges, then was returned without issue, but any small faith Henry'd had in the production crew had evaporated.

Those same assistants now headed toward Tristan's station. That had to be a damn heavy cake, and a nice one. Too nice to fall on the floor. Henry couldn't live with himself if he let that happen. *Am I insane?* He only debated that for a moment. Then he marched up and grabbed the other side of Tristan's cake base before the black-clad production folks could get in there. "Ready?"

"What are you doing?"

That's a hell of a question. "If you're anything like me, you trust a baker to carry your cake more than a backstage assistant." Plus Henry had come here to compete, to prove himself; he didn't come to win because the crew didn't know how to transport a cake. "Ready?"

Tristan scoffed, hesitated, then nodded and slipped his hands under the other side. "Ready."

Slowly, they lifted it, and the thing was definitely heavy. Heavy and not evenly balanced, and Henry had ended up with the heaviest side.

They got Tristan's cake up to the table. He nodded once to Henry, his mouth set in a tight line. "Thanks."

Henry didn't respond, just headed back to his station. The cameras tracked him all the way until he sat. *Maybe my nice-guy persona will get me a little extra time here.*

Dexter broke the silence first. "It's certainly striking. Remind me of your flavors in this one."

Tristan pointed from the top down in turn. "Peppermint, butterscotch, and cotton candy."

"First-grade dream, then, right?" Dexter chuckled at his own joke. "Well, the quilting is nice and even. You've managed to get all the dragées in place, nothing missed. More than I can say for some of the quilted cakes I've seen." He tapped a shiny, pearlescent dragée with his fingertip. "Here, I would have punched in with a coning tool. It would press in the lines to better imitate puckering on fabric. But that's the nitpickiest nitpick I could possibly come up with. It's not even a problem, merely something to consider." He winked at Tristan, then glanced back at Eli. "Anything?"

"They are incredible colors. You don't miss this cake. You can't miss this cake." Eli sighed. "And personally, I want to cut into it. Rita?"

She pulled out a fresh knife and sliced a thin section of each layer. Then she laughed. "You really went for your color choices, didn't you?"

The color of the fondant carried through the layer of buttercream and into the cakes themselves. Green for peppermint, orange for butterscotch, blue for the cotton candy. Henry let himself smile this time—it was clever and striking and the sexy little bastard was good. That fact was considerably less annoying than Henry might have expected. It was almost . . . admirable.

Rita commented on the flavors first. "Everything is exactly what you said it was. They're flavors that can easily be heavy and sickly, but I think you've skirted around that. The mint is subtle and bright, the butterscotch is slightly burnt, and the cotton candy has that signature lightness to it."

"It does." Dexter narrowed his eyes at Tristan. "Genoise?"

Tristan shook his head. "I don't know about you, but I can't think of a genoise that would support a cake this size. It's my basic chiffon."

"It's an amazingly light chiffon, then. Nicely done."

Eli stepped in next. "Your buttercream carries the flavors exceptionally. The cake itself is not terribly sweet on its own, which helps you get the balance right. I definitely wouldn't eat this buttercream straight out of a tub . . . which I may have done before. But it controls the balance on the sugar when you put it with these cakes. Especially this cotton candy one. That's *so* impressive."

Henry chewed on his lower lip. It was going well. The *only* critical comment to be had was that small suggestion on "puckered fabric." Henry couldn't say there was anything else he saw on the cake, either. Flavor he couldn't judge yet, but he doubted very much that Tristan had screwed that up.

"Thank you, Tristan." Dexter stepped back behind the table. "It was a . . . monument to everyone's childhood."

Tristan nodded. Production assistants whisked the cake back to his station—since judging was over, Henry was far less concerned about it being destroyed—and when Tristan turned around, he was grinning. Not at anything in particular and he covered his mouth almost immediately, but Henry had definitely seen teeth and dimples. Goddamn dimples. Real, nonfictional people didn't have motherfucking dimples.

"All right, Henry," said Sylvia, "let's see your cake."

Henry lifted it on his own. Hauling it would be a struggle, but like hell he was leaving it to the crew. Then a second pair of hands appeared under the bottom board. Slightly rough, slightly reddened hands with flecks of dried buttercream sprayed across the knuckles.

"Now we're even," Tristan whispered from the other side of the cake.

Henry chuckled. "Except I'm the better baker."

Tristan didn't miss a beat. "You're certainly the cockier baker."

"Careful. Your mic might pick that up."

"Rivalry's good for ratings, right?" They delivered his white behemoth to the front of the room. Tristan nodded at him. His cheeks bore the slightest tinge of red as well. "Good luck."

"I don't need it."

The red expanded over Tristan's face. He shook his head as he walked away, and Henry felt the tiniest twinge of guilt for acting quite so much like himself. But now wasn't the time to address that. He needed to be judged.

"I have to say, this is spectacular." Sylvia backed up, making a big, theatrical display of taking it in. "Very bridal."

Henry stood stock-still as the three judges swirled around his cake like sharks on the hunt. If there was some missed flaw—an uneven buttercream coating, or God forbid a gap or a crumb on his otherwise pristine white monolith—not only would they notice it, they'd ream him for it. On national television.

This thinking isn't helpful. His stomach clenched and unclenched like his fists. Far too much sweat squelched in his palms.

Eli stopped and fixed his eyes on Henry. "How many flowers did you make for this cake?"

"About two hundred." It was time-consuming, and he hadn't actually counted, but a cake of this style and size should take that many. "Plus leaves and other little filler flowers."

"It's quite impressive. Some of these are not small flowers, either, and to get them so perfect." He shook his head. "Admittedly I hate making buttercream flowers, so I'm biased, but this is so impressive."

"It's very clean," said Rita. "Monochrome cakes are notorious for looking dull, as I'm sure you well know. White in particular. You almost always want to include another color like ivory or silver to give yourself some contrast. But I don't miss it." She reached out and stopped a millimeter short of actually touching his cake. "And you didn't use any fondant for this?"

"No. It's all a classic Swiss meringue buttercream."

"Then that is particularly astounding. People use fondant *because* it's so hard to get that flawless finish with buttercream. But you've done it."

And Henry waited. Dexter made another full circle around, hand to his chin as his eyes raked over the cake. And then he finally stopped. "Beautiful. We have eyes, so we can see that. It's technically wonderful, but it has to taste up to par too. What were your three flavors?"

"It's spumoni. Cherry on top, pistachio in the middle, and chocolate on the bottom. And they're all chiffon cakes."

"Well, I hope you make a good chiffon cake, then." Another clean knife appeared. Henry hadn't seen them deliver that one. Maybe there was a secret stash somewhere under the table. Dexter slivered out a bit of each layer and laid them on one plate together. "You've got even distribution of your ingredients in all three layers, which I like to see. The colors aren't so intense that they clash with the clean, classy appearance you had on the outside." A muted green for the pistachio, deep brown for the chocolate, and a reddish pink on the cherry level.

The judges ate from each layer in turn. He had his simple white buttercream running between each layer. He'd considered adding in something more for moisture. A quick fruit reduction or a curd or *something*. But he'd syruped his cakes and his buttercream was far from dry. Hopefully the judges would agree.

"I *love* pistachios." Dexter bore a bright smile. "I do. Pistachio gelato is my absolute favorite treat. I use it as a reward to bribe myself into doing things I hate." He gestured to the muted-green cake with his fork. "That is a good pistachio chiffon. Better than the one I turn to. It's not easy to get the flavor to stay strong all the way through with pistachio. It has a tendency to throw off the ratio of oil." He nodded, twiddling the fork between his fingers. "The cherry isn't overwhelming. I'm guessing you used maraschino syrup for your color and flavor in the actual sponge?"

"Yeah."

"But only just enough. It's not sickly sweet. And the chocolate, well . . . I think that's your weakest point. It's not a very intense flavor. When something looks this elegant, I also expect it to be decadent. The first two layers are, but the chocolate falls a little flat for me."

"Don't listen to him," said Rita. "All of your flavors are refined, which *I* appreciate. The subtlety is good in my book."

I should have amped the damn flavors up. He knew it was one comment. He knew everything else was good, but it still burned to hear that, and from Dexter Wilson no less. That single comment introduced a niggling fear that he really didn't appreciate.

Rita's judging continued. "The balance of the whole thing is spot on. You could take a bite of each tier together and you wouldn't lose any of the other flavors. I think you could make a brilliant marble cake with this."

Not a bad idea. He didn't know how marketable it would be—his Neapolitan loaf cakes sold pretty well, but spumoni wasn't nearly as popular—but it would probably taste great.

"All right, thank you, Henry." Sylvia smiled. "I'll be taking the rest for further testing, nothing to concern yourself with."

Henry cracked a smile as his cake was whisked away. He eyed Tristan on his way back, and an apology almost fell over his lips. He *did* feel like a dick for that *good luck* exchange. But the moment was wrong, and the emotions were wrong, and before he knew it, he was once again behind his station without saying a word.

As he kicked himself for keeping quiet, his gaze fell on Katherine, the last baker in the row. She gave him a weak smile but . . . well, if Henry had to follow himself *and* Tristan, he wouldn't have been too confident either. Especially not with three-tiers of different fruitcakes covered in boiled icing. Boiled icing could hide a lot—*No, no, it's supposed to look messy, I promise*—but not the severe tilt to her tiers. Not even the most perfectly executed Swiss meringue buttercream would distract from that particular mess. It was a shame too: her first two rounds had actually been solid, especially that coconut cake, even rivaling Bertha's.

Once more, they stood behind their cakes. Tristan's whole body chilled. Not from fear, but . . . he was close to taking this round. Many of the critiques had been middling to poor, with Katherine taking the worst of it for her sloppy presentation. The judges had made a few remarks on the dry texture of Dorian's lemon cake, and had been "uninspired" by the combination of vanilla, spice cake, and too-pale chocolate that Hezekiah had gone with. Tristan was pretty certain he'd bested both of them. Even in his overthinking cynical little heart, he knew he'd done a damn good job and had gotten it recognized by the judges.

He turned to face Henry. This wasn't the most sportsmanlike conduct, but fuck it. It would feel damn good to gloat. "So, five bucks that it's me? Assuming you still think you're a shoo-in."

Henry shook his head gently, not making eye contact with him. "I don't take losing bets."

Tristan struggled against the heat rising slowly up his cheeks. Not that it did him any good. The heat rose all the same. "I don't think it's *that* much of a sure thing."

"It might not be. But you wanted to know if I'd bet. I'm not betting against a wedding caterer on a three-tiered cake challenge. Especially not after hearing your critiques."

"You weren't a hopeless slack-ass or anything. And yours looked a lot more like a wedding cake than mine."

All Henry offered in response was another of those shrugs.

Sylvia stood in her black pantsuit, coming across too much like a funeral director for Tristan's comfort. But it wasn't the death of *his* run, not this time. He had a safe spot for sure. But would he have a *coveted* spot?

Or was he fooling himself and about to get his beautiful three-tier cake chopped in half by a cleaver? Moment to moment, he flip-flopped between the two thoughts, so fast his stomach threatened to unmoor and jump free from his mouth.

Sylvia clapped her hands. "Now, we saw some really amazing cakes from all of you. From the humblest butter bundt to towering, three-tiered behemoths, everyone put out quality product, but one of you was a *slice* above the rest, with clever flavor incorporation and some even cleverer design choices." She paused, then turned to the left. Toward Henry . . . or maybe not? "Tristan, congratulations."

Gentle applause from all around washed away the cold of Tristan's nerves. He'd won. Second set of challenges and he'd *won*. Sure it was cake, but to be the best out of a group of professional bakers and pastry chefs? With a candy-flavored, off-the-wall cake like his? Not to mention against that flowered giant Henry made? Tristan couldn't hold back a smile as warmth bubbled through his veins. *Classic wedding cake didn't cut it, but my ideas got the job done.*

Sylvia's husky voice broke through Tristan's stupor. "Yes, well done, Tristan. Your candy-inspired confection was truly a sight, not to mention an experience for the taste buds. A well-earned victory." There was a little more applause, then Sylvia went dour. "But unfortunately, not everyone's cake was quite at the same tier."

She paused, building the drama. Tristan rolled his eyes. *Katherine. No way they're letting her stay with that mess she presented.*

Sylvia sighed. "Hezzie, I'm very sorry to say, you'll have to head home."

It was a little punch to the chest. Not in a sad way. But Tristan *would* have bet money on Katherine going home. By all logic, she should have been the one out. What did it mean that she was still standing?

"The judges liked your coconut cake, but your Victoria sponge was a touch on the safe side, and they didn't think you handled your time well enough on the tiered cake. And unfortunately, someone has to go." Sylvia shook her head and approached, arms open.

"That's a wrap," said Jacob from backstage.

A wrap? No explanation of what had gone down? From the bewildered looks on everyone else's faces, Tristan wasn't the only one taken aback. Katherine herself had a thousand-yard stare. The *only* explanation that made sense to Tristan was that Katherine, at least, had strived for originality. She'd swung for the fences and failed. And maybe that was worth more to the judges than something well-executed and predictable.

There was no way to be certain his hypothesis was correct. *I'll have to run with it anyway. No safe plays.*

Henry clapped him between the shoulder blades, pulling Tristan back into the current reality just in time to watch the crew carry a cleaver and step stool over to Hezekiah's cake. "Told you I'd lose if I bet against you."

Henry's hand landed a second time, then he was off, leaving nothing but goddamn motherfucking coconut. That couldn't simply be the shampoo, and they'd made the coconut cakes hours ago.

Soon, though, he was distracted from thoughts of natural coconut scent and assaulted by a rush of congratulatory back-patting and phony encouragement from the other competitors. None of them could actually be happy he'd won. Impressed maybe, but these weren't his friends. None of them actually felt good about coming in third or worse.

Because Henry was *definitely* second.

Willa, though—she showed more interest than the rest. Dark eyes twinkled as she smiled. "Congratulations, Tristan. I'll make sure I try these award-winning chiffon cakes."

"I wouldn't call them award-winning. Not yet." Tristan chuckled under his breath. His chiffon had brought him some mentions here and there around Seattle, but no awards. "Thanks anyway."

"You like doing those kinds of flavors? A little weird?"

Didn't everyone? "Sometimes you need something different. Shake things up. I don't get to play with food this way very often at work, so it's nice to stretch my wings."

"Well, I know about shaking things up. Don't fly all the way across the country at seventy-five because you like to avoid a shake-up." She winked at him. "Congratulations again."

And off she went, leaving Tristan . . . pleased, sure. But he was pretty certain he'd never talked to her before this. It was nice but unexpected. *Maybe she was shaking things up.*

All in all, though, Tristan felt good. As good as he could imagine feeling on this show.

He'd beaten Henry fucking Isaacson at cake.

He felt pretty *damn* good.

Chapter Seven

Henry toweled off his hair, then flopped down onto the bed and grabbed his phone. Nothing interesting on Facebook. He wasn't allowed to post, anyway. Not until he got back, and he couldn't mention the show until it had aired, and even then only things that had actually happened so far in the broadcast. That cut Twitter right out of his schedule too. Emails? He never got any that weren't business related, and those were being handled by Athena while she headed up the shop. He'd already texted Carrie, and if he sent her too many messages in a row, she might get worried about him.

I need company. He could watch TV and it would give him noise, the facsimile of not being alone, but he'd been doing that since he got to the hotel. It hadn't helped. If anything, it made him miss nights out at clubs and lunches with Carrie that much more. Still, even if he could have gone out and socialized, he couldn't risk exhaustion or a hangover. He needed to be one hundred percent on his game tomorrow.

Henry stared at the ceiling again. He did that a lot when the internet bored him and he wasn't taking extra-long showers. It made sense why people had had so many children before entertainment was freely available. Sex had been about the only thing to do. Even if it was with yourself. But Henry didn't want to do it with himself anymore. Unfortunately, the one person he wanted to entertain himself with was not an option.

Henry hopped up and went to the fridge. He needed to get off the bed or he'd be in for another round of fantasizing, and although his libido might have thought he was teenager, every other part of him knew otherwise. He pulled out the paper plate with the slice of acid-green cake on it.

Tristan's peppermint cake wasn't quite as good as decent sex . . . but it was better than bad drunken sex. Henry didn't bother with a fork, just picked it up with his hands. The sponge held together well enough that he didn't get crumbs everywhere. As he bit into it, his mouth cooled, and he relished each tiny shard of leaf studded through the chiffon.

He's got a better chiffon than I do, the wedding-catering bastard. Lighter and more evenly textured, but still perfectly firm.

I have to get the recipe from him. If he'll share. Maybe I can trade something.

An inkling of a notion peered out of Henry's thoughts. A strange half-idea, half-fantasy, with maybe a sprinkling of apology on top. Tristan was down the hall and, if Henry really wanted to, he could see what it would take to pry that chiffon recipe off of him.

The fact that Henry's idea/fantasy ended in naked-shower-time was irrelevant. That wouldn't happen—he knew that much.

After finishing the cake, he threw on a shirt and his pajama pants. His plate could stay where it was, but he was sure to grab his key card from next to the TV. At the very least, he had *an* excuse to leave his hotel room. And if the excursion went well and Tristan was as God-awful *bored* as him, he could have some stimulating baking conversation too. Maybe they could set enmity aside in the name of them not going stir-crazy.

This is incredibly stupid. Tristan didn't like him, and Henry had been a dick about the whole *good luck* thing not two hours ago. He hadn't been able to quite apologize for it when they'd been talking after the filming session. But he was making the stupid decision anyway. He walked out of his hotel room, marched down the hallway to Tristan's door, rapped a few times, and waited.

After about ten seconds, the door swung open on a broad, half-exposed chest. *I should have prepared for the visual onslaught.* There was another tattoo too, partially hidden. A brightly colored sugar skull visible on his left pec.

Tristan yanked his bathrobe tighter over himself, covering up the ink, the chest, and the beginnings of a dark happy trail that had sent

Henry's mind spiraling. "Okay, why are you at my door at nine o'clock at night?" He pushed his glasses higher up on his nose. "If this is some weird sabotage attempt where you're going to kill me, I'm pretty sure that's against the rules."

The gears of Henry's mind clunked and ground past the momentary block of all that exposed skin and those hard lines and muscles. *I should have thought this out better.* Suddenly, a late-night recipe swap seemed not only unlikely, but stupid and a *little* bit rude. But he was here and Tristan was staring at him, waiting. Henry cleared his throat a couple of times. "Your chiffon cake. It's really good."

"I'm aware, thank you. Chat over?"

Henry shook his head. "Can I trade you for it? Now that cake week's over, I can't use it to beat you." Heat rose in his cheeks, hot and ragged. "Okay, it sounded stupid in my head, and it didn't get better when I said it out loud."

"I imagine not." Tristan yawned wide, showing off straight white teeth and a nice thick tongue and—

Focus, damn it. You're here for the chiffon recipe, not the sexy pastry chef.

Except he was partly here for the sexy pastry chef.

Tristan finished his yawn and locked eyes on Henry. "I'm not giving up my chiffon. Yours is plenty good, anyway." He cocked an eyebrow. "That it?"

Okay, so recipe retrieval was a bust. Time for mission number two. "About today, when I smarted off to you before? I'm sorry."

One corner of Tristan's mouth quirked upward. "You'll have to be more specific. You have an ego the size of Texas; you smart off a lot. Especially at me."

Ouch. But not inaccurate. "Right. I meant when you wished me good luck and I was an ass."

Tristan nodded. "Oh. Well, apology accepted, then. Anything else?"

This isn't going smashingly. Henry hesitated a moment, then sighed. "I'm dying of boredom, I don't do well alone, and I want someone to talk to."

"And you're picking me?"

Henry shrugged. "You're good at what you do and I know where your hotel room is. Plus nothing I do is going to *lower* your opinion of me."

"Plenty you do could lower my opinion of you. But probably not this." Tristan dragged his gaze up and down Henry before he finally broke the quiet. "The restaurant downstairs is cheap and open until eleven. It would do me some good to eat something that's not cake today. And you were nice enough to come apologize. Eventually."

Holy shit, the plan had worked? This outcome wasn't the naked, sweaty shower fantasy Henry had left his room with, but it was a lot more than he'd expected. "If you want to."

Tristan shrugged, revealing the sugar skull for a fraction of a second. And a peek of nipple that shouldn't have done *anything* for Henry at all. But it did. "Let me put clothes on. A bathrobe probably violates the health codes in California as much as it would in Washington."

"Are you planning to go into the kitchen?"

"Depends how bad the food is."

Henry rolled his eyes as Tristan walked back into the room, but his body betrayed his excitement, tingling electric at the surprising... not quite victory, since he didn't have the chiffon recipe. But not a failure, either. His crazy plan had gotten him dinner with someone. It had gotten him company. It had gotten him out of his hotel room and out of his own head.

I wonder how many other tattoos he has? One tatt was a drunken night in Cabo. Two was a habit.

Henry cupped his hand around his mouth and leaned closer to the door. "I'll be back in two seconds." Then he slipped back to his room and hastily tossed on some clothes that wouldn't embarrass him. And he deodorized, ran a comb through his hair to tame it into shape, and sprayed some of his fancy cologne to walk through. It was a luxury he'd considered not bringing. Did he really need to smell like a tropical jungle to bake cookies? *Of course not.* But wearing it, he could carry himself a little higher and with a heapful more confidence. And a heapful was about the right amount for tonight.

Henry sniffed himself—he smelled good. *Hopefully Tristan'll like the scent too.* It shouldn't have been important, but Henry told himself he didn't want to be an insensitive dinner guest. He didn't believe that was the reason, but he told himself that anyway.

Tristan almost had to laugh at the absurdity of the whole situation. He and Henry now sat together in the very lonely restaurant. *I expect Hell to freeze over any second now.* Dinner with Henry fucking Isaacson? He wouldn't have bet on that in a million years.

A haggard waiter stood with them, wearing a surprisingly convincing smile. "What drinks can I get started for you guys tonight?"

Tristan almost asked for coffee before remembering it was after 9 p.m. "Do you have any herbal teas? Chamomile would be lovely."

"The only herbal we have is peppermint."

"That'll be good."

"I'll have the same." Henry smiled and nodded to the waiter. "I love peppermint. Just had a brilliant peppermint cake, but that's not the most nutritious dinner."

"Okay, I'll bring out the hot water and the tea bags so you can steep it to your taste." The waiter's smile widened for a moment. "Be back shortly."

Tristan leaned forward. "You had peppermint cake in your room?"

Henry shrugged. "I *really* like peppermint, and your peppermint cake was *really* good, so I took a slice with me."

Tristan snorted and broke eye contact. "Thanks." The restaurant was suddenly getting warm. "The key is candy oils instead of extracts and emulsions. And fresh mint." He suppressed his cringe. Mostly. "And I shouldn't have told you that."

"It's okay. I promise to only use it to crush you in the competition."

"So nothing to worry about. Considering I've already come in first and you . . . what, you lost two weeks in a row?" Smack talk didn't roll off his tongue, exactly, but like hell was he going to let Henry fucking Isaacson best him at it without a fight.

Henry shook his head. "I didn't lose." He pointed to Hezzie, sipping away at her martini glass at a corner table. "That's what loss looks like."

"So you'll be drinking whatever fruity monstrosity that is when you lose?"

"Hey, that fruity monstrosity is probably delicious. I love the taste of red number five."

Tristan snorted. When he breathed back in . . . coconut. So much coconut. And some oranges and vanilla and wood, but the coconut was still so prevalent. "What cologne do you wear?"

"Oh, it's not bothering you, is it? I kind of wondered if I should wear it at all."

"It's not a bother. You just smell like coconut all the time and I want to know where I can get it."

"I buy it online. It's called Seas of Trinidad. But please don't judge me when you see the price. It's a luxury I allow myself."

"Oh, I'm absolutely judging you when I see the price." He sighed. "But then you don't have a smoking habit to support, so I bet you can afford it." The only reason he still smoked was the thought of dealing with the world sans nicotine. *Maybe I can quit after this competition. Life should seem easy then.*

"Here we go." Their waiter trudged back with a white ceramic teapot, a couple of mugs, and a little green box of tea bags. He spread them out across their table. "We had a spill in the kitchen and we're running a little lower on staff for the night." He finished his setup. "You guys need longer to look at the menu?"

"Yeah." Tristan felt bad for the guy. He'd probably been looking forward to a nice, easy late shift. "Just a couple minutes, we got to talking."

"No problem. I'll be back."

Tristan glanced to the single-sheet menu they'd provided. The fare wasn't beautiful or gourmet, but it seemed perfect for a late-night meal. Lots of classic, simple food, and most of it under ten bucks. Within Tristan's price range. "You know what you're going to get?"

"Umm . . . the chicken club. That should keep everything clean for them. Last thing I want to do is give an understaffed kitchen a big, complicated order right before closing."

Surprising. So far, Henry's ego didn't seem to be dominating. At least not all the time. "Sounds good."

Henry sighed and ripped open a tea bag wrapper. "So, thanks for humoring me."

"Well, you know." It wasn't a totally comfortable conversation, but it wasn't painful or awkward. No worse than average small talk. "I'd already called my sister, and I wasn't ready for bed yet."

"Yeah, but you were close." Henry winked at him. "All warm and comfy in your bathrobe."

"Well, I'm not highfalutin enough to have a bathrobe at home, so I took advantage of it." Would Henry pick up on his use of the word?

It didn't have any *visible* impact.

The waiter came back up with his pad and pen. "Okay, what'll it be, boys?"

Tristan jumped in first. "Can I get the croque monsieur?" It wouldn't make much extra mess for the kitchen either.

"And I'll take your chicken club." Henry picked up both menus and handed them back. "And could I possibly get some cream?"

"Cream's no problem. I'll get that ASAP, and the sandwiches should be out in a few minutes." The waiter headed back toward the kitchen.

Tristan gaped at Henry. "Cream? Please tell me that's not for your tea. For your mint tea."

"Don't judge me for that either."

"I'm absolutely judging you for the cologne *and* for this. You wanted to know what would make me lose respect for you? Putting cream in your mint tea is the answer."

"Have you tried it?"

Tristan rolled his eyes. "Of course not. It's an abomination."

The waiter dropped off a little metal pitcher without a word. Henry pulled his tea bag out of the hot water and set it on his napkin, then grabbed the cream. He dolloped some into his mug, stirred it, and handed it across. "Try it."

Tristan took it, examining the milky, pale-green tea. Like jade in a mug. It smelled fine. How bad could a little cream make mint tea taste? Then again, he'd thought the same about putting cream in his coffee one disastrous morning—never again. Black all the way.

Tristan raised it to his lips and took a slow drink. There was an immediate hit of strong mint—he'd have to make sure to get that brand if he could find it at home—followed by a nice creamy finish. Like . . . like a liquid version of those peppermint puffs that showed up around Christmastime every year. Not sweetened, but the same besides that. Although sugar was an intriguing thought. "It's not bad." He handed it back. "It feels very indulgent."

"I like it with sugar, but I don't want any more sweet today."

"Valid point." Tristan hesitated a moment, then grabbed the cream and poured some into his own mug. He set the tea bag aside and drank a lot deeper from his mug. "Okay, I cede to you on the cream and mint tea."

"Stick with me and I'll never lead you astray." Henry winked, and Tristan liked it a little too much. But luckily, he was in for a rescue.

"All right, guys." Their waiter was back again, food in tow. "We've got your croque monsieur and your chicken club. Are you good on the tea?"

"I think everything's fine," said Henry. "Thank you." He didn't wait for the waiter to leave before biting in. Tristan *always* waited for the servers to leave before eating. He didn't eat out much, but it seemed rude to make someone working for tips stand there and watch you stuff your face.

Once their waiter had left, Tristan cut the croque monsieur in half and picked up one side to examine. There was the gruyere and the nice boiled ham. Hopefully boiled, if they were going to call the thing a croque monsieur.

"Well, this is an unpleasant meal." Henry had his sandwich up too, a frown on his lips. "No offense to present company, I'm talking about the sandwich. I'm not sure about this tomato at all." He picked at it with one fingertip, and his frown cut deeper. "And I swear they used mechanically separated chicken I could buy at the supermarket."

"That doesn't fill me with hope for the ham."

"It probably shouldn't." Henry sighed, then took another bite. He swallowed and didn't die, but he was still frowning. "It's not only mechanically separated chicken. It's under-seasoned mechanically separated chicken. And what the hell is this bread?"

"They put bakers in a hotel with bad bread?"

"I'm putting my money on mass-produced commercial Pullman loaf. So yeah, bad bread." Henry gestured to Tristan with the partially eaten sandwich. "Well? I'm not the only one going to be suffering through this. Eat."

"Is this how you sell so many pastries?"

"Absolutely. Guilt, insults, and peer pressure."

Tristan snorted and rolled his eyes. But he risked a hearty bite of the croque monsieur. The crust on the bread was flaccid. The ham tasted like salt, the gruyere may as well have been warm vinyl, and the béchamel tasted of raw flour. "I apologize for inviting you to dinner here. They got zero parts of this sandwich right." He set it down on the plate. "Not even *you* deserve this."

"Flattered." Henry also set his down. "Mine's a little better, then." He pulled out a strip of bacon. "They didn't mess this up." He noshed on that and then retrieved a second, unbitten strip that he handed to Tristan. "For putting up with my late-night recipe call."

"Sure." Tristan took the bacon and, for a second, his hand brushed against Henry's knuckles. Then he pulled back. "So, you ready to fess up on how much that cologne costs you?"

"Not particularly." He sounded nonplussed, but pink worked up from his stubble, headed for his ears. "I normally don't even give away the name so no one can see it. Gives the wrong impression."

"Hey, as far as I'm concerned, you're still a cocky, egotistical Seattle pastry chef. What do you have to lose?" Tristan hesitated a moment, then gave Henry a little shove he hoped came off as playful.

"That's how you think of me?"

"Honestly?" Should this happen? *Doesn't matter, because it is.*

"Well yeah, honestly." Henry gestured to their food. "We're not eating this crap, so let's feast on the decadence of our mutual tension."

Tristan would have laughed if it had been anyone else. "Yeah, then. You think pretty highly of yourself, and you make sure everyone knows it. Like your cracks about beating me."

"Hey, I made cracks. You still kicked my ass, so what do they matter?" Henry sighed. "I could be pissed off about your assessment, but I thought you were an arrogant, elitist bastard, so I don't have much of a leg to stand on."

"'Highfalutin' was the word you used, if I remember correctly." Another chance to get that word back in.

"Yeah, that does sound familiar." He took another attempt at his club sandwich, then set it down with a disgusted grimace. "More honesty?"

Tristan shrugged and left his response at that. But it was apparently enough.

"I wanted to bust into catering *bad*. It's a market that would have expanded business opportunities for me, maybe freed me up from the same old, same old. And I thought I had a good chance until Carlita's took off with some ingenue pastry chef." He gave Tristan a shove back. "Not your fault you're amazing, but that didn't stop me being ticked off."

"It's entirely my fault. But I wouldn't say 'amazing.'" Still, it warmed his belly hearing that from Henry of all people. "I didn't know you wanted into catering. Can't imagine why you'd give up all that freedom of choice to instead stand around, making the same white wedding cakes, day-in, day-out." Although if Lucia was right, then it would slot right into the jealousy theory. That was about the only way someone could be jealous of him.

"Yeah, well, I'm happy with the shop. But like you said, I've got an ego bigger than Texas. It was a blow to lose out on that business. Not to mention you're up by two on awards and accolades and shit around Seattle."

"You actually keep track of that?"

"How else am I going to know which one of us is winning?" He sighed and pushed his plate aside for his mug. "And the cologne's two hundred dollars, but the bottle lasts me a year, so I don't want to hear anything about it."

Tristan blinked, trying to process not only the price tag, but also everything else that had just gone down. It was easier to focus on the cologne. "You're going to hear everything about it. Two hundred dollars?"

"In one year. It's not that bad." Henry wafted his arms toward Tristan. "Besides, I smell great."

He did. The cologne was coconut and tropics, all underpinned with something distinctly male that clawed into Tristan's middle and growled demandingly, urging him to keep eye contact with Henry as his mind wandered to . . . unhelpful places. Bedrooms with sweat and coconut cologne in the air, warm hotel sheets, and all the too-many pillows tossed aside to make room for two bodies.

Two bodies passing the time between rounds of baking.

Henry sighed again and leaned back in his chair. "Yeah, I probably don't need to spend what I do. Lance thought it was stupid and overpriced too."

"Lance?"

Henry shook his head. "My last mistake. Hated that I was spending so much on cologne when he'd buy whatever was next to the shampoo and razors." Henry gave a dry little chuckle. "Among other things he hated." He got quiet for a couple of seconds, then waved his hand through the air. "Who knows? I'm sure there's a cheaper cologne that smells as nice. But this one makes me *feel* good when I wear it, you know?"

We're not talking about Lance, I guess. Got it. "Well, it better for that kind of money." Tristan chuckled as his nerves unspooled. "Sorry for calling you cocky."

"Why? I am cocky. I know what I can do, I know I'm good at it, and that's okay. I'm gay, if you missed that tidbit, so I have to be self-assured and confident and over-the-top to make any dent in society. Wouldn't want to be a disappointment to my parents, right?" Henry shrugged. "I also know when other people are good at shit, but I don't like to talk up the competition too much."

He was gay, so he had to be cocky. It explained a bit more about Henry. When you started on a lower rung, you had to work that much harder, be that much more bombastic, and draw that much more attention for the same . . . everything. Tristan had always chosen disappearing as a coping mechanism instead. "It must have been a big deal to come to my door and ask for that recipe, huh?"

"You bet your sweet ass it was. First time I've come across a chiffon cake I like better than mine, and I like mine a hell of a lot."

"Well, I still can't give it to you."

"I figured you wouldn't. You don't owe *this* cocky son of a bitch the time of day." Henry drained his tea and sighed. "But thanks for spending time with me, anyway."

Tristan smiled honestly, completely. "Yeah. No problem."

Small problem. If Henry had been sexy before—and he certainly had—now he was . . . gravitational. *Thank God there's a table between us.* Tristan wasn't about to let himself fall headfirst into a relationship that was all passion and charm. That's what screwed his family up. Every time.

But damn it if this didn't test his self-control.

Chapter Eight

Three days later, Henry furiously beat his dough, eyes flicking between his bowl and his oven and the clock above the café table. Zero difficulty during practice, and now filming day? Everything had decided to explode. He'd made one batch of cookies perfectly fine—his gingersnaps were cooling to be decorated with white chocolate. They'd already crisped nicely. But his chocolate chip had been a nightmare. For two batches. Now he was cutting it far too close, and this time, they had to work. *If I'd fucking been paying attention to my oven, it wouldn't have happened.* His first dough had been an utter catastrophe. He couldn't explain it. He'd made the same cookies a half dozen times in their practice days. But today they were tough and didn't spread out the way they were supposed to. His recipe was designed to be crisp and served with milk, not chewy and pillowy. They'd also come out too salty. If he hadn't known better, he would have diagnosed it as too much baking soda, but he'd *definitely* measured it out the same way he always did.

The second batch had burned because he lost track of time. He'd been paying attention to the other bakers—like Nina, who'd loudly tossed an entire plate filled with cookies into the trash—and especially to Tristan. But Henry had been *sure* he was okay that time. He'd made these bedtime chocolate chip cookies a hundred thousand fucking times. They always cooked exactly the same way.

But they hadn't.

And they'd burned.

It wasn't even a small, mahogany around-the-edges kind of burn. If it was like that, he could have at least served them and taken the hit if it came to it. These had gone black along the bottoms.

Now he had his dough ready and he quickly plopped balls of it onto his lined pans. He'd have time to get them cooked. They only took about ten minutes. Decoration was another matter. He wasn't a "rustic" chef. He was a precise machine and prided himself on that fact. That meant clean lines, not messy, half-melted icing. He wouldn't be satisfied with half-assed cookies, and if he wasn't satisfied, what the *hell* was he actually proving?

He tossed his pans into the oven, set the timer, and had to move on to his gingersnaps. They were both classic flavors, and he knew he had to perfect them. No hiding behind exotic spices or fancy techniques today.

He drizzled lines of tempered white chocolate all the way across his gingersnaps, then again in the other direction at a slight bias to make his crosshatch. The chocolate gleamed—hopefully some of that shine would carry through once it set.

"Fifteen minutes, chefs!" Sylvia said the awful words loud and far too joyously. "Get those cookies cooled and plated. We may not have Santa Claus, but we do have three hungry judges. And me."

Henry glanced into the oven, patently ignoring the camera that hovered near him. The barest edges of his rounds had browned, but not enough, and the middles hadn't started their fall. He willed them to cook faster, or for time to go slower, or for his asshole to unclench for half a second. Any or all of those things would have been welcome.

Another minute and his cookies had collapsed properly in the center. He whipped them out, transferred them to cooling racks, and started to wave his pan at them to cool them like an idiot. But what the hell else was he going to do? Royal icing would slide right off his cookies at this temperature. They were bedtime because they went with milk, but they were also bedtime because of the royal icing moon in the center.

"You're not done?" Tristan had turned around to look at him as he plated up his own cookies. "You know you're screwed, right?"

Gee, thanks for the update. "Not if I pray hard enough." He waved the pan and checked the clock and waved a different direction and checked the clock. The time wasn't slowing down at all. He only had ten minutes left. He glanced his fingertips across the top of his cookies and . . . the tops were cool. Not the core, but he had two dozen chocolate chip cookies to ice and needed to start now if he wanted a chance at finishing in time.

"I don't know if you can do this." His mom's voice played through his head once again.

Can't fall down that rabbit hole right now. Henry set down his pan and grabbed the pale ivory icing, doing his best to ignore the constant itch at the back of his skull, the old words resurfacing yet again. Carefully, he edged out twenty-four crescent moons, forcing himself not to watch the clock at all lest he screw up one of his outlines. He wasn't going to trip, not if he could help it.

"Five minutes, bakers! Anything not plated can't be counted!"

Yeah, give me a goddamn minute. Or ten. He switched to his flooding icing, which was slightly thinner and . . . *Please set up in time you filthy bastards.* Luckily, he had a lot of time to let them sit. The judges started at the other side of the room and he would be nearly the last one to present. If anyone needed to be worried, it was Nina. She'd also had to start over at least once.

His hand quivered and that was okay. This flood icing didn't need to be neat. It just needed to fill the crescent outline. He worked each in turn with a toothpick to force the icing into the very corners of the moon, and by God, he managed what he set out to do. He didn't like his cookies being so warm. The icing could still melt slightly and sink in and throw off the flavor balance, but it didn't seem like it was slipping *off*.

"One minute, chefs, sixty seconds!"

Fifty-eight by the time she got done talking. He dropped his cookies onto the platters, not worrying too much about stacking nicely and neatly. As long as nothing sat on his icing to dent it or peel it away. Henry's stomach clawed up into his throat, and only sheer will kept it from jumping out of his mouth along with the bagel from craft services.

"And that's time, my lovelies!" Sylvia clapped a couple of times. "Step back, close your eyes, and we'll roll on with the judging."

"And we're cut!" The director walked back out. "Get into final positions, then new shooting in sixty."

The cameras winged around into a familiar pattern, the same one they always took during judging. *Breathe. Just breathe.* He had good gingersnaps, peppery and crisp and well-spiced. It was the stupid chocolate chip giving him agita, but surely *someone* had fucked up worse than him. Anyone would do.

Breathing is good. The anxiety was easing, the longer he waited, the longer he had for his icing to set up and his cookies to cool. And there was still no leakage on his crescent moons. He was good. He was good enough and, as much as it burned him to admit it, good enough would have to work today.

He took a moment to scan the room. Tristan was still sexy, no change there. Willa was sitting on her stool, grinning like the damn cat that ate the canary. Nina wasn't ripping the hair out of her head, which was good news for her. She'd recovered. Henry really, really hoped he could say the same about himself.

Backstage, Jacob cleared his throat loudly. "Okay, and we're rolling in five, four, three, two—" Point.

Sylvia stood with her normal, final-judging expression: a slight smile and sober eyes. "Katherine, if you could come on up and show us what you've got."

Henry's stomach dropped like a stone. They were starting with Katherine. They were starting on his end, right behind him. What the actual fuck! He watched in abject fear as Katherine carried up a two-tiered platter of precise, attractive cookies. Farmers' market baker or not, Katherine had proven too capable for comfort this round.

"You okay?" Tristan's voice was barely above a whisper. "You look like you're going to pass out."

Henry shook his head, forcing the easiest smile onto his face that his current level of nerves would allow. "I'm good to go. No worries." TV cameras be damned, there was no controlling his expression. "A little less sure than I'd like, but I'll be fine." He could go home. He could lose out on this, prove he hadn't been worth inviting here. He could be another gay boy who fell and never got back on his feet . . . the way society expected, the way his mom had confessed to worrying herself sick over.

All because of stupid fucking bedtime cookies . . .

"Thank you, Katherine. I'll just be stealing a few of those."

Katherine laughed at Sylvia's closing joke. Her closing joke. The judging was over. He hadn't heard a word of it and it had to be him next. He leaned closer to Tristan. "How did she do?"

"You were right there."

"I wasn't paying attention, okay?"

"You really are nervous, aren't you?" Tristan shifted his stool closer to Henry's station. "She had an okay critique. They liked the Russian tea cakes, but weren't blown away by the clove cookies." He sighed. "Where's the cocky fucker I hate? What'd you do with him?"

"He left when I burned the second batch of cookies today."

Katherine passed by, and Tristan quieted his voice even more. "You're good, Henry. You're really good, and your cookies look good. I'm not going to tell you you'll be fine, because what the hell do I know, but if you go out, I bet it's on a damn strong bake."

Sylvia's voice came from the front. "Henry, let's see what you've got to bring to the table."

Henry took a few deep breaths, smiling weakly at the flashed thumbs-up from Tristan, then carried his two platters up front. He gave them a last once-over, then waited for the judging.

Eli smiled at him. "So, what do we have here?"

"These are gingersnaps with white chocolate, and my bedtime cookies, which are chocolate chip and pecan with some quick-setting icing on top." Although probably not quick enough.

"Bedtime?"

Henry nodded. He pushed himself into customer-service mode, explaining things like he would in his shop. "I designed the recipe to go with warm milk. They're still good on their own, though."

Eli chuckled. "Well, I think I'd like to start with the bedtime cookies, and let the irony be damned." He picked up four and handed them out. One to each of the other judges, one to Sylvia, and the last one for himself. Eli broke his in half. "Your icing isn't quite set. It's not liquid, but it's a little messy." He flashed his fingers, smeared with sticky pale icing. "Cookies are still warm."

Of course they're still warm.

Eli bit into it and chewed for several centuries, at least. When he finally swallowed, he nodded. "It's got a good flavor. I like mine chewier than this, but you did what you set out to do. It really would be great with milk."

"Yeah, I agree." Dexter set his down. "In fact, it almost *needs* milk. I wish you'd given us a jug of it or something to go along with them. They cling to the mouth a bit."

Why the hell didn't I warm some stupid milk up?

"I like the pecans. They're different than the traditional walnuts." Rita smiled, then grabbed a gingersnap. "Now these, it's hard to go wrong with, and they look completely impeccable. You didn't overdo the white chocolate, which is normally the main downfall for me. Covering all of it or even half of it in white chocolate makes it overpoweringly sweet."

They each took one and bit down. Crunching filtered over from the table. Henry was still clenched tight, every muscle tense and hard.

"It's a nice gingersnap." Dexter gestured with the cookie as he spoke. "But any of us in this room could make a good gingersnap and drizzle some white chocolate on it. I do wonder if this wasn't a bit safe?"

That was the punching, gnashing word that iced Henry's stomach. *Safe.* He'd played it safe. Nothing good came out of the safe zone. Scientists didn't learn exciting new things by only exploring the universe between Earth and Mars. Jewelers and painters and sculptors didn't innovate by following textbook examples their whole careers.

And Seattleite pastry chefs didn't prove their worth by making safe gingersnaps and substandard chocolate chip cookies.

"I think there *is* something good here." Rita held up half of his gingersnap, staring intently at the cookie instead of at Henry. "Indian sweets aren't like the stuff we have in America. They're less sweet and rely a lot more on different combinations of flavors." She lowered the cookie. "Well, maybe not *gulab jamun*, but as a rule. You get cardamom and milk and pistachio nuts." She tapped a fingertip on the half cookie. "There are some different spices in here, which I appreciate. I'm getting black pepper and anise and even some proper cardamom. But it's not quite enough to cut through the molasses for me. I wanted twice as much of all your spices, maybe. They're there, but I have to *try* to find them. They're a touch too subtle for my tastes."

God, Henry had somehow fucked up his perfect, clean gingersnaps. They didn't taste right. They were either boring or missed the mark. Neither option put his stomach back inside his abdomen where it belonged.

"And I have to agree with Dexter." Eli nodded, a tiny frown on his face. "For a two-hour challenge, they seem slightly basic to me." He bit into the gingersnap a second time. "It's a good, proper gingersnap, though. I could eat a box of these, but I think we were really looking for absolute perfection and innovation and these fall solidly in 'good cookie' territory."

Good cookie. Before coming on *Get Baked*, Henry would have taken *good cookie* as a compliment. But no one in that room could think it was a good outcome. He nodded. "Thank you." Production assistants scurried away with his cookies, and Henry forced himself to walk back, though his feet all but dragged. Tristan locked a silent gaze on him as he passed by, brows furrowed, but nothing more than that.

Henry sat on his stool, hands in his lap. It sucked. He didn't even feel sick with nerves. He was just *cold*.

Tristan stood towards the back of his station as they waited for the results. He wanted to say something to Henry. He felt sorry for him. That critique would have sent Tristan into the fetal position. After all, they'd seen Hezekiah go home on a safe bake. As safe as chocolate chip cookies and gingersnaps.

After their conversation over that lack of dinner at the hotel restaurant, Tristan saw new angles of Henry. He still seemed like a walking ego in a lot of ways, but for the first time, Tristan felt like he got where that cockiness came from. He understood why. Henry wasn't the first gay guy Tristan had met who thought he had to do more, push harder, be stronger. And let everybody and their grandma know about it.

And because of that newfound understanding, Tristan didn't want to see him go home. Not because of those cookies. They weren't indicative of Henry's skill. Every baker—every person—had an off day. Tristan himself had had plenty. Days when the scars from his past stood out too starkly and threw his entire world off-balance.

Henry's off day just happened to have lined up with this round of the competition. And although Tristan would probably stay, he wasn't sure he could be happy about it if Henry went out now. Tristan would rather have the stiffer competition and see Henry fucking Isaacson stay than win against someone less skilled.

What did he do to me that I actually . . . like him?

Sylvia smiled beatifically, dressed in brilliant crimson. "You all provided us a spread that would bring life to any Christmas cookie swap." She scanned the room. "But one of you has churned out cookies that would make even Mrs. Claus herself blush with envy." She settled her gaze on Tristan and Henry's side. "For the second time, congratulations to you, Willa. You made crisp and crunchy biscotti, and your spritz cookies were sheer perfection."

Willa beamed bright and swept a white curl behind her ear. Tristan applauded softly. She *did* know what she was doing. Her leftovers were consistently some of the best on the table at the end of the day.

On the other hand, so were Henry's, and he was certainly on the lower end of the pack today. It wasn't all a matter of skill. The competition was as much temperament as prowess. Managing your stress, not cracking under pressure. And sometimes it was down to not having bad luck.

Sylvia shook her head. "Now unfortunately, we're going to be losing someone. I'm never going to like this part, and it's certainly not getting any easier week to week, but it is the way the cookie crumbles." Tristan's belly tightened in the seconds of apprehension.

Sylvia sighed. "This week, we have to say goodbye to . . . Nina."

Henry drew in a sharp breath, and a camera whipped around to capture him. Tristan looked too. All the flush poured out of Henry's cheeks, leaving behind a pallor, and he stared wide-eyed across the set.

Nina strode up out of her station to shake Sylvia's hand. "I figured as much." She was a stout, doe-eyed woman with long dark hair. "Thank you for the opportunity."

It wasn't a complete surprise to Tristan either. While he'd been candying the orange peel to go with his molasses cookies, he'd checked in on the competition. Morbid curiosity to see how far behind he was. Nina had been tasting and adjusting and tasting again, and the furrow had never quite left her brows. Plus, in the judging, they'd pointed out how runny the raspberry filling was. Tristan couldn't help but feel a slight wash of relief that it was *her* leaving. *It's not because I like Henry. But I don't think he should go home because of some bad luck.*

Best not to acknowledge that Nina's luck might have been bad too.

Dexter moved out from behind the table and draped an arm around Nina's shoulders while the crew handed Rita the cleaver this time. Everyone watched as she settled into position, raising the knife up high. It gleamed in the overhead lights before she brought it crashing down. Off to the side, Nina cringed and flinched back as one of her oatmeal thumbprints split straight in half, splattering raspberry jam up across the blade and along the countertop.

A few second of ringing silence through the set, finally broken by Jacob's voice. "Okay, we're clear!"

Henry rushed over to Nina, and Tristan followed. Did he know her? It didn't seem like it, but he was an extrovert. He could have easily known everyone by now.

Henry grabbed Nina's hands in his. His comment was barely audible. "It should not be you going home. It should be me."

Nina rolled her eyes. "Bullshit. Try my flavorless, sloppy raspberry oatmeal cookies and say that to me." She shrugged. "I don't know what went wrong with them, but they weren't right. This is the consequence."

Tristan hated the idea of dealing with people, but Henry needed *someone* to pull him out of there. There was no socially appropriate response left to be made to her, so Tristan moved up, smiling morosely at Nina, and led Henry away. "Don't give the judges ideas. Think that might be a smart decision?"

"I was *sure* I was going home on that. They thought my cookies were boring. Why did I stick to stuff that was so simple?"

"No one said boring; they said safe."

"And you know it's exactly the same thing."

"What if it is? Safe and boring executed well is better than anything executed poorly." Which was a crock Tristan knew neither of them bought.

"I didn't come here to be safe. I came here to prove that I was worth paying attention to. I didn't come here to be second to last."

"You don't know where you were, other than not first and not last." Tristan spotted the plate of oatmeal thumbprints being carried past and snatched one. He broke it in half and offered part to Henry. "Try it. This is what she made this last round."

Henry rolled his eyes, but he took the lumpy little cookie and bit into it. He chewed. And chewed. And chewed. And chewed. Then he finally swallowed. "Okay, mine are better than that, but it's not a high bar."

Good to know. Tristan led him around to the café table, which was slowly being filled with cookies, and dropped his half back on the plate. "You're right, it's not. But you don't have to be perfect at everything. No one can be. Not any of the judges, damn sure not any of the contestants. Not even Ms. New York's Treasure Willa." Who was currently shaking hands with the judges. Again.

Henry sighed. "There's a reason I don't make a lot of cookies, but I make these ones all the time."

"Well, you won't have to make them again while you're here if you don't want to." There weren't any other cookies on the list they'd been given. "And remember this pep talk so you can give it to me when I fail miserably at bread in four days." That was the one round Tristan wasn't looking forward to. He was a pastry chef, and bread was distinctly *not* dessert. "You owe me one for doing this."

Henry shook his head. "You'll be fine."

"You will be too."

Henry finally cracked out a chuckle. "Those oatmeal cookies were pretty underwhelming."

"Ragging on other bakers. That's the Henry I remember."

"You make it sound so bad. I'm delightfully catty." A bit of proper Henry crept back into his face. "That's what I tell myself, anyway."

It *shouldn't* have mattered to Tristan at all if Henry was broken or worried or delightfully catty or just an asshole. And yet it did. In the pits of his stomach, in a place he normally choked off from everything else, there was turmoil. He . . . Damn it, Tristan liked getting that glimpse of authenticity, that humanity.

He wanted to see more of it, peel back further layers. Tristan could *identify* with the anxiety, but what else lurked underneath the surface?

"Oh God." Henry pulled up close, whispering. "Finn's macaroons. How do you fuck up macaroons?"

Tristan stifled a laugh and went along with Henry to the plate of coconut cookies. *Henry fucking Isaacson.*

Chapter Nine

Henry stood under the showerhead. He'd been there for at least twenty minutes, because hotel hot water heaters were a godsend and he intended to take full advantage of this one as long as was possible. As long as he was *allowed* to stay.

I seriously could have gone home. He turned around so the water cascaded down his back. Tristan had made him feel *less* awful, but there was no denying the truth. He had to kill it in all the other rounds if he was going to stay. This cookie debacle felt like a free wake-up call from the universe: *Get your shit together, because I'm not going easy on you anymore. Nut up, buttercup.*

Apparently the universe is a real asshole too. Or it just hurt a hell of a lot more when you fell from a pedestal you'd put yourself on. Cockiness, confidence, all that shit? It usually kept Henry happy and functional in the face of adversity, even if it did make a lot of people think he was arrogant. But when a blow *did* land, like the fuck up with those cookies? It was all the worse for having held himself so high.

Henry cranked the water temperature up another notch. Soon, steam billowed over the curtain. He breathed in all that humidity and warmth, rubbed up and down his arms. He felt *okay*. That was something he could settle for, in the given situation. Okay, and hopefully with improvement in his future over the next few days' baking.

Bread was next. Henry could do bread. There were probably a lot of pastry chefs in that kitchen who didn't really handle "traditional" baking in their day jobs, but while it wasn't Henry's bread-and-butter, to use a far-too-apt pun, focaccia and rolls and filled loaves weren't uncommon sights in his life. They just made their appearance on his table at home instead of in the shop window. He could rebound on bread.

Then why doesn't my stomach believe me? It was still protesting—jumping and leaping around, trying to make him toss his cookies in quite the literal sense. His cookies, Nina's cookies, Tristan's cookies, and even Willa's prize-winning spritz. Which had been pale golden, buttery, and flecked with delicate, fragrant pineapple mint. Who the hell even thought to pick pineapple mint of all the available options? Not him. *But then, I didn't win, did I?*

As some small consolation, his bedtime cookies had been among the most widely smuggled offerings. They were good enough for the public . . . but not for Dexter, Rita, and Eli.

Henry turned the shower off and stepped out. He dried himself quickly and unthoroughly, then walked into the hotel room proper and the quiet that came with it. Always so quiet. He still hated that. There was no company save for Lucy, Ethel, Ricky, and Fred, since the only channel worth watching at the Hotel Majestic showed black-and-white reruns. And the programming director liked *I Love Lucy* even more than Henry.

He sat on the edge of the bed and grabbed his phone. Carrie had tagged him in a picture. She was out clubbing and had ordered a grasshopper. Not her drink of choice, but when Henry got enough liquor in his system, he inevitably wanted one.

Seeing his friend deepened the ache for company. And he'd have to settle for leaving a comment on the picture. *Don't try to drink like me, hon. You'll get alcohol poisoning.* Then he pulled up her last text message and shot back another missive. *Miss you. Almost got kicked off today.*

Talking to her was some salve to his wounds. But it didn't take away that terrible loneliness. Henry didn't do alone well. That was what had made Lance walking out last year so painful.

That last fight hadn't been their first. Hell, it hadn't even been their first fight where Lance had called him self-centered, and the biggest sticking point always seemed to be how much time Henry spent on the shop. They'd gotten together a couple of months before Henry had made the big move and decided to open his own place, and had broken up just short of him getting it stable. Lance's protests had begun as simple requests that he not be forgotten, and Henry would oblige . . . until the work overtook his brain again. Had it been wrong of him? Of course.

Knowing that still hadn't prepared him for the blowup when he'd come home that night. No chill, no attempt to talk. Lance had *"been through this too many times"* and wasn't *"going to play second fiddle to a stupid pastry shop that still hasn't taken off."*

His final admonishment still played through Henry's head when he was down enough and alone enough, reaching from the depths of his mind to torment him. *"I've been trying to chip out a spot for myself in your life since we met. But there's no room for me. You're too in love with yourself for that."* Then the slamming of the door.

In the morning, after a fight, Lance always came back.

But Henry had woken up alone. And he'd cried for a while, but not for too long because he was running a pastry shop, and his peak hours were early, for breakfast.

In spite of Lance's continued absence, a tiny spark of hope had burned inside Henry that he'd see Lance back when he came home that evening. Instead, he'd seen a closet half-filled, bookshelves partway emptied, and a couple of lamps missing.

And the key to the apartment with that stupid panda sticker Lance had stuck onto it.

That was close to a year ago, and the memories still managed to creep into his thoughts and cut him up from the inside. *This is why I hate being alone. It's an invitation for ghosts from the past.*

The residual water cooled against his skin in the emptiness as he held his phone, hoping for a text message. The mild, unwavering churn in his stomach was nothing compared to the clawing of loneliness he felt in that moment. A sick, squelching, gnawing in the pits of his soul. One that begged him to run from it but refused to leave. Back home, he could have headed out to one of his usual haunts and found some companionship. He would have been out having that grasshopper with Carrie.

But even if his normal social reprieve was off the table, he couldn't sit and wallow another second. He dressed himself for some level of propriety—pajama bottoms, baggy T-shirt—and marched himself out of that godforsaken room and over to the only company he could think of: Tristan. This time, there was no mangle of confusing or unhelpful emotions as he made his way down the mass-produced hallway. Henry knew exactly what he wanted: company. It didn't matter what form it took, what they did, where they were, as long as he wasn't alone with himself in that room.

He might have been willing to give up his own chiffon recipe if it meant not having to sit with his thoughts anymore. Not that Tristan would want *his*.

He knocked, and a few seconds later, the door pushed open. Tristan held a slim black cellphone to his ear. His eyes widened at first, but then he nodded to Henry and waved him in without ever breaking the stride of his conversation. "I'm glad I caught you while you were still up. How's Karen handling staying at the apartment?" Tristan laughed as he gestured Henry toward the bed. "Tell her she can fight me if she doesn't like the bathroom décor. And it's autumn harvest, not orange. Yes, I know it's orange too, but . . . stick up for me, would you, Lucia? Abuela's bathroom was the same color." He cringed. "Okay, point taken, I'll consider changing it. So you're both good?" Pause. "And you'd tell me if you weren't?" Pause. Tristan turned to face out the window and lowered his voice, but Henry could still hear him. "Robert hasn't been hanging around? You know he's not allowed there. Well, I have to check over and over. I'm your big brother and I'm not going to let you get hurt, even if I am eight hundred miles away."

Sounds serious. Henry considered disposing of himself in the bathroom for a while. At least for a few minutes. He could take the time to send Carrie one more text. But Tristan held up a finger at Henry before he could move.

"Okay, Lucia. I'm at the same number as always. You *call* me if something happens. No bullshit, and I don't care how many times you've heard it already. Send Karen my love. And make sure you tell her she can fight me about the bathroom. I love you." Tristan hung up the phone, then sat beside Henry. "Sorry. I promised my sister I'd call every day. And I wasn't expecting company."

"It's not a problem with me." Henry smiled at him. "Everything going okay? That convo sounded a little heavy."

"Oh, that's nothing. She doesn't do well alone . . . I mean, I don't do well with her being alone. Makes me nervous. Regular big brother stuff."

"I wouldn't know. Only child." Henry stuffed his hands into his pockets. "But I get it. Family."

"So, were you looking to try the hotel restaurant again?" Tristan slipped off his glasses and massaged the bridge of his nose, finger and thumb right against the indents they'd left behind. "Because I don't think my taste buds are up for that."

"No. I was just in that room and I was getting into my own head a little too much. Again. I tend to do better around other people than by myself. Like your sister, I guess." Henry looked at the walls that were identical to his own, yet somehow twice as inviting and welcoming. "But if you'd rather be alone, I'm sure I can manage. I just . . . figured I'd give it a shot."

"Oh god, it's totally fine. I was even dressed this time."

"Not like you've got anything I haven't seen."

Tristan slipped his glasses back on. "You don't know what I've got, so don't assume." He smiled tightly. "I've actually got a portal to the netherrealm hidden somewhere on my body. But keep that under your hat."

"Mum's the word." Henry chuckled. Loneliness and memory no longer clawed away at his stomach lining, but that *comment* sure did. His mind spun right back into teenage, hormone-fueled imagination. *If this was a porno . . . Okay it would make a weird porno, but we'd totally be naked now. Or soon, anyway.* Maybe Tristan had some more tattoos that hadn't yet peeked their heads out of hiding. "So, your sister's living with you?"

"It's a temporary thing. She needed a place quick." Tristan stared at the floor, twiddling his thumbs. He stayed silent a breath too long to seem natural, but not long enough for Henry to try to change the subject. "She . . . well, she had a rough time with her husband."

"Oh." Henry didn't press for what that meant, exactly. *None of my business.* "I hope everything works out."

"Yeah, me too. I was going to stay, but she made me promise I'd come and I'd try to win. She didn't want me to lose out on it because of her." He glanced up with a small, quiet laugh and unlaced his fingers.

"I was *not* sold on it, but she's doing okay, and she's got someone I trust staying with her, so I'm able to relax a little bit." He shook his head, like a dog getting rid of water. "I'm absolutely positive you came here for my intense family drama, right?"

"Hey, I've got company. That's all I needed." Henry stretched and tried to look somewhat natural. "So you call her every night?"

"As long as we're not getting in at 3 a.m. or something crazy like that."

"That's some devotion." Some real devotion. To something he cared about. *Someone* he cared about. It made him all the more attractive. Hard to accomplish—he'd always been pretty—but this dug deeper. It was like finding out a guy could also sing or dance or was a black belt.

Or make a damn good chiffon cake.

Maybe not as cock-twitchingly exciting as a singing, dancing, black belt pastry chef, but every part of Henry's body warmed as he took in what Tristan was all about. A deep, sinking-into-a-hot-bath-on-a-winter-day warm.

Tristan rolled his eyes again, and the tiniest bit of red crept up dusky cheeks. "How are you holding up? I'm guessing you were in your head about the baking?"

There was the subject change Henry had forgotten to make. "The judging was a little bit surreal. I don't want to say it was like almost getting shot, because how the hell would I know, but that kind of thing." Henry mimed a gun and fired his finger at the window. "If the judges' sights had been an inch to the left, so long Henry."

"Well, I guess I wouldn't know about that." Tristan gave an exaggerated sigh. "I've been right at the top of the pack, haven't I?"

"And *so* humble. I thought *I* was the cocky one, here."

"I'm trying it on for size since you don't seem to have any self-confidence to bring to the table." Tristan clamped his mouth shut and shook his head. "Sorry. That was too far."

Henry snorted. "That was *not* too far, trust me." Maybe too true, but it wasn't malicious. Besides, trading barbs back and forth? That was the most natural interaction he could think of with Tristan Delgado. "I think it's impressive you can be so full of yourself after losing to Willa twice."

Tristan chuckled and his face relaxed. "At least it wasn't three times."

A week ago, Henry would have fought the urge to sock Tristan for that. Now he didn't resist it, but punched him right in the shoulder while laughing. A little punch. "Douche."

"Hey, assaulting the competition is probably grounds for removal." Tristan punched back, light, playful, with a broad smile. "Anyway, I'm going to get my ass handed to me on bread. I'm a pastry chef. Carlita has someone else she uses to make breads if we need them."

"You'll be fine. Bread's the easiest thing in the world. Don't underprove it and the rest'll probably fall into place." It wasn't quite that simple, but now wasn't the time to overcomplicate. "I'll show you tomorrow if you want."

"You're just making up for punching me." Tristan got in another shove at Henry's shoulder, a little harder than before. "You help the competition like that, you're going to end up losing. To me. How will you ever show your face in Seattle again?"

And Henry shoved back, a strange and sudden giddiness bubbling electric through his veins. That warmth was only increasing too, and no matter what he tried, he couldn't keep from smiling. "Maybe you're right. I shouldn't help. Make sure you pour your salt directly on top of your yeast. *Really* helps that first rise."

Tristan shoved again. Hard. For a pastry chef, he had decent strength. Probably some nice, firm muscles that Henry failed to stop thinking about.

"Even I'm not that hopeless with bread." Tristan got in a second shove. "And if you're going to start something, you've got to be faster than that."

"Come on, hitting a guy with glasses? That wouldn't be terribly fair."

"That's your excuse?" He slipped off his frames and set them on the end table. "There. Now I'm fair game, Mr. Chivalry."

Henry had punched Tristan because he hadn't known what else to do with the mess of emotions in his belly begging him to *touch* the tawny-skinned catering bastard *and* his sexy-ass biceps. And now? Now Henry was reading a hell of a lot into the way Tristan played back.

"Fair game." There was a hitch in Henry's breath, a renewed lightning pulse in his muscles, and then he did more than shove. He pushed Tristan back on the bed and willed his cock to stay soft as he shifted, climbing on top of him.

And his will to stay soft? That did nothing to help.

Henry straddled him in such a way it *hopefully* kept his "growing problem" a secret. "Did I mention I was a wrestler in high school?"

"I always *knew* that was a gay sport."

"It's the ultimate gay sport." Henry patted Tristan's cheek, then jumped off and sat back down, adjusting himself so he wasn't *too* obviously erect. "Of course football was a close second. Spandex-covered men in piles fighting over balls."

"You could say that about most sports."

"And I do."

Tristan sat up. His face was more than tinged pink. It flushed his skin, especially his ears. "So do you always get a hard-on when you wrestle, or is that a recent development?"

So much for keeping it a secret. Go me. Henry shrugged nonchalantly, avoiding eye contact. "Not every time. Only when the guy I'm pinning is cute and I haven't had any in a while."

"Oh, well then, no wonder." Tristan was totally red, and a glance in the mirror told Henry he was matching. Tristan looked into the far corner by the window. "I am pretty sexy. For a guy who makes a living eating wedding cake and buttercream."

Henry couldn't think of anything to say. Sweat trickled cold down the back of his neck, and his limbs suddenly locked into place, leaving the room still and silent for too long.

"I guess I made that kind of awkward." Tristan cleared his throat, but it didn't strengthen his voice when he spoke up again. "I didn't mean to point it out and embarrass you. It sort of—"

"Embarrassed?" Henry shook his head, finally breaking through the quiet that hung around him. "I mean, I was, but not because you said something. Because I popped a boner at a boner-free event." He smiled sheepishly, finally looking *near* Tristan, but still not making eye contact. "Wasn't quite expecting that."

"Join the club." After another couple of seconds, Tristan jumped up. He apparently wasn't frozen like Henry. He drew the blinds and the curtains, then jogged over and flicked all the locks on the door . . . but not before slipping out the *Privacy Please* placard. "You know . . . you're hot, right?"

Henry nodded, resisting the nervous giggle that pressed to escape. "I've been told."

"And you're gay?"

"Two for two."

"And you know that I'm gay too?"

"I'd guessed."

Tristan was apple red, but he nodded. "So . . . this is . . . stop me if this isn't cool, okay? Because this is not something I would ever do normally."

Don't read into it. It could mean anything. Henry's dick didn't listen and didn't soften at all. It was certainly ready for things to go in an amorous direction if that's how the evening turned.

And *God* did Henry hope it would.

Oh god, what am I doing? Am I really trying to do this? One hard-on and some mild compliments from Henry, and Tristan was jumping to all sorts of conclusions, making plans . . . and ready to get down and have naked time. It was two hundred and fifty percent crazy, and already in motion.

"You can either bang it out of your system or you can ignore it."

Lucia's comment played in his head, and before he knew it, his lips were moving. "Just . . . stay there."

Henry quirked an eyebrow. "What?"

"Do you trust me?" *He has no real reason to.*

A nervous chuckle slipped past Henry's peachy, all-too-inviting lips. "I mean, unless this is a whole Tonya Harding, Nancy Kerrigan kind of thing."

"I have no idea what that means."

"You're gay and you don't immediately recognize violent early nineties figure skating scandals?"

"Oh, that one. I'm not going to break your knees with a police baton."

"Then I trust you."

Tristan nodded with a smile, then reached over and turned off the lights, plunging the room into the endless dark that only hotel rooms seemed able to produce. Now hidden, he raked a hand across his hair and swallowed hard. "Like I said . . . chime in if you're not cool with anything."

Henry cleared his throat in the dark. "You got it."

Of course, all that darkness, with its glorious ability to hide Tristan's imperfections, also hindered him getting back to the bed. He already didn't see too hot without his glasses. Surprisingly enough, his night vision wasn't amazing, especially without them on. He stepped slowly, trying not to stub his toes.

Which he did. He banged against a hard edge on his way over—probably the stupid dresser/entertainment center—and fell to the side. His face didn't hit the floor, though. It hit . . . soft cotton that smelled faintly of coconut. His cheek grazed against something hard and warm that confirmed his suspicions.

Henry's voice growled from above, just in case there'd been any doubt left. "Did you . . . fall face first into my crotch?"

"I may have." Tristan spoke without removing his head. Past the coconut and the smell of detergent coming from the fabric, there was sweat and musk and arousal . . . and cookies. Henry still smelled like cookies under it all, and they were the sexiest cookies in the world. "I can't see very well. This was supposed to be a lot smoother and suaver."

"It's, uh, working fine for me." Henry's voice cracked a bit there. He coughed quietly before speaking again. "If I'm reading your signals right . . . you were going to end up down there anyway?"

"That was the plan." The blessed dark hid Tristan's blush. Not that it really mattered. This was hardly the first time his face had gotten all hot and bothered this evening. "I figured we could . . . make a tabloid-worthy scandal for the show." His heart leapt higher, out of his chest and into his mouth to make speaking nearly impossible. "Just . . . if you're not comfortable with it—"

"Are you kidding?" Another little vocal crack from Henry that was way more endearing than it probably would have been from anyone else. "Sexy guy like you with your face . . . where it is, and you think I'm saying no?"

Tristan's cheeks and ears blazed. "Okay." Slowly, he walked his fingers up to Henry's waistband. He stroked down until he hit the hard plastic button. He fumbled for a second or two, then slid it through the fabric to reveal . . . "Commando?"

"I didn't think you'd be seeing me with no pants on. I got dressed in a hurry."

"Well, I'm not seeing you." Still unbreakable black in the hotel room. "Feeling you, sure, but not seeing you."

Henry breathed a sparse laugh, and Tristan let his hand rest against the warm, hard shaft. Tentatively, he explored it, certain in the back of his mind Henry would put a stop to it soon, or that he'd come to his senses himself and back away. But his fingers brushed the head, down the thick, corded curve of the shaft. He joined thumb and middle finger around it, taking in the girth and the velvet skin.

Henry repositioned himself but made no sound, and Tristan continued down until he hit prickly bush. Obviously shaved. Even in the invisibility of darkness, Henry's cock was *noticeable*. Thick enough, long enough—admirable without being terrifying to think about. Though maybe, in this moment, *nothing* about Henry would have been a turnoff or a terror or a worry.

Tristan slid his hand down, feeling the full, heavy balls rest against his fingers and palm. For a moment, he considered diving deeper, farther back toward the ass, but stopped himself. Fingering wasn't the kind of surprise you sprung on a first date, let alone . . . whatever this was.

So Tristan shifted himself around and pulled Henry's shaft all the way out of the fly. He held it around the base. Tighter than before, pulling the skin back slightly. And he pressed his lips to the tip. He hesitated half a second, to let Henry back out if he wanted to . . . No protest, just silence and his heartbeat in his ears.

Tristan took the head into his mouth. Salty pre-come coated his tongue, and Henry moaned. A guttural, animal sound that thrashed through the dark and drove Tristan's cock higher. *Now I wish I wasn't wearing underwear.* So restrictive. And way too awkward to try to shimmy his bottoms off with one hand.

Tristan took in another inch of the shaft, then another. He ached to explore Henry—mouth, ass, however. It was like all his building passions finally cracked the dam, and there was no stopping the flood, even if he'd wanted to.

Henry's moans turned into tight groans, which buzzed electric down Tristan's spine. His hands landed on Tristan's shoulders, squeezing hard and melting him with the strength of those callused hands. Another inch. The head pressed against the back of Tristan's throat, and his nose filled with coconut and sweat and clean flesh. He wanted nothing more than to envelop himself in those scents and never surface again. He reached down to his own crotch, slowly massaging the hard growth as he bobbed up and down on Henry.

"Jesus. I thought you were just a pastry chef." Henry's one hand grazed up Tristan's neck and cupped the back of his head. He pushed Tristan forward a little harder, a little faster, forcing his cock a little deeper into Tristan's mouth. "When did you find time to learn *this*?"

Tristan had to catch a breath. He pulled off Henry's dick and wiped the barest tears from his eyes. "Even pastry chefs need a hobby."

"Sucking dick is your hobby? You don't seem the type."

"No, it's macramé. Sucking dick is a God-given talent."

"Well, then praise be to God." The hands left Tristan's body. A slight rustle of fabric, and then Tristan felt more heat, more skin. "You still can't see?"

"I'm not wearing my glasses." The sheets rustled as Henry stood, no longer in the blowjob receiving position, that was for sure. "I thought I was good. Too much to handle?" *Or did you finally give up on this insanity?*

The hands returned under Tristan's armpits, guiding him to his feet. "I'm returning the favor." Henry's voice was quiet, breath humid against Tristan's ear. His hands glided over Tristan's ribs, sliding ever downward and taking his pants and boxers with them. Tristan's cock sprung free, almost touching his abdomen it curved up so high.

As warmth and wet pressure surrounded the head, then the shaft, his knees weakened. Henry's hands cupped his ass and forced him deeper, until Tristan felt lips near the base of his cock. Tristan's stomach churned lightning, tossed it into his chest, into his head. Every inch of him sparked and crackled, and the bare shapes he could see vanished under the shroud of passion. He struggled with each breath to keep from moaning or whimpering or letting anyone else know the hot ecstasy that raced under his skin and through his veins. It was— This was for him and for Henry, not the whole rest of the hotel. Like all the heat and energy, it was there to pass between *them*.

But damn it all, it wasn't *easy* to hold back. Tristan chewed his lower lip, clenched and unclenched his fists, but he stayed silent. Even as Henry's speed increased, lips tightened around the base of his cock, fingers brushed against his balls.

"Jesus, I'm not going to last long at this rate." Tristan barely let that out as a whisper in the darkness. He couldn't manage a lot louder without letting go all the way.

Henry pulled off. "Lay on the bed." His voice was gruff, and the rough edges of it grazed and caught against Tristan, raising goose bumps across his skin. "I'll take care of you."

Tristan gingerly lowered himself onto the bed and leaned back. Henry barely gave him a couple seconds before diving into the fray again, giving him warmth and wetness and so much suction. Tristan balled the blanket in his fists as a storm blustered and blazed through his body. Henry apparently didn't intend to slow up. His fingers pressed against Tristan's chest, then down to his abdomen, his thighs. Fingertips turned to fingernails, scratching across too-sensitive skin, and still Henry bobbed. Sweat dripped down Tristan's nose and lips.

"Fucking Christ, Henry." He stroked Henry's hair. Everything about him was fire. Fire and *fucking* coconut that wasn't going away, no matter how much sweat or how many blowjobs. *I've got to get that stupid cologne. Maybe if I win, I can afford it.*

Henry went faster still, and the oncoming eruption swelled. The storm condensed again, gathering in his abdomen, all electricity and light and motion. Like one of those plasma globes firing and arcing brilliant blue in some erratic pattern. Until something touched the glass and attracted that errant bolt of lightning.

Henry was the point of conduction. Tristan's muscles tightened. No words could pass his lips. As the electricity pooled and tightened and flowed down to his crotch, cold and hot burst across his body. His stomach to his chest to the top of his head. His back arched away from the mattress and his balls pulled higher. Henry kept up his pace, the pressure of his sucking and bobbing, the tightness of his lips.

In spite of all his self-control and effort, a strangled groan crept past Tristan's lips. His lightning storm shot down and out, released through thrust after thrust of boiling ecstasy. Henry stayed put, even as the come spilled from the tip of Tristan's cock. Tristan relished being taken care of, attended to even as his body tensed. His skin tingled, and coconut cut through the fog, filling his lungs. Then his muscles gave out, going slack like snapped cables.

The storm dissipated and he collapsed, still in Henry's mouth. His chest heaved, shoulders bounced up with each breath in that unbroken darkness. And there was nowhere he'd rather be.

Henry backed off, leaving Tristan's cock to fall limp. And apparently . . . swallowed. "You satisfied?"

"Immensely." Tristan patted the bed, trying to still and even his breath. "Come here. By the window." A few seconds, then Tristan felt warmth and a presence to his left. He fumbled over until he found a hard shaft, then led Henry closer, closer, up to his lips.

"You don't have to do that. I can take care of my own stuff. Been doing it since I landed."

"Not as well as I can. Unless you had your bottom ribs removed." Tristan wrapped his lips around the head. Salt and man and . . . he wasn't turned off at all, which was unusual in its own right. Normally he was spent and disinterested in sex after he'd finished. But the thought of *not* blowing Henry barely crossed his mind. He bobbed up and down, taking Henry's shaft as deep as he could, even when his eyes watered and the back of his throat burned. Henry had no more words, apparently, reduced to groaning and whimpering and making subtle, almost silent movements in the dark room. The sparsest strands of light slipped past the blinds and curtains. Not enough to see anything still, but enough to make out a semi-defined outline. An awfully sexy outline, but maybe that was all Tristan's baggage and desire weighing down his perception.

"Oh God . . . oh God . . ." Henry's voice pitched higher, tighter. "Jesus Christ . . ."

Tristan took every inch of Henry, swirling his tongue from the head of Henry's cock and all the way down to the base.

Then a groan instead of a voice. And then heat and salt and musk against Tristan's tongue. A spray, two, three. He slowed, only sliding gently along the shaft as Henry finished.

After a moment, Tristan pulled back and swallowed. A sparse, lingering taste of Henry remained in his mouth. He rolled over and fumbled for the light . . . and he stopped himself. He wasn't quite ready to show his body.

Henry had been nothing but wonderful, and the closeness felt unlike anything Tristan could recall. Each touch remained against his skin, a mark of connection. But that was still a step too far. So he slipped the covers over his bare legs and exposed bits—thank God he'd kept his shirt on—then flicked on the bedside lamp.

Henry's blurry body was still naked from the waist down. He picked up something from the bedside table. "Your glasses."

"Oh, thank you." Tristan slid them back on and got a proper look of the half-naked Henry Isaacson. Soft, sparse hair across his legs, a well-trimmed bush of chocolatey brown above what Tristan already *knew* was an impressive package. And when he stepped around the other side of the bed, the two firm, pert globes of his ass slid against each other. Not the pale, untouched skin that Tristan would have expected. Sun-kissed, in a very nonexposed place. Tristan's imagination betrayed him with thoughts of nude sunbathing, and he had to stop them or he'd be raring to go for round two. "Do you think you could get my pants?"

"Oh, yeah." Henry grabbed the sweats and tossed them over, then slipped into his own pajama pants. "You're being shy after that?"

"A gentleman has to have some modesty." He slid his sweats back on under the covers, then kicked the blanket off because he was already way too goddamn hot and sweaty. "Even if he did trade blowjobs in the dark with a relative stranger."

"I don't know about us being strangers, exactly." Henry stretched up, showing off his belly button and his abs and his happy trail and pressing his cock against the loose plaid fabric of his pants. "I think we pretty well hated each other when we showed up. Can't really hate a stranger."

"*Hate's* a little strong. You could call it *disdain*, maybe. Mixed with a healthy dose of jealousy." Sure, they'd blown each other, but *that*—admitting his own envy to Henry—was what threatened to heat up his ears and cheeks. "I don't know if that's better or not."

"A bit better." Henry winked, then sighed. "Since we're talking about it anyway, can I ask you about that first time we ran into each other? That awards ceremony?"

Tristan's chest twisted, but he nodded. "You want to know why I ran away?"

"It was a kind of weird."

Tristan combed his fingers back through his hair. How to go about this without embarrassing himself? *Carefully and vaguely.* "I had a total panic attack, then when I tried to approach you and apologize, you rightly didn't want to talk to me."

Henry stayed quiet a few moments before responding. "I didn't know you were trying to come talk to me after that. I guess . . . Well, what's done is done." He rubbed his arms as if the room had suddenly gone cold, then nodded seemingly to no one. "I should get going, then. Use the bathroom and stuff."

Tristan didn't want him to walk off. Not on that awkward note. "Believe it or not, they've included a bathroom in my hotel room too."

"Yeah, but you'll want to go to bed, right?" Henry shifted in place. "I interrupted you, and you were probably close to getting to sleep."

"Not exactly. And I could sleep with you around too."

"You're . . . you're sure?"

What the hell is he talking about? "Dude, seriously, we can be in the same bed. Unless *you* don't want to? I don't want to guilt you into sticking around."

Henry stayed silent a second. Two. Three. Then he gave another wink. "I'm happy to stay here for the night. Just don't want to keep you up or make you late or uncomfortable or anything like that."

Tristan smiled at him. "Thanks for the consideration, but . . . thanks. Bathroom's right next to you and the bed's plenty big. But it's bread practice tomorrow, so I'm getting up bright and early. Fair warning."

"We can catch a cab together." Henry smiled sheepishly, then jabbed a thumb toward the bathroom. "I guess I'll be back."

He disappeared through the door. Tristan stretched out on his bed and stared at the ceiling. He'd assumed Henry would stay. After that, why wouldn't he? But . . . Henry had wanted to leave so that he wouldn't bother him. So that Tristan could get his sleep and be prepared to bake. He *cared* whether his actions would impact Tristan.

"I'm acting like an idiot." It was nothing, after all. It meant nothing.

His heart wouldn't believe that, hot and tight in his throat. His face wouldn't believe it, equally hot and undeniably red when he glanced into the mirror. His stomach and his fingertips wouldn't believe it either, dancing and light and begging him to dance with them in glee because Henry wasn't a completely useless tool. "This is afterglow, and I need to get higher standards." He wasn't even melting because he got paid a *compliment*. He was melting because Henry wasn't an irredeemable tool. Henry had thought about someone else's well-being for half a moment.

Tristan sighed. "He thought about *my* well-being." And aside from Karen and Lucia, there hadn't been a whole lot of that going on in his life the past handful of years. Not until he ended up here in this culinary competition with Henry fucking Isaacson.

I need to go out there. What will he think I'm doing in here this long? Henry had already used the bathroom, washed his hands, washed his face, stared at himself, and washed his face again. Now he was leaning against the counter, back to the mirror.

Even Henry's wild, impossible fantasy outcome had involved him going back to his own hotel room after all was done. Henry had been okay with that, had known it was coming. But it hadn't. Even when Henry had offered Tristan ways out . . . they were sleeping together.

Just sleeping.

Tristan . . . wanted him around. Sure, he wasn't going to be the one *leaving* in this situation like so many other guys—Henry hosted a lot more often than he liked—but there was no rule or kindness or etiquette that said he had to let Henry stay. Hell, maybe there was, but gay guys didn't follow it.

Tristan wants me to stay, though. And probably not in the bathroom. Henry turned around and splashed cold water on his face once again for good measure. It didn't make him feel any different, but it bought him another few seconds to get himself under control.

His phone bought him a little longer. He fished it out to see Carrie's reply. *You okay? Need to talk?*

Henry thought about it: what had happened, where he was, how he felt. And honestly, when he was in that room with Tristan, even when they weren't crawling all over each other, his problems didn't seem so bad. *Naw. Just got some action, so I'm good.*

This time, she responded immediately. *Deets?*

A lady doesn't kiss and tell. Call later and maybe I'll forget I'm a lady.

Deal. I'm here if you need me.

With a sigh, Henry turned off the light, opened the door, and walked back out into the continuing comfort he'd been looking for. Tristan lay there, staring up at the ceiling. When Henry stopped, he looked over, a gentle smile on his lips. But no requests or demands. Henry was clearly welcome to share that space, and Tristan didn't seem to expect anything more of him. Henry smiled at the scene. It *was* nice to be greeted by the sight of Tristan, and to know those expectations didn't exist here. Not between them.

Henry's mind flashed to another sight, a memory of Lance lying around in a faded concert T-shirt and some briefs. He turned and smiled at Henry—this had been before his mouth would go off and spout accusations at Henry, scream that he was too selfish for anyone's good . . .

Henry shook himself loose, walked over, and gingerly sat on the edge of the bed next to Tristan. Lance was long gone, nothing but a coal in Henry's mind to fuel his furnace, push him forward. "So, do you want to sleep on that side or . . ."

"That's fine." Tristan rolled over, smiling sweetly. "I'm . . . glad you decided to stay."

"I figured you'd have wanted your privacy."

"I would have figured that too." Tristan shifted himself higher. "But I get the feeling you're worth giving up some alone time for." He sighed and pulled out his phone. "Can I get your email?"

"Oh, was I good enough for a comment card?"

Tristan shook his head. "I'm thinking maybe you're worth giving up a recipe for, too. Don't waste time, otherwise the afterglow might wear off and I'll come back to my senses."

Henry couldn't do anything but blink for a few seconds. "You don't have to."

"Maybe I want to. Since that's what started this whole thing anyway."

Henry couldn't help but grin as he rattled off the address. Within a few seconds, he had a file-sharing notification. "You have your chiffon cake recipe on your phone?"

"It's in the cloud." Tristan set his phone back on the table. "Even I'm not *that* anal-retentive."

"We didn't go far enough to find out how anal-retentive you are." Henry lay down, enjoying the space shared with another body at long last. The chiffon cake . . . he probably would never change from his own. But regardless, Tristan thought highly enough of him to hand it over. He nuzzled closer to Tristan, let himself fall against the warm, hard chest. "Any time you want company for the night again, you know where to find me. I'll be here."

"Careful." Tristan chuckled, then slipped off his glasses, set them aside, and closed his eyes. "You don't want to make any promises you can't keep."

"I never do." Henry reached behind him and clicked off the light.

Chapter Ten

A couple of days later, Tristan sat on the stool at his station, resisting the urge to stare into his oven at the dinner rolls. He'd made four batches during these practice days so far, and they were close to perfect when they worked. Sweetened with molasses and flavored with nigella seeds and hazelnut. They always *tasted* good; however, the additional flavors sometimes led to a charred undertone, or even kept the rolls from rising properly. They weren't as hearty and full as Dorian's far-too-delicious rye rolls—the bastard apparently made them all the time at his hotel—but at their best, they could stand on even footing. Even Henry said so . . . while he stood behind batch after batch of perfectly risen, shiny challah rolls with poppy seeds, or black salt and roasted fennel focaccia. That was Tristan's problem: Was his presentation up to snuff? He couldn't tell and couldn't afford to have a slip with such stiff competition.

The cinnamon raisin bread, at least, was something Tristan had no problem pulling off. Of course, nobody else seemed to be having any problems with that either.

He'd take his smoke break after this. He hadn't gotten one in the morning like he normally would have. It wasn't great etiquette when you woke up next to a nonsmoker.

They hadn't fooled around since that first night—exhaustion helped keep their libidos in check—but ever since they'd blown each other, Henry had spent every night in Tristan's hotel room. He always asked if it was all right, and Tristan always said yes. He liked having Henry in bed next to him. More than he would have possibly guessed. His being there, scruffy and aggravating and sweet and masculine, led

Tristan into hotter, steamier, crotch-tenting thoughts that often had him rolling onto his side so Henry wouldn't notice.

He wanted Henry. He wanted him in the bed next to him, and he wanted to keep peeling away deeper layers of Henry. If he was honest with himself, he liked that he could let down his own walls, as well, actually breathe. This kind of infatuation was familiar, but something about Henry made it headier, left his body tingling and his mind focused on nothing except Henry.

Tristan blew out a long, slow breath, then looked behind him at Henry, also sitting. "Waiting game?"

Henry nodded. "You tried Katherine's focaccia?"

"Not yet."

He leaned over the counter and whispered, "Terrible. Dense, soggy, way too salty."

"Hasn't she made four loaves already?"

Henry chuckled. "She's good, but she's still a farmers' market baker."

Tristan rolled his eyes. "Be nice. She's here for a reason."

"Hey, I said she was good. But that doesn't change the facts on her focaccia or her rolls. I felt bad enough to go help her. Willa did too. Well, she was bouncing between Katherine and Bertha. But with both of us on the job, Katherine was still making hard, crispy rolls last time I checked. Don't know what the hell she's doing wrong, but she can't get either recipe to work at all." Henry sighed. "I told her to talk to Dorian; maybe he can figure her shit out."

Tristan nodded. "Well, I wouldn't have gone *that* far." Dorian could probably figure out her shit if anyone could. "I would have hooked her up with . . . I don't know, Finn or someone."

"Dorian makes the best bread here, as far as I've tasted. And I'm not here to win against someone making easy mistakes. I'm here to prove I'm better than the best chefs. Even if I do badmouth them mercilessly."

Tristan checked on his rolls, which were puffing in the oven. "I guess that's a little nobler than deliberately sabotaging her."

"I wouldn't call your idea sabotage. Finn couldn't make anything worse for her. Sabotage would be telling her to pour salt on her yeast to help it rise."

"Oh, like you told me a few nights ago?"

"Exactly." Henry leaned back and looked in his oven too. "My focaccia's coming out soon, so we can have a good nosh. And we'll see if your rolls are somehow better than last time."

"They'd better be if I want to keep going."

"Oh, come on, they're good rolls. You're just a perfectionist."

"Yeah? It's not a bad thing."

"It's not. But you're fine. I guarantee it. Even *Dorian* isn't going to save Katherine. Although if *he* doesn't win, I'll eat two loaves of her wet disgusting focaccia myself."

Tristan chuckled, then leaned down to peer at his rolls. They'd browned, the egg wash shining, the little black nigella seeds standing out even against the slightly darker bread. He hopped up, opened the oven, and tapped the rolls. They sounded hollow, they felt right. He sighed contentedly and removed his pan. Then he went for the clarified butter to brush over the top. He didn't *quite* like the color with only egg wash. They needed that tiny bit of extra shine, extra salt, extra flavor. And the butter let him get some fresh nigella seeds on there at the end. Exposed to direct heat, the nigella seeds got too bitter, which wasn't quite right with a slightly sweet, nutty roll. Since the rolls were already dark, bitterness contributed to the impression that they were overcooked. Plus adding them after gave an extra hit of oniony crunch as counterbalance. He brushed the butter over, then sprinkled his seeds on top. They adhered fine enough, as long as he did it when the rolls were hot and the butter was cooled slightly. And a few potentially loose seeds were better than bad flavor.

But . . . that was it. He couldn't fuss anymore, had to taste. Tristan pulled one roll free from the batch. The bottom was solid, and the top had only a bit of give, in no small part thanks to that butter soaking in. The final product would firm up, but if he had to serve them a little too hot like they were now, at least it wouldn't be the end of his run.

Yeah, it wouldn't be. He smiled. He'd probably never be truly, completely *happy* with anything he produced for *Get Baked*, but if he was honest with himself, he was confident this wasn't the bake he'd leave on. Bread wasn't his forte, but if he kept producing as well as he had in these practice days, he'd be golden.

Well, not golden. But maybe bronze. Or maybe he'd win a *You Did Okay* ribbon with a smiley face on it. He'd take that to losing and being tossed out on his ear. Every extra day here was extra money, and he and Lucia needed that money coming in from somewhere. He needed that money to make leaving her behind worth it.

He broke open the roll to be absolutely sure nothing had gone wrong. Immediately, the smell of warm nuts and sharp onion struck him, then an underlying note of heady sweetness. When he bit into the roll, it was perfectly soft. Not doughy, but wonderfully fluffy with everything evenly distributed through the body of the roll.

He turned and handed a roll to Henry. "I think these ones might do it. Maybe."

"Well, you're a wellspring of self-confidence now, aren't you?" He tore it open and popped a bite into his mouth. He shook his head, lips curling upward. "I think you might be right. They're good." Another timer buzzed. Henry bent down, and he came back up with a perfectly crusty round of bread, festooned with strips of golden-brown fennel and flakes of black salt. It certainly sent a message: *Look at me, notice me, I'm different and exciting and probably way more expensive than any other foccacia loaf you've ever had. Don't you wonder how I taste? Bite into me!*

Henry grabbed a bread knife and sliced a couple of hanks off the thin, dimpled bread. He handed one to Tristan. "In trade."

Tristan took the bread, which was full of irregular air pockets with a thin, crisp crust in spite of the potentially wet fennel—and bit down. It was definitely light and dry on the inside, slightly fragrant from the olive oil. The fennel wasn't overbearing; most of the anise qualities had cooked out to a subtle depth and now it had a sweetness and brightness that played against the earthy black salt. It had more than just an impressive appearance. "Do you make *this* for the shop? Because I would tolerate traffic in the U District for this."

"It's a pâtisserie, so no. I saw that they had the black salt and . . . well, it sounded interesting, so I tasted it and went from there." Henry bit in too. "The fennel came late in the game, but I think it adds something special."

"I would say so. You might actually beat the pants off Dorian this time."

"Apparently you haven't tried his focaccia. Mine's good, but that would change your tune." Henry gestured to the café table, which was laden already with some of the day's experiments and practice runs. "Go on. I'll *guard* your rolls."

"In your stomach?"

"Some. Some in my bag to take back to the room so I don't risk trying the hotel restaurant again."

"Well, I wouldn't want to subject you to that." The ease of their banter stacked one more warm feeling on top of everything else that seemed to be going so surprisingly *right*. Henry liked his rolls. Sure, maybe he was being flattering, but then again, maybe he wasn't.

Tristan picked up his sheet pan of rolls, which was already cool enough to handle thanks to the wonderful AC in the studio, and headed over. But not before giving Henry a tiny glance, just to see the fake betrayal on his face.

Instead, Henry followed him up to the table and grabbed a roll as soon as Tristan set it down. "Go on and try the focaccia, then tell me I could still win this thing."

He pointed to a textbook-perfect bread round: dimpled top, studded in bronze roasted garlic cloves and crisp flakes of prosciutto. Tristan poked it with a bread knife that had been left on the tabletop. It felt sublimely like focaccia. Thin and crisp with a firm middle and a bouncy recoil. And it sounded hollow. He sliced a hank of it to reveal a slightly yellow interior with a delicate structure, and the instant aroma of thyme and rosemary leaking from the hundred pockets, although no herbs speckled the bread itself. *Infused oil?* "Looks as good as yours."

"Try it before you flatter me anymore."

Tristan rolled his eyes and bit in, and all those flavors instantaneously exploded across his tongue: the sweet-but-bitter roasted garlic, the herbs coming from somewhere, the intense salt and umami from the prosciutto. They blossomed and mingled, everything held in check with the yeasty, dry bread.

Tristan swallowed, then glanced back at Henry. "Second's not bad, right?"

"Second's not bad at all if that's what I'm coming second to." Henry cut his own slice and crunched into it—because this focaccia crunched properly. "Third or fourth wouldn't be bad against this. Hell, I'm pretty happy with not last when I'm making bread against that brilliant son of a bitch."

"Well, I firmly believe you have 'not last' in the bag."

"Oh, such glowing praise. I knew there was a reason I picked you."

Tristan bit down a little harder than necessary on the bread. He missed his tongue and his teeth thankfully, but had to close his mouth fast before anything slipped out. He collected himself in spite of the churning heat in his belly. "You picked me, huh?"

"Whose hotel room have I been trying to get into every night lately?"

"And succeeding."

Henry shrugged. "I guess you picked me right back, then, didn't you?"

"Maybe I did." And maybe Tristan suddenly wanted to shove something else in his face. He went for the nearest loaf of cinnamon raisin bread, already precut, and popped it in. It was better than talking further about that in public.

"So, you boys ready for tomorrow?" Bertha had trundled up and stopped with her hands on her hips. She smiled at them. "Early, early rising so we can get our bread . . . risen." She chuckled and pushed her way to the table, where she grabbed one of Tristan's rolls. "These things are good. I'd eat the hell out of them with some roast chicken."

Tristan nodded. "Thank you. I, um, I don't think I've gotten to try yours, yet. Unless I did without realizing it."

"Oh, it's nothing special, trust me. Tried-and-true recipes I've been making for years. Except that cinnamon raisin loaf. I hate raisins and I've never made anything like that before. Tried making a fruit cake for Christmas once. Never again." She tore apart the roll and shoved some of it into her mouth, chewing and swallowing before continuing. "But I think I'll get enough done to get by. Nothing wrong with a classic. Plus I might be sweet-talking Finn and Dorian for a helping hand. Hard for such nice young men to say goodbye to someone who could be their grandma." She narrowed her eyes and grinned at the pair of them. "Don't suppose I remind either of you of your grandmothers, do I?"

Tristan shifted uncomfortably, and from the way Henry moved his weight foot to foot, he wasn't feeling it either. "My grandma was a tiny Salvadoran schoolteacher who could barely heat up leftovers. So no."

Bertha laughed and winked. "Well, I guess I'll try Willa again. Solidarity among decrepit old ladies, right?"

Filming day had come again. Henry had gotten so used to being on camera, he no longer struggled or felt jittery when they flipped on. He'd already baked his focaccia and cinnamon raisin bread, received good reviews on the focaccia flavors, and the judges had appreciated his use of sultanas and cardamom in the cinnamon raisin loaf. Now his rolls were coming out of the oven. They looked as perfect as he could have hoped, with the poppy seeds evenly distributed across deep, brassy rolls, all baked together on his sheet pans. He slid them off to cool and checked the clock above the café table. Seven minutes left. His rolls would still be warm when tasting rolled around, but not blazingly hot or so soft that the textures would be off. He tapped on top to check everything, and it seemed perfect. A tiny bit of give, but a hard enough crust to be a proper challah.

He'd even bitten the bullet and used margarine instead of butter. An older lady, Eva Rosenbaum, had worked for him early in the days of the shop, and she'd told him up and down that *"Real challah uses margarine. Pareve margarine. Butter doesn't taste right, and you won't convince me different."*

Of course, the shop had never sold challah. Henry imagined she spouted that information off whenever there was a lull in conversation, in a kitchen or on the bus.

Maybe it was true, maybe it wasn't—Henry had tried it both ways and never tasted a difference himself—but he wasn't taking any chances. Any of the judges could have an opinionated little Eva Rosenbaum whispering in their ear about margarine.

Henry actually had time to clean up his station. Sure, the network staff would do it again no matter how good of a job he did, but it kept him from focusing too much on his singular niggling worry:

Had he gone too simple? Not on his focaccia, and cinnamon raisin bread could only be stretched so far before it wasn't what it claimed to be. But maybe he'd finished his rolls so early because he'd just done a basic challah topped with poppy seeds. It would have to be perfect, and maybe perfection would have taken the full three and a half hours instead of falling seven minutes short.

But cleaning kept that out of his mind. He wasn't thinking about it at all. He definitely wasn't thinking about Tristan, either. He wasn't thinking about the possibility of Tristan having to go home. He wasn't thinking about being left alone here again. He wasn't concerned about Tristan's fate in the competition alongside his own. No, the cleaning definitely kept *all* those thoughts at bay.

When everything was clean and clear, Henry checked out his rolls one last time but saw nothing he could attempt to fix. They were baked, they smelled like wonderful eggy challah and poppy seeds. Now his fate was in the lap of the gods.

Tristan pulled his sheet pans out with a couple of minutes left. He tapped the rolls, pressed against them, then sighed contentedly and grabbed his butter and nigella seeds and finished off the bread, leaving them shiny.

"Looks good." Henry leaned closer over his counter. "I have competition, I guess."

"Competition for second, maybe." Tristan rolled his eyes. "Feeling good?"

"Not as good as I did yesterday. But okay. I'm probably not going anywhere." It felt a lot more *probably* than it had when he'd talked with Tristan the day before, or even an hour ago. He had to have earned himself some credit with the focaccia, though. It had been even better than when he'd made it in his practice days, and it had been a good hank of flatbread then.

"Okay, that's time!" Sylvia clapped her hands up at the front of the room. "Roll your rolls onto their display racks, and then we'll roll them on up front." She smiled right up until the director came out, then shook her head. "Can I reshoot that later? That was bad improv even for me."

Jacob nodded. "No problem." He looked around at everyone. "Five minutes, then we'll reset for the final shoot."

Henry nodded, as though they hadn't heard some variation of that spiel every three days since they got to San Francisco. He tapped his rolls again to make sure nothing had magically gone wrong in the past five minutes, which it hadn't. *I think I'm a little too concerned.* Then he transferred everything to his two big platters.

The set smelled absolutely divine. The past few filming sessions, there'd always been an underlying scent of char. Someone had inevitably burned something, at least a bit. But not this time. *Guess we've weeded out the rabble.*

In any show like this, even with the most accomplished chefs in the whole world, there would be some people who would bend to the pressure of being on national TV, or wouldn't handle cooking outside their own kitchens or being away from their own business well, or would just hit a plain old streak of bad luck. Once they were gone, the real competition could start.

Consider it started.

"Good luck." Tristan winked at him, smiling. "You'll need it to do better than me, after all."

"Hey, let go of the cocky schtick. That's mine." Although seeing him open up and smack talk was awfully endearing. And Henry would have taken any excuse to see him smiling. It brightened up Tristan's face, brought out his dimples, and made it hard to believe he was the same semi-dour introvert Henry knew.

"Okay, guys. Let's get going." The director stepped off the set. "In five, four, three, two—" He pointed to Sylvia.

She smiled for the cameras. "Okay, then. Katherine. Let's bring your rolls up to the front and see what we can see."

Katherine passed by Henry on her way up, and he had to admit they looked a ton better than when he'd tried to help her. Maybe Dorian knew magic. If nothing else, he seemed to have straightened out whatever-the-hell problem Katherine had been having. Of course, she'd been doing fine up to the rolls too, so she was no longer out of the running the way she had been the past few days.

When she went by the front station, he noticed that Willa straightened up and her mouth seemed to turn down, though Henry was too far away to be sure. Something about Katherine had her annoyed. Annoyed enough she wasn't pretending for the cameras, anyway.

Eli tore off a row of Katherine's rolls, then split them up. "They're nice. Potato rolls, correct?"

"Yeah. Garlic and herb potato rolls."

"They're nicely uniform, and I can smell all the garlic and the rosemary already." He split the roll open and held it up to his nose. "Good, strong aroma on this." He prodded the roll, pulled it apart. "I would have expected more moisture and give on the inside, however. Especially from a potato roll. This is almost crumbly. I'm guessing you overbaked it, but I'm a pastry chef, not a baker, so I'll let Dexter take a look at it."

"No, I agree." Dexter tore off a bit and tasted it, then nodded. "It's a good flavor, it's a good chewy crust, but the interior is almost stale. Obviously it's not—it has that good fresh-bread flavor—but the texture isn't helping you. Cooked about five or ten minutes less, these would be a fine roll."

"Exactly." Rita nibbled some gently. "But it *is* hard to go wrong with rosemary and garlic."

Katherine's shoulders raised slightly, her spine straightening. But she said nothing.

"Thank you, Katherine." Sylvia smiled, production assistants carried everything off, and Henry prepared to carry all his shit up to the front.

A few minutes of reset, then Sylvia started again. "Henry, roll on down and show us what you've worked up."

He balanced both platters on his arms, then carried the lot up to the front and set it all down. No nerves fired in his stomach or tingled across his skin. He felt almost as calm as he had during the cake round. More so in some ways—with cakes, he'd known he had a shot at taking first, so *that* had been on the line. Today, he felt safe, but not like he could take the top spot.

Dexter grabbed the rolls and handed them out this time. "Now these look suspiciously like challah."

"They are challah."

Dexter smiled slightly and his eyes narrowed. "With butter?"

"With margarine. Pareve margarine." *Bless you, Eva Rosenbaum.* "I'm not an animal."

"Good man." He tore his roll apart and sniffed the yellow interior. "I'm always a butter fan . . . with the exception of challah. It makes that little bit of difference." He ripped off a sizable chunk and played it around his fingers. "A good bake. Moist, eggy, which I happen to like in a challah. It's not too dense, so you managed to get a good rise in spite of the extra eggs." He popped the manhandled piece into his mouth and, for a few moments, Henry's stomach twisted and clenched. Just in case he'd managed to do something wrong like not add any salt.

"It's a good challah. Not the most innovative roll out here, but to get that proper rise on a loaf with that much egg and margarine in it in that amount of time? It's a solid showing."

"I agree." Rita smiled sweetly with a bitten roll in one hand. "The crust isn't as hard as challah would normally have. It strikes a nice balance between a roll and a traditional bread. It still has that beautiful color to it."

"I do wish it would have been done in little knots." Eli held his roll up to the light, spoke while examining it. "There's not anything wrong with it, but challah is traditionally braided. It would have been a nice nod to that, given away what it was more readily."

"All right." If *that* was his criticism, then Henry was in a damn good place. Joy buoyed warm and full in his chest. "Thank you." His rolls were whisked off, and he grinned as he walked back, even winked at Tristan and mouthed, *Good luck.*

Another reset, then Sylvia rubbed her hands together. "Now, if you don't mind keeping the ball rolling, Tristan, let's see what you've got."

Tristan blew out a long breath, his shoulders dropping visibly on the exhalation, then grabbed his trays and carried them up front. Henry scooted his stool to the far end of the station so he could see around Willa.

Keeping with their pattern, Rita started this time. "These are attractive and fragrant. That's my first impression." She carefully separated the rolls to be passed out. "What flavors are we working with?"

"They're a molasses bread roll with hazelnuts and nigella seeds."

"Sweet, then."

"Mildly."

She weighed it in her hand. "It's substantial. I'm really hoping it's risen when I look inside."

So am I. Henry wasn't ready to deal with Tristan leaving. He hadn't been last time, either, but where they were now? He was *doubly* not ready.

Rita tore her roll open and prodded it. One second. Two. *God, if I feel like this, what's it like for Tristan?*

Rita smiled. "It's risen. I think it's heavier because of the hazelnuts. But everything is well distributed, the crumb is even on the inside, and it's got a lovely color." She bit into it, as did the others.

"Now *that* is good bread." Dexter spoke out of turn, and he grinned wide. "Back in Jamaica, we have coco bread. It's got coconut milk in it, so it's a little bit sweet, you know? American bread doesn't have that, brioche doesn't hit it right, but the molasses and the hazelnuts in here are bringing me that same experience. And I love nigella seeds." He raised his half-eaten roll in salute. "It's good by me."

"Well, I'm not having quite the same love affair as Dexter, but it *is* a nice roll." Eli nodded. "It would be great with a roast or a turkey for thanksgiving, or ham. It begs for some kind of salty meat to balance out the sugar and the density. But for what it is, it's still a good roll."

"Well, I'm going to need that recipe," said Sylvia. "Anything to make Dexter fall in love with me."

He cocked his head to the side and grinned at her. "I love you enough to get you a job in California, don't I?"

Laughter rippled through everyone as Tristan turned around and his rolls went away. He grinned wider than Henry had ever seen. Sure, he'd only been in reliable proximity with Tristan for about two weeks, but still—that smile was bigger and better and brighter than usual, dimples on full display.

When Tristan swung back into his station, Henry reached over the counter and gripped his shoulder. "Nice job. Think you beat me."

"Only with Dexter." Tristan chuckled softly, then lowered his voice to the barest, sparsest whisper. "Assuming there's no fluke with the results, let's get drinks to celebrate."

Drinks would mean one drink, max. But Henry was down for it all the same. "Oh, how daring of you. Braving humans."

"I know. So take advantage of my temporary insanity before I come to my senses and realize how bad people suck."

"Take advantage of you, got it."

Tristan laughed a little louder, shaking his head and unfortunately covering his mouth. When he was finished, it was back to whispers. "That's after drinks."

"All right, but I'm holding you to it." Henry eyed the camera and really, *really* hoped they'd been quiet enough not to be on mic. Or at the very least, the network wasn't willing to run something so risqué as light innuendo.

"Perfecto." Tristan sighed, then turned around. "Well, let's see what the darling of New York's managed to pull off."

Henry looked him up and down, now that he wasn't paying attention . . . and as always, Henry liked what he saw. Was it objectifying, and risky with the cameras rolling, to be checking out Tristan's pert ass in those jeans, his broad shoulders under the beige shirt? Of course.

I don't plan to stop anytime soon, though.

Tristan stood behind his platter of rolls, waiting for the final verdict to come down. He knew bread wasn't his strongest point, and that he'd be riding somewhere in the middle for this round. The middle wasn't safety. Not in the long run. But he'd take it.

That's how Tristan felt, anyway. The judges *had* spent their sweet time deliberating this round, calling crew from the back and whispering to them. It had taken twice as long as normal before the competitors got arranged behind their stations. So maybe things were tighter than Tristan assumed.

"Well, we saw more rolls than an ensemble cast and flatbreads that were anything but flat in flavor." Sylvia's spiels seemed to be getting better as she settled into the job. "But one of you baked us simply the best rolls of the bunch and an herbaceous, vivacious focaccia to beat all the rest. The winner this week . . . is Dorian! Congratulations!"

Tristan nodded. No shock there. Even Dorian himself looked like it was fated to happen that way. It probably wasn't going to be one of their more exciting episodes of the season. Not unless the editors put in some real work.

When the accolades died down, the three judges stepped in front of the table. *Not good.* They clearly had something to say, and Tristan wasn't sure that he wanted to hear it. There was no way in hell the three of them breaking the flow of the show could be *good* news. *At least they're making things easier on the editors.*

Dexter was the one to speak up first. "Before we finish this out, we need to address something that was brought to our attention by one of the competitors." His voice had no lift or lightness to it; instead it was severe, each syllable landing like a cinderblock. "We wanted to address it now, so that everyone would know what was going on. In case this wasn't made clear when you all agreed to appear on the show."

What happened? Someone must have violated some rule. Tristan tried his best to pull up everything they'd been warned off doing, everything that had been in the contract he'd signed before flying out. But without context, his rushing thoughts were a cloud of worries with nothing he could cling to, nothing but

After what felt like an eternal pause, Dexter continued. "This is a competition to find the best of the bakers and pastry chefs in the United States. We want everyone here competing on their own merits. Some camaraderie and advice is one thing, and it's admirable. But there's a point where we have to begin to question whether the work presented is your own, or if it's more of a collaboration." He glanced to Rita and Eli on either side of him. "A situation like that, it muddies the waters. Receiving that level of assistance is not the spirit of this competition."

Do they know about me and Henry? How could they possibly know? Do they have cameras in the hotels? We haven't been helping each other . . . but what else could they be talking about? Tristan's stomach tightened. The judges thought he and Henry weren't competing fairly. This relationship of theirs, however new and burgeoning it was, had put Tristan's money at risk.

And without the money to support him and Lucia, would she go back to Robert?

"It's an unfortunate thing. The person we've decided to send home today was *not* the weakest baker among you today, nor have they been in prior weeks. But this isn't the sort of issue that we can ignore." He sighed, shaking his head.

It took everything in Tristan not to glance at Henry. Nothing untoward had happened between them, but who would believe that? If anyone knew he and Henry had been sharing a hotel room, they'd assume the worst.

But goddamn it, something *had* happened. Tristan's mind flicked to the recipe he'd shared. His stomach threatening to launch out of his mouth, but he choked it down and stood as stoic as he could manage.

Dexter nodded once, as though steeling himself, then spoke gently again. "This week, we've chosen to send Bertha home. We have fair reason to believe that the recipes you used for your rolls and for the cinnamon raisin loaf weren't entirely your own."

Bertha. Tristan's body slackened as the tension wicked out. *Not either of us. Bertha.*

She stood at her station, somehow paler and more drawn than usual.

Rita finally spoke up, her face soft as she looked to Bertha. "Do you want to . . . dispute that?"

She can dispute it. Good. It's not trial by accusation. We could defend ourselves . . . because being in a relationship wouldn't sound bad at all. Tristan glanced finally to Henry, to see if he was panicking. He was staring across the way at Bertha, but that was the only sign that he was at all *interested* in what was happening, let alone concerned.

Bertha stepped up and all the cameras swung around to focus on her. "I—I got some help from . . . someone." Her words stuttered off her tongue. "I don't know if it was too much help, but I suppose I have to trust your judgment on this."

The whole set was silent, not even a breath breaking the quiet. Bertha was willing to go without a fight. What had she done? Who'd helped her out that much? And who had turned her in? *Who do we need to be watching out for?*

After a few more beats of silence, Sylvia cleared her throat and waited for a couple of the cameras to focus on her before speaking.

"Well . . . Bertha, I'm sorry, it looks like you'll be heading home this week. We're . . . we're all sorry to see you go."

With that, Jacob stepped onto the set. "Okay, then. That's a wrap." He pinched the bridge of his nose with one hand and slipped his headset off with the other. "Bertha, hate to be a bother, but you're probably going to have to stay around another day or two. This is going to take some serious cutting and editing to get a good episode out of it."

She nodded, and slowly the set crept back to life. There wasn't the big show of cleaving her bread in half. It happened, but it wasn't the affair it usually was, mingling with all the other action on set. People crowded over to Bertha, offered condolences. A few people came up to give congratulations to Dorian as well. But the whole of the set seemed shaken: the walls, the floor, the ceiling, and everyone in it. It was all a touch off-kilter after . . . that.

Tristan took off his mic pack, then stepped away from his station and headed toward the table loaded with the round's offerings. Henry followed shortly behind. He grabbed one of Katherine's potato rolls and tore into it. He put it into his mouth, chewed, and swallowed. "I'll be damned, she got it to an edible place. They're not terrible. I wouldn't buy them myself, but they taste like what she said they were."

How the hell was he not panicking? Tristan could barely hold himself together.

Henry offered the other half, and Tristan took it despite that less-than-stellar review. It was a soft, flaky bread, aromatic and sharp with garlic and thyme and a good dose of black pepper. Maybe too much for some people, but Tristan could handle twice as much heat as that. "Pretty good." He wasn't able to keep up the charade nearly as well as Henry was. "Aren't you . . . Didn't that freak you out? That whole situation with Bertha and competitors working together and—"

"You mean did I shit my pants when I thought they were talking about us? Absolutely." He kept his voice to a sparse whisper, barely audible with Tristan standing right next to him. "But they weren't, apparently, and the last thing we're making time for in that hotel room is helping each other. With baking, anyway." He smirked and cocked one eyebrow. "I know I didn't do anything wrong, and I don't think either of us can afford to focus on what might have happened if reality was different."

"Well, you're a hell of a lot calmer than I am." *Which is one more reason to keep him around.* Still, Tristan's whole body was tense and tight, and his brain wouldn't quiet. Was spending time with him worth the risk?

Henry smiled and nudged Tristan in the side. "If we're drinking, we should probably fill up on bread at least a little bit so we're not getting too drunk."

Were they still drinking? Suddenly it didn't feel like the right call. Henry might have been cool and collected over the whole thing, but why? How?

Two desires pulled at Tristan. He had to help himself, and help Lucia, but he also *wanted* Henry. He wanted to hold on to what had grown between the two of them, but without putting his sister at risk. He needed a path that could balance both options, and he needed it fast.

Only one real option presented itself. Tristan leaned close enough that he could whisper and be heard. "You can swing back up to my room. If you want. We can have our celebratory drinks up there. In private." He had never gone to that extra step of inviting Henry. He always confirmed that it was okay when Henry asked. But an invitation would keep Henry around, and moving the drinking out of the public eye would hopefully add a layer of protection. It was the cleanest solution he could come up with. "If you want to. No pressure."

Henry smiled, and the knots in Tristan's stomach loosened. "I'll stop by my room to get my cologne and . . . toothbrush?"

A toothbrush meant a long-term stay.

Tristan nodded, hoping his words came out nonchalant and not as a spew of vomit as his stomach did backflips. "Well, I hope so. Don't want your baking off because you can't taste shit right."

"You're so considerate." Henry raised a hand, lowered it, raised it again. His face reddened, and eventually he patted Tristan's cheek. Gently, in *just* the way to pierce through all the nerves and skitter electricity across his skin. The tiniest stirring at his crotch, as much as he hated to admit *that* in what should have been a tender moment. But his tightening pants weren't going to be ignored.

Tristan made himself stand there instead of melting into a pool of hormones or backing away from Henry. "I'm sure there's a store nearby where we can get a bottle of vodka."

"I'm sure there is too." Henry chuckled a little bit. "I'll run out and get supplies. Then we can shower."

"Oh, so we're showering together?"

Henry shrugged. "Conservation of water. It's important."

Tristan wasn't going softer. But the thought of being in the shower . . . it would mean the lights on. Was he ready for that on top of everything else that was going down?

In that moment, standing in the studio, turned on, and barely resisting the urge to take Henry in the middle of the bread display, it seemed like that wouldn't be quite as bad as he'd built it up in his head. If anything, he could use some stress relief. *As long as it doesn't get me sent packing.*

Chapter Eleven

Henry dropped the paper bag from the liquor store onto the bed. His tongue barely wanted to move, his palms sweated. *Fucking stupid—we've done this before for Christ's sake.* It didn't make sense for him to feel nervous, and yet he did. It was probably a holdover from the competition. Much as he wanted to put on a good show for Tristan—who was currently unpacking their liquor store haul and setting it up next to the TV—he couldn't stop a niggling worry from churning through his belly. Bertha was gone, and who'd turned her in remained a mystery. It could have been a few people. Practically everyone had interacted with her at some point during the bread practice days, trying to address her issues.

Any of them could have spotted a suspicious discrepancy. Whatever it might have been.

She had to have done something significant, that much was clear. Several people had lent Katherine a hand, and she wasn't being tossed out.

Henry desperately needed a drink and an orgasm to get his nerves to unspool. "So, I'm going to jump into the shower. If that's good with you?"

After a second's hesitation, Tristan nodded. "I . . . Does that offer to join you still stand?"

Henry nodded back, projecting as much calm as he could muster. *So probably not a ton.* "It's your shower."

Tristan sucked in a sharp breath, then took off his glasses. "Okay. Yeah. But . . . don't say anything, okay?"

Henry nodded, resisting the urge to laugh at such a ridiculous comment. What did he think Henry would *say*? "You have my word."

"I mean it." Tristan's ears reddened and his mouth turned down slightly at the corners. "I . . . Okay, I turned the lights off for a reason the other night. And I keep my shirt on for a reason . . . I don't show off my body a whole lot. So no comments. Please. I'm already stressed out enough today."

Henry nodded again. "I wouldn't say something to make you feel bad. I mean, okay, maybe I would have before when I thought you were a son-of-a-bitch caterer, but not now."

"I think the word you used was 'highfalutin.'" Tristan cracked a little smile. "I was a 'highfalutin caterer.'"

"You're not letting me live that down, are you?"

Tristan shook his head. "Did you really expect me to?"

"Color me . . . hopeful."

Tristan sighed, then wrapped his arm gingerly around Henry's waist. "Let's get you your precious shower."

They walked into the bathroom together. Henry slipped off his shoes and socks, then his pants and his shirt. *Better if I go first. Maybe it'll help. Or maybe I think too highly of my own contribution to this whole thing.* Either way, he was down to his underwear, standing there in the bathroom. He wasn't going to pressure Tristan into anything, though. He reached back and turned on the faucet. "How hot do you like the water?"

"Umm, flesh-scalding?" Tristan chuckled, then slid off his shoes. His socks, followed by his pants to reveal strong, thick legs dusted over with dark hairs, and awfully flimsy cerulean boxer shorts with off-white pinstripes running down the legs. He hesitated, then slowly pulled up the hem of his shirt. Henry watched a little more closely than he should have, given Tristan's nerves. *Forbidden fruit.*

Slight, wispy hair led up from his waistband, across his belly button and over well-defined abs and a dark treasure trail. More tawny skin was revealed with each inch Tristan's hem rose. His ribs pressed slightly against his skin as his arms stretched higher.

Another inch up, just at the bottom of Tristan's left pec, a curving scar. Slightly jagged along the edges, but still very well-defined. On the other pec, a puckered burn mark. Those definitely weren't normal baker's scars and injuries, unless he was working shirtless during all those catering events. And juggling burning-hot pieces of metal. Suddenly, it made sense why he'd jerked away at that awards ceremony.

The small marks continued down his biceps, mixed in with bigger ones. Some were clearly cut marks. Others were something else entirely, although Henry couldn't have said what. *Now I know what he was talking about.* They weren't grotesque, but Tristan definitely had a lot of scars. A lot.

Finally, Tristan stripped off his shirt, all the way up and over his head. He turned to set it on the counter, and Henry noticed some thicker, much fainter marks left on his back. Across his shoulders, mostly. But before long, Henry was distracted by other sights. Like Tristan's ass, barely covered by the thin material of his boxers. And the barbed-wire tramp stamp completely visible and inviting. *I guess that's the one-time barbed wire says, "Come touch me, you'll love it."*

Tristan faced forward again, cheeks and ears bright scarlet. "Ta-dah."

"Nice trick. I'd rather pay to see you undress than David Copperfield make a rabbit disappear."

"Does David Copperfield do that?"

"Hell if I know." Henry hesitated, then gingerly grasped Tristan's shoulders. He ran his hands down hard, muscular arms and burn marks and another tattoo, this time of a poinsettia, which was faintly scribed a few inches above his left elbow. The ink was faded, barely red and barely green with a graying outline. Henry traced the outline of the petals with his thumb and stared straight into Tristan's eyes. Unendingly dark and deep. They had their own gravity, begging Henry to come forward even as his stomach tightened around the thought of what he was doing, what he couldn't keep from doing in that moment.

His lips pressed gently to Tristan's. He stayed there with that barest contact, holding Tristan's arms, waiting. A second. Two. Three. *He's not responding. It's too much for him.* Henry pulled away . . . and Tristan wrapped his arms around Henry's middle so they were skin to skin, heartbeat against heartbeat. The tension wicked from Henry's body as he leaned into Tristan's embrace, relishing each point of contact.

Finally, Tristan leaned back in, made full lip contact. Henry let him control the pace, crackling with the thrill of the moment. Tristan, exposed, nervous, and still choosing him.

When Tristan finally broke away, he swallowed hard. His voice came out brittle. "I . . . Wow."

"A closed-mouth kiss like I gave Samantha Nelson in sixth grade gets a wow?" Henry chuckled, and then drew in a lungful of Tristan's warmth and sweat and the pervading smell of too much yeast and wheat and herbs that clung to his skin after so long working in the kitchen. Henry slid his hands back, clutching Tristan even closer: underwear to underwear, bulge to bulge. Tristan grew hard, and all Henry wanted was to strip him down and take him there against the counter. Legs in the air, dripping sweat, shower be damned.

But he pulled back. Tristan's body *wasn't* his. With whatever issues he had going on, Henry was going to be as careful as he could.

But his *own* body was his. He stood against the tub, hooked his thumbs into his waistband, and dropped his trunks. His cock sprung free and all the confidence in the world wasn't keeping heat from rising up his chest and neck and face as Tristan took him in.

After a few seconds, Henry stepped backward into the shower. "You can join if you want. Or you can watch. Of course, if you don't participate, you'll have to put up with watching me jerk off."

Tristan chewed on his lower lip, but didn't step forward. "You don't want to ask?"

"About what?" Henry let the steaming water pour over his hair, trickle hot down his spine. Nothing was doing a thing to get him softer, which was probably for the best. His physique was more impressive when he had a hard-on than when he didn't, after all.

"Well . . . you know?" Tristan gestured to his chest, down his arms. "All this?"

"Oh. Yeah. Why a poinsettia? I mean, barbed-wire tramp stamp was probably a right-out-of-high-school decision, right? And the sugar skull because you're a pastry chef and you're proud of your heritage." Henry cringed a bit at that. "Sorry. Guess I don't even know what your heritage is. I bet your family's from Allentown, PA or something like that and I look like an ass."

Tristan shook his head, smiling. "First generation, actually. My parents lived in San Salvador when they were younger."

Henry nodded, glad to have avoided that particular faux pas. He brushed soaked hair out of his face. "And the poinsettia?"

Tristan shrugged. "I think they're pretty, and I like the story. Minus the Jesus stuff."

"Well then, tell me the story, because I'm a clueless rube."

Tristan chuckled, then dropped his boxers to the floor. His cock was impressive, with a rosy head and a thick, curving shaft that leaned to the left. Neatly trimmed bush of black curls. He didn't have a bodybuilder V, but there were some noticeable sex lines running down from his abdomen. He stepped up and into the shower, then pulled the curtain around them. "You're making a mess and you're going to get the maids pissed off at me. Honestly."

"Sorry." Henry bent down and grabbed the tiny hotel shampoo from the corner of the tub. He scrubbed it through his hair, then turned in the too tight, too hot, too steamy confines of the shower. If they hadn't been pressed together before, they certainly were now. "Story?"

"Yeah. Just let me have the water a second."

Henry obliged, flattening himself against the wall as Tristan slipped past, his ass rubbing against Henry's crotch.

"Poinsettia . . . a poor kid didn't have anything to leave to honor Jesus at Christmas. So rather than leave nothing at all, he picked some weeds from the side of the road and left those. They sprung to life into beautiful red flowers. The poinsettia."

"So it's about transformation." Henry couldn't even make eye contact. There was something about a man under running water . . . and maybe specifically *Tristan* under the pelting flow of the showerhead—hard-bodied, broad-shouldered, skin like fresh nutmeg. And god*damn* the things that man could do with chiffon cake. That was no small part of the overwhelming attraction.

Neither was his clear devotion to his sister. *Nice to see a guy who cares about the world past the end of his own dick.*

"It's transformation, and about the power of belief. Again, not Jesus." Tristan plucked the shampoo bottle from Henry's grip, his touch lingering several seconds longer than necessary before taking it and popping the cap. "How if you really hold an idea in your heart, even the worst, most useless thing in the world can become special. It just needs enough love and affection to grow."

Henry smiled and watched the suds wash their way down Tristan's chest and shoulders. When he looked up, he fell toward the gravity of those eyes again until they pressed lips to lips. This time, Tristan's mouth parted. His breath tasted of yeast and oil and flour, and his tongue pressed forward, hard and unrelenting. Henry could barely catch his own breath, and he relished every lightheaded second of the kiss, stretched it as long as he could stand it, because separating was unthinkable in that moment.

But eventually, he had to breathe, and he drew back enough to draw in oxygen. Tristan's face was flushed, though from the kiss or the shower wasn't clear. "What, I don't get a wow from that?" Henry quirked up one corner of his mouth.

"If you need constant ego stroking, I don't know how well this is going to work out. When you give away compliments, they lose all their meaning."

"Oh, I don't know if I can agree with that." Henry reached down for the bath's corner again and grabbed the body wash. He lathered up his hands, then scrubbed that soap across Tristan's shoulders, down his chest and ribs and sides and the scars that weren't any of his business. "You're gorgeous and sexy and I want to fuck you. That's three compliments in a row. Did they lose their impact?"

Tristan's skin flushed somehow redder. His voice quivered as he replied, and it only got worse as Henry slid his hands farther down Tristan's frame. "Absolutely. By the time you said you wanted to fuck me, I was completely turned off." He gestured to his hard-on, still as stiff and curved as ever, even as hot, soapy water flowed on either side and over the head. "See? Absolutely no attraction to you anymore."

"Bummer." Henry had hit the make it or break it moment. He rubbed the body wash through Tristan's sparse happy trail. His breath caught in his chest when he brushed the bottom of his hand against the first coarse bit of pubic hair, but he stayed the course until he hit the iron-and-velvet cock. "I was hoping this could turn into more than a shower." Slowly, he stroked from the base up to the head, watching the bubbles build and lather, then wash off and cascade down strong, solid thighs. "I know I kept my ulterior motives flawlessly secret, but I figured it was time to come clean."

"Oh." That single strangled syllable betrayed Tristan. "Well, then I should probably be honest too, if that's . . . the path we're headed down."

"Go ahead." Henry kept up "cleaning" Tristan's cock. "I'm all ears."

"I wasn't turned off—at all—Jesus fuck, dude. Do you *want* me to come right now?"

"I could think of worse outcomes." But Henry finally let go and finished his pass down Tristan's body. Thighs, calves, then back all the way up to standing. He pressed his lips to Tristan's again, then relathered his hands with body wash and scrubbed his own chest, under his arms, his crotch. He *did* need to get clean, even if the plan was to get dirty right again after the fact.

Or *during* the fact, in this case.

When he was soaped up, he pressed himself flush against Tristan, relishing the hard cock against his navel. "Sorry. Have to get rinsed."

"No problem." Tristan grinned wide. He combed his fingers through Henry's hair, down his back, below his waist. He dug between the cheeks, barely brushing Henry's hole with electric ice.

Henry's whole body tensed and his balls pulled higher. "Fuck . . ."

"Yeah, I thought that was the idea." Tristan pulled one hand back and slicked his middle finger, sucking on it all the way to the base. Then around again. "You can tell me to stop."

That finger circled Henry's hole, teasing.

"Why the hell would I want you to stop?" Henry leaned his head forward as he felt more pressure. He locked his lips to Tristan's for a minute as his hole finally loosened. All breath left his body, poured forward into Tristan's mouth. His cock throbbed against Tristan's hard abs, and suddenly the shower was everything and nothing. He couldn't possibly hope to track every sensation, let alone piece them all together. The slow movement inside, in and out and in and out. Hot water pelting his skin. The lingering perfume of yeast mingling with the artificial coconut and lemongrass of the shampoo and body wash. And skin and sweat and *Tristan*. Tristan was the world.

Henry slid his hands into the too-tight space between them and wrapped his hands around both of their cocks. Slow up and down, but speeding quickly as Tristan fingered him faster and harder and deeper, reaching *that* spot. Lightning and frost veined and split through every inch of Henry's body every time Tristan got that deep.

Henry stared into Tristan's eyes as best he could manage being so close. Whimpering groans and moans escaped Tristan's throat, and his head slowly leaned back. But still, he pushed his finger deep into Henry, circled it around the inside, pressed against the edges.

"Fuck, fuck, fuck, fuck . . ." Henry couldn't keep from saying *something*. A string of whispered obscenities was the *least* offensive and extreme reaction he could manage. He wanted so much beyond that, but there was no articulating any desires. He just had to stroke and feel the pressure inside himself and let his balls draw ever higher as steam filled his lungs. Steam and sweat and every tiny smell of Tristan's body that Henry hadn't yet had time to parse out. Yeast and wheat and herbs. Kitchen smells. Comforting, warm, perfect perfume.

Tristan pulled his finger free, and all that electricity and ice pushed to the surface, riding under Henry's skin. An overwhelming emptiness filled his core, but his skin crackled and his cock throbbed in his grip.

So did Tristan's.

"I'm close." Tristan's voice was even more strangled than before. Tight, barely creaking out.

Henry sped up. His balls crept higher and his belly tightened.

Tristan's full lips opened wider, displaying straight white teeth. His head tilted back and his words were barely audible. "I-I'm . . . coming . . ."

Henry slammed his fist up and down both of their cocks. Tristan's pulled and twitched away but stayed restrained by Henry's hand. Spurts of white shot up, landing on Tristan's abs, into his bush, onto Henry's cock. It all washed away with the flow of the water.

When Tristan had finished, Henry pulled back, stroking madly. He wouldn't last much longer, given the build, the pressure, the heat in his belly desperately clawing to burst out. His knees quivered, calves tightened so much they almost hurt. Numbness spread through his extremities as he struggled to hold back, to ride the wave longer. He leaned against the far wall of the shower, out of the shower's stream and absorbed the view: Tristan panting, chest and shoulders heaving, hard muscles working gently under his skin, cock still semi-hard beneath dark bush.

Finally, Henry's whole body exploded. The heat in his abdomen burst down, along his shaft, and out of his cock. Four, five, six, seven. He shivered with the explosion, barely able to hold himself upright. Yet even as he came, he longed for Tristan back inside him. His body shivered with the memory of that fullness, and his desires growled unintelligibly from his throat.

Henry slid down the wall. Tristan was right with him, nestling between Henry's legs so his back pressed against Henry's chest. He sighed, running his fingers in gentle circles up and down Henry's thigh. "I hope that was good for you."

"Good? Jesus Christ, yes."

"Okay." Tristan leaned his head against Henry's chest. His hair tickled Henry's nipple, a gentle sweeping and scratching sensation that was almost too intense. Tristan sighed loudly, and the water kept pounding its symphony against the tub. "I wanted to do more, but it felt too soon. Sorry."

"Don't be sorry." Henry brushed Tristan's hair back from his forehead, then kissed the top of his head. "I showed up here expecting to thrash all the competition. So far I've gotten a bonus blowjob and a sexy shower." *Plus I got over my weird antagonism with Tristan.*

Tristan snuggled in deeper. With his foot, he reached over and popped down the diverter on the faucet. Hot water quickly crept up the tub and up their legs. "Well, I had to give you *something*. As a consolation. Since you're not going to win."

Henry snorted a laugh. "Right. I wouldn't get too cocky. Or did you have some burningly brilliant insight about that stupid bee-sting cake thing? Because I sure as hell haven't yet."

"Maybe I did, maybe I didn't." Tristan leaned his head all the way back and puckered his lips.

And Henry kissed him.

After their shower, Tristan lay on the bed next to Henry, both of them in their underwear with the AC turned all the way off to account for their lack of clothing.

Henry lifted his glass—one of those cheap ones hotels always left in the bathrooms—to his lips and drank the mostly-vodka-and-partially-grape-juice cocktail. His face screwed up a little, but not as much as when they first started drinking. "So, are you *totally* sure you're okay with me sharing your hotel room? I do have a perfectly workable one down the hall."

Tristan shook his head. "I offered this time. I promise it's good with me." He picked up his own glass off the floor and clinked the edge against Henry's glass.

"I'm glad. I like spending time with you."

"Well, no one else is giving you sex, right?"

"That's not why, thank you very much. I thought you would think a *little* more highly of me by now."

"I do. I think *pretty* highly of you, actually. Believe it or not." Tristan sighed and took a slow drink, an attempt to brace himself for being incredibly stupid and bringing up the past that he'd struggled and fought hard to keep private. Opening that door was incredibly, *monumentally* stupid, but the thought of it wouldn't leave Tristan alone. Not with Henry lying there, not saying anything and just letting the scars be the way no other guy had ever managed to do. Tristan felt he almost *deserved* to be told. It was like one of those weird ancient riddles: as soon as you stop wanting something, that's when you can have it.

Tristan lowered his glass once he'd drained half the contents, the terrible lack of flavor be damned. "So . . . why didn't you ask me? I was expecting it."

"I asked you about your tattoo."

Tristan rolled over to look him in the eye. "You know what I mean, Henry."

Henry sighed and set down his drink, then fixed those bright and piercing eyes straight on Tristan. "The scars and stuff aren't my business. Hell, the tattoos aren't, either, but at least you picked those, so you must be a little okay with people seeing them." He shrugged.

"So it's whatever. If it makes you uncomfortable, I'm not going to harp on it."

Tristan smiled at him. His stomach tightened and churned around what he was about to say. But he forced his lips and tongue to make the sounds anyway, and it wasn't nearly as weighty as he expected it to be. "They're ... My dad was an asshole. A *real* asshole. To my sister and my mom and me all through our whole childhood."

"Oh." Henry's voice quieted. He sat up and broke eye contact. "I'm sorry."

"Yeah, me too." Tristan blew out a slow breath. He hadn't told anybody *any* of this in years. Karen was probably the last one he'd gone into it with. As far as Carlita was concerned—she'd caught sight of the scars at an event once and asked—they were from an accident he had as a stupid preteen with an ATV. But now something in his core pushed at him, and the truth scratched to be let out.

For Henry.

"It went on for a long time. I took the brunt of it sometimes for Lucia, and our mom took the brunt of it for the both of us. That's also why I'm checking on my sister. Her husband's, um, the same way."

"That's why she's staying at your place."

Tristan nodded. "Yeah." He still had more to say, though. Now that the door was open? He wasn't quite ready to shut it. "It got a lot worse once I was out. I got extra for being a 'good for nothing faggot.' So that was fun for me." Tristan sighed, and it quivered past his lips. He sat up too. "Most of the time, we healed up fine, but obviously I still have ... some marks. So I don't like to take off my shirt. I don't like to wear short sleeves. I don't like when the hems on my shirts ride up. Even if I do have a tramp stamp back there." That had been a super drunk, impulsive decision, one night when he'd felt okay. Tristan blew out a shuddering breath ... and he was all right. Not great, but all right. "It's easier that way. No questions, no extra worries."

Henry finally looked up again. "But you were willing to show me."

"I wanted to be close to you and ..." Through the icy embarrassment of that whole story—*Why the hell does that embarrass me in the first place?*—heat managed to rise, bubbling from Tristan's core and into his face, and giving him a whole new *hot* embarrassment to contend with. "I wanted to be close to you. If we were going to shower together, it kind of had to happen."

Henry scooted across the bed. He rested a hand on Tristan's exposed knee. He had hot, hard, callused fingers. "I'm glad you decided I was trustworthy and everything. And I really am sorry you had to put up with that. I mean, a kid. That's fucked."

"Yeah. Fucked is about how I would describe it too." Tristan's whole body lightened, and a laugh escaped his lips. "I can't believe that went so well."

"What did you think was going to happen?"

"The best reaction I've gotten is a fake 'I'll call you' after we're done screwing. So maybe something like that." Most guys didn't ask about the scars, simply used him to get off, but damn sure didn't want anything to do with him after the fact. Most of them would respond if he tried to touch base with them, but they never made the next move. "The worst is calling me a suicidal freak and storming out of the apartment. Which I wish I could say only happened once."

"Jesus. Even if you were in that mental space, the reaction to have isn't leaving. It's . . . I don't know, not running out of the house while insulting a suicidal guy seems like a good starting point."

"That's what I would say, but I guess everyone has a different opinion. I think they're probably wrong, but . . . that's the past. It doesn't matter anymore." Tristan scooted over too, until his legs touched Henry's. "It's been a long time since I've spent time with anyone like this. Just . . . relaxed."

"And naked."

Tristan scoffed a laugh and rolled his eyes. "I'm covering my shame, thank you very much. Give me some credit."

Henry leaned back and looked below Tristan's waist. "I'll give you . . . three credits. Because those boxers are still damp and they aren't hiding much."

"Three, huh?" Tristan reclined onto his pillow. It was *nice*, not having to worry about covering himself up. Especially here in fucking San Francisco. All those long-sleeved shirts were *fucking* hot.

Henry reclined next to him and smiled serenely. He draped an arm over Tristan. "Just so we can get it out of the way . . . am I here tomorrow night too?"

Would he be? They'd been sent a pretty strong message earlier that day about getting too close together, and Tristan had been functioning entirely on autopilot when he'd told Henry to bring his toothbrush. He'd been trying to get the conversation over so that no one would hear.

But then this. Henry was being so good about the scars when no one else seemed able to be. If his biggest rival could treat him with respect . . . what did that say about the quality of men he'd been with before? Tristan couldn't remember the last time he'd felt this calm and relaxed. If Henry could make him feel that way . . . maybe it was worth risking the competition.

Maybe *he* was worth the risk.

Tristan kissed him on the biceps. "You can consider yourself officially invited to stay here every night until further notice."

"Oh, I don't know if you want to do that. I'm like black mold: you'll never get rid of me."

"Well, could be worse." Tristan kissed his mouth this time, then nestled into the pillow and the embrace. Tomorrow, he could start to worry about pretzels and bienenstich and black forest cake. He could worry about keeping their budding relationship a secret from the production crew. He could worry about whether he was making the right decision.

Tonight, he only needed to worry about coconut, a hard body spooning him, and Henry fucking Isaacson.

Chapter Twelve

Henry stood at his station, whipping cream by hand for his cake. He could have more easily used the stand mixer, but there was something particularly visceral about doing the whole thing manually. It was like a good workout . . . really, really like a good workout. His arm already ached from the effort. *I've gone soft. I can't even whip my own cream anymore.* Admittedly, he should have frozen the bowl and the whisk before he started, but had it always taken *this* long? *Maybe I'm remembering those halcyon days of culinary school with serious rose-colored glasses.* At least it was a practice day; he wouldn't be this stupid during the actual competition.

"Jesus fucking Christ." Tristan tossed a length of dough onto his countertop, then turned to Henry. The corners of his mouth bowed in a scowl. "These pretzels are going to be the death of me."

"Are you boiling them in the baking soda too long?"

Tristan snorted. "I can't even get that far. I can't shape the damn things. They look like little piles of dog shit when I'm done with them. Super appetizing when they bake up to a nice dark brown, I'm sure."

Henry came around the edge of his station and offered Tristan the bowl. "You whip this, I'll show you how to shape them the lazy way."

"Are you sure about that?" Tristan glanced side to side and lowered his voice. "What if they catch us out? I mean, we don't need to get caught."

"I'm not giving you the recipe. I'm showing you how to shape them. If they want to toss me out for being a decent person . . . fuck 'em." Though Henry kept his voice low for that too. In case the higher-ups were listening and didn't like the way he referred to them. "Besides, we can obviously help each other a little. Katherine got to stay."

He still wanted to find out exactly how much help Bertha had gotten, and who had ratted on her, but the production crew were closed-mouthed and she hadn't come in to film any extra pieces yet today.

After a few moments, Tristan nodded and grabbed the proffered bowl. "Done and done." He stared into the bowl. "God, you whip your cream by hand?"

"I was bored and felt like reconnecting with my roots. And don't mock me when I'm helping you." Henry moved in front of the long, thin strands of dough. Eleven of them were all laid out together, and one of them in a mess well away from the others. "Okay, they aren't too bad to shape. It's getting everything down in your head first that's the tricky part." Henry picked up one of the strands. It was a good consistency for pretzel dough, felt right against his fingertips and moved easily enough. He laid it down and Tristan stepped up closer, whipping the cream furiously . . . and loudly. "You can stop whipping for a second."

"Thank you, oh mighty overlord."

Henry shook his head, chuckling. "Okay, so you want to twist it twice, then bring the arms down." At this point, he could make pretzels in midair, but that was useless for teaching. He did it a little more slowly than he would have normally, showing each twist. Then he wet the ends of the dough and laid them against the bottom curve. Some slight finger adjustments to get the holes proportioned correctly, then he stepped back and gestured to it. "See?"

"Oh yeah. I can do that." Tristan rolled his eyes and handed Henry back the cream. "Don't go anywhere—unless your timer goes off—because I totally don't have this at all."

"Yeah. I picked up on your ever-so-subtle sarcasm."

Tristan offered another eye roll, but he grabbed a new length of his dough. He laid it straight on the counter, then a curve, two twists, and he wet the ends to place them together. It looked . . . not entirely offensive. He didn't have enough actual body, and the arms were too long, but it was clearly a pretzel, which seemed better than he'd been doing before. No dough tossing, at least.

"Thanks. I guess it's not that bad. I was getting too frustrated." He picked up another piece of dough, and this one turned out much better. A lot more evenly spaced. "If you still need someone to whip that cream, I owe you one."

"I've got it." Henry moved back behind his own station and glanced at the timer. Eight minutes until his first check on the cakes. No way they'd be done by now. He examined his partially whipped cream. *That means I have time to pop this in and chill it down.* It would whip up a lot better from cold. With a sigh, Henry put the whole thing in the freezer. *It's no longer amusing to whip it by hand, either.* Once it was good to go, he'd pull out the electric hand mixer and do it up properly.

Henry stood back and watched as Tristan made the rest of a fairly even batch of pretzels. Time still wasn't going to be his friend, and preserving all that work on the shape when he dipped them into the baking soda bath was just one more frustrating part of the process, but the shaping wasn't so far off they were unrecognizable. A lot better than some of the testers people had been producing.

I didn't expect the German round to be the really hard one. Go figure.

As Henry stood waiting and contemplating, a familiar head of white curls stepped out from backstage. Bertha, being escorted by Kristin, the tiny blonde production assistant who'd led them all here that very first day.

Henry left his cakes to bake on their own and met up with her. Kristin stumbled, apparently not expecting a tall scruffy gay man to get in their way.

Bertha smiled at him. A small, somewhat tight smile, but a smile. "You coming to say goodbye? I'm only here to get some filler shots. They didn't have enough footage of me looking devious."

Kristin put on a fake laugh. "Now that's not it. We want to get some extra footage to stitch everything together."

"I know, darling." Bertha nodded at her and flashed the same smile. "Let a sad old cake lady have her jokes."

Kristin apparently didn't know what to do with that either, since she just walked off and started talking to Jacob and the sparse camera crew they had on hand. Which gave Henry enough time to do some reconnaissance. But he didn't feel like he could launch straight into that, so he started cordially. "How are you?"

"I'm okay. I knew it didn't feel right, what I was doing, but I was desperate." She shrugged and sat on the stool in her old station. "Let's be honest, I wasn't taking home the big prize here."

"You might have."

"I can make good cakes and I didn't win the cake round. If that's not a poor omen, I don't know what is."

Henry could have spent time telling her that she'd have been fine, trying to make her feel better. But he wasn't sure how much time he had before they started filming, and the question burned against his tongue. "Can I ask what you actually did?"

Bertha nodded. "Figured someone would want to know eventually." She sighed. "I'm no good at making bread. Never have been. When it comes down to it at a family get-together, I buy the frozen rolls or make a loaf of beer bread. Willa shared her foolproof roll recipe with me during one of the practices. It wasn't what she was making, so she said it would be fine, and at least I'd get something out for the last challenge." She shook her head and chuckled softly under her breath. "Guess the judges disagreed that it was fine. Definitely make sure you're providing all your own recipes."

She'd used Willa's recipe. Henry relaxed, though he tried not to make it too obvious. The chances of him crossing that line were nil.

Kristin led two cameras over, offering him a convenient out from the conversation. "Sorry, Henry, but we need Bertha back. Faster we get this filmed, faster she can get home to her family."

Henry nodded, smiling at Bertha, and retreated to his station as the timer clipped to his lapel chirped. She was going home for a legitimate reason. Still, the specter of rule-breaking hung across his shoulders. Mostly, it was the shock of it all, the sudden nature of it. One slip up—a bad one, admittedly—and that was that.

Someone *had* brought it to the judges, though. Not Bertha, and not Willa, but someone. And that fact alone made him uneasy. *I wouldn't turn someone over for something like that.* Maybe that had more to do with his personality, or his reasons for being here. Or maybe he was assessing himself wrongly.

As he removed his cake from the oven, he sighed. Fretting wouldn't get him anywhere. He had to muscle forward and take the fact he was still here at face value. It was good. He was around. And he would win.

Chapter Thirteen

Tristan took advantage of their filming break to step outside and smoke his much-needed cigarette. The bienenstich hadn't been too hard, once he had it figured out, and his pretzels looked and tasted like pretzels, which was a nice little surprise. Still, his hands had started to shake there at the end, and he had this crawling, creeping pit of despair in his stomach that *somehow* wasn't all that comforting.

Tristan flicked his lighter to life and started up his cigarette, muttering to himself around it. "These things'll kill me, but they'll kill my nerves a hell of a lot faster." And before he made his towering Schwarzwälder Kirschtorte, he needed those nerves gone.

"Don't suppose you could share that with me?"

Tristan dragged deep as he turned. Henry had slipped out the door and leaned against the wall next to him.

"You don't smoke." Tristan's words rode out on billowing blue smoke.

"Nope, but maybe I should take it up. Now seems as good a time as any. Calm my nerves."

Tristan rolled his eyes and dragged in the warmth again. "I'm not getting you hooked, and the only reason this shit relaxes me is because I have a nicotine addiction. Don't think it's going to work for you. Try downing half a bottle of kirsch and call me in the morning."

"Spoilsport." But Henry smiled and winked and the whole thing was over and okay. Tristan pressed up close to him in spite of the California sun, and Henry put an arm around his shoulders. "Good pretzels, and your bee-sting cake seemed to get the job done."

It had. He wasn't used to making yeasted cakes, but it had gone all right, in the end. He'd even managed to throw together a quick honeycomb to add some texture—and it felt nice and on brand for bee-sting cake. Plus it was good to know he still had the chops for something different. The fact his honeycomb had turned out right on the first try had been a hell of a high. "Wish my custard hadn't been quite so thick." It had been very solid compared to the other smooth, silky custards that had come from the other bakers.

"Well, I think you're safe. Only a couple people got as good of a rise out of their bienenstich as you." Henry nudged him in the side. "As long as you're confident you can pull off a cake. I know it's uncharted territory for you."

"Yeah, well, I'll be fine with it once this cigarette's gone." Tristan dragged a little more smoke off it, letting the nicotine wash over his fraying nerves and meld them back together into something cohesive. "You think *you* can pull it off? I mean, black forest cake, that's pretty seventies."

"First of all, I make them for the shop, remember? We talked about it first day of filming."

"Oh yeah, we did. I guess I forgot. That was back when we hated each other."

Henry snorted a chuckle. "Second of all, I did a whole seventies party for someone back during my short-lived foray into catering. For their thirtieth anniversary. They met in high school back then. Baked Alaska, black forest cake, rum baba, battenbergs, some monstrosity called mock apple pie . . . I think I can handle this little bit of retro flair popping back up."

Tristan pulled the butt from his lips and ground the cherry out against the wall behind him. "Mock apple pie? Because it's . . . not pie?"

"Oh, it's pie. It's not apples. It's crackers. It was a Great Depression thing, but it resurged in the seventies."

"Crackers?" Tristan shook his head. "Fucking crackers instead of apples?"

"Yeah, I know. But it honestly wasn't *that* bad. It tasted like cinnamon and cloves more than anything."

"Still . . . it's not the Depression, and I assume they were living in Washington if you did the catering. They could have had real goddamn apples." Tristan pocketed the snubbed cigarette butt to trash it once he went back inside, then turned to look at Henry dead-on. "I guess that doesn't hit that same nostalgic button, though, does it?"

"No. But at least it wasn't hard to put together. The black forest cake was a much bigger pain in the butt." Henry stretched his arms above his head and leaned side to side, showing off a flash of abs and underwear and *goddamn it* he was sexy.

Tristan glanced down both ends of the street. He didn't *really* think there would be anyone, but better to be safe than tossed out ... Once he confirmed they were alone, he sidled closer. Close enough that he could press his hands to that exposed skin, slide them a little ways up Henry's too-hot back.

"Are you feeling me up?"

"I'm touching your back. If you think *this* is feeling you up, you're going to lose your shit if I slap your ass."

"I would *definitely* lose my shit if you slapped my ass." Henry turned too and wrapped an arm around Tristan's waist. "I mean, out here in public in front of God and everyone? Not to mention with the producers right behind this door? Scandalous."

Tristan slid his hand out from under Henry's shirt, and he did *exactly* what was expected. He slapped Henry on the ass. Not hard or loud, but enough to feel how fucking *firm* it was. No real give. For a man who made a living off cake and pastry, he was surprisingly not soft anywhere.

Well, one place. Tristan quickly kissed those soft, supple lips. Henry tasted of honey and salt and vanilla, and his tongue pressed forward, strong and unwaveringly confident.

Then the door opened. Tristan's stomach clenched into a tight ball, but there was no discreet way to remove yourself from someone's tongue in a hurry. So he just pulled back and smiled at the intruder. It was Finn, the Irish bastard. He at least looked properly embarrassed for walking in—or out—on the situation, averting his eyes and blushing. "They want to start filming, so if you guys want to sneak back in real quick?" He propped the door open with one arm and gestured them through with a tilt of his head.

"Right. Thanks." Together, Tristan and Henry slipped in, and the door shut behind them, clanging like a prison cell. Every inch of him was frigid. They'd been spotted. They'd been seen by someone in the competition, all because Tristan couldn't keep it in his pants until they got back to the damn hotel room. Would Finn rat them out? *If he wants to win, that would be the smart thing to do.* Tristan tried to speak, but nothing would come out, and Finn quickly darted around them and back onto the set, leaving them still on their way.

"Hey." Henry grabbed his shoulders, stopping him out of view of the set. He must have noticed Tristan silently exploding. His brows furrowed, and he stared straight into Tristan's eyes. "It's fine."

"How is it fine? What if Finn was the Chatty Cathy who turned in Bertha, and he's going to get all righteous about us, now?"

"It's fine because we're not sharing recipes, for starters. I told you, that's why Bertha got kicked off. Plus Finn's not going to go running to the producers."

"How could you possibly know that?"

"Trust me." Even Henry didn't sound convinced by his own statements, but he kept on making them, and somehow, Tristan's stomach calmed. A little. "It's going to be fine, okay? Let's go make cake."

But Tristan's calm only lasted a few moments before his stomach was back to churning and his thoughts back to racing. "What does it matter if he throws us under the bus?" Finn was now armed against them if he chose to fight dirty. "Why bother baking?"

"Because he might not say anything, and the last thing either of us need to do at the moment is give up when we're not even sure he's going to blab." He locked those chocolate eyes straight on Tristan. "Your sister insisted you come, right? You're going to give up and let her down?"

Maybe Tristan was being too nervous, but then maybe Henry could act a bit more concerned. This competition was more than a chance at glory for Tristan. It was about that very same sister Henry had just played against him, for starters. Sure, Henry wasn't privy to the whole situation, but Tristan was upset. He was freaking out. Shouldn't that have been worth paying more mind to instead of *assuming* everything would turn out fine?

With a sigh meant to steel himself—though it didn't do much good—Tristan held the door open for Henry, and they walked together through the back of the set. Maybe Henry couldn't understand Tristan's anxieties. Worse, maybe he couldn't respect his concerns.

Tristan made sure to leave a little space between them.

So much goddamn chocolate cake. Even as a baker, Henry was struck by how much they'd all produced. The manifesto called for a minimum of three tiers, which was a heck of a lot of cake anyway, but most had gone for at least four.

Henry had made a five-tier, and it was a pretty motherfucker, too. Whipped cream piped all around the tiers in perfect stars, but not covering the dark chocolate cake—he'd gone with black cocoa powder, because why the fuck not? It made the contrast all the starker and more striking. Kirsch-infused cherries, cooked down with allspice and cinnamon and clove.

I really am good. It was a bit egotistical, but he also couldn't deny it, looking over the product he'd whipped out in four hours. Four goddamn hours. It would have been impressive for eight hours' work. A five-tiered cake was an investment of some serious time and effort.

Not to mention he'd been splitting his focus between his own work and Finn's station. He didn't know what he was looking for exactly—there were no neon signs flashing to say Finn was going to turn them in to the higher-ups at Eatery TV—but he couldn't help keeping watch. Whatever he'd said to Tristan, he was nervous. The last thing he wanted to be sent home on was some damn misunderstanding.

He glanced at Tristan's equally impressive stack of cakes. It was very modern and sleek, like most things Tristan made. The sides were smoothed out with a thin layer of dark chocolate mirror glaze, and whipped cream was piped in alternating seashells around the border of each of the four layers. Whole cherries adorned the top, each on its own little pillow of whipped cream. Offset tiers too. It was nice, and a big counterpoint to a largely classic presentation from everyone else. Maybe it would work in his favor, maybe it wouldn't.

Henry caught Tristan's eye and flashed him a smile and a wink. Tristan's spine straightened, he nodded curtly, then faced fully forward. Fully and pointedly *away* from Henry. It was an icicle straight to the stomach. Henry wanted their lightness back. But there was no recourse. Not now. So that icicle stuck around, a weight in his gut to slow him up and bog him down.

As judging commenced, the judges changed up the order again, going from one side to the other all the way up both rows of workstations. Katherine had impressed wholeheartedly with rum-infused cherries that Rita called "sinful," and beautiful, clean linework on her frosting that made Henry question his prior assumptions about her and her farmers' market bakes. Dorian had just gone back to his station after a fair to middling critique—the cake needed more seasoning, but the accoutrements had impressed, especially his handmade cherry cordials—and Henry sucked in a deep breath.

Sylvia—today in a dark-plum blouse and cream slacks—smiled straight at him. "Now, Henry, let's see what this *towering* behemoth is. If you can bring it right on up. Do you need a hand?"

Henry waited to see if Tristan would move to help, even though that seemed unlikely. But still, he gave it a few seconds, silently imploring Tristan to move.

Nothing doing though, and a new layer of ice formed in his chest. "If you don't mind." With no other choice—this was a massive cake— he left his fate to the crew of production assistants, all dressed in black. It took three of them, but they lifted it and started the slow hike up to the front of the set.

Thankfully, the cake arrived in one piece, and Henry let out a breath he'd been holding the whole time.

Dexter started stalking around the cake. "This is impressive. I think you've officially won the prize for tallest cake."

Henry nodded. With five tiers, it *was* approaching the three-foot mark. It was *really* close if you counted the tiny mounds of whipped cream all along the top.

Dexter gently pressed into the side with his middle finger. "Moist, springs back to the touch. Lovely, dark color, how did you do that?"

"Black cocoa powder."

He nodded slowly. "Nice choice. Offsets the decoration. But let's see how it tastes."

Eli cut an excessively thin slice from each tier. *I guess to see if they're all good. I could have hidden Styrofoam in the middle one.* He laid them each out on a cutting board rather than a plate, all in a row from bottom to top. All three judges dived on them, going in order from the bottom to the top tier.

Rita broke the silence first. "They're definitely all the same. Either you made a truly massive amount of batter at once, or you managed to keep uniformity across a number of batches."

"It's a familiar enough recipe."

Rita scraped up a bit of whipped cream and spooned it into her mouth, then popped one of the spiced cherries, chewing carefully before swallowing. "And your flavors work well together. It's classic, but it's still different enough to keep me interested, which isn't that easy when I have to eat six black forest cakes today."

"Yeah, I enjoyed this," said Eli. "The black cocoa powder is bitterer than a normal cocoa powder, and that lets you amp up the sugar for the cherries and the whipped cream and everything else. Nicely done."

"It *is* good." Dexter picked up what remained of one of the bottom-tier slices and stretched it gently between his fingers until it tore apart. "It's a good crumb, properly risen, no streaks of egg white. This many tiers in four hours isn't a sloucher move by any stretch. And it really is beautiful." He smiled. "Well done. Very well done."

Sylvia nodded to Henry, smiling broad. "Thank you for a splendid showing."

He walked back and actually felt *good* about his chances as they carted his cake back to his station.

That confidence took a minor hit as Finn, Tristan, and Willa went up for their judging. It wasn't that he thought any *less* of his own feedback or accomplishment. No, he'd still made a five-tiered chocolate sponge, and a good one. A different one, according to Rita.

But then Tristan's was apparently different too, with his sleek presentation and the stewed cherry compote between the layers. Willa's wasn't different, but it was "perfectly nostalgic," whatever that meant for her chances. And Finn's was impressively decorated, which Henry couldn't deny—with swirling ropes of whipped cream roses that somehow weren't losing a bit of their definition, even clinging to the side of the three-tiered cake. The center of each rose was a bright red glacé cherry, and the whole cake was dusted with powdered sugar.

It might not be enough. After all, I haven't won one, yet.

"I don't know if you can do this." On cue, at the worst possible moment, the familiar sabotage tightened his stomach around a core of ice.

Soon, they all stood behind their own cakes, waiting for judgment. Tristan was pointedly looking forward, not conversing, not glancing back to Henry. Was this his overblown nerves about the competition, or had Henry done something to earn this cold shoulder? Was he too self-centered to notice some flub?

Sylvia actually broke into light applause as the cameras started rolling. "You *all* deserve that. Judging is getting harder as the weeks go on, but this was far and away the longest deliberation I've sat in on. Back and forth, over and over every minute detail." She held her thumb and middle finger up, pressed together. "The margins were this slim. Everyone tackled our German round with an amazing amount of fervor, and it showed in your final products."

Oh God. How was Henry supposed to feel? If the competition was that tight, maybe he was in the middle of the pack after all. Or the bottom. God, *no* one stood out as particularly error-ridden.

This is what I came here for, damn it. Real competition. His gaze darted to Tristan. *But I guess there's even more at stake than my pride. I guess he's more than a maybe.*

Sylvia sighed. "One of you pulled out all the stops and made something truly *ausgezeichnet.* Sometimes, there's nothing better than the classics, executed to perfection."

Perfection. Classics. It's Willa, it has to be Willa. Again.

Sylvia gestured toward the middle. "Congratulations, Katherine. It was your bienenstich that really pushed you over the edge for the judges. It was tight, but you were a busy bee and *buzzed* right past the competition."

Katherine stepped out from her station, hands to her mouth. Henry wouldn't have picked her. But that was likely on him more than anyone else. Katherine had proven herself as nothing if not absolutely capable. So when everyone was clapping, he clapped for her . . . and he actually meant it. She deserved this victory.

But that means I'm still not safe.

Sylvia clasped her hands in the now all-too-familiar *bad news* stance. "Unfortunately, a close competition means that the person going home also turned out an incredible product. This final decision came down to microns, but it had to be made." She sighed again. "The person who has to leave us this week . . . is Finn."

Finn? Are you shitting me? Henry's jaw clamped tight. If Finn was going to try to drop some bomb about Henry and Tristan, now would be the moment. He was on his way out, and a wounded animal would attack. Another chance for Henry to fall, to bring his mother's worries to life. Henry glanced surreptitiously at him, trying to get some clue as to how he was feeling, but his taut stance revealed nothing.

Dexter cleared his throat and the cameras whipped toward him. From the wide-eyed, open-mouthed look on Sylvia's face, this wasn't anything they'd planned. "You may be going home, but you really turned out an amazing body of work this week and during the whole competition."

Finn was obviously trying to hide his confusion, but he was failing, brow furrowing.

Dexter smiled at him, eyes bright. "And I say this wholeheartedly: if you ever need a change of job, you have a spot in my kitchen. It's not often you run across someone who works with the sort of precision you've demonstrated under pressure."

Finn's face reddened, his body relaxed, and of course the cameras swung back around to catch it for posterity. "Thank you. Really."

"And that's a wrap!" Out came the director, Jacob. He walked straight to Dexter and didn't even attempt to whisper. "A little heads-up would be appreciated before you decide to go rogue, again."

"Sorry. It was in the heat of the moment."

Jacob shrugged. "You do what you want with your business, no skin off my nose. That shit makes for good TV. It has to be usable footage, though." He turned to address the whole line. "We're going to have you guys do your interviews and voice-overs tonight before you head home. I hope none of you made pressing dinner reservations."

Henry released a breath. His whole body went slack as the nerves wicked away. He was here for another round. Four more days to spend with Tristan. Icy responses or not, he was looking forward to any morsel of that man he could get. Plus another chance to prove himself against the other bakers. And that was key, because although he'd gotten to stay, he hadn't yet lost, he was also the only one left who hadn't yet won. Willa had two. That put Henry firmly at the bottom of the pack.

But next week is viennoiserie. Viennoiserie I can do. He made turnovers and cinnamon rolls and kites all day, seven days a week. And damn it, if he couldn't pull *this* win off, then there was no real hope for him.

Henry turned to the other bakers. Surprisingly, they weren't all crowding around Finn. Apparently their condolences had already happened while Henry was hanging out in the dark corners of his head. Either that or they thought getting a job offer from Dexter Wilson was enough of a prize.

Willa was there, though, a leathery arm around his shoulder, smiling and chattering away. Would he say anything to her about them, or would he keep that a private issue, the way it should be? It wasn't Willa's business. It wasn't Finn's, for that matter, but fate had intervened to make sure he knew regardless.

Henry glanced at Tristan, and he was still closed off, still avoiding eye contact, standing at his station and clutching his arms around his chest. He wasn't the Tristan that Henry had been spending all this time with, the one that was digging in under Henry's skin and making a place for himself. It was *painful* to see him so closed off, so hurt, so worried.

And if there was a way to fix it, Henry was damn sure going to try.

He leaned in closer to Tristan. "Hey, I'm going to handle something, then I'll be right back." Henry didn't stick around long enough to hear Tristan's answer, instead jogging after Willa and Finn.

"—really a shame you're heading home. I liked your style, kid."

"Thanks, but it's the way the cake crumbled. My time to head back, I guess."

They're not talking about me or Tristan. Relieved, Henry laid his hand on Finn's shoulder. "Hey, you left your phone back at the station it looks like." It was a shitty excuse, of course. He probably had his phone in his pocket, but Henry wanted him separated for this.

Finn rolled his eyes. "I'm always losing that thing. Good chat, Willa."

Once they were away from everyone else, Henry stopped. "Listen, about what you saw out there . . ."

Finn blinked a couple of times before shrugging. "Saw? Who saw anything?" He grinned like an idiot, his smile pushing up the mole on his right cheek. "Don't worry about it, Henry. Who cares if you like to kiss boys?"

"But . . . with what happened with Bertha . . . you could have taken that to the judges."

"Are you telling me you did something wrong?" He shrugged. "The way I see it, you deserve to be here. Both of you boys. I lost out. What kind of bitter, loveless bastard would I have to be to throw you two under the bus for getting a little action on the side?" He clapped Henry hard on the shoulder. "I'm not saying a word to the judges. No worries."

Henry breathed a sigh. "If you're ever in Seattle, I owe you."

"I'll keep that in mind if I make it that far north. Until then, farewell." Finn left with a wave.

When Henry turned, Willa was right there, and his heart almost blew out of his chest. "Willa. Didn't see you."

"Did Finn get his phone back?"

"Oh, it was in his pocket. Don't know what I saw." *Apparently I'm shit at lying today.* "Must be my exhausted brain after all this baking."

She nodded and smiled at him. "Well, go get some good rest. This next round's not going to be easy."

And she left too, leaving a glimmer of unease with Henry. He didn't love trying to juggle partial truths and secrets and all that crap.

But unease aside, for now he could take his three extra days with Tristan—assuming Tristan would have him back. But one problem at a time. For as long as he could manage.

Henry didn't ask that night if he was coming back to Tristan's hotel room. That niggled at Tristan a bit, considering how clear he'd tried to make the separation between the two of them, but he said nothing about it. *I gave him permission, after all.* And if he turned his brain off, it *did* feel good, walking through the door together and not having to go through the motions of Henry asking. Just getting to go back and spend time together, albeit with Tristan surreptitiously glancing over his shoulder every minute or two.

So turn his brain off was exactly what he did. He pushed his worries and stress aside at the door as the hotel room ensconced them away from any prying eyes. He could tackle his worries about Finn—and about how Henry reacted to his worries worry—a little later.

For a few hours, Tristan wanted to pretend everything was fine.

Henry sat on the edge of the bed and immediately slipped off his shoes and socks. "You make a good chocolate cake."

"Not as good as yours." Tristan sat on the opposite side, facing the window and the darkened parking lot below. He pulled off his shoes and socks and tucked them into the far corner, then immediately fished out his phone. "I need to give my sister a call, then I'm yours for the night."

Henry flopped down so his head was next to Tristan's hip. His stubble, now quite visible at the end of the day, was like the outside char on a campfire marshmallow, dark over silky and pale skin. "You really never miss a night."

"Of course not. I made a promise."

"I thought, with everything that happened today . . ."

Tristan balked at the mention. "Bad day, sounds like I need my sister more than usual."

Henry nodded, then popped back up. "I'll go over to my hotel room, though. I can talk with Carrie and give you your privacy so you don't have to send me for ice again."

Tristan's skin flushed hot. "Was I that obvious?"

Henry chuckled. "Did you think it was subtle?"

"It's not you. I just . . . you know . . ."

"Hey, she's family, she's having a hard time. I don't have a problem leaving you to talk to her." He stood, walked over, and kissed Tristan on the cheek, his stubble barely scratching. "Come get me when you're done. No big deal. God knows I should probably use the room they're paying for, for a few minutes, anyway. I mean, what must the maids think?"

Tristan's face stayed hot. Honestly, why was he keeping the call private at all? Henry knew Lucia's situation already.

"You don't need to go."

Henry's brows furrowed. "You don't have to try and make me feel better about it."

"Look, you don't need to. I know I made excuses, but . . . stay. Please." He wanted to keep connected to Henry, even when talking about his sister. He didn't want any gaps between them. "If you want to use your room after that, I'm all game for it."

Henry's lips pursed tight for a second, then he sat back on the bed. "If you're okay with it, I'm okay with it."

"I don't want you to feel like you have to leave because I'm calling Lucia. After all, she's the one who told me to hook up with you in the first place."

"Oh really?" Henry's face relaxed into an easy smile. "Maybe I should call her, then. I seem to owe her."

"Right. Maybe postpone *that* conversation a bit longer." Tristan unlocked his screen and flicked through his contacts until he hit the apartment's number.

Two rings, then Lucia picked up. "Hello, Tristan. How many wonderful admiring fans have you acquired?"

"At least fourteen today. You know, kind of mediocre ones, but they can't all be perfect."

She laughed slightly. "You're done earlier today than usual."

"Yeah. It was only a ten-hour day today. Piece of cake."

"Are you getting enough sleep? There's no point killing yourself for this show, no matter what Carlita has to say about it."

Tristan cringed. Lucia didn't know what the financial situation was like at home . . . or that she wasn't making it better. He wasn't about to go into that with her, not with everything else going on in her life. He was ready to support her as long as he possibly could, because goddamn it she wasn't going back to Robert, but still . . . it *was* worth killing himself a little for the show. Every round he stayed on meant another bit of pay he could take home. "Come on, you know I barely sleep anyway. I think I can handle this."

"If you burn out for this show, I'm never letting you out of my sight again."

"Yeah? If I recall, you're the one who insisted I had to come down here and compete."

"Don't go turning the facts around on me." She sighed and the line crackled with static. "So, how's your new lover coming along?"

Tristan flushed hot immediately and glanced at Henry, wondering how much of Lucia's end of this conversation was bleeding through. From his placid expression and seeming lack of attention, all was well. "It's coming along... all right." Aside from the whole *getting caught by one of their fellow contestants* part. "Pretty well. But I don't really want to talk about that right now."

A pause. One second, two seconds. "He's in the room with you, isn't he?"

"Possibly, yes."

"So I could screw with you and talk about all kinds of embarrassing things, right?"

"And I could hang up the phone."

She laughed, *not* softly this time, and Tristan couldn't help but enjoy it. He loved to hear her laugh, and it was so rare in the past months. Years. He certainly never got to hear her laugh around Robert. So if it was at his expense now, that was fine.

She finished with a sigh. "I'm sorry. I won't do that to you. But I'm glad you called. I'm glad you keep calling."

"Of course." His stomach clenched, and all the sudden he wondered if maybe Henry shouldn't be there after all. "Is everything okay?"

"Yeah, of course. What makes you think something's wrong?"

"You were saying you were glad I called."

"You're my brother. I kind of like you. I don't know if you'd put that together yet."

"You know, I had a suspicion. Thanks for the confirmation. Now, are you sure you're okay?"

"I am better than I've been in months, Tristan. All right? Do you believe me? Or do I need to put Karen on so she can tell you too?"

"It would be nice ... but I guess I can trust you. As long as you promise you're not fibbing."

"'Fibbing'? Jesus, what are you, seven?"

Tristan's belly relaxed. Yeah. She was fine. Acting more like real Lucia and a lot less like Robert's meek, polite, unopinionated wife Lucia. "'Fibbing' is a perfectly valid word. But I believe you. You're fine. And you love your big brother so much that you'll definitely call if you're not. I'm sure of it."

"Of course I will." She sighed. "Really. Thanks, though." He could almost see her squirming and fidgeting over the phone. She was probably flicking her fingernails off each other right then and there. "I mean, you know, you're always there, and you always let me stay, no matter what."

"Don't even worry about it." It was Tristan's job to worry. It was Lucia's job to stay there, to stay away from Robert's manipulative ass. And to hopefully take the time away from him to recover as much as she could. "I like having you around. Plus, God knows how many people would have broken into my apartment if I didn't have you there while I'm gone."

She chuckled. "Glad to know I can be of service. You could have just asked me to come watch your place for a while, though."

And have Robert constantly there, and have him hitting her while Tristan was gone, and, and, and. "Well, it worked out either way." Another glance to Henry, who was lying back on the bed, staring up with an unfocused little smile on his face. Tristan couldn't help the corners of his mouth pulling up at the sight. "Okay, Lucia. I'll call you tomorrow."

"I'd tell you that you don't have to, but you wouldn't listen and I like the conversation. Karen's great . . . but she's no you."

"Oh yeah, me, the stunning conversationalist. Often compared to a rock at parties."

"People at parties are too busy getting drunk or getting their rocks off to have a conversation with you. No one as smart as you with your job could possibly be bad to talk to."

"Maybe not, but I can sure convince people otherwise."

"All right, I see I've run into self-deprecation o'clock, so I'll leave you to it."

"Thanks, the flagellation begins in ten minutes. With or without you on the phone. Night, Lucia."

"Yeah, yeah. Good night, Tristan. I love you."

She'd said it first. She was *really* missing him, then. "Love you too. I'll be back soon." Tristan hung up the phone and set it aside, then flopped back on the other side of the bed. His hand moved gently to Henry's thigh, all of its own accord. He didn't creep closer or pull back. He just rested there and let the moment exist.

"So . . . I heard something about flagellation?" Henry rolled over and looked Tristan in the eye. "I mean, I would have thought this was a little early in the relationship for bringing out the whips and flogs, but I guess I'm game for it if you are."

Tristan chuckled and shifted closer, wrapped his arms around Henry and relished the firm muscles and the heat and the weight of him there in that bed that had seemed so perfectly, wonderfully devoid of people when he first showed up at the hotel.

Tristan knew, in the logical parts of his mind, that this was the time to have all these hard conversations with Henry. They were probably comfortable enough to handle any extra stress those would present.

But Tristan shied away from that cold spot in his thoughts. He wasn't ready. So he slid his hand up underneath Henry's shirt and rested it against Henry's abdomen. It was easier, better to skirt wide of the actual issue. Every word sat heavy on his tongue. Too heavy for liftoff.

"Thank you for staying."

"Of course. Thanks for letting me." Henry sighed, his stomach moving up and down with his breath. "I'm glad you're starting to relax. I like it better that way."

That niggled at the back of Tristan's mind, joining all the other niggles. It was better for *Henry* when Tristan relaxed.

But Tristan wasn't ready to let conflict into the space. So he swallowed back his frustrations, leaned in, and kissed Henry on the nape of the neck, then lay back down, sliding closer, letting the comfort wrap him tighter and try to choke out the rest of his concerns. But one still slipped out, loosed from captivity. Maybe to make room for his own thoughts. Maybe because only so much stress could live in one human body. "I just . . . need this money so much."

Henry moved closer. "Really?"

Tristan shrugged, not able to make eye contact against that question. It was a safer release valve to open than the one to do with their own relationship, but that didn't make it easy to talk about, to fess up to. Instead, he focused on the corded muscles in Henry's neck. "I've got Lucia living with me, and she doesn't work. I don't know how long she's going to stay at my place. Maybe she'll need a divorce lawyer. She might need therapy to help her deal with all this." His stomach clenched as he tried to ignore the sums swimming through his gray matter. "And finding that extra money is my responsibility. Robert never let her get a job, so it's going to take a while before she can get employed, and I'm not going to push her. But at the same time, my credit cards are a mess, and I need all this money from somewhere. It's life, you know?" Finally, he gazed up into the chocolate depths of Henry's eyes, and he both hated and adored the concern blossoming in that gaze. "Pastry bitch doesn't pay that well. TV baking competition star does."

Henry nodded and visibly tried to erase his frown. It was a good gesture, but he still had that slight anxiousness in the tone of his muscles, the set of his jaw. But he lay down and slipped his arm underneath Tristan's shoulders, and he placed a gentle kiss on Tristan's cheek.

And they lay there together, neither of them acknowledging what had been said. Tristan continued to pretend that he was okay and everything was okay and he wasn't feeling a little unseen and unheard by Henry.

Pretending was nice. But exhausting.

Chapter Fourteen

The first day of practice for the next shooting flowed past Henry with no obstruction, no catch. More than any of the cooking in the previous weeks, whipping out turnovers and cinnamon rolls and pain au chocolat felt like his everyday life with some extra strangers tossed into the mix. These were tried-and-true recipes, the kind he could bust through without even trying. Hell, if he was back home in the shop, he probably wouldn't have measured. *Guess that's the other difference here. In my kitchen, a batch of puff pastry only has time and resources on the line. Not a quarter-million dollars. Also I don't make my own puff when I can help it, and nobody notices the difference.*

They finished up the first practice day, and he and Tristan left the studio separately, didn't even ride together, at Tristan's behest. Henry thought it looked a hell of a lot more suspicious for them to be changing things around all of a sudden, but he wasn't going to push it. Tristan was the one with the major nerves.

Henry took the elevator of the Hotel Majestic up. Tristan's door stood open the tiniest crack, and he let himself in. Here, Tristan was utterly different. He'd already lain belly down on the bed, pants tossed off so he was in his boxers, shirt riding up to show off his tramp stamp and the barest corrugation of his spine. No tensions touched his shoulders, no nervous twitches or twiddles. In here, Tristan truly relaxed. *And I'm the only one who gets to see it.*

Henry couldn't resist. When he stepped in, he slapped Tristan right on the ass, then slid his hand up. "Hey."

"Hey yourself." Tristan rolled over onto his side and set down his phone. "You know, you spank a little hard."

Henry coiled back. "Shit. I didn't mean to trigger anything. I didn't even think."

"Hey, hey. I'm fine." Tristan sat up and grabbed Henry around the shoulders, his touch firm. "This isn't about my past. I'm just making a normal complaint. I have to sit on a big hard stool when I'm on set, so I need to preserve my poor tender ass."

Henry nodded, taking a moment to collect himself. He didn't want to push the wrong buttons. Tristan had seemed off ever since Finn saw them kissing, and Henry was maybe a little on edge himself, ever since Bertha had gotten kicked off. He wanted to play it safe.

That was why he had decided not to bring anything up. He was going to hold to normalcy. Or what passed for normalcy while they were here. So he took a calming breath, then leaned against Tristan's bare shoulder. "So, did you try my turnovers?"

"The fig? Yeah." Tristan took off his glasses, polishing them on the bedsheet. "I love figs."

"Cool. Can you tell me what's wrong with them?"

Tristan slipped his glasses back on. "Is that going to be too much?"

"We've conferred on flavors before. I helped you with your pretzels. I helped Katherine with her focaccia." Henry wanted to get off the subject, steer into light territory. "I throw myself at the mercy of your baking prowess, oh mighty one."

Slowly, a grin split Tristan's face. "Since you're prostrating yourself before me, your icing was too sweet. Try using grapefruit instead of orange. The bitterness will help balance everything out."

Grapefruit. It was a solid pull. "I guess I owe you if I win."

"Nope. Don't joke about that." Tristan sighed. "As far as the judges and everyone else is concerned, that was your own idea."

This new awkwardness niggled at Henry. Not because he *blamed* Tristan for being cautious. Because it wasn't the way they should have been, wasn't the relationship they'd tenuously cobbled together during their time here so far. It was a dark spot in the middle of all this lightness, and one that bloomed resentment through Henry.

Tristan chewed on his nail a few seconds before continuing. "Even without the icing change, those turnovers are good enough to win. Everything you made is good enough to win this round."

"Your stuff isn't exactly dog shit."

"Yeah, but you do this every day." When Tristan looked back at him, his face was oddly calm. He smiled slightly—not enough to show off his dimples, but there was a definite upturn to the corners of his mouth. "You'll win this one, and you deserve to win it. I'd bet on it. And I don't throw my money away."

Henry couldn't keep his frustration under that amount of ego-stroking, or the assault of sincerity from Tristan. He lowered himself down onto the bed, and for a few moments, everything felt right, back to the way it had been. "Sometimes I wish we could stay up here and forget all this."

Tristan nuzzled him. "I've heard worse ideas."

Henry sighed. "Then it's a plan." And he pressed his lips against Tristan's warm throat, feeling his breath moving.

A couple of days later, the evening before filming, Tristan was doing his best to act nonchalant, even as his palms sweated. *Don't want to tip Henry off to this little surprise.* Currently, he was on the bed, scrolling through his phone. Tristan took a few calming breaths that did jack shit to make him feel more at peace. But he had something to attend to, and until he *did*, his nerves and stomach wouldn't settle.

Of course, it was entirely possible they wouldn't settle *after* he took care of his little errand, either. But that hope was all he had to lean on in that moment. "So, I need to head to the store real quick. I'm out of some personal amenities."

"'Personal amenities'?" Henry sat up. "Sounds to me like you're trying to hide what you're talking about."

Probably because I am. Tristan wasn't going to come out and say what this was about. Not to Henry. There was a plan in Tristan's head, a set of contingencies to be met that would get him to the goal. *I want this to be an occasion.* "It's just something I need to pick up. Humor me."

"Well, I can come with you."

Tristan waved that concern away. "Trust me, I'm the worst person to shop with. Up and down every aisle deciding what I actually want. It'll be better for our relationship if I go alone." Tristan lay out on the bed next to Henry and kissed the back of his neck. "Besides, did it occur to you that I'm spending my meager funds on you and don't want the surprise wrecked?"

"Oh, don't buy me anything."

"I don't know if I will, now. Nosy McNosyFace."

"Not even if I'm super cute?"

"You're contradicting yourself." Tristan rolled his eyes. "I'm going to the store for some stuff that's none of your business. There, problem solved." He kissed Henry's neck again. Then he forced himself back up into the cruel world. He had a damn job to do, and he was *going* to do it. "It *shouldn't* take that long, but this is San Francisco, so I have no clue what the reality is going to be."

"I'll hold vigil for you if you aren't back by sunrise."

"Gee, such comfort." Tristan winked, then darted into the bathroom. He futilely slid his hair into some shape resembling normalcy—it would be out of place again by the time he was in the actual store—slapped on a little extra deodorant, and double-checked his hands and face for flour. Everything checked out and he whispered to his reflection, "Okay, let's do this." Then he stepped back and grabbed the door handle. "Wish me luck while I travel the intestines of the beast."

"Sounds like fun. If I'm not here when you get back, come knock on my hotel room door." Henry sighed and winked. "But I'll probably be here."

"Well, I have my key anyway. So worse comes to worse, I can at least get back in."

"Glad you have your priorities straight." Henry rolled over onto his front, resting his chin on his hands like a 1950s' slumber-party girl. "Have fun shopping."

"Fun. Right." Shopping wasn't fun. Especially not shopping for this stuff. But he ached for connection, to really *be* with Henry. He wanted something special and *right* between them. They both *deserved* this.

Tristan headed out the door and, of course, patted his pockets for his wallet after he'd already left the room. But it was there, and his phone was there, so he headed for the elevator. It opened straightaway and he took it down to a rather empty lobby. "Suits me fine."

He walked over to the desk and waited until the dark-haired woman nodded to him. "I'm sorry, I'm looking for the nearest general store. Maybe one with a pharmacy if it's not too far away."

"Oh, no problem." Her brows had raised at the word *pharmacy* though, and her eyes kept shifting over to him as she typed. "There's one here on the corner. Four blocks down to the right. I hope you get to feeling better soon."

"Oh, I'm not sick. I figure a store with a pharmacy is going to have the best chance of having cotton balls." He shuffled through his thoughts for something else, since only a weirdo would just go out to buy cotton balls. "And Benadryl." *Because that's a totally normal shopping list.*

"Oh, all right." She appeared relaxed now that Tristan had confirmed he didn't have the plague. "Well, the one you want is Highland Drug and General."

"Highland Drug and General. Got it." He backed up and gave her a wave, then stepped into the heat and noise and sea smell and too many people. *Henry's worth it. He's goddamn worth it.*

There was never a question of that. To Tristan, Henry was important enough to bear through even *twice* that many people.

The drugstore itself was a quiet enough affair, but the back wall sent Tristan's anxieties into full bore. Did the world need this many kinds of condoms and lube? How much difference did they really make? What would Henry find the most . . . pleasurable?

The only thing that snapped him out of his fugue was an elderly woman coming by, smiling too knowingly at him. Getting away from *her* took priority, and he grabbed an average-priced pack of condoms and a small bottle of lube, and took those up to the cashier, who thankfully didn't make a single comment.

Ten dollars later, he was walking out with his surprise, and a growing sense of anticipation brewing in his belly.

The hard part of this wouldn't be getting to the sex.

The hard part would be practicing patience until he could.

Henry stood behind his station, waiting to learn the results of the viennoiserie round. It was getting *sparse* in that kitchen, with only five of them remaining. But he couldn't muster any real nerves about his chances this time. He'd gotten glowing remarks, especially on this final set of pastries: Aztec chocolate palmiers for the sweet, and little puff pastry pockets of chicken thigh, morels, and caramelized onions for his savory. Tristan hadn't been far behind him, showing off a nice command of simple flavors. Onion and Monterey jack for his savory, and mango with a crumbly, Salvadoran dulce de leche for his sweet. Not that anyone had done *badly*, but in Henry's opinion, they both had solid spots in the next round.

Sure, I want to win this one. But at least I'll be here next week regardless. And I'll have long enough to figure out what's going on with Tristan. He'd come back the day before with a bag Henry wasn't allowed to look in, so of course there had to be *something* worthwhile in there. *Even if there isn't, I have to know.* Would he be disappointed to learn it was a chocolate bar? Maybe a little, but solving the damn *mystery* would be enough.

Sylvia cleared her throat, and the cameras all whipped around into their usual end of filming positions. A few focused up front, and the rest were set to pan and zoom through the kitchen and all the contestants. Once they stilled, Henry barely noticed them, anymore. *I guess that comes with the territory.*

"Well, you all took us on a trip to Vienna … Or is it France? I can never keep viennoiserie straight." She paused a moment, some forced laughter went through the line, and then she picked her spiel back up. "There's one among you who proved absolutely capable of handling the layered challenges viennoiserie brings with a cool, level head." She scanned the room, then turned and pointed open-handed to the left. To Henry's side. "Henry, congratulations."

His face immediately split into a smile. He'd done it. And this time, the applause didn't feel trite or obligated, even though it had to be the same as it always was. But on the receiving end of it … Yeah, Henry felt damn good.

I did it.

The applause subsided, and Sylvia offered a little wink to Henry before she continued into the second part. The less pleasant part.

Sylvia clasped her hands in front of her and scanned the room one last time, her mouth losing its smile. "But as these things always go, someone will have to leave us this week. You're all great bakers and pastry chefs. No one is leaving now because they did a bad job with the challenges, but the judges need to be especially exacting. You *all* deserve to be here, but the rules have to be followed." She groaned exasperation, her brows furrowed, and she pulled her cerulean lapels straight. "Dorian, I'm sorry. You'll have to leave this week."

Dorian nodded and smiled. He took handshakes and claps on the back, and even Henry himself gave him a tiny salute, while he had Dorian's attention. The man deserved it. He'd been solid all the way through. *But we're getting down to the meat of the competition, now.* Skilled chefs were going to be heading home every single session.

Eli carried the cleaver back to his station. They'd set up his worst showing, apple and pecan turnovers with cinnamon puff pastry that hadn't quite puffed up correctly, on the cutting board. Normally, whoever lost looked a little contrite or upset during this part. But Dorian watched rapt as Eli raised the cleaver and, in spite of his slender frame, slammed it down with a satisfying clunk, sending shards of not-quite-right puff pastry and glistening chunks of apple flying.

"All right, we're clear!" Out came Jacob with a clipboard. He pointed the corner at Dorian over on the right. "Once you're done and said your goodbyes, I'd like to have you record some voice-overs and interviews. Everyone else, we'll get you next time like normal. No need to rush in early for filming on this next round. It's just choux pastry. Won't take very long." He actually gave them all a smile, which was something Henry couldn't recall seeing from the director before that moment. "Congratulations to the four of you, by the way." He gave a brief nod to each of them in turn: Katherine, Willa, Henry, Tristan. "You've made it this far, and that's a feat all on its own."

Ouch. Couldn't even wait until Dorian left? Henry glanced at their newest lost baker for any sign that it affected him, but got nothing. Still, it felt a bit cold for the director to congratulate them, and specifically *not* Dorian.

Jacob cleared his throat and lowered his clipboard to his side. "All right, we'll be in the interview room when you're ready, Dorian. No rush."

He left and the line slowly broke apart. Production assistants carried out the day's baking—the café table wasn't looking nearly as full as it used to, anymore—Dorian said a few more goodbyes and thank-yous before heading backstage, and the judges . . . well, Eli and Rita left, but Dexter stayed behind, talking to Kristin.

Henry turned away from what was probably a private conversation and looked across the fare laid out, then stepped up and made a grab for one of Katherine's sausage and fennel kites. She might have had a lot of issues making rolls, but the puff pastry on her kites was absolutely perfect. Dozens of layers of crisp, buttery delight, all surrounding a center of fragrant, sweet sausage and thin strips of fennel. She had a command of flavor, that much was certain.

But then at this point, who among them didn't? Wasn't that part of the reason they were still here? Flavor. Technique. Creativity. Flat-out skill and talent and training being brought to bear by the lot of them. It's what had made the competition worth bothering with, at least for Henry. Competing against people who could do amazing things with flour and sugar and fat. *Well, it sounds fucking stupid put that way.* But it was true. Like alchemists, they could turn those base ingredients into incredible wonders.

And Henry had to damn well beat every last one at it.

"It's a good spread, isn't it?" Dexter slid to the front and, after a few seconds, he reached for one of Tristan's cinnamon rolls and tore it apart. "You know, when I brought this idea to the network, I had this picture of all these professional chefs, all this high-quality food laid out just like this . . . and it's real. You guys are actually making it real, and that's pretty impressive." He lowered his voice. "And so were your turnovers. I love proper use of figs. I know they're out of vogue, but I can't help loving the stupid wasp fruits."

He'd won, and now Dexter Wilson was having a conversation with him about figs. *I never could have predicted today. Never.* "I'm a big fan too. Even after I found out about the whole wasp-pollination thing. I was that kid who liked it when we had Fig Newtons in the house."

"I didn't get to ask, what kind of figs did you use?"

"Oh, um, calimyrna."

"I thought so. Butterscotch. Weird little figs, but undeniably good for sweets." Dexter bit down on the cinnamon roll as he turned to Tristan. "And you, too. Those cheese and onion blossoms you made were outstanding. Monterey and smoked gouda, right?"

Tristan swallowed visibly, then nodded. "Yeah. The bite from the Monterey against the sweetness of the . . . the caramelized onions."

Dexter winked. "It was a good choice. You put out an impressive spread. I mean all of you did, but . . . well, a standout's a standout." He backed up and shrugged. "Good work, boys." He waved to them. "Nice chat. See you in three days, I suppose." Then he moved in Katherine's direction.

Tristan slid next to Henry. "Did . . . Was that strange, or was it just me?"

"I don't know. What do you mean by strange?"

"I don't think he normally does that, does he?" Tristan's gaze darted around frenetically as he spoke. "Maybe he's got suspicions. Maybe he's trying to scope us out."

Henry rubbed his chin. He still hadn't taken a bite of any of the food he'd grabbed. "Or maybe he liked what we made. Come on, Dexter Wilson likes your onion blossoms. How many people can say that?"

"It could be." Tristan shrugged. "I'm sorry. You're probably right, but . . ."

"Hey, I get being concerned. Given everything." Henry nudged Tristan in the side. "Those cheese and onion things were damn good. Simple, but when you nail it, you nail it."

Tristan nodded, shaking himself. "I may have nailed it, but you really nailed it. Winner boy."

Henry chuckled. "I have to admit, I'm feeling pretty fucking decent."

"Yeah, no shit." A string of nervous laughter crept past Tristan's lips, and he finally stepped up to the table to grab something. Of course, he went straight for Henry's turnovers. "You have reason to feel good. I mean, seriously, congrats on winning."

"Well, it's about time I catch up to you. You won the second fucking challenge, right? Don't think I forgot it."

"Yeah, but that was close and you know it. We both know how to make cake. Mine's better, that's all."

"Oh, how humble of you." Henry sighed and stepped away. "You're right, but still. *Some* humility might be in order, don't you think?"

"We're in the final four people here." Tristan moved away from the table too, a sampling of pastries in his hands . . . and two fig turnovers. "Come on, final four. I know the show means exactly shit in reality, but we're better than everyone we've beaten so far, right? A *little* ego seems appropriate to me. I expected yours to be *huge* by now."

Henry shook his head. "Hell no. If anything, taking this long to win, and seeing that *Katherine* is in the running with me? I'd discounted her out the gate, but I obviously judged her wrong, and I'm eating that crow now. Being wrong this much is . . . humbling. And there's no room for ego if it's going to get in the way of me winning."

"Buzzkill." Tristan nudged him in the side in a very non-Tristan way. "Enjoy the moment. You won. I won't even mock you for being cocky. Much."

Henry laughed. "You're in an awfully good mood." He almost didn't want to say anything else, in case he scared it away.

"I finally get to show you that surprise I bought for you."

Ah. So he'd been waiting for Henry to win. "Then we should go fast."

Then Willa walked up, smiling wide and bright, and Henry knew their hotel room foray would have to wait. She grabbed Henry by the shoulders and looked him in the eye. *I guess this is considered A-OK in New York.* "Congratulations are due to you. You're a good baker. Blew everybody ten feet back with those turnovers, didn't you?"

"Well, we all do what we can do and try to make it work." He shifted back enough to get out of her grip and grinned gently at her. "I got lucky this time."

"Lucky? Don't be modest. If I had been able to bake like that at your age, I'd be rich enough to retire by now." She winked at him. "Seriously. Good job, kiddo."

And she wandered off. Tristan smiled coyly, and once she was out of earshot, said, "Should I be worried about you two?"

"Long-distance would never work."

Tristan nodded with a chuckle. "So . . . same as usual?"

That meant separate rides back to the hotel, meeting clandestinely in Tristan's hotel room. Apparently even his excitement about this surprise of his wasn't enough to wash that caution all the way off. "Of course." Still, Henry was endlessly curious about this surprise, enough to overcome his annoyance with the situation. *What the hell do you have planned, Delgado?*

Chapter Fifteen

Tristan stared into his reflection in the bathroom mirror. "Come on, you can't keep it to yourself forever." He had been fantasizing about this moment since that first wrestling match/blowjob, and fantasizing even harder since he'd made his excursion to the drugstore. They were in the final four now, so it was time for a celebration. That didn't keep his stomach from jumping. Exciting or not, this was a big step. A step Tristan hadn't taken in a *long* time.

It was good jumping, though. The kind that wound him up as he stood there. In spite of all his rules and his desire to keep himself out of the Delgado curse . . . he cared more about Henry than he should have. What would Henry say when Tristan brought up sex? He could say no, after all. He could deny Tristan. He could freak. He could *laugh*.

But Tristan didn't actually think those things would happen. He knew the way he felt around Henry, and he'd only felt anything close to it with one or two other guys. Then it had been nothing near this level of intensity, but similar, and unmistakable.

Tristan was ready. As ready as he was going to be for a "let's have sex" talk. He drew in a breath meant to steel his nerves, grabbed the bag that was meant to make an amazing night, and stepped into the room that was originally meant to be his alone.

Henry was sitting on the bed cross-legged . . . and shirtless. Damn it, why was he shirtless already? Tristan absorbed the vision of his hard, wiry body and little tuft of chest hair, his happy trail across softly defined abs, well-muscled arms ending in the gnarly, rough hands that could only belong to a professional baker.

New knots tangled into Tristan's nerves. Knots of passion and longing and fire that burned hot and bright. "So . . . your surprise."

Taking in Henry's slight smile, the expectant glint in his eyes, Tristan couldn't find any words. So he dumped out the contents of the bag on the bed next to Henry. KY and a variety pack of Lifestyles tumbled out. He swallowed to try to wet his throat, but no luck, so his voice came out weaker than he intended. "Surprise."

Henry shuffled the contents of the bag around with one hand as scarlet fire blazed up his cheeks. Redder than Tristan had ever seen him, including when he'd been standing over a steaming pot with the clock ticking down. "You . . . Wow."

"Wow good or wow bad?"

"Wow bad?" Henry shook his head. "How could this be bad? I *want* you. Like . . . a lot. I know things haven't quite moved that far yet. And I was fine waiting." He nodded. "I still would be. We don't have to take that step if you're nervous. But . . . did you think I was going to turn you down?"

"I mean, maybe a little."

Henry chuckled and rose, then wrapped his arms around Tristan's chest and shoulders. He smelled like coconut and sweat and flour and his touch untied all the knots in Tristan's middle. His words soothed away all the rampant stress and worry in Tristan's head. "I want you. Any way and anywhere you think is good and right. As long as you're comfortable."

As long as I'm comfortable. Tristan smiled and leaned into a kiss, mouth parted. He tasted the remains of the cheap hotel coffee on Henry's breath as their tongues passed and tangled . . . Tristan leaned back just far enough to speak. "You're the first guy I've ever pulled who's not a complete asshole." It was hard, in that hazy moment of relief, to think of him as selfish. Even slightly selfish.

"High praise."

"Yes and no." Tristan couldn't help smiling. Not that he tried that hard to stop it. "I mean, it puts you at the top of the list by a big margin. But it wasn't exactly a fair fight. You probably still would have blown them all away when I thought you were a douchebag."

Tristan kissed Henry again before he could speak. Slowly, he moved them toward the bed and let himself fall on top of Henry: body to body, chest to chest, crotch to crotch. Tristan struggled to get his shirt up and off with one hand while he brushed the fingers of the other through Henry's hair. Eventually, he had to lean up and pull his shirt all the way up and off. His scars crossed his mind, but only for a fleeting moment. They didn't matter. His body barely mattered.

Only Henry was important.

Tristan tossed his shirt aside, then lowered himself back against Henry and into the cocoon of those wonderful smells and heat emanating from Henry's body. Their lips met again and again, and slowly they shifted on the bed. Before he knew it, they'd turned and had their heads against the massive sea of pillows. Henry's nails scratched along Tristan's back, shooting electric fire through his belly and down to his cock and balls. He longed to be free, to be touched, to be fully *connected* to Henry.

Henry's hands cupped his ass. His grip was firm, squeezing, digging deep into the muscles. Through the fabric, his fingers edged closer and closer to the cleft. Tristan's cock throbbed heat and pressure and *God* couldn't they hurry this along?

Henry pulled his head as far back as the pillows would allow. "Take off your glasses. And everything else."

"Happily." Tristan couldn't jump away fast enough. He set his glasses carefully on the bedside table, then stripped off his pants and underwear and he was finally, *finally* loose. He watched ravenously as Henry stripped naked, then took in the full glory of that lithe body stretched out on the bed. Coarse bush and gleaming, stiff cock turning up toward his belly button. Rough hair covering muscular legs. Patches of hair peeking from his underarms. And a huge, ridiculous smile plastered across his face, the kind that flooded Tristan with warmth and light. He laughed, a faint, breathy sound. That joy and excitement and pure exhilaration needed some escape.

Tristan lay back down and wrapped his hand around Henry's hard shaft. Slowly, he stroked up and down. He didn't think it could get any harder than it was, but he *had* to touch it, to touch Henry. He needed that contact like breath or water.

Henry's head tilted back even farther, raising the pillows to either side, and his eyes closed, but Tristan kept on. He reached to his own balls, caressed them with his free hand.

"Jesus." Henry bucked against Tristan's hand. "We're not going to need the condoms if you keep that up."

"Oh, come on, you can take a little more than that, can't you?" But Tristan slowed, loosening his grip until he just *barely* had a hold on Henry's cock. Pre-come dripped down the shaft, slicking Tristan's subtle movements. Damn it, he wanted every inch of Henry. Now. "So, we didn't talk about specifics . . . but I'm a bottom. I mean, I can do whatever you need, but—"

"I'd rather top. At least this time." Henry lifted his head and winked. "I mean, you *did* buy a full pack of condoms, and I assume we're only fucking once tonight. So we'll have at least a few more opportunities to switch things up."

Tristan laughed and leaned in to kiss Henry again. First his mouth, then his jaw with the stubble that scraped Tristan's lips. Down to Henry's neck, where he felt the gentle pulse. To his chest, where Tristan wrapped his lips over one of Henry's pert nipples. He nipped it with his teeth and Henry whimpered. He passed his tongue over the bud and a shiver raced across Henry's skin.

"Fucking Christ, I want you." Henry's voice crept out hoarse and tight. "I want you right now and I don't do well with impulse control. If you hadn't noticed."

"I noticed." Tristan wasn't going to move first, but if Henry wanted to jump into it this fast, he wouldn't argue. He shifted himself around to lay at the edge of the bed while Henry stood. Tristan fumbled to get a pillow under his head so he could watch, so he could see everything.

"You one hundred percent about this?" Henry blew out a slow breath. "I might be the stupidest man in the world questioning that *now*, with you laid out like this, but I want to make sure. Do you want this?"

Tristan chuckled. "I am a shut-in pastry chef. I don't like people or interacting with them. Yet I walked into a drugstore and bought literally nothing but condoms and lube, and believe me the cashier was *amused* by that. But I did it anyway, and I'd do it again with a smile on my face." Tristan locked eyes with Henry. With the tiny blur in his vision, any minor flaws Henry might have had—though Tristan couldn't think of a damn one in that moment—faded away and he was . . . beautiful. "I would say I want this, Henry."

Henry nodded, then draped himself across Tristan. He came back with the lube and the condoms. Condoms went down on the bed and he popped open the KY. The plastic *click* thrilled up Tristan's spine. They were really doing this. Henry smeared some along one finger, then reached down, his eyes flickering between Tristan's face and his own hand. Tristan tensed at his touch, but only for a second before he dragged that natural reaction back under control. He gazed up at Henry as the pressure increased, taking in each detail on that scruffy son of a bitch's face. The crinkling around deep brown eyes, the cherry-colored flush moving through his neck and chest, and the stray lock of hair that hung in his face. God, he was gorgeous. *And he's all mine.*

Tristan lifted his legs up to better expose himself, and felt the first knuckle slide in. His back lifted off the bed as lightning spiked through him, but he forced himself to keep watching Henry in spite of the cascade of ecstasy. The second knuckle popped through, forcing sounds from Tristan he couldn't recall ever making. Above him, Henry worried his lower lip with his teeth, tensing his jaw in the most stunning way. Tristan quivered as more pushed inside him until, finally, he couldn't hold eye contact anymore. He moaned and let his head fall back.

Henry swirled slowly and deliberately inside him. Every now and then, his fingertip would brush against *that* spot. The one deep inside Tristan that shot fireworks across his body. Heat and stars whizzed wildly through every inch of him, all pooling as static in his head and tingling in his balls.

Henry pulled back a little, then a second finger pressed in. Tristan's back arched, and there was no *allowing* his moans, anymore. They simply came free, past his lips as Henry worked inside him, scissoring his fingers, slowly but surely stretching Tristan wider. Almost without noticing, Tristan wrapped a hand around his own cock and stroked slowly from base to tip. It took all the self-control he had not to pump furiously, but he wasn't going to finish, wasn't going to squander this experience in a flash of recklessness. What never even crossed his mind before coming here, now seemed like the ultimate bliss, the moment he'd unknowingly been striving toward for so long.

Tristan's moans gave way to words, guttural and coarse, as he peered unblinking at Henry. "Fuck me."

Henry chuckled and shook his head. "You don't waste time, do you?"

"I'd say I do— Oh God . . ." Henry had sped up as they spoke, as though *that* made it easier to have this conversation. But Tristan wasn't about to stop him. "I wasted the whole however-long-we've-been-doing-this *not* getting fucked. And nothing could feel this good." The sensations, the fullness, the connection, they all washed through Tristan, a salve to cover the anxiety from the past week. He closed his eyes and let out the shuddering groan that had built in his throat. "I mean . . . goddamn it, you're like figs and honey and cinnamon and whipped cream." His rational brain was fading into the background, leaving him with only food metaphors and Henry's fingers twisting and working inside of him, slowly plunging deep, then sliding back out against the too-sensitive ring of muscles. "*Fuck* me."

"I just want to make sure you're ready."

"I think I sound pretty ready." Tristan forced himself to focus right on Henry's eyes. "I want you. Henry Isaacson, I want every part of you."

Henry pulled his fingers free, leaving Tristan with aching emptiness that longed to be filled. Tristan lifted his head to watch as Henry slicked his own cock with the remaining lube. Then he ripped open the box of condoms and pulled out a blue one. It stretched taut and gleamed over his cock as he rolled it on, and Tristan's stomach tightened in the most electrifying way. Like in that moment of hesitation at the apex of a roller coaster.

Henry popped the cap on the lube and dolloped some on the tip of his cock. Slowly, he spread it down the length . . . or maybe it wasn't slow at all. Maybe it was just Tristan's longing that made it take forever and a fucking day.

Finally, Henry went back to the bottle for more. He spread it around Tristan's hole, circling in as he went, until his finger slid inside again and, for a few moments, there was fullness. But it wasn't *satisfying*. Not when Tristan could see what was there on the horizon. The spit of land for a desperate traveler. With everything he wanted and needed within reach, a finger of fullness wasn't going to cut it.

Henry passed Tristan the bottle of lube. "For his pleasure."

"His pleasure is already here, I think." Still, Tristan slicked his cock, and the lube tingled and warmed against the stiff shaft . . . and especially his head. Goddamn it, the head was sensitive. It was *always* sensitive, but riding that wave of expectation doubled, tripled that sensitivity.

Henry's rough, strong fingers wrapped around Tristan's legs, holding him right at the knees. He shifted Tristan closer to the edge of the bed and raised his hips a little higher. Tristan fumbled for another pillow and slipped it under himself to prop his ass up. He felt so exposed. A tiny flame of embarrassment burst to life in his core, but it paled in comparison to the ravening that shook through his every cell, waiting for Henry in the too-long seconds it took to get in position.

But finally, Henry was ready. Soon a slick, hard tip pressed against his hole, and he forced himself not to tense, to relax. Even as Henry's shaft pushed forward, he relaxed, and it slid in quickly, a restrained gasp blossoming from Tristan's lips. Just the tip in, and he already felt so much fuller, so much more connected. He resisted the urge to fall into closed-eyed ecstasy, and instead stared at Henry's face as his cock made slow progress. Henry's eyes crinkled at the corners, his smile faded into open-mouthed panting, and the blood rushed into his cheeks and ears, the sweat dripping down his nose and off onto the bedsheets. Henry in ecstasy. *I'd buy that painting.*

And all the while, the pressure increased, inexorable as the rising tide. And somehow so soon and yet after so long, there was the telltale scratch of coarse bush against Tristan's ass. The tension visibly dropped from Henry's face and body, and he loosened his grip on Tristan's legs . . . although Tristan had never noticed his fingers tighten to begin with.

Henry sighed and looked down at Tristan. There was a softness in his eyes, contrary to the raging animal in Tristan that clawed at his middle and scratched and howled to be satisfied. Henry even *smiled* at him. "Are you okay?" There was a sharp, rough edge to his voice, and the redness remained in his face, but he *meant* it. God, he actually wanted to know if Tristan was okay.

"Yeah." Tristan felt his own lips curve upward. Once a guy got this far, how often were they willing to stop? That simple three-word question only set the beast within raging stronger and harder.

Tristan slowly slid his hand all the way to the base of his cock. He tightened his hole as much as he could, hungry for deeper connection, more points of contact. Judging from the shocked-but-ecstatic expression that flashed across Henry's face, it was appreciated. Tristan was warm, ravenous for more.

He drew a ragged breath. "I *need* you to fuck me, Henry. More than I've needed anything before." He bit down on his lower lip and focused on the full feeling, the way it shot lightning and light and power in tendrils through his body. "Come on."

Henry nodded and rocked his hips backward. If being filled was ecstasy, the receding was almost unbearable. At once Tristan longed to have that fullness again, to be completely, intimately connected with Henry, and just . . . So. Much. Sensation. It was always greater than the going in. There were no waves, no manageable burst of feeling like there was on the thrust forward. The out was . . . every nerve ending, blasting and crackling simultaneously. Tristan sweated, caught between moaning and begging for more. If being with Henry was figs and honey and whipped cream, then that goddamn pull out was passion fruit and champagne and blood oranges—bright and overwhelming and decadent, all at the same time.

When Henry pushed back in, it was a little faster. Waves of pressure rocked through Tristan, followed by that brilliant explosion of nerve endings on the pull out. The red spread from Henry's face and neck and crept slowly down his chest. Exhilarated, Tristan pumped his fist, syncing with Henry. There was no pain, no worry, no *anything* beyond the joining of their bodies.

Now Henry was really going, his pelvis slamming into Tristan's ass. His gentle, quiet breathing turned to ragged panting, and Tristan could barely pump his cock fast enough to keep up with his own desires, with Henry's thrusts. Nothing else mattered, and all control wicked away from Tristan. "Fucking Christ . . . do it harder . . . Goddamn it . . . Shit."

And Henry obliged. At this angle, going so hard, pushing so deep into Tristan, his cockhead kept hitting *that spot*. But with the thousand other sensations careening through him, Tristan couldn't even follow the lines of fire that snaked through him. They mingled with the lightning and power and pressure. Everything flowed through Tristan to try to sate the beast, and it begged for more. It begged to do this in Henry's hotel room, and in the shower, and in the airplane bathroom on their way back to Seattle, and in Henry's kitchen, and on Tristan's couch.

Henry's fingers tightened again, and this time Tristan *did* notice. Henry's eyes had squeezed shut, his lips parted, sweat drenched his hair and plastered it to his forehead and the sides of his face. Each breath raised his shoulders visibly, and still he humped, pressing harder and harder and . . . Oh God. Oh *God*.

Tristan swallowed hard as his walls finally broke down. The currents of power and pressure shifted and eddied and swirled back toward his crotch. His balls pulled higher, his toes curled above him. "I'm—I'm gonna come—" He struggled against it, held on to that wave for a second, two, three . . . then his breath caught, pushing out in rough, ragged grunts. His cock vibrated with each spurt. One in his bush, then up by his navel, then his chest. It came and came, seven, eight spurts before it calmed.

Tristan slackened and let the bed support him fully. The bed and Henry's hands behind his knees.

And Henry pulled out too. He peeled away the condom and tossed it in the trash, then lay next to Tristan and pumped. Fast and hard. Tristan breathed in the scent of him, the coconut and sweat and sex. He reached across and took over, running his fist the full length of Henry's cock.

Soon he heard the telltale groaning, saw the tiny spasms. Henry's cock pulsed out white heat. It landed in little pools on his stomach and his thighs and all across Tristan's hand. Warm and pungent and sticky and . . . Henry. It was all Henry.

Eventually it stopped and Tristan let go. They lay there, pressed side to side, just breathing for a while. Tristan's mind raced. This wasn't *him*. At least not the normal him. This was a guy who didn't care about showing off his scars, or lying around naked in a hotel room, covered in come. Goddamn it, it was nice. He draped an arm over Henry's chest, relishing the sweat and the heaving movements of each breath and the tufty hair right there in the middle.

"That . . . was good." Henry spoke between pants. "That was . . . amazing."

"Yeah. Lived up to expectations." Tristan laughed at himself. He didn't know what else to do. "So congrats on the win. I couldn't afford a trophy or anything like that, so I hope this was a good enough prize."

Henry snorted. "Is this up every time I win?"

"Well, I don't see why not. And when you lose, I can *console* you with sex."

"So it's like selling your body, but not quite."

"I mean, if you want to start paying me, my landlord would appreciate it." Tristan pulled up closer and nuzzled his head right into the crook of Henry's neck. Coconut and sex. That was Henry . . . his Henry, with all the baggage stripped away.

"I don't think I could afford you. A night like that's got to run at least ten grand, right?"

"Ooh, I get to start as a high-class hooker. No working my way up."

Henry chuckled, and another minute of silence fell over them. Their breathing settled, regulated. Henry gripped Tristan's hand, twined their fingers together. Then he twisted his head around to glance a kiss off Tristan's lips. "So, we should probably hit the showers."

"You don't *like* laying here soaked in sweat and semen? My God, what am I going to do with you when pride rolls around? That's my favorite part."

"Well, I don't know about pride, but maybe if we make it down to a White Party. Special occasion and all." He shifted, then sat up, bringing Tristan with him. "But I think the shower is a good idea tonight." He finally let Tristan go to get up and walked away, swaying his hips exaggeratedly, swinging his pert, tanned ass from side to side. "I'll even let you watch."

Tristan rose. The beast within was sated, for the moment, and it left room for a hot, bubbling joy to fill the empty space, unfettered by his worries. "You know I'm going to be walking funny tomorrow, right?"

"That means I did my job. And if anyone asks, you tell them you obviously had way better sex than they did last night." Henry held out his arm, and Tristan walked up, let him drape it around his shoulders as they headed toward the bathroom. "And thanks. For letting me. I hope you weren't feeling pressured."

"Oh, I absolutely was. By my dick. It really, really, *really* wanted you." Tristan stopped Henry and kissed him right on his hard chest, next to his nipple. "You saying you wanted me was the excuse I needed."

Henry laughed loud and hard, and it echoed in the bathroom. It was a sound of such pure joy that Tristan couldn't help joining in.

Henry's upper arm ached—half his body ached after last night's romp—but his choux pastry was *almost* smooth. Choux was cooked once on the stovetop before being baked, and letting it sit in the pan would cook the damn thing too far and ruin the batch. So he stood there, beating at it with a wooden spoon and willing it to finish. *Why is it that everything I make for a living is a pain in the ass?* And he had to do three preparations: éclairs, gougères, and a full, proper croquembouche. A two-foot-tall croquembouche, minimum.

Nothing about the making of the components in these recipes was exceptionally challenging, which was a godsend in some ways. But *everything* was finicky in some way or another, and when every component was finicky, that stacked. The pâte à choux had to have their tips moistened and molded back into shape before baking, each individually. And that was a lot when you had to make eighty-plus cream puffs, two dozen éclairs, and three dozen gougères. The caramel had to be kept at the right temperature to work with for the croquembouche, and that meant dipping shit by hand into nearly 350-degree molten sugar, while keeping it from *actually* crossing the 350-degree mark.

Finicky shit everywhere. Henry sighed and set his dough down. It was finally together, and he let his arm rest. On a normal day, he could do choux pastry without issue. But he'd already made four batches that morning, and had many more on the horizon.

With only four people left cooking, it *should* have been pretty quiet. But making pâte à choux was not a quiet process, no matter how gentle your intentions. It involved beating the *crap* out of your dough. At least it did if you wanted it to be light and airy and crisp like it should be.

Tristan finally backed off from his own bowl and turned around. "I hope I never see another cream puff again in my life. I haven't even made them yet, but I *guarantee* I'm going to hate them after my fourth croquembouche of the week."

"You ever made one before?"

"I work weddings. So yeah." He rolled his eyes, then slipped off his glasses and massaged the bridge of his nose. "There was a while there where every other bride wanted a croquembouche instead of a wedding cake, since it was *so* original and she hadn't seen one before. Meanwhile I'd just made a dozen."

"Ouch. I'm surprised you still have fingerprints left."

"I'm not sure I do. Haven't been arrested yet." He put his glasses back on and blew out a long breath, puffing his cheeks in the process. "And we have to work with everything fresh this time, so that's even worse. With catering, I can make some of this stuff ahead of time."

"Yeah, making stuff in advance must be nice. I once decided it was a *great* idea to celebrate National Cream Puff Day. Cream puffs for fifty cents apiece as a loss leader. I had to make a thousand. A *thousand*. It was a nightmare, and I had to do it all on the day."

"Why would you ever do that to yourself?"

"Business decision." Henry groaned thinking about that particular circle of hell he'd conceived for himself. "It was a great sale. Made my quarter. Sure, I had to surgically remove the piping bag from my hand, but I *guess* it was worth it." It had also been a hell of a distraction after Lance had dumped him, though he didn't bring that part up. No use dredging up the past with his . . . with Tristan.

Tristan laughed, shaking his head. "And when *exactly* is National Cream Puff Day?"

"January second. A day that will live in infamy." It *had* been an excellent way to get him in the black, he had to admit, but not good enough that he was going to consider it again. At least not with a thousand . . . maybe five hundred. Five hundred would be doable . . . *Don't go down that road. Circle of hell.* "But you'll recover. I did. Still love cream puffs and profiteroles and all that stuff." He stared at his choux pastry and sighed. "I actually really love a good croquembouche, when I don't have to assemble the fucking thing in five hours. Especially when I don't have to make it at all."

"Those are *definitely* the best croquembouches." Tristan stretched his arms up high and groaned. "God, I'm fucking sore today."

"Is that a surprise?"

"A little." Tristan turned back around too quickly. Henry'd said the wrong thing again, apparently—had pushed too far into suggestion in front of the wrong people. *I still can't navigate the minefield.* All he wanted was to be open. He wanted to talk to Tristan like a normal human being, but even after they'd had sex, he kept stumbling and getting shut down out of nowhere.

Henry sighed, then picked up his dough again. The arm-burning part was over. Now it was time for finger shredding. He loaded his dough into the pastry bag—not a clean process, but much, much better than royal icing or buttercream—then started to pipe his dough into tiny ... well, blobs. He had circular templates on the silicone sheet for macarons, but with these he didn't need to be quite as precise. No matter how lovely and round the dough he piped, they wouldn't stay that way once they baked and rose. As long as they were the same *size* and not in any particularly weird shapes, he'd be golden. They were all going to be dunked in hardened sugar and stacked up, anyway.

Tristan was loading up a pastry bag himself. His dough was slightly darker and yellower, but the same consistency. Probably had more eggs and some other amazing, unthinkable flavor to go with his crème pat.

Henry's eyes fixated on his ass. It was a *great* ass. Or those were particularly great, tight khakis. Or he was wearing them higher so they hugged the curves better than usual. *Or I'm seriously infatuated. That seems most likely.*

He had reason to be. Tristan was nice and understanding and devoted. Sure, he was hot too. Yeah. Lots of guys were hot. In fact, most of the guys Henry slept with were hot. But hot didn't mean near as much as how Tristan called his sister every day, or let her stay at his apartment to get away from some asshole husband. Hot didn't count for anything next to his utter devotion to his craft. Hot wasn't a damn thing compared to how far Tristan stepped out of his own comfort zone for Henry. Time and again. He gave up his solitude. He went to the store and bought the condoms. He showed off his scars even though they'd sent guys running in the past. He ... he really did a lot.

It made staying quiet, leaving him alone, and keeping their relationship confined to that hotel room a hundred times harder. Henry wanted to be close, to interact. The passion burned under his skin. He couldn't stand there and pretend they were strangers who didn't talk.

Food, at least, should be a safe subject. "So what's going on with your choux? Cloves?"

"Cocoa powder." Tristan angled himself and made eye contact with Henry, and his face was relaxed. Just a little bit. "To go with the orange filling."

"Chocolate and orange. I love it."

Tristan smiled, showing off his dimples again. He was magnificent, in his own subtle fashion. He was unlike anyone Henry had ever met, and when he smiled, Henry could still be taken aback by him. Like now.

"It makes the pastry a little firmer than usual, but it's not bad." Tristan nodded to himself. "I still have time to experiment, though."

"Sounds like I need to watch myself, otherwise you might get your second win."

"Bet that would be a blow to your ego, huh?" Tristan was still smiling, and he brought his voice down low. "Maybe if I win, it'll chip out enough space that I can stick around."

I've been trying to chip out a spot for myself in your life since we met. But there's no room for me. You're too in love with yourself for that.

Lance's parting words played through Henry's head as Tristan returned to his pastry. It was sheer, absolute coincidence that Tristan had used those words in particular. The English language only had so many words, so many turns of phrase. And Tristan had said it with a smile, unlike Lance. But more than Tristan winning ever could have done, that simple, glancing remark blew through Henry's layers of ego and blasted out his core.

"Henry!"

He snapped his gaze up and saw Tristan chuckling. Then he realized that he'd piped four perfect little mounds of choux pastry right onto the countertop. "Wow. That was special."

"You in there now?" Tristan winked at him. "Better not do that when it comes time for filming. Otherwise they might toss you out."

"I'm good." The haze of memory was already clearing, leaving just a lingering shadow of the past behind, a touch of bitterness on the air, that continued to fade as he spoke. "Hey, Tristan."

"What's up?"

"I . . . What do you want to do tonight?"

"I want to go back to my hotel room?" He shrugged and lowered his voice. "We'll talk later. Not here."

Right. They still needed to be careful. He couldn't let a moment's recollection throw everything into turmoil.

There was too much at stake for that.

Once Tristan had turned back around, Henry slipped out his phone and pulled up Carrie. *Tell me again how Lance was wrong and I wasn't a selfish prick?*

She responded straight away. *Uh-oh. What's up?*

I'm in my own head. Don't want to blow this whole thing.

A brief fit of flashing dots while she typed a response. *You're good. You're not selfish. Lance was unreasonable. Breathe.*

She was right, of course. Not that it completely erased the fear from Henry's mind. But if he could have someone *else* reassuring him, he could make it through this.

Tristan almost considered setting up for another night where they could be good together, feel as good as they had before. He still had lube and condoms left. But he decided against it, stashing all that stuff back in the nightstand. He did strip down to his shirt and boxers, though.

Right in time for Henry to slip through the door. "Hey."

"Hey yourself." Tristan sighed and sat on the edge of the bed, breathing in the company. *Me? Actually appreciating company? Blasphemy.* But he did. He liked being around Henry. He liked it even more when Henry lowered himself down next to him, wrapped an arm around his shoulders, slid a hand down his back and played with the waistband of his boxers.

And then Tristan's phone rang. He rolled his eyes. "Let me check that. Just in case."

"If you insist." Henry let him go. "But hurry back."

Tristan hopped up and saw that it was coming from . . . Karen. His stomach immediately tensed, but he answered anyway, tried to sound cool. "What's going on?"

"Robert's going on."

"Oh my God." Tristan sat back down on the bed. "Where's Lucia? Is she okay? That *bastard* is *not* allowed in my apartment, and he knows it." Tristan tried to control his breathing. It didn't work. "Start with the first one: Where is Lucia?"

"Lucia's fine."

"He only left four bruises where no one could see them fine, or fine fine?"

"Fine fine. I promise. She's in the living room giving her statement to the cops, and she specifically told me not to call you, but . . . if you ever mention that I did this, we're done, okay?"

A strong hand landed on Tristan's shoulder, fingers digging in. Tristan grabbed Henry's fingers as he spoke. "What happened?"

"Robert fucking showed up."

They'd been here before. Too many times for Tristan not to ask Karen, "Did she call him?"

"I checked her phone's history myself. Which you're also not allowed to tell her about. I guess there's only so many places Lucia would disappear to. He was going to figure it out eventually." Karen blew out a breath, the sound crackly and staticky over the phone. "When he showed up, she wouldn't unlock the chain, so he started reaching in to get at her. She tried to shut the door on his hand, force him out, but he just busted through and started screaming. I promise you, she wasn't expecting this. She didn't want him anywhere near her."

Some of the knots in Tristan's stomach loosened. Robert had such a magnetic hold over Lucia that, even with her seemingly determined to stay away, Tristan had to worry Robert would find a way to persuade her to come back. He always had in the past. *But maybe not this time?*

"Did I mention he's a bastard?"

"Yeah, you don't need to convince me." Karen huffed harshly. "He tried to rough her up when she wouldn't cooperate. I maced him, he ran, and Lucia marched over to call the cops."

Tristan breathed out a long-held breath and caught the end of it turning into a laugh. Lucia called the cops. She called the cops on Robert. She never, ever did that before. But then, he'd never broken into someone else's apartment to come and get her.

"How is she?"

"She's shaken up, but I don't think he hurt her. No marks I could find."

That was something. "Karen, can they actually charge him? If he didn't mark her up, like, what's the recourse?"

"Man, my *dad's* the cop, not me."

"Come on, Karen. I'm not using you as legal counsel."

He could almost *hear* her eye roll, but she did answer. "They can get him on breaking and entering, destruction of property—he *did* rough up your place pretty bad—probably even robbery and an aggravated assault charge. Maybe some other incidental stuff. Enough to get him in jail for a while, pay a fine."

"For a *while?*"

"Yeah, I know. He's scum and deserves a long, long time in jail, but this is the only crime we have him on. It'll hopefully be enough time for Lucia to get herself in a better situation, get a restraining order, start divorce proceedings, all that stuff."

Tristan sighed, not letting the "divorce proceedings" bombshell break through yet. "You really think she will?"

"You know, I do think so. It's not like the other times, Tristan. It's hard to describe, but if you saw her, you'd get it. You'd totally get it."

"I trust you." Not enough to stop worrying, but enough that his stomach unclenched a little further, and his shoulders fell. "Are *you* okay? Sorry for not asking before."

"Yeah. Everyone's fine, except Robert. You know, mace hurts. But your apartment took the brunt of the damage. He broke the chain, did some damage to the door and the wall where it was attached. And he smashed a lot of stuff in your kitchen while he was throwing a fit. You're, um, going to need a new oven, I think. And I'm pretty sure your mixer isn't going to go back together. Your laptop hit the wall pretty hard, too. I haven't exactly taken full stock of the damage. But you know Robert. He gets violent when he gets angry."

Shit. His door and decorations didn't matter. But his kitchen? How was he supposed to test recipes if his kitchen was in shambles? How was he supposed to do his fucking job? Still, he shoved that aside for the time being. "It's fine. Fuck, Karen, I'll take all of that over you and my sister beaten bloody. It's not like I've filled my house with Chihuly glasswork." This wasn't the place for his own personal panic.

"Well, look, they're going to want my statement, and Lucia's probably going to call at some point. You don't know anything I just told you, understood?"

"I got it. And I'm glad you're safe." Tristan blew out a nervous breath. "I'm glad you were there. I don't think Lucia would have been able to mace him, even if she'd *had* mace in her pocket."

"Thank God I'm a cop's kid, huh?"

"Yeah. And thank God he trained the shit out of you."

"That too. Okay, I need to get off the phone. But everyone is fine. Everything's good. Go bake something, I guess."

"Right, yeah, I'll whip out a nice Devil's food cake in the hotel microwave. No problem."

"Ingenuity, thy name is Tristan. I have to go. Good luck, everything's copacetic, you know nothing."

And she hung up. Tristan set the phone aside and leaned back on the bed. "My sister's piece-of-shit husband broke into my house and tried to attack her or take her or something."

"Shit. Is everything good?"

"Surprisingly, yes. My kitchen took the worst beating." He swallowed down a surge of icy panic at that thought. "And Lucia called the cops on his ass this time, so maybe he won't get off scot-free."

"It sounds like it went as well as a home break-in possibly could."

Yeah. Yeah, it had. Tristan grabbed Henry's hand and held it tight. "It's weird, you know? She did what I wanted her to do all this time, and all I can think about is how I should have been there. Though honestly, it's probably better that I wasn't. Our friend Karen's staying there, and she maced his ass when he went after Lucia. I don't own mace."

"Okay, so look at it straight on, then. She's fine and you're here doing what you love. Plus, if she called the cops, maybe he'll get the message this time."

"Maybe." But his baby sister had been left to deal with her abusive husband alone because he'd gone to this baking show.

"You're where you need to be. I don't buy into any kind of God and Jesus crap, but I believe there's an energy to the universe. There's potential, and there's places where we make choices that are important. You being here was an important choice. You're going to be a hit on TV, assuming this show takes off, which is going to help you make the money to support her through this. And you met me, which . . . you know, not to be an egotist, but I'm pretty great."

Tristan chuckled. A little chuckle, but it was there. "You are pretty great. And I know this is the best place to be, if I'm totally objective. But it still feels like I should have been there for Lucia. At least been *available*."

On cue, his phone rang. It was a call from home. Henry smiled and winked at him. "You seem available to her. Now that she needs you."

Henry was right. Talking to her was all he'd be able to do at home. It wouldn't be any different over the phone. And now that she was definitely going to be staying with him longer term—he had every intention of insisting once she came clean about what happened—he needed the money from this competition even more. Not to mention for the repairs to his apartment, maybe a divorce lawyer if she was finally cutting Robert all the way off.

Henry silently disappeared into the bathroom, and Tristan picked up. "Hi, Lucia."

She started with a heavy sigh. "So I assume when Karen went to wash her hands for fifteen minutes, she was filling you in on everything?"

"*That* was her excuse? I promised her I'd feign ignorance, but you'd think she could give me a better lie to work with."

"I knew she'd call you as soon as I told her not to."

"Hey, go easy on her. Slayer of giant angry men, right?"

Lucia laughed. "Yeah. I guess I can give her this one. But I was going to call as soon as I was done talking to the cops."

"Well, it's done, now." Tristan tapped his fingers on the end table. "So you're okay?"

"You know something, Tristan? I haven't felt this good in years. Probably not since I married Robert. Standing up to him, like, calling the cops to finally fucking report him? It's . . . amazing." Though he didn't miss the clot in her throat, the telltale shake in her voice.

"I'm glad you did it. I'm just sorry I wasn't there to see him getting maced." *And to support you.*

"I'm not. It made me stand up on my own two feet and . . . Goddamn it, Tristan, I've been an idiot."

"Lucia—"

"No, Tristan. I've been a complete moron for the past six years with that bastard. And you constantly put up with me." Her voice thickened further. "You never told me to leave him or pressured me. You just gave me your stupid hide-a-bed until I dumbed up enough to go get back with him."

"First of all, you're not an idiot, you're not a moron, and you didn't dumb up enough to go back. Robert is an abusive shit-bag. What happened is on *him* not on you. And second of all, that's what I had to do. You needed space, and I needed to be in your life. And in case no one's told you yet, you're brave as fuck for standing up to him." He needed to tread carefully on the next part. "And if you ever do go back—"

"I'm done with him, Tristan." For the first time in the whole conversation, her voice bit out, fiery and sharp. "I'll swear it on Our Lady of Guadalupe if I have to, but I'm not going back to Robert."

"Swear it on Tia and I'd believe it more than you swearing on the Virgin Mary."

She didn't hesitate one second. "Done. I swear on the soul of Tia Conseulo, Robert can rot in Hell before I *ever* take him back. I'm filing for the restraining order tomorrow as soon as the county clerk opens up." She cleared her throat. "Also, like, until I can get everything squared away, I don't really want to go back to that house. Other than to get some stuff I left so Robert doesn't destroy too much of it, but I'll have Karen for that—"

"You can stay on my hide-a-bed, as long as you admit it's not stupid."

"It's the most glorious contraption I've ever slept on besides my own bed."

"You stay as long as you want, Lucia. I'm not turning my baby sister out on the street."

"Thanks." The line went silent for a few seconds, and when Lucia spoke again it was quiet. "Do you forgive me?"

"Forgive you for what? I told you, this is on Robert, not you."

"But . . . I fell into the same trap Mom did, and everything she put us through—"

"Mom didn't put us through anything. She put up with Dad to keep us as safe as she could. She's not to blame and you're not to blame because someone else is an asshole." Damn it, he was going to cry real, big, manly tears if this conversation didn't wrap up. "Why don't you take care of whatever else the police need, then rent a movie and order takeout or something? You could probably use a good night at home after this."

"Okay." She was still quiet, but calm had begun to bleed into her voice. "Thanks, Tristan. And you'll call tomorrow?"

"I'll call tomorrow. And I should be home soon."

"Good. Just don't get stupid and throw the competition to come home."

"I'm not going to throw it. Night, Lucia. I love you."

"I love you too."

He hung up the phone and lay back. His stomach unclenched all the way, and cold relief splashed through his veins. If she was willing to swear on Tia Consuelo, then she was serious. It was one thing to make promises. It was another to risk the wrath of a six-foot-seven lesbian biker. Even if none of them admitted to believing in her ghost, none of them were willing to take the chance she might be real, either. Better to be safe and not have her impressive silhouette looming over your bed at night.

The fact Lucia was so completely done meant that she'd be around a while, and she'd need that divorce lawyer after all. Plus Tristan had still unknown damage to his apartment, and was down at least one computer, an oven, a mixer . . . plus Lucia had no money of her own, so he *needed* to stay. He needed the money. He needed to win.

And he *really* needed to get out of his own head and be in the moment.

Henry slipped back out of the bathroom. "So, everything good?"

"Yeah, I think it's going to be fine. Karen says that Robert should be in jail for a bit, anyway. Assuming he doesn't get some abuser-sympathizing judge or anything like that." Tristan blew out a long, slow breath and fought back a tickle of sheer, unadulterated relief behind his eyes. "Lucia's going in tomorrow to file for a restraining order, and hopefully that won't take too long to go through. And she's staying with me. My apartment and my *kitchen* were fucked up by that rat bastard. I'll have to fix that. But she seems to be okay."

Slowly, Tristan turned his head to the side and smiled at Henry. Wonderful Henry, standing there just for him. When the chips were down, he showed up. Tristan scooted closer to him. "For once, my sister and I are both in happy relationships at the same time."

"Happy relationships? I thought she was alone."

"Yeah, well, we normally do best alone. She needs to be in a relationship with herself for a while."

"And you? If Delgados do best alone."

"I said 'normally.' I happened to get lucky with you."

Henry lay down on the bed next to Tristan —not close, but still within arm's reach. He brushed those beautiful, rough baker's fingers down Tristan's cheek. "I am certainly glad you got lucky, if that's the case."

"Yeah. Me too." Tristan sighed and slid a little closer to Henry. "And I really, really did."

"Yeah. Now all we have to do is trounce the competition and hope that our relationship survives a head-to-head bake-off."

"Our relationship *started* as a head-to-head bake-off. We can manage."

And there, in a weird San Francisco hotel, waiting to wake up and make choux pastry, with Lucia finally away from that abusive bastard, they *could* manage. Just fine.

Chapter Sixteen

H enry glanced between his oven and the clock. It had been a *stupid fucking* decision to include the chopped hazelnuts to top his croquembouche. Sure, if he was in a restaurant, or even back at his shop where he could try and fail and perfect his recipe before anyone but himself had to taste it, then it would be fine. But he was on the set of *Get Baked*, competing for real money, with fewer than ten minutes to go. Not much testing time to speak of. *And of course I mentioned them to the judges. Now they'll be expecting hazelnuts.* If they weren't there, that meant explaining that he screwed it all up.

He definitely had enough time to get his hazelnuts right. Once. If he had to toast them again, then they'd just have to go missing from the final croquembouche. It was an impressive tower of profiteroles: two and a half feet tall, covered in perfectly amber caramel. If he brought his nose up close enough, he could catch the smell of the crystallized ginger hidden inside the pastry cream. Not too pungent, at least when he tasted it before. There was just a subtle touch of heat to balance out all that sweetness.

Another glance inside the oven, and his nuts were perfect. He had five minutes left to get them in place and make it not look like complete assbaggery. He pulled out his pan, then set to work applying them. Super-hot chopped nuts were basically embers from the deepest and fieriest pits of hell. *Thank God for asbestos hands.* Working with molten sugar and hot metal for the past several years made him . . . well, not exactly fireproof, but certainly heat-resistant. He quickly shook the nuts free and started to place them the best he could. His sugar work was still slightly tacky, so it caught the nuts and held them in place. Mostly. A little "decorative sand" around the base of the tower wouldn't be a completely unconscionable design decision, though. *I can at least make a run at defending this if they bring it up.*

The time ticked down, and the kitchen had never been so quiet. There was a weight, a gravity in the air. Henry glanced around just enough to get a glimpse of Katherine and Willa. Production had redistributed them to fill up the set, since the remaining contestants had all been working on the same side. Henry and Tristan got to stay on their side, and Katherine and Willa worked on the other side. Willa's croquembouche was, expectedly, a sight to behold. It towered, more than any of the others. Her flavors were good, a touch hit and miss from time to time, but her presentation was always worth writing home about. She made shit that was New York big and New York stunning. The kind of things that rightfully drew your eye.

Katherine's were as humble as Willa's were extravagant. Normally, Henry didn't hold with "rustic" preparations. They were an excuse to be messy and not have to answer for it. But he had to make an exception for Katherine. *I'll call her a shabby-chic baker.* She made some awfully attractive "shabby chic" bakes, even if her skill was occasionally questionable. The éclairs she'd pulled out earlier in the day were showstoppers. Rose-petal whipped cream with a cinnamon and honey icing on the top.

And then there was Tristan. Tristan, still comfortably set right in front of Henry, where he'd been the whole time, with his fantastic ass and amazing baking skills. His croquembouche was completely *him.* The profiteroles were made with a chocolate choux pastry, because he couldn't do anything simple, it seemed. His sugar work was considerably lighter in color than all the others, and he'd covered it in silver dragées and silver luster dust that made it so Goddamn elegant. *He does some beautiful fucking work.*

"Okay, that is time, bakers. Drop the spatulas and step away from the cream puffs!" Sylvia clapped her hands a few times, smiling at them.

I guess this is it. This is fucking it. Henry stepped back as far as he could and looked up and down his croquembouche: evenly sloped sides, sturdy, few spaces between the individual profiteroles. He had to resist the urge to tap it, to check if it was all hard and ready to go. He didn't want to risk anyone thinking he could be cheating this close to the end.

Sylvia nodded as she scanned the room. "All right, if you all want to bring your towering croquembouches up to the table, I can get eating— I mean, the judges can get started." She gestured to the right. "Willa, if you can go ahead? Or do you need some help with that beauty?"

Willa scooped up the tower with a smirk and brought it forward. Now was the time to see how this was all going to fall out.

Rita immediately picked up a spoon and cracked it against the side of the croquembouche. "A good, stiff caramel. Properly cooked, not raw or sticky. What flavors are we working with on this one?"

"It's a basic choux pastry, filled with a chocolate and Irish cream filling, and then obviously the chocolate-covered espresso beans studding the outside. And some spun sugar wrapped around the whole number."

"Well, the appearance is very, very impressive, but let's get a check on the flavor." It was almost painful, watching Rita crack the beautifully constructed tower. They all knew how much work went into that thing, and it was unceremoniously broken and handed out to the other judges, and Sylvia too. They ate in what could have been silence, save for the constant cracking of the sugar under their teeth.

"It's good. Exactly what you said." Rita nodded as she went in for another bite. "I mean, truly, it's one of the most decadent cream puffs I've had in a long time. And I eat more cream puffs than I'm comfortable admitting on national television."

"The filling is on point," said Eli. "And I always appreciate some liquor with my dessert, so thanks for that."

"But, you know, I'm not sold on this as a whole." Dexter's brows furrowed. "I know it's a nitpick, but the espresso beans aren't cutting it for me. I'm all for you going after something a little extra. This close to the end, you have to if you want to stand out. But I think they overpower the dish instead of cutting through all the sweet and the decadence, which is why I assume you went with them. All in all good, but maybe a bit too much."

Willa nodded silently and, after a few seconds, she walked back to her station. She hadn't hit a home run. Henry's stomach flipped; they all still had a shot.

Sylvia smiled, then gestured back to the right. "Katherine?"

And it continued. Henry sat on the stool and stared up at his croquembouche. This was torture. The judging got shorter every time, as they lost people, but it always felt twice as long as the round before. He didn't even watch now, just listened.

Eli first. "Good structure, nice appearance. Flavors?"

Katherine. "It's a vanilla and Earl Grey pastry cream, and the choux has finely ground Earl Grey mixed in as well, and then a caramel and some candied citrus rinds."

"Color me intrigued."

Henry shifted his focus to watch Eli break apart the individual profiteroles. He was much more delicate than Rita had been, carefully cracking the sugar apart, then passing a couple to each of the other judges. Henry watched their faces. No obvious disgust. Rita went back in for another bite after her first, and so did Dexter. Not Eli, but all their initial reactions seemed positive.

Eli broke first. "It is good, but your choux pastry has some problems. The Earl Grey I don't think was ground down finely enough, so I'm getting pockets where I bite down on tea, and there's this overall *gritty* texture that I'm not in love with. But the candied citrus is a lovely touch. Even with the tea, the profiteroles are a little on the sweet side, and the bitter and sour from the rind helps balance that right out."

They really are being picky, aren't they?

"I'm not bothered by the texture," said Dexter. "And your pastry cream is incredibly flavorful. It's never easy to get tea to carry through, even harder when you're working with something as potent as vanilla to go with it. But you managed it. I do agree that's it's a little on the sweet side. I would have liked some of that citrus in the pastry or the cream instead of only on the side."

"They're both crazy. This is perfect." Rita leaned over the table, smiling. "How much tea did you have to use for this pastry cream to taste like actual tea?"

"It was about half a cup."

"Good to know. Very good to know." Rita jotted something down on a slip of paper. "Thank you, Katherine."

Katherine nodded and walked back to her station, and off went the broken croquembouche with the production assistants, following behind her. Judging by the split of her critiques, Henry wouldn't bet on her taking the top spot. You needed more than one judge on your side to pull that out.

Sylvia switched her gaze to the other side of the room. "Tristan, if you don't mind?"

He nodded, then gave a tiny glance back to Henry, the smallest wink and smirk imaginable before carrying the choux pastry tower up front to the café table.

As expected, Dexter went first this time. He performed the same spoon-cracking test and it glanced off the sugar. "Nicely held together. Looks like a chocolate choux?"

Tristan nodded. "Chocolate choux with a red chili and blood orange crème pat. And then some luster dust on the outside."

Dexter nodded. "That is an exciting flavor combination, isn't it? I hope you're not going to kill us with that pepper."

"Yeah, I hope so too."

Dexter cracked into the tower and passed two profiteroles to everyone. He bit in. A strange tableau, seeing a man of such impressive musculature delicately biting into that dark, crisp profiterole. It was apparent on the judges' faces that *something* was going on inside those tiny cream puffs. Dexter stopped chewing for a moment, and Rita's and Eli's eyes both closed. *But is it a good thing or a bad thing?* After all this, could Tristan be headed home? Could this little pocket of time—the pair of them, separated off from the world—end because of that tiny pause?

The fact was, Henry didn't *want* to win the competition against anyone else. Sure, beating Willa would be impressive enough, and Katherine had proven herself remarkably talented in a way that, honestly, Henry was worried about. Their styles were so different that the judges' personal tastes could decide a final showdown between the pair of them.

But Henry wanted to face off against Tristan, because Tristan was the kind of crazy bastard who would make . . . well, blood orange and red chili crème pâtisserie. Henry wanted to prove himself against *that*, and if he came up short, then what else could anyone expect? Somehow the idea of losing to Tristan was more palatable than that of losing to anyone else. Henry wouldn't just be a gay boy getting run over by the world at that point. He would be part of a duo, first and second place gays against the world.

Finally, Dexter swallowed and broke the silence. "How did you get the blood orange flavor in the crème pat?"

"It's blood orange juice reduced down with sugar, and I steeped the rind in the syrup to boost up the flavor that way too."

"And the pepper?"

"It's ground cayenne. Neutral flavor, and it sort of disappears in the crème pat once you get the color going from the blood orange."

Dexter nodded. "You know, I thought your idea was interesting, but I was waiting for it to go wrong. Too much cayenne or, God forbid, a curdled pastry cream from all the acid. But it wasn't. It was good." Dexter reached across the table and clapped Tristan on the shoulder. "Nicely done, Tristan."

Tristan nodded silently, and he was at the right angle that Henry could see the edge of his grin, wide and bright and pulling in the dimples on his cheeks. Henry smiled too. Tristan had gotten some credit for his ideas and innovations and, goddamn it, that made Henry happy to see.

Eli gestured to Tristan with a half-eaten cream puff. "I think the flavor really is something great. The chocolate has a good, strong presence, so it stands up well to the citrus and the bite from the pepper. But I think your dough was a bit tougher than I would expect from a cream puff, and my guess is that it's because of the cocoa powder you used for the chocolate. It normally makes the dough stiffer, and it takes more work than a normal pâte à choux. More work means more gluten, all that stuff. It's not bad, just not *quite* what I'm used to. But absolutely excellent flavors."

"And flavors I love," said Rita. "The cayenne I could take or leave, personally, but I understand it. It works, it makes sense, and it wouldn't stop me from buying the cream puffs by themselves. And the croquembouche part was nicely put together. The silver for the caramel stood out against the dark dough, so it was really an eye-catching piece. Plus, I love anything that includes dragées. They're cheap, but they make me feel like a princess all the same. But I do agree that the dough could be a little less tough. It would have given you a lighter shell. But that's being super nitpicky, of course. I'm not convinced I could have done a better chocolate choux in the same amount of time."

Sylvia nodded and smiled. "Thank you, Tristan."

The critique had been good. Not perfect, but Henry hoped it was enough. Now he had his own hurdle to jump. His belly, already uncomfortable at the possibility of Tristan leaving, tightened further around the idea of going up there. So much was at stake. So much more than usual, even if choux pastry was part of his daily life at the shop. He didn't know if this batch had turned out. He didn't know how his pastry cream stacked up against everyone else's, although he doubted it was up to snuff compared to Tristan's. Blood orange pastry cream sounded good, and it had apparently performed well enough for the judges.

Sylvia locked eyes with him. "Henry, if you can come show us your tower?"

Henry lifted his croquembouche and carried it up the long, long aisle toward the front. He set it down and waited. Who was going to come out and judge him?

Rita. Right in order. She popped her spoon against the side and the caramel cracked cleanly. She nodded at the tower, then turned to face Henry. "It's classic and pristine. Everything we've come to expect from you over these past weeks. What are your flavors?"

"It's a vanilla bean pâte à choux with a raspberry diplomat cream filling, and then spun sugar all around the outside, with toasted hazelnut for a little more depth."

She nodded, then casually broke his beautiful stack of profiteroles apart. It was still painful, after all that, to see it broken apart with such lack of care. But it had to happen eventually. No matter how painstaking to assemble or how much work and time went into the end product, even if it was really, truly the most beautiful food ever created, it was still food. And more important than anything else, food had to taste good, to feel perfect in the mouth.

His profiteroles were particularly dainty. Each judge had three, and they popped a whole one into their mouths. Henry stood by, waiting for a response.

Rita first, again. "The profiterole itself is crisp and delicate, and it tastes very strongly of vanilla, but it's not overpowering. It stands up to the tartness of the raspberry cream in the middle. And your spun sugar is, honestly, some of the nicest I've seen that was made without a cotton candy machine. An even texture all the way through, delicate, and not so thick that it makes shards in the mouth."

Dexter took a second profiterole in one bite. "Your caramel is good. Dark but not scorched, and there's not so much of it on here that you ruin your texture." He nodded. "I have no complaints."

Jesus, no complaints from Dexter Wilson. That has to be worth something.

"If you don't mind, I want to break one of these open." Eli gently pulled apart a profiterole, then held the two halves open. A camera swooped in and shot it up close and personal for several seconds before Eli continued. "So the diplomat cream is an interesting choice."

Henry nodded. "I wanted to lighten up that pastry cream a little." Whipped cream hadn't been holding up to the raspberry puree properly, and it had seemed *wrong* to have a raspberry-flavored crème pat all by itself.

"It's a good call." Eli stuck a tiny spoon in the cream and popped it into his mouth. "I mean, I'm a sucker for diplomat cream as it is. Nobody uses it, it's incredibly underrated, and this is a good one. But it works beautifully with the raspberry. It's not so thick and heavy that it kills the natural tartness of the berries, which I think you would have gotten only using a pastry cream. It's almost like an old-fashioned fool: fruit and whipped cream, but with that extra bit of richness from your crème pat. I would honestly eat this out of, like, a crystal bowl and feel perfectly classy and at peace. If you're *trying* to make something like croquembouche higher-end than it already is, then I think you've nailed it. I'm sure if you dipped the whole thing in chocolate and gold leaf, it could be classier, but that's about all that's coming to mind."

Henry fought against the rise of heat in his cheeks. That was some high praise. Hard as Eli tried, he couldn't find *one* negative comment about it. And he seemed like he was a couple of steps away from having sex with that croquembouche, he liked it so much. *And wouldn't that just ensure us a primetime spot?*

Sylvia beamed at him. "All right, thank you, Henry."

He walked back, his croquembouche following swiftly behind him. The judges began their quiet deliberation, and Jacob slipped into sight. "Okay, prepare yourselves. We're running a little longer today than intended, so the faster we can buzz through this, the better. The extras, we can catch up on tomorrow."

Henry breathed deep, taking in the other competitors. Willa smiling even as her fingers tightened into fists. Katherine absently curling and uncurling her hair around one finger. Tristan back to twiddling his thumbs. The four of them had been through so much here. They'd each had flops and successes along the way. This competition was brutal, as baking went. No singular baker kept up this pace of recipe development and statement pieces in everyday life. But they'd all lasted it out. Henry couldn't help a warm wash of camaraderie through his middle, competition or not.

Once the judges had apparently reached their verdict, Jacob counted them back in. Sylvia clapped and scanned the set. "Congratulations to each of you. You've done alarmingly well, and I like to imagine my waistline is expanding so that it can give you all hugs. Your éclairs and croquembouches were no exception. Stunningly delicious and staggeringly impressive. But there was one outpouring of baking prowess that slightly edged out the others. Perfect execution of classic flavors . . . Henry, for the second week in a row, congratulations!"

Holy shit. Henry's eyes widened, and he blinked at Sylvia a few times. Then the applause came and reality flooded through. He'd won twice. In a row.

That shouldn't have meant anything. Hell, if there *were* two rounds in a row where he'd win, it would be viennoiserie and choux pastry. Still, Henry's body tingled with the excitement, the knowledge he'd won and the feeling that, somehow, it *meant* something. And it did, to beat out the best of the best. The top four. He was the best out of the best four bakers they'd managed to find for this show. Henry won out over all of them, and damn it, that was worth *something*. Surely this proved that he wasn't going to disappear or be run over by the world at large. He could do take this all the way to the end.

Sylvia took on her dour face, and the room fell silent. "This is the most painful one yet for me, but someone does have to go. I don't envy the judges any day, and I especially didn't envy them the task this time." She sighed. "Katherine, I'm sorry. Your pâte a choux wasn't quite down pat." Sylvia marched over and wrapped Katherine up in a tight hug.

Katherine smiled as she took the hug, but a little sparkle of water in her eyes betrayed her actual feelings. Henry couldn't blame her. It was bittersweet, at best, to make it this far and fall short. He wasn't sure he'd be able to control his emotions that well in the same situation. Sure, yeah, you were still a good chef . . . but it was almost better to be tossed out first than to get this close to the prize and miss out.

Willa put her hand on Katherine's shoulder, but that was it. Henry glanced to Tristan, then walked over to Katherine and got in his fleeting contact. She *had* pulled together some amazing flavors. It wasn't all that fair to judge her on one baking session with bad rolls and a few appearance-based missteps. The kitchen without her . . . well, seeing the others go home before her had been doable, but somehow Katherine leaving made the kitchen feel a little emptier. Maybe a little too empty. *Who am I going to silently judge, now?*

Seeing the cleaver in Dexter's impressive grip was bothersome. The sore muscles and expertise put into a croquembouche, all about to be shattered.

All four of the bakers clustered together to watch that one, and all of them—even Tristan—had a hand on Katherine as the cameras lined up their shot. Dexter had to swing up well over his head to make it work, and as he crashed the knife down, shards of caramel shrapnel shattered over the counter along with a spray of pale gray pastry cream. Katherine flinched, and Henry gave her shoulder a squeeze.

"And we're cut!" The director waved. "I don't want to rush you out; however, I'm going to rush you out. Sorry. Executive bull-crap, but I'm a slave to it, which means all of you are too."

As the room emptied, Henry smiled at Tristan. "I won again. I don't know if you remember what happened last time, but . . ."

"Pipe down." But Tristan smiled too. Just a touch.

Katherine walked off with the disgruntled director for her last interviews and whatnot, and Dexter walked over to the three of them who remained, wiping a smear of crème pat from his cheek. He grinned wide at them and rubbed his hands together. "Well, we're down to three. What do you say to dinner?"

"Really?" Willa raised one eyebrow and looked him up and down. "Dinner with you? What if the neighbors see?"

"Let them talk, *mon ami*." He winked at her. "Besides, I could never land a woman as lovely as you."

"You talk as pretty as you bake."

"I try." He sighed. "But the dinner is with all of us. We want to take out our final three for a nice dinner. Although knowing the final three are from Seattle and New York, I might be tempted to skip it. God knows nothing we picked is likely to stand up to what you can get at home."

"Oh, I think we'll be okay. Right boys?" Willa turned toward them.

Henry nodded, then looked at Dexter. "I feel like I *might* trust your taste."

Dexter laughed, loud and booming. "You're only saying that because you won, aren't you?"

"It certainly doesn't hurt."

Rita came around the table, closing a surprisingly out-of-date flip phone as she came. "I confirmed with Marguerite, and we have the terrace." She beamed at the three of them. "I'm sorry, I don't know if Dexter told you, but . . . they're sending a couple cameras too. We let it slip that we wanted to take our semifinalists out for a meal, and the executives thought that was a great idea for a TV spot. I hope that doesn't bother you."

Henry shook his head. Willa shook her head. Tristan stood there wide-eyed and very, very pale. If they were alone, Henry would have given his hand a squeeze. But instead he just smiled. "What's the plan?"

"Well, like I said, I got the terrace reserved at Bluestone Lotus. Renata has a full eight-course tasting menu for us."

Tristan swallowed hard and Henry *got* it. It clicked. It had to be a high-end place, and he probably hadn't budgeted for that. Neither had Henry, but he had more wiggle room, especially considering how much time he and Tristan spent gorging on takeout and craft services instead of eating real food in real restaurants.

Rita sighed and slipped her phone away. "We'll all go together, of course. The car will be at the hotel at seven thirty, so plenty of time for a shower, shave, and everything else?" She smiled wide, clearly oblivious to the tension radiating off Tristan. "Is that good with everyone?"

Henry nodded, Willa nodded, and Tristan finally found some motor control and nodded as well.

Rita rubbed her hands together. "Wonderful. Even if it means I have to wear heels again."

Eli came from backstage. "Congratulations, you three. Really. None of us are exactly slouches in a kitchen, but I think we've seen some things worth paying attention to. Particularly from the three of you."

He smiled, and Henry saw why he was the big baking heartthrob. He carried himself with a subtle confidence, and at least when he wasn't judging you, his whole demeanor was warm and inviting. What wasn't to love?

But he's no Tristan.

Which could be said of anyone. Anyone but Tristan, anyway.

Rita looked over to Sylvia. "You'll be joining us as well, of course."

"Oh, no, not me. A fine-dining experience like that would be wasted on someone with my palate."

"Nonsense." Eli walked out of the group and pulled her over to stand with them. "You're a part of this as much as anyone. And besides, there's nothing like your first foray with real gourmet food. We can all be privy to that and enjoy watching your head explode."

Sylvia blushed a deep red. "I suppose if I'm providing the entertainment, it would be rude of me not to go."

"Perfect." Eli gave them all one last smile. "Okay, then. Seven thirty, car will pick you up at the hotel, so you have an hour and half to get back there and get ready."

"Oh, you're pushing me." Willa bounced up her white curls. "I haven't gotten ready that fast in years. Guess I'll have to pop some speed or something."

Dexter snorted a laugh. "I can't *condone* that, but reservations are reservations." He patted an oversized hand on her dainty shoulder. "All right, we're off, you're off. They're probably annoyed that we're still here as it is."

Sylvia and the judges all filed away, leaving Tristan, Henry, and Willa to stand around the set. Willa sighed and shrugged. "I need to get my hair done and pull out that nice dress I'm glad I decided to bring after all." She winked. "You boys have fun and behave yourselves."

Henry fought a surge of panic. *What does that mean?* He closed his eyes and counted a slow breath. *It's nothing. I'm being paranoid.* And right now, Tristan needed a rock, not a mirror to his own anxieties. So Henry nodded and winked at Willa as she headed out. Then he turned to look straight at Tristan. "You . . . heard anything about this Bluestone Lotus place? You're way more plugged in to all the trendy stuff than I am, especially outside Seattle." *Compliment him, get him to talk about something other than the money. Get him out of his own worries for a second.*

"Umm, yeah." Tristan pulled off his glasses and massaged the bridge of his nose. "It's a new, high-end molecular gastronomy joint. I haven't really checked out the menu, just seen it in passing, but it's gotten some attention. Not, like, Osteria Francescana attention, but attention." He slipped his glasses back on. "We should probably get going if we want to look presentable."

"Right, yeah." Henry wanted to wrap his arm around Tristan as they walked out, but fought down the urge.

As soon as they crossed the threshold, Tristan stopped. "Do you think you could get ready in your room? It'll be easier than trying to share the shower or go in turns or anything like that."

Henry nodded. Best not to push the issue when Tristan was obviously already nervous as hell. "No problem. Meet back at your room?"

"Yeah. I'll leave it ajar, in case I'm not out of the shower yet." He brushed his fingers gently against Henry's hand. "As long as you agree not to get too handsy until we get back from dinner. Showing up in come-stained dress clothes might not be the classiest decision."

Henry chuckled at the joke, even though it didn't seem funny. Not the way Tristan delivered it, with uncertainty quivering in his voice and worry flashing gray and lifeless behind his eyes. "I'll restrain myself as best I can."

There was an easy way around the financial concerns, at least. They just needed to make it back to the hotel.

Chapter Seventeen

Tristan stood under the scalding flow of the shower, hoping it would boil out or wash away all his worries. "You're being ridiculous. The fucking network's going to pay for this like they pay for everything else. An eight-course dinner is a drop in the bucket to them. They probably spend more than that a day on hair and makeup." Still, the worry remained. Especially since there would be cameras. It was bad enough already, possibly having to show off his finances—or specifically the lack thereof—in front of Dexter and Rita and Eli. But good lord, that would be such juicy drama, him asking the price of the meal and checking his wallet and bank account. That clip would be plastered all over every trashy tabloid website for the rest of his life. Were there still restaurants in the world that would make you go back and wash dishes? Or was that only a sitcom trope?

Once they paid him for the show, he'd be fine, but what would he do tonight? Ask for an advance on the check to pay for dinner? "I should have brought the stupid credit card." Except he'd specifically left that with Lucia in case there was an emergency on that end.

"I should just ask them if the network's covering it." But that would *also* be a revelation of his financial hardship. There was no face-saving solution other than magically pulling money out of his ass. And if he thought that might have worked, he'd have tried it right then and there.

A gentle knock, then Henry's voice filtered through the pounding water and closed door. "Hey, no need to rush, okay? I can wait."

"I'll be out in a minute." Tristan had washed right away. The rest of his time in the shower had been spent taking advantage of the industrial-strength water heater, something his apartment definitely lacked. Hot water and plenty of time to ruminate and spiral through scenarios that would never play out. Unless of course they did.

He shut off the water, toweled off enough that he didn't leave an ocean for housekeeping to wipe up, then pulled on his bathrobe and stepped out. Henry was sitting on the very edge of the bed again. He wore black slacks and a deep burgundy button-down that caught the light just so. He'd shaved off all notion of stubble, which Tristan could have easily seen as a shame—he liked that stubble, had *uses* for that stubble—but it worked. He looked crisp and wonderful and every bit the young socialite out on the town that Seattle had trained both of them to be. Hell, Tristan was pretty sure he'd almost bought himself that same shirt, once. He remembered the breast pocket with the satin-covered square button. "You clean up pretty."

"Yeah. I hate doing it, but I figure I might as well put my best foot forward. I checked out the restaurant, and then I compared myself, and we did *not* match up well."

"Oh, you would have been fine." Tristan pulled out the only really nice clothing he'd brought with him: a brilliant green dress shirt and dark slacks. Toss a black undershirt on underneath and he could almost be presentable. "If it were up to me, I'd let you in anywhere. Even if you showed up stubbly and sweaty and naked as a jaybird." Okay, *that* was trying too hard to sound natural and coming off plain weird, but it was better to go with it. Tristan turned and winked at Henry. "I might be *more* likely if you were stubbly, sweaty, and naked, but that's probably personal bias."

The last thing Tristan wanted to do was let Henry in on his worries. This was set to be a good night for him. For *both* of them, because realistically, Tristan knew he wasn't going to have to pay. Probably. He knew it wasn't going to be a face-melting embarrassment, but that did jack shit to stop his anxiety.

Tristan walked over to the dresser and pulled out a fresh pair of boxers. Blue and white houndstooth and, far more importantly, not worn for hours and hours in a very hot kitchen. They'd been a gift from his ex, Jacky, before Jacky had turned out to be an asshole and Tristan had sworn off men for the third time. But they were the only pair of underwear that made him feel confident.

He slipped them on, then dropped the bathrobe and continued dressing. "So, it sounds to me like Rita must know the people at this restaurant pretty well. I mean, it's a Saturday night, isn't it? Getting outdoor seating at an expensive-ass restaurant is . . . well, you're aware. You've lived in Seattle even longer than me."

"Yeah, but a personal connection can remove a lot of obstacles. I bet she got a good deal, too, if she knows people there." Henry sighed, but not his contented sigh. A tiny flutter of warmth traveled through Tristan's chest—he could recognize Henry's damn sighs. But then the flutter died. This sigh signaled a heavy subject incoming, and it was better to rip off the bandage in one damn fell swoop.

Tristan pulled on his T-shirt as he turned around, then fixed his gaze right on Henry. "Okay, what is it?"

"What?"

"You have something you want to say, so you may as well say it now."

"God, am I that obvious?"

Tristan rolled his eyes. "Maybe not to everyone, but to me, yeah." He glanced at the clock on the end table. "And we need to be down in the lobby in twenty minutes, so if there's going to be a fight, I guess we should expedite it."

Henry let out a strained chuckle. "No fight. At least *I'm* not planning one." He stood and smiled at Tristan. "You're . . . Look, I noticed that you were nervous when they brought up going out to dinner." Blush bled into Henry's face, even more blatant than usual with no stubble to obscure and blue it out. "Is it about the money, or about the two of us, or something else?"

"God, it's not about us." Conflicting sensations burst through Tristan's core. Hot, flickering embarrassment exploding against a steady, calming thrum. "You really noticed that? I thought I hid it pretty well."

"You totally froze when they brought up dinner. I knew something was going on."

Tristan scrubbed his cheeks, trying to formulate the words. "It's the money. It's *always* the money. I have all the same expenses I did before, but now I also have repairs to my apartment to handle when I get back, and maybe my sister's going to need more support.

It's probably not the last time he's going to try and get her back even with a restraining order. Catering only pays so much."

"I mean, there's no reason to think the network isn't comping the whole meal. Especially if they're filming it."

"Yeah, I know. I've been trying to convince myself of that since I got back in here." Tristan walked back to the closet and grabbed his slacks. "But my brain keeps telling me that maybe they aren't and I'm going to be outed as some poor little baker."

"You're not some poor little baker, though. You're Tristan and you're amazing and you made it this far."

"I'm very flattered you think that, but I have no money." He slipped the button-down over his shoulders, then pulled it straight as he turned to face Henry again. "I don't have money for this meal, and I know it's a small concern in the grand scheme of things, but it's a problem *tonight*. I have all this money on the horizon for filming this show, let alone if I win the full quarter million, but none of that will help me cover dinner in a few hours. Which again, small worries. God forbid you compare my stupid problem to world hunger and war and people getting killed overseas for being gay and nuclear stockpiling—"

"Dude, dude." Henry gripped him hard by the shoulders. "Is this what it's like to live in your head?"

"When I'm panicking? Yeah." Tristan grabbed Henry's hand, worried his thumb across Henry's scarred, pockmarked fingers. "I'm sorry. It's just frustrating."

"Hey, it's fine." Henry sighed. A normal sigh. A let's-continue-the-conversation sigh. "I have extra money, and I want you to hold on to it. In case."

"What. God, no. No way. No." Tristan stepped back and started buttoning up his shirt rapidly. "I'm not taking your money."

"Tristan, if I can help you out with this, I want to."

"Yeah, but I don't want you to." Tristan finished buttoning, then sat on the bed with his socks, head spinning. "I'll figure it out."

"Come on. We both acknowledge that you're probably not going to even need it. It's extra, and you can give it back at the end of the night. Let me be the highfalutin one today."

Tristan sighed as he pulled his pant legs down over the socks. "I appreciate it. I really do, Henry. But it's not okay. Not with someone

I feel about like I do about you." An urge struck him there, one that nearly made him say something too honest. "We already have to hide what's going on here from the production crew. I don't want anything as stupid as money to put our relationship on the line."

"I get that. I just . . . I don't want you to worry."

"Oh boy, if you don't want someone who worries, you've hitched yourself to the wrong wagon." Again, the urge to speak came over him, to lay out every feeling currently pumping through his veins. What was this? He got a modicum of kindness and suddenly his heart wanted to pour out.

For Henry, though.

That was the lynchpin, wasn't it? It wasn't simply that someone was being nice. It was that, in spite of all Tristan's problems and ghosts and demons, not only was Henry still here, he was trying to ease some of those worries. At the cost of his own pocketbook, no less.

"Do it for me. For *my* peace of mind." Henry held the money out again. "I don't want you to stress about this dinner and ruin it for yourself. You deserve to have a nice time tonight as much as anyone else. And if I can give that to you, I want to."

This time, Tristan didn't hold back the surge of emotion that built across his tongue. He let it loose, even as it chilled him and tightened his stomach around that unique ball of lightning. "But I might be in love with you, and taking your money is no way to start a committed relationship."

And Henry faltered. His hand dropped to the bed, and he blinked for several seconds. Other than that, he seemed frozen in place until he finally spoke. "That's the same reason I want you to take it. That, uh, that first part."

The room was silent for a long time, or maybe not long at all. They sat together in the quiet, close as could be, but Tristan couldn't seem to touch Henry. Nothing had changed, but somehow everything had.

"Did you mean that?" Henry slowly, carefully twisted his head and made eye contact, his cheeks flushed. "If you didn't, and it just came out, that's fine."

Tristan chuckled and inched his hand over to rest on Henry's knee. "I think I might love you." It came easier this time, and he grinned at the shape of the syllables in his mouth. "So I'm not taking your money."

After a couple of seconds, Henry smiled. He slipped the cash back into his pocket. "But aren't you going to panic your whole way through dinner if you don't have it?"

"Maybe. Like I said, if you're not up for me being a worrywart, then you're not tall enough to ride this ride."

"Yeah, but the ride is so good." He kissed the nape of Tristan's neck, shooting flames out from where his mouth made contact. When he pulled back, he was staring dead into Tristan's eyes. "If . . . if we're talking the big L word here, then can we compromise? If you end up needing the money, I'll palm it to you under the table or something."

Tristan sighed, and he nodded at those chocolate eyes. "Deal." And, much as he hated to admit it, it felt good to know he had a safety net for the evening. "Thank you."

Henry pressed his lips to Tristan's.

"Jesus Christ . . ." Henry gawked at the view from the terrace, along with the others. He'd thought his hotel room had a picturesque view, but this shit was postcard worthy, the bay of San Francisco lit up by the moon with the Golden Gate gleaming all on its own and some other part of the city glimmering like diamonds in the distance.

Marguerite, the maître d', stood off to the side of the terrace, which was private. He hadn't expected that. "You can go ahead and take your seats. Antonio will be serving you tonight, so if you need anything, ask for him. He'll be here momentarily for drink orders, and Renata will come out before the first course to talk with you."

Henry shook his head in amazement. This was more than a three-star restaurant. This was the kind of service reserved for celebrities, and it was being pushed at them like it was nothing. He glanced to Tristan and raised his eyebrows. Tristan smiled back and took the first seat around the one very large table.

Henry sat next to him. On the edge of his visions, he could see cameras and audio being set up. But they weren't filming quite yet.

It was a good chance to try to assuage Tristan's concerns. He started talking with Rita—dressed in a blazing gold brocade cocktail dress—as soon as she sat down. "Before the cameras get rolling, I have to ask . . . what's something like this cost?"

"Cost? No idea. It's a special thing I set up with Renata. I'm sure the network will itemize it out though. There's probably some tricky deduction they can take for filming here so it won't cost them a cent."

Well, there was confirmation on that: the network was for sure footing this bill. Henry's eyes darted to Tristan, just long enough to see the flash of contentment pass across his face.

"It's not something *I* could justify paying for, that's for certain." Dexter sat next to Rita, Eli next to him, and Willa between Eli and Tristan, leaving one empty seat.

Henry looked behind him. "What happened to Sylvia?" She'd gotten out of the car with them.

"Sylvia's fine, I'm sorry, I'm sorry." She walked in, for once not dressed in a blazer and khakis. Instead, she wore an impeccably tailored black suit jacket and a razor thin black tie over a white blouse. Black high-waisted pants and black wingtips. She looked austere and put-together. Even more together than usual, which was impressive. She took her seat next to Henry and immediately shifted her coat off and onto the back of the chair. "Ladies room. Also, that jacket gets hot as a mother."

And there goes the class. Henry grinned at it all the same. At least she wasn't faking.

Eli turned and gazed out over the ocean. "This is a great view. Really, really great. Or maybe I'm so used to the New York skyline that anything else looks amazing and exotic."

"I'm with you there," said Willa before winking at Tristan. "I bet you two both feel the same about Seattle, too, right? I mean, it's no NYC, but Seattle's got a hell of a skyline."

Tristan nodded. "Especially at night. I don't live in any of the posh neighborhoods, but from my bedroom window, on a clear day, I can see the Space Needle and the EMP. It's a striking view. But so is this."

Willa nodded and sighed, then turned to Rita. "Thank you for setting this up. It's a nice way to destress before I have to give these boys what for."

"Oh, confident?" Dexter chuckled. "Well, looks like we're about to be filmed, so get all your cussing out of the way now."

"Shitting fucking Christ on a dick," Sylvia rattled off quickly, almost like it was rehearsed. She smiled sheepishly at them. "I didn't expect to be doing that alone. Sorry. I say it before every filming to, you know, get rid of it. Please stop staring."

Henry busted out laughing and clapped her on the back. "I think any of EateryTV's shows would be a lot more interesting with Christ on a dick, myself."

Dexter joined the laughter, and soon all the others did too. But Dexter, of course, was louder than the whole lot of them. "I think *some* of the hosts would shit themselves, though. So probably not the best idea. Don't want to give poor Martha Edelstein a heart attack."

Willa snorted. "Who says I wouldn't? How much do they pay her for her little . . . program?"

Dexter chuckled. "No idea. But she's the biggest thorn in my side in the whole network. Everyone else I can stand, but I'd much rather watch any of you three on a cooking show than her, that's for sure."

"Well, you're going to get to." Tristan's voice was barely loud enough to break through the din, but hell, he'd *said* something.

Dexter smiled and, without his guffaw and bellow, the terrace was considerably quieter. "Right you are. I'll get to see all three of you at once on a TV show, so all the better." He glanced to the cameraman in the far-right corner. "Okay, you can get filming. I think we're as ready as we're going to get."

After a second, the little red lights flicked to life. And almost as soon, Henry forgot about them, so used to being recorded now that the glowing specks faded into the rest of the glimmering lights out there on the horizon. *There's something I never thought would be normal.*

Either she was waiting for some cue from production, or it was pure luck, but a black woman in chef's whites and a toque strode through the door right then, hands clasped in front of her. "Welcome. I'm Renata Dixon, I'm the chef here." She waved wiggling fingers at Rita before continuing. "So, I don't know how much you got filled in on, but tonight you can consider this the chef's table. I have six courses for you, and my pastry chef has two to finish off your meal." A waiter walked in, notepad in hand. "So, I hope you really enjoy seeing what I and my kitchen can pull off. And we've got enough to keep these poor intrepid camera people fed. It wouldn't be fair to make them stand there all night watching you eat." She sighed, and then smiled broad and bright. "Your first course will be on its way shortly."

And it was. Henry was impressed with the service to be certain. They'd obviously been working on the meal, because as soon as Antonio dropped off their drinks—Henry ordered what turned out to be the best whiskey sour he'd ever tasted—in came the opening plates. They each had a thick card with the contents of the dish scrawled in royal blue script. Native whitefish ceviche with seeded puff pastry crisps. The ceviche was . . . well, ceviche. And the crisps looked like the beginnings of mille-feuille, rectangular shards of puff pastry but studded with a mix of sesame, poppy, and caraway seeds: an earthy, nutty accompaniment to the briny seafood. When Henry took a bite, the fish was saline and pungent, barely kept in check by the acidic lime juice. But the meaty texture of the fish with the incredibly thin, flaking layers of puff pastry was incredible. The whole thing practically fell apart in his mouth.

And like Eli had said, it was worth watching Sylvia. Her eyes widened at the first bite, and they seemed to stay that way through every course. The three little soup dumplings filled with classic French onion soup and served with gruyere and parmesan toast. The vampire-killing levels of garlic in the cubic Caesar salad. The three perfectly seared and perfectly seasoned lamb chops with champagne beurre blanc. The deconstructed carbonara, with lightly dressed pasta and fried guanciale. When each new course was delivered, Henry eagerly watched Sylvia to see her shock and involuntary laughter at the new flavors.

When the very clean plates from the last main course was taken away, Sylvia leaned back, hands above her head. "Do you people eat like this every day?"

Dexter shook his head. "If we ate like this every day, none of us would be able to fit through the doors in the morning. But every now and then is always welcome."

"I think people should eat gourmet at least once a year, if they can swing it." Tristan seemed to have relaxed considerably, though he was still talking comparatively little. "Just pick a day out of the year, set aside money for it, and then go all in on a real, high-class meal like this. People deserve to know what real, good food tastes like."

"Agreed." Rita held out her glass for a toast, and Tristan clinked against it. She swallowed the last bit of Riesling from said glass. "You must have access to all kinds of good food. I love eating in Seattle. There's something so special about it."

"Well, I have to agree with you on that one." Tristan chuckled. "Although I'm biased, and we probably lose any objective comparison to New York City."

Willa laughed at that. "Oh, you can't boil down the spirit of a food city like NYC or Seattle or New Orleans into a nice, digestible rating of quality. New York does what New York does and Seattle does what Seattle does. I mean, I wouldn't expect to walk in downtown Seattle and stumble on a Gray's Papaya, but I also don't expect to narrowly avoid flying fish back home."

Henry smiled and took another drink from his second whiskey sour. *The studio can afford it, after all.* "Pike Place is a beast all its own, I have to admit. Fresh seafood, tons of restaurants, the best little spice market. I wouldn't trade it for the world."

"Two of you from Seattle, I don't know." Eli finally slipped off his jacket, let it hang over the back of his seat the same as Sylvia. "I had preconceived notions about what I'd see from you guys. I thought you'd do a lot of stuff the same. And, well, you know, it would have made for more exciting TV if you'd brought a little history. We knew you ran in similar circles."

"No need to be coy, Eli," said Dexter. "We heard scuttlebutt that there was a little rivalry there and were hoping it might show through. Alas, seems the rumors weren't true."

Tristan rolled his eyes. "Maybe we were fighting when this whole thing started. But we got over it."

"You got over it?" Eli leaned in. "Do tell."

Tristan flashed a sideways glance to Henry. "Even in Seattle, the baking and catering circuit is only so big. We knew about each other. And perhaps there was a little rivalry going on, but . . . I mean, look at what he can do with chiffon cake and royal icing. How can you stay mad at that?"

Henry took a quick drink so that his inevitable blush could be blamed on the alcohol. Then he felt able to jump back into the conversation. "What I can do with royal icing? What *he* can do with flavors. It's *his* fault that we're not sniping at each other anymore." *Him and his stupid delicious mint cake.*

As a cap to that, Renata came back out along with Antonio, both carrying long, rectangular plates. They passed them out as she spoke. "Now, this is the last of my contribution. The last two courses are all Destiny's work. But I hope everything was as perfect as possible."

She scurried off and left them with their cheese plates. Henry checked over the card that came with it. Half a dozen small tasting samples of gouda. Different ages, preparations, and origins. Served with thin slices of apples and different citrus, plus water crackers. It was damn ingenious. Low work and high concept, minimal financial output, but big impact.

Henry sat there and soaked up the night. There, overlooking San Francisco Bay as the sky blackened, surrounded by other chefs, eating a fine meal that he didn't have to pay for. There was a magic and electricity in the air.

Quietly, so that no one else would notice, Henry reached under the table and took Tristan's hand. And crazy as it was, as though the universe was approving, a spark gleamed on the edge of his vision.

Fat and happy, Willa, Henry, and Tristan unloaded from the car. Tristan *might* have had more than an appropriate number of Manhattans, but the food had been so *fucking* exquisite, he'd fallen into the trap of decadence. He rarely got to indulge so much. For all his "gourmet food once a year" talk, he didn't come anywhere close to pulling that off. Most of his meals were quick, throw-together one pots or baking-sheet dinners, unless he was at an event. Then he ate whatever the guests did, but in the tent.

Even the dessert fare had been incredible, and Tristan knew how stressful that had to be, serving desserts to six professional pastry chefs. But the crème brûlée with the pomegranate molasses had been to die for, and the white chocolate mousse with powdered olive oil and balsamic vinegar had been a brand-new experience. Tristan had little interest in participating in the molecular gastronomy craze. He'd adopted a couple of techniques here and there—sous vide zabaglione was a damn sight easier than using a water bath and ramekins—but the powders and chemicals and liquid nitrogen weirdness wasn't working for him. So the fact he'd scribbled out *tapioca maltodextrin* on some scrap paper so he could track it down was a testament to that dish.

Tristan watched the car drive away, then sighed and smiled at Willa and Henry. "Good food. Good company. Good night."

Henry nodded. "See you two in the trenches again tomorrow." But the look in his eye told Tristan there was more in store for the pair of them that night. Naked, tangled, sweaty time. *Thank God I'm not the only one thinking about it.*

"Let's not cut the evening short quite yet." Willa set her hands on her hips and stepped away from the two of them. Not inside, not toward the doors, just *away*. Her eyes narrowed, and Tristan's spine immediately straightened. That wasn't a friendly face.

"You know, you two are looking awfully close, lately. I saw your hand-holding act under the table, in case you thought you were being subtle." She pulled her phone out of her purse and waved it at them. "Even snapped a little evidence when you weren't paying attention. I know what's up. Caught something in the air between you, and now I've seen it with my own eyes."

Henry spoke softly, but his voice was full of venom. "The flash . . . you bitch."

Tristan jerked his head around. "What flash?"

"When I grabbed your hand. I thought it was a reflection off a glass or something."

Tristan nearly swallowed his tongue, and his palms went clammy.

Henry stepped forward, closing the gap with her. "You *really* think gay bashing in downtown San Francisco is a smart decision?" His voice edged cold and sharp. "You really, *really* think that, with all your years of experience in this world?"

"I'm not a bigot. I could give half a shit if you're gay. Go be gay. Do it now, I'll watch." She rolled her eyes and swept a stray white curl away from her forehead. "But fraternizing isn't the best decision on a competition show. Especially where someone's already been kicked off for working too closely with one of her competitors. Be a shame to get caught up in something like that."

Henry snorted. "Not what we're doing."

"Hey, if you think everyone's going to buy that you two are fucking and not helping each other, take the risk. Let's see how that turns out."

Tristan's whole body burned, and all the good stupor from their dinner blazed away with that heat. "You can't win on your own damn merits? Have to try and throw us under the bus?"

"I've been in this business for a quarter of a century. I deserve a break, and I deserve it way more than you young up-and-comers." She shrugged. "I'll make this really simple. One of you throws the next round, then we won't have any problems. I don't care which one of you it is. Decide between yourselves: draw straws, thumb war, whatever you need to do. Whoever it is gets paid, gets some nice publicity, and I'll *deal* with whoever gets to the final with me." Her eyes narrowed. "Or you can ignore my beneficent offer, refuse to throw the competition at all. Then the producers find out, and if they don't like what they see, you won't get a dime. So it's up to you how much you want to wager on a roll of the dice."

"Fucking asshole." Tristan stepped up next to Henry. "I actually kind of liked you. And you turn around and do this?"

"Turn around? Please." She rolled her eyes. "I knew you two were competition from the start, and I'm here to compete. You think I've been sitting with my thumb up my ass? Please. This is just the first real dirt I've managed to get on you, and it's pretty clean dirt. You're good guys. Don't let hubris get in your way, boys."

"So this show isn't even about competition to you? This isn't about honor and baking?" Tristan wanted to punch her. A couple more Manhattans, he might have been seriously tempted, but he was still sober enough to know clocking an old lady was in bad taste. "You want to turn us in to the producers for going against the spirit of this competition, but this is how you've been playing?"

"I don't *want* to do anything. Ball's in your court. I'm giving you a chance to not go out like Bertha did."

"Like Bertha did?" Tristan shook his head. "It was your recipe. Did you . . . set her up?"

Willa just turned, lips barely curling upward, and walked her smug ass into the hotel.

What was this? Tristan couldn't quite pull himself together. His thoughts swam and chased each other in fruitless circles. *Willa and Bertha. Chiffon cake. Losing the competition. Losing the money. Lucia. Robert. Henry. Willa. Bertha.* Willa had to have been the snitch. That was the only way that her comment made sense.

Henry whipped around. "I am calling the producer in the morning and telling him about this."

"Telling him about what? That Willa threatened to report us? She's *supposed* to. Or should we mention that I gave you that chiffon cake recipe? Is that what you think we should tell them?" Already, Tristan's mind followed out the lines of probability, tracking the worst-case scenarios, looking for a solution if there was one to be had. Most of them led to this all being for naught. "If anyone goes to McCall, then all of that gets laid bare. And if they decide the possibility of us having cheated is too high, it doesn't matter if Willa was trying to cheat. We still lose."

"She all but admitted that she sabotaged Bertha."

"Plausible deniability. That's how this works."

Henry punched the air as though that were going to do anything. "Well, fuck her."

"If we'd been a little more careful, this wouldn't have happened. I got too into the moment. I was riding the high. I—"

"Hey." Henry grabbed him by the shoulders and led him over to the wall of the hotel, his brows knitting. "Tristan. Chill."

And then Tristan was back in that hall at the award show and everything felt hot. He identified the snap coming a second too late. "Just stop." He knocked Henry's hands away. *I need space. I can't breathe.* "You know how important this is. I've made it clear how scared I've been. But you still grabbed my hand under the fucking table?"

"What? Tristan, you need to calm down."

"Do not tell me to calm down. No." If he lost his place here, he'd lose all the money from his appearance. He'd lose any chance at the quarter million. He and his sister would be struggling to eat, let alone to sever her legal ties to Robert.

When he was around Henry, he felt like he was flying. But now he'd gone too close to the sun. "We have as long as we want back in Seattle, Henry. Why couldn't you wait it out?"

"Tristan—"

"I might lose everything. It all got put at risk, and I didn't even get a say."

Henry's lips curled into a sneer. "You're acting like I don't have anything on the line here. I have to prove to—" His jaw clamped shut over the end of that sentence. "What about my *reputation*? What do you have that's so import—"

His eyes widened and he started into some stuttering defense, but the words were out.

Tristan couldn't let them go. "My *sister*. My apartment. Maybe my job if Carlita doesn't like the way this plays in public." How could Henry be acting like this? He knew—he knew everything. Tristan had dared to open up about . . . everything. He'd laid himself out for Henry, and yet it didn't seem to mean jack shit.

"I know you have a lot at stake." Henry's voice was quieter. "I'm not trying to belittle that."

"You're not trying to belittle it? A couple people say you're not the best baker in the country. Boo-hoo. If this ends for me, I'm opening more credit cards, and Lucia's God knows where. All you have at stake is your ego, and you've got enough of that to go around."

"Tristan . . ."

What kind of brother would he be if he put Lucia at risk for this relationship? He had to stay, no matter the cost. And maybe if Henry didn't think that was *important* enough, Tristan didn't need him.

He shook his head, and almost couldn't believe this was only a few hours after that heady exchange in the hotel room. Just like then, his emotions spilled past his lips. "I think . . . I want my own bed tonight."

Henry stared slack-jawed. "Tristan, that's ridiculous. We need to be together, work this out. We need a plan."

"For fuck's sake, no, Henry." Tristan's voice gruffed, sliding sharp out of his throat. "If you love me like you say you do, then *listen* to me. I know you mean well, but you're being self-centered. Make room for me . . . go sleep in your own bed. Please."

Each step he took away from Henry ached in his middle, and he fought the tears prickling against the backs of his eyes. But no footsteps followed him into the lobby, into the elevator, down the hallway.

He flipped the swing bar closed once he got inside, slumped down, and clutched himself. This room of his—of theirs—was so large, so empty, so cold and quiet. So he filled the emptiness with sobs.

Chapter Eighteen

Henry sat down in the lobby of the hotel, clutching a cardboard coffee cup from the shop down the block. He hadn't been able to sleep, still felt the claws of exhaustion ripping away at him even as the caffeine battled to keep him upright. But his empty bed, the lack of a warm body beside him, no gentle breath filtering through the space, they had been bigger distractions than anything that happened with Willa.

In his sleepless fugue, Henry had thought through dozens of possible solutions. He could murder Willa—that would sate his rage, at least, but it wouldn't fix anything. He could knock on Tristan's door and force him to get up, but that would doubly prove he was selfish.

And that wouldn't have been an incorrect conclusion. After all, Henry had done everything for himself, and had ignored what Tristan needed. The emptiness and cold enveloping him now proved it. He'd *needed* Tristan, and hadn't stopped until he'd fulfilled his own desires. Not once had he considered what Tristan needed in return.

That selfishness wasn't limited to the big picture, with Lucia and Tristan's finances and how much Tristan *actually* needed to stay around here. It had been present in every little interaction. Henry was the one who'd called on him out of the blue because he couldn't stand being alone anymore. He was the one who had asked for the damn recipe. He *had* grabbed Tristan's hand because he'd wanted to touch him. And he knew he wasn't keeping his mouth shut enough on set. He got too wrapped up and forgot himself too often.

Now not only had he blown up his own happiness . . . Tristan's *home*, his *family* were at risk of implosion.

He fumbled out his phone, nearly dropping it in his daze. It was early, but hopefully not too early. He tapped Carrie's name, and she picked up after one ring. "You're up early."

"Yeah. Couldn't sleep." It was good to hear her slightly guttural rasp again, even over the phone. Especially right now. "I may have screwed some shit up. By being selfish."

"This isn't Lance baggage again, is it? Because you know where I fall on that son of a bitch."

"It's not Lance this time. But I think I majorly fucked up, Carrie."

And he launched into the whole sordid story. Well, not the *whole* story. He left out the parts that were private to Tristan, only mentioning that *he* needed the money and Henry flat out didn't.

When he'd finished, Carrie sighed. "Sounds like you messed up."

A cold shock spiked down his middle. "You're not going to disagree and try to boost my spirits, here?"

"I love you more than fucking life, Henry. And you're not some ass-bag waste of skin like this Willa lady—I'll happily put the smackdown on a grandma if that's what you need me to do to her, by the way. But you're right. You screwed up this time. You don't need to dwell on it, though."

"I'm just supposed to move on? Like that wouldn't be selfish too?"

"No. You're supposed to make it right. If you're this crazy over Tristan, try to fix it. Then if he doesn't want to get back into that business, at least you'll know you owned up to your shit."

It made sense, even if it sucked to not get reassurance. "I wouldn't forgive me."

"Yeah, well, you hold yourself to impossible standards. Maybe he won't be so exacting." She yawned. "Listen, got a big day at the office. I need to jump my happy ass in the shower. You want to come in with me, or are you good?"

"You know I'd always shower with you, but I think I'm okay." As okay as he could be, anyway. "Thanks for being around."

"Anytime, sweet cheeks. You call anytime you need to. And I don't want to say to hurry home, but I can't wait until I can see your face again."

In spite of everything, Henry couldn't help a tiny smile. "You too, hon."

He hung up and sighed. He *did* want to try to correct the situation with Tristan, whatever that looked like. It wasn't as if he didn't have ideas. A night of not sleeping had left a lot of time for overthinking.

Henry doubted either Willa or Tristan had awoken. So he'd wait, ready to catch whoever showed up first. His plans were all half-baked, but he wasn't about to wait around for things to get any worse. So he sat, keeping his eyes peeled.

In the end, Willa stepped out of the elevator first, just before seven in the morning. She wore a simple navy T-shirt and jeans that belied her dastardly, scheming ways. Henry rose and met her outside on the sidewalk. "We should talk." This wasn't his preferred plan—he would have preferred the fantasy plan where he ran into Tristan and they decided love was enough and they'd be able to get by—but it might be the best.

"We talked last night, Henry. Cavorting with *all* your fellow competitors, now?" She faced him head on. "What didn't I make clear?"

Nothing. She'd left not one damn thing unclear, but Henry needed to do something, do whatever he could manage to make this up to Tristan. To *save* Tristan from Henry's own damn selfishness. "If you leave Tristan alone, fight it out fair and square in the final, I'll leave without a fuss. Please."

"You actually do care about him." She smiled, shaking her head. "If you're worried about him dealing with me by himself, then tell him to throw this round, then *you* can join me next time."

"He doesn't need to know about any of this." Would anything Henry said get through to her, make her have half an ounce of compassion? "He's struggling, okay? He needs this money. I will step out of your way gladly, but give him a shot. Be a decent human being and let him have his chance to win."

"Why?"

Henry sighed. "Because you have a heart, and I'm coming to the negotiating table and willing to do what it is you want. I may have my life under control, but he's still trying to sort his out. So I'm begging you. I'll get down on my knees if I have to." If she asked, he would drop down right on the pavement. "Let Tristan have a fair shot. Your business is going to amp way up anyway just from being in the finals."

She had to give him an inch here. This was his only way of getting Tristan a chance.

A car pulled up at the curb and Henry checked his phone, but his ride was still on the way. Willa opened the back door. "Negotiations have fallen apart, Henry. I want to win this. I'm old, I'm tired, and I'm not making you any promises."

Damn it. Only one option left to try. "Then consider this." His stomach was tight as he spoke, but this wasn't about *his* feelings. For once, it wasn't. "You agree, or I out the whole thing. The blackmail. Bertha. We can all go down with the ship."

Her eyes narrowed. "You wouldn't. Not if it hurts him."

"You don't know jack about me. You were right that I'm a threat, though. Being gay's given me a lifetime of experience dealing with people trying to make my life worse. That might not be why *you're* targeting me, but I can handle you too." That realization had been the only silver lining of the evening. It had cleared some of the baggage from Henry's head. He was a contender. Being gay *hadn't* spoiled that. His mother's worst fears *hadn't* come to pass. "Don't know if you're familiar with your gay history, but we've always fought back. Sometimes with bricks, sometimes with lawsuits, but we fight. *I'm a fighter.*" And unfortunately, in a fight, sometimes there were casualties. Throwing Willa under the bus *would* hurt Tristan. Materially. But Henry had minimal leverage here. He had to pull every single lever at his disposal. "If the options are you get away with this and we both lose, or you don't get away with this and we both lose?" Henry shrugged, feigning as much nonchalance as he could. "And maybe I've been recording this conversation. Did you consider that?"

That seemed to knock her back a little, and Henry shook his phone. Her face tensed. Henry raised an eyebrow and shrugged, leaving his comment to stand.

Finally, she snorted, face contorted into a scowl. "I want to see you off the show first. Then we can talk." She slid into the back seat without another word.

Henry shivered. His play had been pure bluff. *Wish I would have thought to actually record the conversation.* But it seemed to have put Willa back on her heels. He felt a little better about leaving. He'd won himself some room to maneuver, and hopefully won Tristan a chance to get the money he needed. It pained Henry to think about leaving Tristan to deal with her by himself . . . but Tristan *needed* the money.

And Tristan's need to protect Lucia was way, way more important than his own desire to prove himself. He would give up every ounce of recognition for Tristan. *And I might have to if I'm going to get us out of this.*

The kitchen didn't bustle, was dead quiet as they all worked their chocolate, fighting with temperature and crystal structures. Tristan pointedly didn't look away from his station. He didn't want to see Willa, and he couldn't risk seeing Henry. His stomach still roiled when he thought about the scrape of his stubble and his coconut cologne. Too many conflicting emotions, all clashing into a mess in his middle.

Tristan couldn't keep his mind off Henry though, looking at him or not. A voice in his head constantly sang Henry's virtues. He was perfect and lovely and talented and he opened Tristan up in a way Tristan hadn't let himself be opened in too long.

He'd also been the one-way ticket straight out of the money Tristan needed for Lucia. Henry was obsessed with his own pleasure, his own wants . . . even though Tristan could have pulled his hand away that night, could have not drank so much that he hadn't noticed the flash from Willa's phone.

"Can you grab that whisk?"

Tristan automatically turned at the voice. Henry stood at the counter behind him as always. Scruffy already in spite of shaving clean the night before, wearing a tight T-shirt. Dark crescents sliced away under his eyes, and he was pale, his body tight. Henry's visage tore apart Tristan's middle. He still cared about Henry. Cared so much that his skin burned to touch him, to be near him. So much that he could wind up doing something immensely stupid like fucking over his sister, his life, if he let himself relax.

So Tristan bent down and picked up the whisk. "Here."

"Thanks." Henry touched Tristan's knuckles briefly as he took it, and he locked his eyes on Tristan. "Something came up at the shop . . . so I might have to head home."

And that one stilted, softly whispered sentence crashed into Tristan, shattered all his conflicting feelings and left a gaping maw in its wake. "Henry."

"Good luck if I have to head home." Henry briefly washed the whisk, then went back to his ganache.

Tristan turned off his burners and his oven, forcing his breath to steady. A cigarette was the answer. Now. He double-checked to make sure everything was off, that he wouldn't burn the place down, then beelined for the back door. Out in the wide world, Henry wasn't talking about forfeiting, about leaving. There was just fresh summer air that knew nothing of Tristan's panic.

He's leaving for me. Henry wouldn't back down from this fight for shits and giggles. No, this was Henry tossing all his desires aside to get a highfalutin caterer one more round's worth of pay.

Tristan's hands shook so hard he struggled to light up, had to flick the lighter a full five times before he finally got the flame steady enough to light his cigarette. Then he sucked in deep and waited for the nicotine to wind its way around all his concerns and worries and anger and . . . everything.

Nothing. The fragrant smoke did nothing for him as it filled his lungs. No calm. No peace. Not even a glimmer of something that resembled that normal, drug-induced relaxation.

His phone buzzed. It was a notification from his cloud storage. *Classic chiffon recipe.rtf privacy settings changed.* He tapped the notification and saw Henry Isaacson had relinquished access to the file. With a note.

Just in case.

The recipe that Tristan had given him after that first night together. His breath hitched in his throat, and not because of the cigarette currently hanging limp from his lips. If they were coming back to this . . . Was that the end? It felt too significant, too circular for him to ignore. If he'd needed more proof that he could *trust* Henry to do the right thing . . . his phone had given him that.

The door opened and Tristan whipped around, hoping in every fiber for Henry to come outside. It was irrational, against everything he'd been asking for, but he needed that touch.

A production assistant walked out, muttering over a list. She didn't even look at Tristan as she strode past.

How could it end this way? Willa had won so easily. Tristan's chest tightened, fingers tingling with misplaced adrenaline. It wasn't right. It wasn't fair. To either of them. But what was the recourse? Tristan's breath stuttered out, and he hastily snuffed his ignored cigarette before it could fall and burn him. The thing was useless anyway. The nicotine wasn't stopping the itch behind his eyes or quelling his thrashing heartbeat. He leaned against the wall, but his mind wouldn't clarify, buzzing nonstop as pieces of himself collapsed.

His hand shook as he desperately wriggled his phone out, dialed up Lucia. Each ring stretched forever, a lifetime, an eternity between him and someone who could hold him steady. One ring, two . . . finally. "Hello?"

"Lucia." He could hear the desperation in his own voice. "Henry and I had a fight and he's going to throw the competition and I—I called him selfish." Thoughts spewed out of his mouth without coherence, falling forward as they occurred to him. "I don't know what to do and I don't want him gone but I don't want to leave. I don't have any—"

"Tristan!" Her voice was sharp. "You are spiraling. What is actually happening?"

He tried to respond, but no words came out.

"Tristan, breathe with me. Come on." She took exaggeratedly loud breaths, in and out. Slowly, Tristan fell into rhythm with her, tapping the crushed half-cigarette to count the seconds.

After about a minute, he managed a "Thank you." He took a few more breaths to try to collect himself, then gave her a brief rundown. The threat from Willa. The hand touching. He left out how they felt about each other. "And now he . . . he's implying he wants to forfeit. For me." *And for you.*

"Jesus. You have to tell someone."

"But what if they kick us out because of it? How is he going to recover? How can I face up to Carlita? What if this comes out and wrecks *her* business?"

"Tristan. This is your schtick, you know that?" Her voice was soft and full of . . . God, was that pity? From his little sister? "You can't control everything in the whole world. You can't bear all this weight all the time. That's how you end up like Mom. Miserable, then dead."

Tristan wanted to argue, but that had been their mother. She'd taken as much as she could for the two of them, and now she was gone. So instead of arguing, he said, "That's not what this is about."

"You want everything to be okay for you and for Henry, and for Carlita, and you're worried about the competition, and the prize money, and, and, and. Stop when I say something wrong."

"What am I supposed to ignore?" The only way to make this clear to her was to drop the big bombshell. "The money is for debts, and for living expenses, and now repairs to my apartment, and to keep you safe."

The line went silent for quite a while before she said, "To make sure I don't go back to Robert."

Tristan cringed at the hurt and tightness in her voice. "Yeah."

"Tristan. Take me off your list. I'm not. Going back. To Robert. And what, you think I'm not going to get a job now that fucker doesn't have me under lock and key? Come on, Tristan."

"What? You need to recover."

"Oh, I need to recover? Well, getting back into life and getting a job are part of that." Her tone was slightly playful. "Look, I'm going to give you one piece of advice, and for the love of God you're going to listen to what I have to say. Take care of yourself. Not me. Do what's right for you, and from the way you talk about Henry, that relationship is what's right. Money is money. You'll get more. But are you going to be able to live with yourself if you let Henry throw this away without trying to stop him? If you let him walk away? And is your budding relationship going to survive that?"

"Lucia, listen—"

"No, we had an agreement. You're listening to me. You're going to do what I say. You're going to stand up for someone who makes you so happy that the thought of him getting hurt sent you into a panic attack."

Tristan sighed. "But what does that look like?"

"Whatever it needs to look like." She'd taken a clipped, almost militaristic tone, now. And in spite of himself, Tristan felt *better* at the prospect of someone else taking charge. Lucia getting a job wasn't what he wanted, and even if she did, it wouldn't replace his oven or clear out his credit cards. But just talking to her about this had lifted a twenty-pound weight from his shoulders.

Tristan stuffed his half-used cigarette back into the pack, then sighed. "I've been out here a long time. I need to get back in. Unless you have more orders?"

"Take a breath, then forget about protecting me and take care of you and Henry. And uncurl your toes. You always bunch up your toes when you're really freaking out."

And now that she mentioned it . . . yeah, they were all curled up inside his shoes. "Thanks. I love you, Lucia."

"I love you too. Neuroses and all."

The line went dead, and Tristan blew out a long breath, before turning around and heading back inside. *Take care of me and Henry?* What did that look like? What was his plan? He stepped back on set and locked his eyes on Willa, and then on Henry. Her smug, him visibly shattered.

And that just wasn't okay.

It was time for judging to begin. All three of them had plugged away, whipping ganache, making custard, tempering chocolate for their giant centerpieces. Henry wanted to toss Willa off a cliff and into a pool of lava, but there was no denying she was a damn good baker. All of them were. Today, they'd made rich chocolate pies, six beautiful chocolate soufflés apiece, and finally centerpieces and the individual confections to accompany them. Willa had gone booze-themed, spiking all her chocolates with brandy and crème de cacao and whiskey. Tristan had been bold with his flavors, using candied ginger and lemongrass and chili-spiced walnuts. And Henry, in spite of the weight crushing him, had made his mark, or at least he thought so. The judges had all loved his chocolate-covered pralines and the caramelized white chocolate truffles and even his smoky, peaty Scotch cream chocolates.

Their work on the actual centerpieces had been on par, no one obviously pulling ahead as far as Henry could tell. Now the judges were deliberating, and Henry couldn't help but glance to Willa one more time. She smiled serenely at him, as though they didn't all know what the hell she'd done.

It wasn't long before the judges finished and the cameras swung back into place. In the semifinal, there should have been some anticipation, but Henry could only muster the most robotic of customer-service smiles. Sylvia stared at them, no smile on her face. "The final three chefs. You've all come so far at this point and done some amazing things in this kitchen. It's a shame to see any of you go, but that's the unfortunate reality." She sighed. "But first the good news. Someone really pulled out all the stops to bring us something spectacular. An eye-catching centerpiece worthy of any event, perfect chocolate soufflés, and a stunning pie." She clapped her hands once, very quietly. "Congratulations, Tristan. Well, well done."

There was light applause to greet him, but the clapping fell quite short, especially from Willa. No surprise.

Sylvia's smile faded quickly. "And there is, as always, bitter to go with the sweet. Sometimes, it has to come down to the events of one day. All of you are absolutely amazing chefs, but the one who has to leave today . . . is Willa."

She gave zero response. The judges shifted uncomfortably in place, Eli glancing to the other two, seemingly seeking some information. Willa stood stiff and plain-faced, but her knuckles were white, fingers balled into tight fists. He doubted she'd stay quiet long. Henry had to act now.

"Actually, I need to step down."

All eyes swiveled toward Henry, as well as the cameras. He was met with a dozen or more gawking stares, and if the silence when Willa lost the challenge had been heavy, this was deafening.

Rita apparently collected herself before everyone else. "What did you say, Henry?"

"I'm forfeiting."

"No." Tristan shook his head, eyes wide. "Henry, no."

"Yes." Henry tried to calm the rumbling in his stomach. "I can't stay here anymore. I need to head home. There's . . . an issue with the shop. I'm sorry."

"No, Henry." Tristan stepped in front of him and grabbed his shoulders. "This isn't right. You deserve to stay."

"But I can't." He took the opportunity to look Tristan straight on and willed him to understand, willed him to get *why*. "You need to stay and do Seattle proud. I need to . . . get out of the way."

Tristan's eyes widened in his pale face. Then he whipped around and stood straight in front of Henry like a wall. "He's leaving because Willa blackmailed us. Henry . . . Henry and I have been seeing each other, and she threatened to go to the producers and out us."

Holy shit. Henry didn't quite know what to make of that. He'd have happily crowed about their relationship from the top of the Golden Gate Bridge if it had been safe. But *Tristan* had told them? Out loud? What about Lucia? What about the money? Did that mean they were . . . What did that mean for the pair of them?

Willa finally unclenched her fists. "These boys are not playing kosher, and all I tried to do was give them the chance to save face. Guess they didn't want that, so let's lay out all the cards."

Dexter stepped out from behind the café table. "What are you talking about?"

"They've got their little romance on the side, and they're helping each other out for God knows how long. Maybe from the very start."

Sylvia stared slack-jawed at the judges, then to the director tucked in the back corner. But it was Dexter who finally spoke, turning toward the open backstage. "Jacob, I think maybe we should cut for a second while we sort this out."

Little red lights flicked off all over set as the cameras shut down. They were taking the accusation seriously, and that didn't give Henry any hope. Why couldn't Tristan let him make this right? Why couldn't he *trust* that Henry knew what he was doing?

Dexter came down into the aisle between the two rows of stations. "Why don't you be very clear about what you're claiming, Willa."

"They are an item, and they have been for a while now." She pulled her phone out of her back pocket and flashed the screen to Dexter. "That's them trying to be secret and hold hands at the Bluestone Lotus, and Finn walked out on them kissing behind the studio."

Goddamn. Henry's gut tightened a little. He'd assured Tristan that Finn was solid. Apparently not.

Dexter nodded and went back to the other two judges. They huddled together, whispering and . . . fuck. Henry turned toward Tristan. "What was that?"

"I'm sorry. I hope that wasn't too far. But I can't let you throw this away."

Some of the tightness in Henry's abdomen faded slightly. Not much, but slightly. "What about . . . everything?"

Tristan sighed. "I hashed it out with Lucia. As much as you can in the middle of a panic attack." He laughed nervously. "She laid my ass out and told me if I care about you, I'd better damn well try to stop you from leaving."

"I was ready to."

"I gathered from the giant forfeit scene." Tristan shook his head. "Did I go too far?"

"Not unless you think you did. I'm more worried about you and how this is going to play out." Henry looked over at the judges, who were still discussing. "Is this going to fuck you hard? Because I can always try to help you out—"

"Did I take your money last time?" And for the first time in way too long, Tristan smiled. A tiny smile, but it lightened up Henry's entire mood. He'd missed those dimples. "I'm not doing it now, either. I'll fight you if I have to."

Dexter separated from Rita and Eli and glanced over his shoulder. "Kristin, Call Mr. McCall. Tell him we need some info on the rules and we might be able to get a big ratings hike. Whatever it takes to get him down here pronto." He had no smile when he turned toward Willa. "However this turns out, I have to say I'm . . . disappointed."

She snorted. "Rules are rules."

A few minutes later, the short, mustachioed Mark McCall strode out from backstage. He wore a gray suit and a red tie and presented more professionally than anyone else on the set. He walked up and shook Dexter's hand. "You caught me before I headed home. Lucky for you I had to work late today. What's urgent?"

"Rules dispute. Big issue here in the semifinals. We need someone in a higher-up position than us. We discussed and we're at a loss."

This could be it. The end of it all. Tristan would have stepped in for him and lost so much more than Henry'd ever had on the line. The possibility churned his stomach.

If Tristan could risk everything, Henry wouldn't simply stand the fuck down.

The man frowned, cutting deep lines into his face and rustling his mustache. "Well, what's the problem? It was a pretty boilerplate set of agreements everyone signed, I know them backward and forward."

Dexter nodded. "Is there an issue if two of the contestants end up in a romantic relationship?"

"One that's been going on a while," said Willa coldly. "These two are an item."

"I see." McCall turned to them. "Are you two together, then?"

Tristan nodded. "Yeah. It happened while we were here." The slight quiver in his voice betrayed his nerves, but he was otherwise solid. "Once Willa found out, she decided to turn that against us. But I figured that would fall apart if I laid everything out. No more power to her threat."

McCall actually smiled. Then he sighed and massaged the bridge of his nose. "It all really comes down to whether you two worked together, then."

"Well, of course they did." Willa's voice had an angry edge to it now, and her arms slipped to her sides, fists balling. "A couple, and you think they're not out there helping each other stay in this thing?"

"I think that's not a given." McCall sighed again, running a hand through his hair. "And if there's evidence of blackmail on your part, that's not good either."

That was Henry's chance to do something. He slipped out his phone and looked over at Willa. Was she going to call his bluff?

She flinched. "I wasn't trying to blackmail anyone. Like I said, I wanted them to have a face-saving way out. It *happened* to mean they would step aside and I would win. Coincidence."

McCall shook his head. "Frankly, let's not pretend that makes any sense. Whatever your professed reasons are, blackmail is blackmail. Call a duck a duck." He turned his gaze back to Henry and Tristan. "Did you help each other out in this competition at all? We'll start there."

"No more than any of us helped each other," said Tristan. "Put bakers in a room and they're going to talk to each other. Baking techniques are inevitably going to come up. But my recipes were mine and Henry's were his. I'm assuming saying that isn't enough, though."

And there was that smile again, just for a moment. McCall, at least, seemed to like Tristan. Henry didn't know if that was going to help, but it couldn't be *bad* for their case, right?

"The editors have footage. They would have caught anything on filming days. I trust them." He faced Dexter, Rita, and Eli. "Do you three have any reasons to be suspicious of them?"

They all glanced at each other, but Dexter was the one who stepped up. "There's no evidence we could think of when we were discussing. They've put out very unique products. It's a totally different situation than what went down with Bertha." He nodded to Willa. "It's also worth noting, the only reason we found out someone had used her recipe was because she came forward to tell us."

"So this isn't the first time she's stepped in? But you didn't suspect her earlier?"

Dexter shook his head. "The crew and us looked for potential wrongdoing, but her story checked out."

"What was that story?"

"She showed Bertha the recipe to illustrate some techniques. Then Bertha used the recipe in its entirety. Didn't see any clear sign not to trust Willa. As far as we could see, she'd been taken advantage of, and we didn't want to punish someone for that."

McCall nodded and fixed his eyes on Willa. "We can circle back to that later. Do you have *evidence* for your claims about these two boys?"

"I have photo evidence of them holding hands at dinner."

"But do you have evidence of them actually cheating? Because being a couple isn't a violation of the contract."

"What?" Willa marched over to him. "How in the hell can this be okay? A couple that isn't working together? You buy that?"

"What I buy is the lawyers who put together these contracts. I know the verbiage inside and out." He turned back to Henry and Tristan. "There's going to be a lot of paperwork to make sure this is above board. Disclosures, affidavits, that sort of thing. The lawyers need to dot the i's and cross the t's on something like this."

Willa crossed her arms again. "This is completely outrageous."

"No, what's outrageous is that this happened in our first season." McCall tossed his arms out, and the twinge of a smile pulled at his face again. "A scandal like this in the semifinals of season one? Ratings are going to be *huge*."

Willa stood gape-mouthed, fuming at all of them. "And what happens if you let them go forward, then find out they worked on every single round together? What then?"

"The winner won't get the big check for a couple months after filming ends. Plenty of time for us to comb through the footage for any wrongdoing." McCall nodded at Tristan and Henry in turn. "If we find out that all three of our semifinalists were cheating, then third runner up will get the quarter million, and we'll have ratings through the roof from the scandal. It's a very simple setup."

Was this . . . working out? Henry struggled against the warm balloon of hope buoying in his chest. The only worry was the chiffon recipe. He knew their recipes were separate though, had returned the chiffon cake recipe to Tristan to be certain. And no one was going to mistake Henry's chiffon for Tristan's. Well, no one in this room, with the skill sets they had.

McCall turned to face Tristan and Henry full on and shrugged. "Well, boys, mazel on the love and mazel on making it through to the finals. Just promise me you're going to duke it out as hard as ever in the last round?"

Henry rolled his eyes and relished the rage burning through Willa's features as he spoke. "I came here to prove myself against the best. The way I see it, having to go up against someone I'm dating means I have impeccable taste."

Tristan scoffed. "And an ego. Don't forget that ego you have to carry around with you, day in, day out. If I let you win, think how insufferable you'd be."

McCall smiled contentedly, then turned to the judges. "If that's all the drama you have for me, things will continue on as per usual. We'll be in touch if anything comes up, boys." He faced Willa. "As for you, the check will be in the mail to compensate you for your time spent here." He shook his head, laughing incredulously. "An actual romance *and* a blackmailing scandal. We need to get that into the press releases as soon as we possibly can."

Dexter cleared his throat and pointed toward Tristan and Henry. "You maybe want to bring that up with them?"

"Oh God, of course. I thought that was implied." McCall cast his gaze over Tristan and Henry one last time. "You guys mind doing about a million interviews? Because I don't think you're going to escape it once this hits. But we can try to keep it quiet if that'd make you feel better. No promises, though. These things have a tendency to slip out."

Henry looked at Tristan and his slowly fading smile. Then he shrugged. "Let's talk about it after the final. Don't want anything getting in the way of us competing, right?"

"Right." Mr. McCall stepped away. "You can get on with any last filming you might need to do." And off went Mark McCall, savior of the gay romances. At least today.

Willa's face snarled into a deep frown. But what could she possibly say? Even trying to twist himself around to her way of thinking, Henry saw no argument she could leverage. Not without making an even bigger fool of herself.

And to her own credit, she didn't try. She just stood there, frowning.

The director scrubbed a hand over his face. "I don't think we have anything else to film. If we do, well . . . fucking shit, I don't know, let's call it a wrap." He tore off his headset. "Those two backup cameras better not have stopped working."

"Backup cameras?" Henry quirked an eyebrow at him. "What do you mean?"

"Whenever we cut the normal cameras, we keep two recording. This is reality TV, boys. Missing out on something like this is not an option. Especially when you've all been so terribly *nice* to each other up until now." He gestured to Tristan and Henry with his headset. "You and you, interviews. Willa, if you feel like cooperating, give an interview. If not, don't. Either way, the editors and I can make good TV out of what happened."

She snorted. "Pass."

And off she went, taking every bit of blackmail and stress and cheating with her. Plus apparently the two-ton weight that lifted off Henry's chest. The lights on the cameras flickered back to life. The cleaver ceremony was somber this time. But damn was it ever sweet to watch that giant knife slam through all of Willa's chocolate, shattering it apart, just like her plan.

And more importantly, he and Tristan . . . they got to stay. Together. Henry would have to find out what the hell had happened, what Tristan had been thinking. But for now, he let those questions sit in his stomach.

Tentatively, he offered Tristan his hand.

And on set, in front of everyone, Tristan took it.

Chapter Nineteen

"**I** can't believe it actually worked out . . . well." Tristan slid his key card into the lock and opened up the hotel room. Clean and picture perfect, so obviously housekeeping had ignored the Do Not Disturb sign.

"I know. But I'm not complaining." Henry held the door open for him and, as Tristan passed through, slapped him on the ass. "Whoops. My hand slipped."

"Right. I *definitely* believe that."

"Oh, as if you didn't like it."

"That's beside the point." Tristan came around the little dividing wall to the bathroom and saw a large wicker basket set near the head of the bed. "Wow, I guess someone appreciates me." Inside, there was a bottle of champagne—the French stuff, not California Champagne or generic sparkling wine—a vase with an arrangement of lilacs and baby's breath, a rather large box of local artisan chocolates, and a card. He pulled off the card and flipped it open. "'Congratulations on making the final. Good luck. Best wishes. Rita, Dexter, and Eli.'"

"How exceedingly generic of them."

Tristan set the card on the table, moved the basket, and lay out on his bed. On *their* bed. He'd never felt so free and open as he did in that moment. "They probably got this all set up days ago, when they didn't know who was going to make it."

"Then I'm going to head off to my hotel room real quick."

"What? Why?"

Henry opened the door, but turned around and winked. "One bottle of champagne is nice. Two is a celebration."

Tristan slipped off his shoes. "Well then, let's have a celebration."

Henry nodded. "Back in a jiffy. Don't lock me out."

Tristan sighed as Henry left the room. They were almost done. They'd gotten through fucking Willa. They'd gotten through eight rounds of the competition without cracking. They'd gotten through their own bullshit anger with each other.

Tristan slid his phone free from his pocket and dialed up Lucia. "Hello?"

"Hey, Lucia. I didn't wake you up, right?"

"No. Karen and I rented a couple movies. Chick-flick shirtless-actor kind of movies, since we can't watch those when you're around."

"According to who? Those are my favorites."

"Could have fooled me, the way you bitched all through *Her Vibrant Roses*."

"I bitched because nothing happened in that movie. It was literally all set in the same room. Start to finish. Plus the only guy who took his shirt off was Mr. Neanderthal Forehead Ridge with the tiny squinty eyes."

"But his *arms*, Tristan. His arms are wonderful."

"Good luck making out with his arms."

"You name the time and place and I will take that challenge."

Tristan snorted a laugh. There was a knock at the door, and he jumped up to open it. "So I have some good news if you can keep your lips totally closed. Not even a peep to Karen, swear on Tia's grave."

"Awfully secretive for some good news."

Tristan opened the door on Henry. Henry and a completely identical wicker basket. He blew Henry a kiss before continuing with Lucia. "I mean, if you don't want to know, that's fine."

"Jesus, let me save you *and* me the trouble: you're in the final, right?"

"How the *hell*—"

"You do three days of practice and one filming day. I can do math, and I can *also* look at a calendar and do math. It's called multitasking."

Tristan groaned. "So much for my big reveal. It's still best if you don't mention it to anyone."

"I'm not going to. But spoiler alert: Karen knows too. I've got big Xs on the calendar marking the days you've been away and this might shock you, but Karen can count."

Tristan chuckled. "All right, all right. You have anything to say?"

"Aren't you glad I made you go?"

"Anything *else*?"

"Like what? You don't need to hear that I'm proud of you. Not for this. There's a hundred things I'm proud of you for every day. Cooking is down on the bottom of the list, no offense meant. But I suppose it *is* on the list. I'll be prouder when you win."

"I guess I have to win, then." He smiled even though she couldn't see it. "How are you holding up?"

"I'm fine. You don't have to keep asking me. I'm not going back to him, and he's behind bars. I'll have to see him in court, but since the restraining order I just got is miraculously still in place, that's all."

"God, would you believe I missed your sarcastic side?"

"Yeah . . . me too. I was catty as hell in my head. Tried a few times out loud, but Robert made it *clear* he didn't appreciate that. No matter how hilarious I was."

Tristan resisted a sharp gasp. *Stay upbeat, stay light.* "Hilarious? I see you're as humble as ever too."

"I'm being a realist. So, how did stuff go with the whole Willa, Henry, listening-to-your-baby-sister ordeal?"

"What do you want to hear, how brilliant you are?"

"It wouldn't hurt my feelings. I take it things went well?"

"Well enough that Henry and I are planning on some champagne for the evening." He winked at Henry. "All right, go back to your chick flicks, and tell Karen I'll kill her if she lets this slip."

"No problem, will do. Oh, and you should call Carlita. She's constantly on the phone here, trying to find out how long it's going to be until you're back. Doesn't want to call you and distract you with those worries, since you're out there doing publicity for her, but she's anxious. Apparently the pastry chef she brought in while you were gone is . . . How did she put it? 'A goddamn waste of flesh and buttercream.'"

"I'll call her tomorrow at a reasonable hour, but if she gets to you before I get to her, let her know I'll be home inside a week."

"I have something to tell her. Awesome." She sighed. "And I'm glad you're coming back soon. I make major life changes and I don't get to celebrate with my big brother. That's fucked up."

"Maybe next time you won't send him off on the best baking adventure of his life."

"Maybe next time I won't. Now let me go watch my movies."

"You got it." Tristan hung up the phone and smiled. Lucia was herself again. This was the sister he'd grown up with.

"So, do you know how to open champagne?" Henry wiggled the bottle at him. "I feel like there's a good chance I might blow my head off with the cork if I try, but you do wedding stuff and . . ." Another bottle wiggle.

"Wedding stuff has nothing to do with this. FYI." Tristan snatched the bottle and set it aside. "Ice first, because room-temp champagne is going to explode everywhere. Period. But I'll open it for you when the time comes. A champagne cork doesn't have enough force to kill, but it would be such a shame for you to get a black eye right before the final. What would all the pretty girls think?"

"Pretty girls? We're not teenage heartthrobs, we're pastry chefs." Henry scooted over and draped himself across Tristan. "And, believe it or not, I don't care what the pretty girls say, regardless. I wouldn't even if I *was* a teenage heartthrob." He kissed Tristan on the cheek. "I've already found somebody much prettier."

"Oh, I'm the pretty one. Cool, I never get to be the pretty one in the relationship."

Henry rolled his eyes, then rose from the bed. "I'll get the ice, but we *are* having champagne tonight. At least one glass."

"Agreed. Flip the thingy so the door stays open."

Henry wandered back out and Tristan pulled the sheet of paper the crew had given him from the nightstand drawer. It was a long, grueling day they had coming. Cheesecake: six hours. Angel food cake: four hours. And a giant, "whatever you want" round: seven hours. With breaks to reset and all the extra filming, they'd be looking at nearly twenty hours of straight-up work to get through everything. Maybe more, depending on what other kind of shit the network had planned to make the finale big and exciting. Tristan would have to bring two cigarettes . . . maybe three.

Henry came back with the ice bucket full. "Okay, champagne time in, like, an hour?"

"Champagne time in an hour. Perfect. Gives me time to wheedle you for information on what you're making for the grand finale."

"Oh, so we're all done playing with honor? After signing all those extra disclosure agreements?" Henry shoved a bottle of champagne into the ice bucket—Tristan had already lost track of whose was whose—then flopped onto the bed next to Tristan. "What'll it be, then? Car battery to the nipples? Waterboarding? Branding?"

"Easy, now. We've only had two dates so far, if you count that dinner at Bluestone Lotus. We can get to the nipple electrocution after three dates."

"Should I hold you to that?"

"Hey, I'm not *promising*." Tristan nuzzled against the nape of Henry's neck, seeking out that pulse of warmth, and took in a deep breath of flour and coconut. It was Henry. Everything was Henry. "I'm just putting it on the table, but I'm damn sure not slutty enough to go *that* far before the third date."

"You keep saying we've been on two dates. I'm only recalling the Bluestone Lotus."

"Shitty sandwiches, *then* the Bluestone Lotus." Tristan put his hands on his hips. "Honestly, if you're not going to remember our first date, I don't know what to do with you."

"I thought we discussed that already: car battery to the nipples." Henry smiled at him for a few moments, and when he spoke again, his voice was soft. "Why did you step in like that?"

"Because you're worth it." Tristan shocked himself at the ease with which that came out. "I couldn't let you leave. Not like that." Tristan's belly tightened, but he sighed and took Henry's hands, squeezing them gently while he looked into those warm brown eyes. "I know I can't live without my sister . . . but I'm not sure I want to try living without you, either. And if I let you throw your dream away for my sake, we'd never be okay again. I'd never be able to look you in the eye." He didn't want to focus too much on the panic brewing, the building expenses waiting for him. For a moment or two, he wanted to give himself over to Henry. Henry, who had been ready to throw everything away for him.

Tristan kissed him before he could say anything, and he didn't have to worry about the show, and he could touch Henry as much as he liked.

He liked to touch him a lot.

When they finally parted, Tristan adjusted his glasses. "With all the stuff we have to make in one day, the filming is going to be brutal this time."

Thankfully, Henry took the subject change in stride. "Tell me about it." He lay down next to Tristan and kissed his cheek. "You know, now that this is getting real . . . What do you even do with a quarter million dollars? That wasn't exactly on my radar."

"Do you want an itemized list?" Tristan shifted a little higher up. "You lose about half to taxes, so 125,000 left. I'd pay off my student loans, get a better car, pump some money into savings and retirement, pay off as many credit cards as I possibly can, help my sister, fix any remaining house crap. Then if there's anything left, maybe I'd invest it."

Henry rubbed his hand up and down Tristan's spine. "I think you might have a little room for some fun in that budget."

Tristan chuckled. "We'll see."

Henry nodded, seemingly to himself. "I'd get an ice cream machine. I love ice cream. Plus maybe I'd be able to introduce it to the shop if I had a chance to experiment with it."

"There's something special about making your own. I used to do it in culinary school all the time." Tristan pressed himself against Henry's side. "Olive oil ice cream, sea salt, parmesan. And some normal stuff too. Sometimes."

"Well, when I win, you're welcome to use it anytime."

"Still so cocky. Aren't you the one who wanted to trade me for my chiffon recipe?"

Henry shrugged. "Maybe, maybe not. I plead the fifth."

Tristan planted another kiss against the nape of Henry's neck and snuggled against him. And that's how they stayed the rest of the night.

Chapter Twenty

Tristan furiously whipped meringue for his grand finale bake. The top layer of his wedding cake—because of course he was making a wedding cake—would be covered in thick Swiss meringue and torched off in the oven. The oven was really the only way to do it. A blowtorch didn't cook the meringue deep enough, didn't dry it out enough or give it that perfect chewy texture the way a few minutes under the broiler would.

He'd left a little more than an hour on his schedule for assembly and decoration, but he'd been putting the base pieces together the whole time, so it shouldn't end up too tight. He had all his tiers crumb-coated and his fondant was ready and colored. He'd momentarily considered making his own, but there was too much to do, and the quality of fresh-made fondant wasn't a significant enough improvement to justify that much work.

At long last, they'd moved Henry to the opposite side of the room. Cons: it put him and his delicious goddamn body too far away to properly gawk at. Pros: it let Tristan take in what Henry was doing for this last challenge. And all the ones before that.

And so far, they were pretty much neck and neck, based on the judges' notes. They'd universally liked Henry's cheesecake better, as far as texture and finishing. Which was valid, since Tristan's was *slightly* grainier than it should have been. But Henry's flavors—a blueberry and lemon zest compote on top of a classic vanilla cheesecake—had been "maybe too safe" compared to Tristan's white chocolate cheesecake and huckleberry syrup. On angel food cake, they'd been functionally identical.

So it was down to this. And *both* of them, from the looks of things on Henry's side, were pulling out multi-tiered cakes.

The three judges walked over to Tristan's station and he smiled at them. "Afternoon." They were somehow such a part of his life, now, that he could talk to them without blithering.

Dexter smiled wide. "Afternoon, Tristan. How are you holding up?"

"Oh, plugging away." He pulled up his beaters and the meringue was perfect. "Hopefully you like it."

"So, you're the flavor man in this competition. What are you bringing us?"

"You want it in alphabetical order or something else?"

They all laughed, and Dexter leaned in. "Whatever comes to mind."

"Well, it's a four-tiered wedding cake. My wedding cake, so my flavor stories."

"Flavor stories." Eli chuckled. "I'd expect nothing less from you."

Was that a compliment? Tristan knew it was a *little* pretentious to talk about flavor stories, but there was no better term to describe what he was doing. Like a movie, each section of the cake used flavors to evoke feeling. "I wanted a tier for each of the four seasons. Eternal love and all that. So for spring, I've got a cherry cake with rose and sour cherry buttercream." He pointed to each layer as he detailed them. "And that's filled with a quick cherry compote. Then summer needs bright and tropical flavors, so a classic orange cake with pineapple and coconut buttercream, toasted coconut on the outside, and a passionfruit jelly in the middle." Plus maybe the coconut in *his* wedding cake represented Henry a little bit. Maybe. "Fall is all about apples in Washington, so I've packed as many apples as I could inside the layer. Apples in the buttercream, stewed apples, an apple cake, and . . . there's just a lot of apples."

"And I'm sure you could tell us all the varieties," said Rita. "Not to enforce stereotypes, but I've never met a Washingtonian without opinions on apples."

"You wouldn't be wrong." His stewed apples were Granny Smiths. The buttercream had Golden Delicious and Honeycrisp. He had slices of Pink Ladies and Winesaps candied and drying at the moment for decoration, and the apple cake was that super classic Red Delicious flavor, mixed with Jonagolds for a little change and surprise. So many apples. "And then winter is all about indulgence, so I made it my smallest tier, and I packed in the richest flavors I could. It's a coffee sponge cake filled with whipped cream and chocolate ganache. The buttercream is flavored with all sorts of those good warm spices, and then I'll cover it in this Swiss meringue and toast the whole thing."

"That is a *lot* of work." Dexter clucked his tongue. "You going to be able to finish it up in time?"

"No problem." Maybe some problem, but Tristan was feeling too good for that idea to take hold. He'd do it and he'd make a good presentation for judging.

"Well, I look forward to it." Dexter slapped the counter a couple of times. "Good luck, Tristan."

"Thank you." It might take a little luck. However talented he might be—because Tristan couldn't deny he had some skill, no matter how incredible his powers of self-deprecation might be—Henry was just as good. There was no guarantee it would turn out any one way or the other.

And although Tristan would be ecstatic for Henry if he won . . . he'd be even happier if *he* won the money. Yeah, he'd talked to Lucia, and she planned to pitch in when she could. That didn't change his circumstances though. He still needed to get access to the big money.

With the waiting portions out of the way, Henry could relax. He wasn't going as traditional as he maybe had in the past. At least not with his flavors. But if he was going to play to his strengths, this fucker would *look* traditional.

The judges walked from Tristan over to him. Eli smiled. "So, you feeling good about today?"

"I'm feeling great. Everything's going to plan, and I love it."

Eli's grin widened. "Well great, then let us in on the plan."

"So, I have a five-tiered cake, and I honestly just wanted to include things that I love in it. I've got a mixed berry cake with lemon curd and lemon icing, a cake full of all different kinds of seeds that I'm pairing up with a bourbon vanilla buttercream, a pineapple upside-down cake with a twist—"

"Pineapple upside-down cake as a cake layer?" Rita raised an eyebrow. "You're not worried it's too dense and wet?"

"Not in the least." It had been a bit tricky to cut enough moisture from it for structural integrity, but he'd managed it nonetheless. "Now that's paired off with a coconut and rum French meringue, and then there's a nice ginger cake. Just piles of ginger everywhere I could get it in there."

"But that's only four layers," said Eli.

"Well, the fifth layer is a surprise, and I don't want to ruin it."

Eli's eyes sparked. "I wish you luck and look forward to your surprise."

Yeah, so do I. In all his practice runs it had worked fine. No real mess. But there was always a chance that it might not play nicely with him today.

With the judges gone, Henry went on to icing his cakes, starting with his top layer, smoothing the final presentation coat over his crumb coat. Cakes, even this size, weren't hard work, per se. Sometimes temperamental, often tedious, but Henry had made so many cakes that it wasn't *hard* to do it.

Once he had that tier iced and smooth, he popped it back into the fridge, then checked the clock. They still had two hours to go, and that was perfect. He wasn't running tight quite yet. Henry looked across the way at Tristan. He was piping something around the outside of one tier. The cake itself was beautiful and glossy and certainly held its shape well. He'd overtaken the station behind him for his cakes as well. Four tiers, and none of them were delicate little baby cakes. They were all *substantial*, which felt right for Tristan. *Crazy flavors and giant cake tiers in all sorts of bold designs. It's going to be hard to get those out of my head when we get back home.* Would Tristan be happy going back to classic white wedding cakes trying to emulate sixteenth-century Paris?

The sweets and cakes he'd made during this competition? *Those* were Tristan, not some frilly, white ruffle cake that a hundred brides saw in a magazine.

Henry sighed. He could have easily sat there for another ten, fifteen minutes watching Tristan apply decorations, work different batters and confections into perfection. But there straight-up wasn't time for that.

I guess that's on my list to make time for when we're done. Henry turned back around and looked through his list again. *Should probably get the pineapple soaking in the rum now.* It needed time to properly soak up the liquor, and then to sit and mellow some of that boozy bite.

There was work to be done, but Henry felt a lot more in control with "work to be done" than "waiting aimlessly and hoping things turn out." Considering this was the finale, he didn't feel all that panicked. He was almost *Zen.* This was the moment he had come here searching for, one of true competition. And a worthy adversary. Going up against someone like Tristan Delgado was forcing the very best out of him.

He cracked his knuckles, then pulled out his pineapple chunks. *Let's go.*

Judging was on them faster than Tristan could comprehend. But this time, when he was called to the front, Henry could help him again. Which certainly seemed to excite him. As the judges tasted and re-tasted, Henry kept flashing him little grins and winks from across the room.

"Tristan." Rita's gentle voice cut through the quiet. "This was stunning. The layers here flow well together and tell a cohesive story."

"It does," said Eli. "The coconut is exquisite."

"No, it's the apples." Dexter pointed to that autumn layer with his fork. "They make it quite moist. Everything was pulled off beautifully, so I don't doubt you used your time well. But I still can't help but wonder what you might have accomplished if you'd gone a bit smaller on each tier. A touch more complexity, perhaps."

That critique would have sent Tristan spiraling a few days ago, but now he nodded. "That's fair. But I stand by the decision."

Dexter smiled. "Good. You should. It's, as Eli said, exquisite. And not just the coconut."

Sylvia nodded, rubbing her hands together. "Always lovely to have you over for dessert, but I'm afraid we need to move on to Henry." She winked. "If you don't mind."

Tristan didn't bother with pretense. He let the production crew return his cake to his station while he headed straight for Henry. "Ready?"

"As I'll ever be."

Henry and Tristan lifted the cake and carried it to the front. Tristan leaned around the cake to catch a glimpse of Henry: stubble and muscle and a grin full of straight white teeth that he tried not to imagine nipping the nape of his neck. Not a helpful line of thought to go down, however pleasant it might have been. Then Tristan went back to his station to hear it play out. And maybe to check out Henry's ass, since the angle was so accommodating. The judges got their description from Henry, although he still wasn't revealing whatever his "surprise" layer was. Then they began to cut, laying thin slices out on their plates until they hit the top.

"Well, surprise indeed." Dexter laid a slice out on a new plate. The outside was cake, but inside was a firm, jiggly center, fully bound to the crumb on the inside. He prodded it. "Bavarois?"

Henry nodded. "Of course."

"Clever. And you've managed to pull it off."

Tristan was impressed. Getting that layer put together was a task worthy of another trip to the drugstore.

They worked their way through the rest of the tiers. Once they'd finished, Dexter nodded, rubbing his hands together. "That was a delight, especially the bavarois. Creamy and rich, and the genoise has a great texture."

"And that really was the standout," said Eli. "It's an impressive bit of work, especially considering how much bavarois you have inside. Though the others were well-made cakes, good flavor as well."

"They are, but I don't think they're balanced." Rita went back in for another forkful of cake and Bavarian cream. "This is fantastic. The others are a little overbearing, and I don't think they go well together as a whole cake." She gestured to the top layer again. "But that's delicious. Stunning."

"Thank you." Henry turned to Sylvia. "It's been real."

She chuckled. "It has been real. Real-ly bad for my dress size." She patted her stomach as Henry walked back to his station. The crew got all their cameras in place, the judges got hair and makeup retouched, and a bubble of tension expanded in Tristan's middle. This was it. The end.

After fifteen minutes, which seemed like approximately thirty seconds, he and Henry were herded up front to stand next to each other, and Tristan nudged into his side, just to get fleeting contact as their mics got adjusted.

Then the cameras flicked on and Sylvia clapped for what would probably be the last time, and Tristan's stomach lurched into his throat as she started to speak. "Tristan. Henry. You've both been wonderful the whole competition, and today is no exception. I may very well have to fly out to Seattle the next time I need my cheesecake fix, and I'm divorcing my husband and hiring you both to make wedding cakes when we get remarried."

Tristan chuckled and Henry pulled him closer until they stood absolutely side by side, pressed to each other and waiting, ensconced in the smell of coconut. His skin tingled, but his mind calmed at Henry's presence next to him.

Sylvia nodded. "I'd like to tell you that you'll each be given 125,000 dollars and it's a wash, but unfortunately that idea was shot right down. One of you *did* win. You edged out the other by a fraction of an inch of buttercream, but that fraction made all the difference." She gestured to Henry. "On one hand we had classic beauty and flawless execution of five different cakes, including a stunning upset with that Bavarian cream layer. A display worthy of any time from the 1800s to two hundred years in the future." Her hand shifted to Tristan. "And on the other, we have irrepressible style and unique flavor that took us on a journey, from the tropic heat of summer all the way into the fireside cocoa of winter. I tell you, I'm glad I didn't have to make this decision."

At her sigh, Tristan's stomach made another valiant escape attempt, and Henry's grip tightened well into the point of discomfort. This was it. This was the decision they'd been working toward their whole time here. One of them was going to win the money.

But Tristan had already won a prize. He'd gotten Henry.

Sylvia kept her face stern yet again. "The winner of *Get Baked*, and a quarter million dollars is . . ." Her face broke into the widest smile she'd given during their whole tenure there. "Tristan Delgado!"

Did they say that right? His head swam, light and spinning. *Did I hear it right?* His fingers quivered. *She said my name.*

Henry immediately tossed his arms around Tristan and squeezed him even tighter than he'd been holding his hand. Which was good, because Tristan had nearly collapsed.

If it's a dream, then fuck it. I'm making the most of it. Tristan pressed their lips together. Henry leaned into it, locked his mouth to Tristan's with fire and sugar and . . . coconut. *Goddamn coconut.*

When they finally parted. Tristan smiled at him. Just at him. "I won."

"You won. And it could only have happened to one better person."

Tristan shook his head and whispered, "Henry fucking Isaacson."

He heard footsteps approach and, in spite of his desire, he tracked the sound over to a bright grin and a shiny bald head. Dexter approached and leaned in close, covering his lapel mic with his hand. "Director's losing his head, saying we're going to make so much money on this finale. Good news for us, bad news for you: you might have to come in and film some new material to play up the romance angle. But they owe you one if you need anything." He pulled back and shook Tristan's hand.

"I . . . I won." Tristan barely let the words fall off his tongue a second time. "My God, I won." A quarter million dollars. Respect from people in his industry. He could probably even renegotiate his contract with Carlita, if he could summon up the nerve to bring it up with her. *Then maybe I can leave eventually and start my own place.*

Tristan's knees shook, but he forced himself to stand straight and firm and, finally, smile at Dexter. How long had they been standing there, now? "Thank you, thank you."

"Thank you." Dexter smiled, all white teeth and real, sheer glee. "You helped me make this whole show happen."

After that, Dexter pulled back and Rita and Eli stepped in. Rita with a silver trophy engraved with the show's logo and the year, and Eli with a bouquet of roses.

Once he had the flowers, Tristan stared straight at Henry and mouthed, *I love you.*

Henry grinned back with the most perfect grin, even if he wasn't corrected and smoothed out by blur like he had been that first night together. There was nothing Tristan would change, from his rough, burnt-marshmallow stubble, to his peachy mouth that was maybe just a little too wide, to his 62% dark chocolate eyes.

Henry was already perfect.

Epilogue

Henry slipped into the back. He needed a break from the rush of customers. Ever since they started airing promo for the show, plastering Henry's face up on TV a million times an hour, business had ticked way, *way* up.

"Knock?" Tristan's voice came from the other side of the office door. "Knock knock?"

"Come in."

Tristan slipped into the room, carrying a Styrofoam clamshell. "I brought you something from work. Chicken cordon bleu and baby roast potatoes and pearl onions."

"Carlita's work?"

"Yeah. It's for that vow-renewal ceremony. This was apparently their chicken option back when they got married the first time. But it's good. I tested it myself."

"Are you still planning to stay? That offer to come work with me stands."

"If I leave, it won't be for a while. Bills and savings come first, then new business ventures."

"I keep telling you, you don't have to buy your way into the shop."

"And I keep telling you, if I'm going to partner up with you, I'm buying in. That's the only right way to do it."

Henry chuckled and opened the box. It was still steaming. "You really raced over here with this, didn't you?"

"Well, I wanted you to have something nice . . . I mean, it's not the most festive meal. I don't generally care for chicken cordon bleu, but Carlita's is excellent."

"I thought we were celebrating tonight, though? We've got food coming from Veni Vidi Vici."

"That's still on for the premier, don't worry." Tristan's eyes sparkled. "Since you're in the office, I figure I can steal you away from here for a second or two. I've got something to show you."

Henry raised an eyebrow, but he closed the container and followed Tristan out. "This isn't like a strippergram or back-alley exhibitionist sex, is it?"

"Not today, no." Tristan led them through the crush of people—Henry mouthed a quick *Sorry* to Athena behind the counter—and out the front door. He gestured to his car. "Ta-dah."

"You learned to drive like a big boy?"

"I got the money, Henry."

"You got the money." *Jesus Christ.* "Why are you showing me your car?"

"Because I . . . Well, okay, I did get an accountant, but I set aside a little mad money for something special." He walked over and popped the trunk, then took out a box.

A box with a big picture of an ice cream maker on the side.

"Happy Thursday, Henry."

"You bought this for me?"

"I bought this for us." Tristan set it on the sidewalk between them, and his cheeks were cherry red. "I thought maybe it would make a nice housewarming gift, too?"

"Am I moving?"

"Well, maybe." He combed his fingers through his hair. "I know we haven't talked about it much, but . . . want to live together?"

It took Henry a second to realize he'd heard right. "You're serious?" He hadn't wanted to push that at all, even after they'd gotten back. But if Tristan was going to open the door . . . "You want to live with me?"

"We already practically live together most nights of the week anyway. We would just be picking one place to stay instead of swapping back and forth. And now that Lucia's back out on her own two feet, I feel like I can move if we'd rather live at your place. Or have you move in with me. Or find a new place altogether. Please say something so I'll stop talking."

Henry chuckled and wrapped his arms around Tristan. He kissed his forehead, then the tip of his nose, then his full lips. Tristan still tasted of vanilla from work. "We'll work out the details tonight, okay? But yes. Let's live together. Somewhere. Anywhere."

Tristan nuzzled his head against Henry's shoulder. "Thank you. I was worried this might go horribly wrong."

"Nothing between the two of us is horribly wrong."

Tristan pulled back and nodded. "I have one more surprise for you." Slowly, he removed his jacket.

It took Henry a moment to realize what the big deal was. Then it rolled over him like a tidal wave. "Short sleeves."

"I set aside enough for some new shirts too." Tristan smiled. "Mom's dead, God rest her soul, Lucia's getting past our childhood shit . . . me covering up is the last bit of influence my dad had on our lives. So fuck it." He turned his arms side to side, showing off the scars, and the faded tattoo, and his wonderful, ripply muscles. "Besides, I think they make me look all manly and sexy and shit."

"I would *definitely* agree." Henry walked up and rubbed his hands from Tristan's shoulders, down his arms, and grasped his fingers. "I love you, and I'm so fucking proud of you. I can't wait to pick out our first coffee table. But Athena's going to dip my face in molten sugar if I don't get back in there and help her."

"Well, we wouldn't want that." Tristan pecked him on the lips, then lifted the ice cream maker back into the trunk. "Tonight. Your place. Lucia's still invited?"

"Hell yes, Lucia's still invited. Karen, too, if she wants to come. Hell, you could invite Carlita for all I care. I've got Carrie and my crew coming, so you should have a little better representation."

Tristan smiled. "I might just do that. She's a nag at work, but she's a hoot and a half if you get a couple beers down her."

"Okay, but you bring the beer. I couldn't risk being seen buying that shit, they'd revoke my gay card."

"Wouldn't want you to stop being gay." Tristan slapped his ass. "I'll see you tonight."

Henry waved as he pulled away from the curb, then stepped back inside and pushed his way through. "Sorry, Athena. Duty called.

There's some good chicken cordon bleu in my office, but only take half, please."

As he took over serving customers, his mind wandered. There was so much light ahead, so many moments he'd imagined and could finally make. Christening the sofa in their first shared house. Insomnia-fueled baking sessions. Waking up pressed to Tristan's sepia skin every morning. Kissing him goodbye with coffee fresh on his breath.

The show had brought in these new customers, would bring in even more. But none of them mattered.

The show had brought him Tristan, and no other prize could compare.

Dear Reader,

Thank you for reading Alex Danvers's *A Teaspoon of Desire*!

We know your time is precious and you have many, many entertainment options, so it means a lot that you've chosen to spend your time reading. We really hope you enjoyed it.

We'd be honored if you'd consider posting a review—good or bad—on sites like **Amazon, Barnes & Noble, Kobo, Goodreads, Twitter, Facebook, Tumblr,** and your blog or website. We'd also be honored if you told your friends and family about this book. Word of mouth is a book's lifeblood!

For more information on upcoming releases, author interviews, blog tours, contests, giveaways, and more, please sign up for our weekly, spam-free newsletter and visit us around the web:

Newsletter: riptidepublishing.com/newsletter
Twitter: twitter.com/RiptideBooks
Facebook: facebook.com/RiptidePublishing
Goodreads: tinyurl.com/RiptideOnGoodreads
Tumblr: riptidepublishing.tumblr.com

Thank you so much for Reading the Rainbow!

RiptidePublishing.com

Acknowledgments

I've never written a note like this that can properly cover every single person important to the process of producing a book. It's utterly impossible, but I always try to get at least key players. Julia: you not only gave me my first publishing break all those years back, but it was your Facebook thread that got me to write this whole book in the first place. Mom: you were my always companion watching shows like this, following the drama between competitors week to week and acting like we definitely knew better than they did. Caz: you whipped this beastly slop pile into something resembling an actual book, and dealt with me during an alarming spread of emergency surgeries, medical visits, and at least one "Hey, my city almost exploded last night" that pushed the schedule back bit by bit. Thank you for not murdering me. John, Jeni, Rebecca, and the whole Rouxdie community: you've been the best company I could ask for while working on this book.

And of course, dear reader, the largest thanks goes to you. I've been at this a long while, and I know from experience that none of this happens without you picking up the book and leafing through. I've spent a long time contemplating recipes and flavor combinations or telling myself stories about guys meeting up when cameras stop rolling. You and you alone are the one who makes that more than simple daydreaming. So sincerely, and again, *thank you*.

Alex

Also by
Alex Danvers

About the Author

Alex Danvers is the contemporary pen name of Raven de Hart, telling stories with a little less fantasy but just as much steam and emotion. He lives in the middle of the Eastern Washington desert with a pack of spoiled Golden Retrievers. In his pre-publication life, he studied culinary arts, with an emphasis on pâtisserie, and continues to enjoy dangerous levels of fresh pastries, cakes, and confections to this day. When he can be removed from his keyboard, he can be found singing, playing the trombone, or ranting about culinary nonsense in long-winded Facebook posts.

Website: www.ravendehart.com
Facebook: www.facebook.com/RavendeHartMM
Twitter: www.twitter.com/dehartslist
Newsletter: eepurl.com/b64M5v

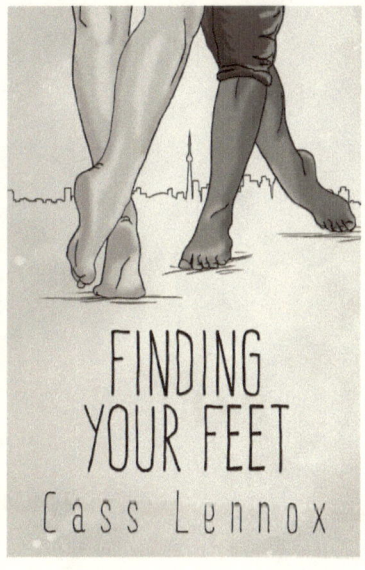